J. J. Connolly was born and brought up in
north-east London. His first published
story was in the *Brit Pulp!* anthology. He
is the author of acclaimed bestseller *Layer
Cake*, which he adapted into the script for
the film directed by Matthew Vaughn.
Viva la Madness is his second novel.

ALSO BY J.J. CONNOLLY

Layer Cake

VIVA LA MADNESS

J.J. Connolly

Duckworth Overlook

This edition 2012
First published in 2011 by
Duckworth Overlook
90-93 Cowcross Street
London EC1M 6BF
Tel: 020 7490 7300
Fax: 020 7490 0080
info@duckworth-publishers.co.uk
www.ducknet.co.uk

© 2011 by J.J. Connolly

A catalogue record for this book is available
from the British Library

ISBN 978-0-7156-4365-5

Typeset by Ray Davies
Printed and bound in the UK by
CPI Group (UK) Ltd, Croydon, CR0 4YY

CONTENTS

What's with the Big Q and A?   9
Shock and Awe   18
A Different Kinda Bank Job   25
Dropping off the Bagwash   32
Madheads, Melts, Mackerels and Headpeckers   39
Morty's Pitch   47
Going Backayard   57
Home Sweet Home   63
Lovely Day for It   70
Nut Down in Chelsea   79
You Like Riddles?   87
Uptown Belly Bumping   94
Cha-Cha with the Devil You Know   106
Lunch at Sonny's Hideaway   115
No Mum – Dog Eat Mum   128
Jesus – *Has-ooze* – AKA Golden Goose   140
Consequences   150
Speculation   157
Made in China   164
Reading Between the Lines   171
Strange Devolvement   180
Bad to Worse   187
Sonny – Santos – Santos – Sonny   197
Some Good News …   208
And Some Bad News …   217
Worried Boys   223
Take Me to Your Leader   227
This Be Dark   236
Pure Toil and Trouble   244
Riddles and Fiddles   250
Another Time Another Place   260

A Dazzling Star Dies   270
Today's Dilemma   278
Cruel Ironies   287
Spick 'n' Span   300
Safe Journey Home   309
Prelude to Madness   316
Who's Sammy Laniado?   323
Jesus' Inferno   333
Patsy, Ya Gotta Love Him   341
Wrong Place, Wrong Time   348
Juggling Big Time   360
Broken Souls   370
What Is Madness?   380
Plan B   384
The Brigadier's Coup   394
Never Trust a Toff   406
Couple of Complications   425
Viva La Madness   432

An interview with J. J. Connolly   446

'YOU LIKE RIDDLES?' HE SAYS.

'NOT ESPECIALLY, NO.'

'HERE'S ONE FOR YA,' HE SAYS, IGNORING MY ANSWER.

'WHY DO PEOPLE GO TO PRISON? THINK ABOUT IT.'

'DUNNO.'

'TRY HARDER,' HE INSISTS STRAIGHT AWAY.

'WHY DO PEOPLE GO TO PRISON?'

'FOR COMMITTING CRIME?' I SAY.

'NO, NO,' HE SAYS, SHAKING HIS HEAD, PRETENDING
TO BE DISAPPOINTED.

'THINK AGAIN. YOU'LL KICK YOURSELF. IT'S NOT
FOR COMMITTIN' CRIME.'

'OH, I GET YA. IT'S FOR GETTIN' CAUGHT.'

'NOW YOU'VE GOT IT, SON. I KNEW YOU WAS A BRIGHT KID.

IT'S FOR GETTIN CAUGHT COMMITTING CRIME. SO BE LUCKY.'

CHAPTER ONE

WHAT'S WITH THE BIG Q AND A?

Grantley Adams International Airport, Barbados
Wednesday, 22nd August 2001

Q. Do you know who I am?

A. Are you having an identity crisis?

Q. Why are you here, at the airport, in Barbados?

A. I'm waiting ... I hate waiting.

Q. What is your name?

A. My name's unimportant. I am thirty-five years old. I own a hotel in a resort on the far west coast of Jamaica, that beautifully corrupt, sun-kissed lunatic asylum. The operation costs me money to run, it drains my resources because, basically, I ain't about a lot of the time, ain't one of nature's hospitable hosts. In fact I find the guests a right pain in the arse.

Q. How'd I get the tank money?

A. I used to supply cocaine – multiples of kilos, back in London, back in the day. I served up a cross-section of London dealers. I had some customers who were ex-public school, polo-set, take five kilos on bail, credit, return me a hundred grand in large denominations forty-eight hours later – no sweaty fivers or tens, please – and at the other end of the scale we occasionally served full-blast lunatics. But everybody paid up. I spun the loot through various legitimate enterprises. I lived the colour-supplement lifestyle. But I had a spot of bother – another time, another story – so I had to ship out quick-sharp. I managed to go through the slips with about half what I'd accumulated, half a million in sterling, but I ended up with a metal plate in my head because some love-struck hero shot me.

I'm persona nongrata back in the UK. The law told me they'd convict me for anything, manufacture evidence if necessary, if I ever stepped back on British soil. I laid low in backwaters, scratching about, running a bar. I'd got people to check with bent cozzers back home to see if the police were *actively* looking for me. They drew a blank. I started to venture out.

Q. How do you sleep?

A. I have a recurring nightmare. Nothing about loud shooters going off in my face or bogeymen chasing me naked. My dream is old-school, Freudian in many ways. I dream a large powerful beast, a cross between a tiger and wolf, is savaging me. It's in so close that if it wasn't trying to rip me to pieces it would be trying to fuck me. That's an image to spin the canister, even in sunlight. The beast's long razor-sharp teeth are embedded in my flesh. It plays with me, crushes my exposed bones in its powerful jaws. My blood sprays everywhere, like a slaughterhouse wall. I always wake up suddenly, covered in a cold sweat, head to toe, breathing hard. I'm relieved but I can taste my own terror in my spit. It takes me till afternoon to slip the feeling, to properly lose it. Apparently fear is a pre-programmed, biophysical chemical reaction, but when I'm in fatal close quarter combat with the Bengal werewolf it's incredibly real.

Q. Can anything be done?

A. Someone suggested I get my head totally checked out, tests and scans – the mad dreams could be pressure on the brain. So I did. And they were right. I've recently come back from Florida where I've had the National Health Service tin can replaced with the titanium private-enterprise model. Apparently the old one had been causing the problem. Some days I couldn't think straight, and I was getting excruciating headaches. Two hundred and thirty grand – US dollars – in cold blood it cost me, with no medical insurance to take the sting outta it. Complex seven-hour brain operations don't come cheap. My memory is slowly returning. Can be a good or bad thing. I can remember some parts of my life in infinite micro-detail and whole chunks I have no recollection of at all.

Wanna tip? Forget crime. Become a brain surgeon. Crime may pay, but there's a price to be paid.

Q. Do you think you're really suited to the hotel and catering business?

A. My thinking has changed. Some guys don't really mind

indulging fuckwits, pandering to their every need. It's not that I ain't got the humility, and I'm not a violent man, it's just I wanna head-butt certain punters when they look down their noses like I'm Joe the Go. When it comes to humility I like people to meet me halfway.

Q. So how did you get into the business?

A. Through a series of defaults. It seemed like a good idea at the time – to buy a share in a loss-making, Art-Deco relic of a hotel for bottom dollar from a desperate, destitute Ivy League drug addict. American royalty in social freefall. He's dead now; nothing to do with me. He started off wealthy but it didn't help him; fucked the guy in many respects, couldn't apply the brakes. He pathetically begged me to buy it. A bit sickening it was, watching him crying, sweating buckets in a white linen suit, his personal hygiene all gone.

Q. Do you regret it?

A. I regretted it as I signed my name. Sometimes you regret things in life as you're doing them – like an outta body experience. There was a chance – a slim one – that I was getting a bargain but in retrospect I was *found*, as they say in London. I've gotta wipe my mouth, crack on, and start looking for someone to sell it to. I could blame my health condition or the strong prescribed medication I was gulping at the time but that would be an excuse.

Q. Have you ever thought about, you know, a happy accident?

A. What, burn the fuckin gaff down? I'd burn the fucker to the ground in a heartbeat if I could get some cover but they're ahead of me, the insurance salesmen. I've tried talking to them in the bar about getting a policy and they laugh. If I could get insured, I'd check the fine print, make sure I was paid up to date then call in a specialist.

I've tried but I completely miss the point of being an hotelier so I keep a low profile, a shadowy presence and an office on the property. I leave the everyday running to managers, ambitious hotel-school graduates who you know one day will open up the rival hotel or even stage their own *petit coup d'état*. The rot at the hotel had set in deep, and trying to turn it round was never going to be easy or quick. The kitchen staff were taking liberties left, right and centre, and sirloin steaks home with them. The front desk staff were blatantly dipping the till. The concierge service could provide the best flake cocaine on that whole bit of coast, delivered by the gamiest hookers, who rinsed out the punters till they were praying to the lord, so *I* had to pay off the local constabulary. All the decent bartenders and waiters were hunting for sugar mamas – who they'd fuck delirious, who'd buy them tickets to Montreal or Chicago, leaving me with the schlumps.

The whole gaff was a free-for-all that I was paying for. I skimmed my whack off the top, obviously pulled rank and dipped the till myself to a greater degree. Couldn't help myself. My partners in the hotel don't really need the money. Give it time, they were saying, but I was running outta time. One day the gaff might even be worth selling but if I knew then what I know now I woulda kept my readies under my mattress and eked out a living from the bar I owned back on Curaçao.

I realise now – now the mist is clearing and the thinking is getting sharper – that I've been sitting out here in the Carib waiting for my wake-up call, like those Cold War sleepers, but absorbing shit I wasn't even aware of. For a while, after getting outta London alive I was content to just plod on, keep my nut down, and not get mixed up in any shenanigans. My heart certainly wasn't in the crime swindle any more.

But one day I woke up and a red light in the cockpit was flashing. Every single day you're observing guys with serious wealth and stunning women and it's going in under the radar without you realising. You start to see ugly guys with no talent or style turning up with the kinda woman kings fought battles over in ancient times. I'm not saying these women only go for seriously caked dudes, but it certainly helps.

Money is sexy. Money is power. Power is sexy. I wonder what would happen if they woke up one morning and a big storm had blown all their money away. How would the lady friend be then? Devoted? *It's only money, darling, we can get some more.* Or out the door sharpish to hook up with the next dude?

You're peeping into a world of perma-tanned middle-aged guys, looking leaner than a pikey's dog, muscles toned from sea swimming, salt and pepper hair, and dressed in that disposable luxury attire they wear once then leave in a hotel suite someplace.

You realise that you're peeking *into* a world from the outside where the smell of Cuban cigar smoke mixes with aviation fuel on private runways, where gorgeous, lithe, tanned women swim naked in cliff-top infinity pools. *Let's play a little game, dearheart. Can you spot my two-hundred-foot schooner moored in the far-away distance?*

You're peeking into a world where guys collect, for fun, fleets of vintage motors, misplaced national treasures, artworks that belong in museums, antiques with stories to tell of murdered czars, deposed princes or star-crossed abdicated kings, or antiquities that cost as much as a street of detached houses in a comfortable part of London.

You're routinely rubbing shoulders with gents in the cocktail lounge who are stepping out of limos after dropping into resorts in helicopters, after stepping off private jets, and block-booking whole floors of the hotel. And they're renting thirty-berth yachts in the harbour, but only using them as floating base-camps while they're fuckin about in speedboats, swagging barracuda a few clicks off the cape. These dudes are keeping the kitchens in Michelin-star restaurants open all night cos they're busy partying with Brazilian models. Ain't got a care in the world. They're dropping bellboys, concierges and barmen obscene amounts of cash. They're parading round like they own the gaff. And I'm thinking *I* own the fuckin gaff!

Q. Would you describe yourself as an angry man?

A. I do get angry. I've got waiters who are *buying* lucrative jobs from *maître d'*s, making bundles while I pay the rent. I had more control of my world when I was a drug dealer.

The Caribbean isn't the place to come if you've come looking for equal distribution of wealth. It's the most unequal carve-up in the history of the world. Some people live in shacks, work hard, go to church, have no known vices, while others live in palaces, do nothing but laze around and come nightfall feast on rich foods and wines, stick powders up their snouts and act like debauched fuck-pigs. Euro-trash, newly rich Russian looters, Columbian commodities brokers, the flash-but-gormless sons of Third World dictators – but these people ain't so silly. People might think they're vulgar, they might look down on these hideously affluent brothers and sisters, but they ain't on the tube on a Monday morning, skint till payday, rushing to punch the clock, wondering what to do with a damp brolly.

Q. What shall I do with my wet umbrella?

A. Stick it up your fuckin arse.

Life is just one long holiday for some people. They follow the sun, follow the seasons and explore the world.

'See you at the Rio carnival?'

'Let's rendezvous in Colorado.'

'Maybe we'll hook up in Monaco? At the Grand Prix?'

Money's no object to some people. The young pups will always live beyond their means but mama and papa always bail them out. These are heirs and heiresses who've had money in their families for as long as anyone can remember, household names, trust fund bubbers, who take it all for granted. These are folks who are so fabulously wealthy they couldn't even begin to count it, have crafty accountants to bury their wealth far from sunlight, on dots on the map that nobody's ever heard of, known only to the razor-sharp bankers. There are islands that only exist to aid and abet tax evasion, with polished brass plaques plastered from floor to ceiling on wooden shacks, safe havens beyond the reach of the inquisitive taxman.

Temptation and envy start to become scheming and plotting. I look at wealth and realise my problem is that I want not a little but a lot. My problem with the rich is I'm more than a tad jealous. I need to make moves that settle me for life. I need to get my money pot brimming. Money goes to money. It's no good letting my mind wander back to London, how I really put in the shovel work to set myself up nicely, earned over a million and a half in businesses and property – taxes paid, no mortgages – but it wasn't to be. I have to look forward. It's time to start making moves again. I've seen opulence with my own eyes; you can never creep back to blissful ignorance.

Q. Do I wanna be *seriously* rich?

A. Are you fuckin serious?

I'd be sat at sunset, on my balcony, drinking a brandy coffee, reading a psychology book. Psychology is stuff you knew but didn't realise you knew. Or a history book, usually a lengthy history of the Caribbean, all pirates, planters and slaves – all history is basically ruthlessness and cruelty – or just gazing out to sea and thinking ...

Q. How would a chap like me accumulate some serious currency?

A. I could sit and be patient, work hard, like a navvy down a hole, legit, year after year, accumulating stock and assets *or* I could go sniffing around for a shortcut. Life, I've worked out, is about being in the right place at the right time. Or, on the other hand, the wrong place at the wrong time.

Q. Why are you here, at the airport, in Barbados?

A. Sometimes our minds are made up for us.

One evening I was stood outside my own hotel waiting, with great humility, in the line for a taxi. A gent, my age, tanned and handsome, strolled outta the hotel and gave the car valet a wink and a green dollar bill, of what denomination I don't know but the kid dashed off to fetch his motor. The guy was trying to relight his cigar and still had his wedge in his hand, held together with a chunky silver bill-clip. A thousand-dollar bill had somehow managed to separate itself from the herd and was hanging half out of the clip. I thought the note was going to catch fire because the gent was holding his lighter so close to it. But instead it detached itself from the clip, fluttered to the floor and caught the lively wind. The G-note spun in tight circles like it was chasing its own tail. I watched it with interest, and the guy watched me watching the thousand-dollar bill doing its spinning dervish dance but neither of us moved. The wind vanished suddenly. For a second the note drifted to the floor and remained motionless but then the wind snatched it up again. The gent watched, more curious than bothered, neither smiling nor frowning. But I could tell he was intrigued; it was the finest distraction he'd had for a while. He didn't want it to stop. The note made its way along a row of privets then went out of sight, was lost. But then it reappeared, skipping along the floor, back towards where we stood. It rushed in front of the guy. He could have stamped on it. But he didn't.

A grand – seven hundred quid – and all he had to do was bend down and pick it up. But he couldn't be bothered. He wasn't showing off; he just saw a thousand dollars as an abstract thing. It no longer held any value, was simply a piece of paper blowing in the wind. It wasn't wages for a week or a month; it's how you score the game.

The note disappeared into the twilight. There was no shrug, no nothing. No emotion either way. The guy's car arrived. He got in and drove away. Out of my life.

But later that evening I left a message for my friend Mister Mortimer in London using our primitive jungle telegraph. Due to a series of events that went down many moons ago it was always in our mutual best interests that we never got into the clutches of law enforcement. We had to look out for each other, same as when we shuffled kilos around town and both ended up with a tidy stash. When I had to get out Morty semi-retired because the law were convinced he'd killed some geezer who got battered to death in a café. Morty, heavy-duty black dude, a generation older, with genuine charm, had been responsible for protecting our firm. Mort would pop over to the Caribbean to see me. The last time he was over this side, a couple of months ago, I started to tentatively sound him out.

We'd set up a freebie email account where we both knew the address but more importantly the *password*. If I needed to contact Mort I would drive down the road to the cyber-café, open up the account and, avoiding the inbox altogether, go straight to the 'drafts' folder. I would find the draft of the last message that either Mort or myself had written. I would then alter it, letting him know in innocuous code what was required. I arranged a conversation between two call boxes using a pre-paid phone card.

I would save the draft and sign out. Most importantly I would not actually send the message so there was nothing to intercept on the very-much-monitored Internet. We would regularly check the drafts folder to see if there were any messages. I sent the message saying I needed a conversation on the weekend, five on a scale of ten for urgency. I suggested noon GMT Sunday, seven in the morning my time. He got back quick – no problem.

The essence of my conversation with Mort was I wanted to either sell the shares in the hotel on the quick and on the quiet, or, after much patient preparation, shift them into an impenetrable offshore holding company and disappear off the face of the earth.

Relocate. What I told Morty was that I was in the market for a whole new profile – a couple of new passports, credit cards and a British driving licence. I had some photos taken in the shopping mall and had them FedExed over. I was open to ideas but I realised I would require tank money.

When we spoke again three days later Mister Mortimer told me to come over to Barbados, to rent a decent sized motor on a passable snide US licence, book myself into a quiet guesthouse. He gave me a flight number. He told me: 'I might have a little something for ya. Someone's been asking about you recently.'

Morty told me to meet him here, so I'm here. I let everybody know back in Jamaica that I was shipping out to Las Vegas – a conference on hotel management. My duplicitous management team doesn't believe me for a minute.

Sitting here in another airport. I hate waiting.

CHAPTER TWO

SHOCK AND AWE

I'd got over to the airport early, parked up the rental motor in the parking lot, ate lunch across the road, then took a leisurely stroll back, retrieved the motor and moved it to outside the arrivals lounge ready for the quick getaway. I wandered inside the terminal building, bought an English newspaper and sat down to wait. I was looking forward to hanging with Morty and getting a plan together. It was good to hang with Mort in the Caribbean. People took to him. He liked to get outta London and relax, eat and drink well, switch off.

As I'm watching the holidaymakers come off the planes through customs and immigration, I do a slapstick double-take. I see two faces from London queuing for their luggage. I don't believe it but it's true. I don't want them to see me if at all possible because they're a right pair of lunatics. I can't see Morty anywhere, but then, cool as ya like, he strolls out of the airside bathroom and wanders over to join them, laughing and joking. Maybe he's met them on the flight, but it's soon apparent they're with Mort.

As soon as I saw Mister Mortimer walking over to Sonny King and Twitchy Roy Burns, I knew it was not gonna be a quiet rendezvous in Barbados. Burning, wrecking, destroying and even possibly killing, Sonny was capable of it all. He's about five foot ten, bulked up from doing weights and 'roids, but carrying a bitova belly after too many rich takeaways. Sonny's a gym bod but I doubt if he could run a hundred yards without keeling over. Make no mistake, he could battle for hours and enjoy every second, indulged in recreational violence as a leisure activity. I'd never really got on with Sonny. I'd always hoped it was because we were at opposite ends of the evolutionary scale, but when I was in London I always kept him sweet as syrup on a spoon because Sonny's your worst nightmare.

Sonny King trades cocaine. Trades it very well, and has got very rich on the back of it because he serves every yard-dog and head-the-ball who can't get served anywhere else. While me and Mort had the occasional lunatic in the Rolodex, Sonny had the complete A to Z of unstable criminality on his beat. In every walk of life there's snobbery. Why should crims be any different? Sonny's posse are the lottery winners of the criminal world. They give criminality a bad name. I know criminals who wouldn't leave the house in the morning without doing the *Daily Telegraph* crossword, while Sonny's guys would struggle with a colouring book. And hierarchies exist wherever you go. I made good money from dealing so it's hypocritical of me to begrudge them their cash, but before powders came along this breed of guys were putting the grip on pub landlords, café owners, market traders for a drop of protection. Never had much in the way of imagination or talent. But times change.

And crime is like any other business these days; if it's not organised its going outta business. The days of getting up at midday, scratching yer bollocks, trying to work out your next move are gone. Sonny, to his credit, could gun a crew, could certainly be the Bilko. Sonny was always a player, but the beautifully insane thing about the drugs business is that you can go from nowhere to stratospheric wealth in weeks and months rather than years. Percentage growth rates, future growth projections – the statistics corporations pride themselves on – couldn't be worked out quick enough. If you drew a box two inches across by twelve high and then got a sharp pencil and drew a diagonal line from bottom to top, that would be Sonny's trajectory. And his business rivals didn't just step aside. Sonny is one of life's assault tanks.

The thing to always remember in the crime game is that you can rapidly go from hero – in the penthouse suite overlooking the harbour at Monte Carlo, surrounded by two-grand-a-night hookers, swigging pints of D.P. and lighting fat cigars with a fifty – to zero, the defendant in the dock at the Old Bailey, surrounded by the Metropolitan Police's paramilitary wing, getting a double-figure sentence.

Sonny was quite happy to swallow non-payment on occasion if

it gave him an excuse to go to town on some poor defaulter, but I don't think making money was the be-all-and-end-all. It's more to do with having heavy geezers look down and check their shiny shoes to avoid your gaze, and having fit birds with short skirts, big eyes and gamey attitudes standing on tiptoes to get a glimpse of you in the VIP.

According to Morty, Sonny had upgraded his grandiose fantasies and bought the ultimate plaything – a nightclub in the West End that was nominally run by an upper-class loon called Dougie Nightingale. Sonny bought in when coke-addled Dougie was on his arse and desperately needed funds. So Sonny's now hanging hard with the paparazzi fodder, skint-member-swells and the dubious chancers who inhabited that scene. Sonny should've been the silent partner but he couldn't stay away. He was no doubt using the club to fire his coke profit through the books. This was a move, buying nightclubs, that was regarded by savvied crims nowadays as being far too obvious, bringing too much exposure. The VIP area would soon be crawling with Sonny's entourage of thicknecks and slappers. Decent punters would give the gaff a wide berth. One brawl or firearms incident and it was all over.

The guy with Sonny, Twitchy Roy Burns, is one of life's professional sidekicks. Royski was called Twitchy cos he had a bad twitch that invaded his face at the first sign of threat, real or imagined. Back in London Roy had a reputation as a completely paranoid nut-nut who could get didgy if an unfamiliar milkman delivered his milk in the morning. Twitchy saw plain-clothes cozzers *everywhere* so he'd end up with a twitch, hence 'Twitchy' or 'The Twitch'. Exhausting business, being Roy.

I thought Roy had gone into retirement after his near misses with the Old Bill – he was incredibly lucky on a few occasions. The Other People – the law – were a millimetre or a minute out a few times in their strenuous attempts to nick him, so Roy started to tell people, seriously straight-faced, that he was gifted, protected by the hand of fate. Because Roy Burns is a belligerent pothouse who would bite your nose off, people would agree to his face – *yeah-yeah-yeah, Roy* – but piss themselves behind his back. The Twitch was of a breed best avoided, a criminal who's not as clever – or as lucky – as he thinks he is.

People in the past have looked at Royski, with his mad ginger hair and rake of freckles, and thought he was a lightweight, the court jester, but this is a geezer who plunges fellow motorists in the face, with chisels, if they take up too much of *his* road. Roy dresses like a slightly deranged golf pro, a straight-goer – consequently a few major dudes have come seriously unstuck by underestimating Royski. He was, back in the day, and probably still is, priceless and mad as cheese. I thought Roy had retired to the Costa del Sol to run a bar for ex-pat criminals so I'm surprised to see him reactivated and getting off the all-inclusive package-tour charter flight with Mister Mortimer, who'd never entertain these two unless it was serious business. This isn't a jolly for Mister Mortimer, but our coded chat had made no mention of Twitchy or Sonny.

The flight's luggage is starting to tip up on the baggage reclaim carousel. One after the other three massive, identical, brand new Samsonite cases appear. They're shrink-wrapped in industrial cling film that makes them almost impossible to ransack. I know from intuition that those cases belong to Mister Mortimer and his travelling companions. I'm proved right. Sonny barges roughly through the waiting passengers and starts wrestling with the first case. It's almost as wide as he is. Sonny pulls it off the carousel and starts wheeling it self-consciously across the arrivals lounge towards the customs and immigration. He sails through after a polite glance at his passport but now he's telling the airport porters who hustle a few dollars by shifting luggage to fuck off.

Roy and Morty wait and then follow the same procedure, and now all three of them are heading across the stuffy arrivals lounge towards me and the exit. The lovely-northern-lass holiday rep, with her canary yellow uniform and clipboard, is trying to shepherd all her flock but this trio – fifty stone of London villain – marches straight past, eyes front, ignoring her. She looks at them anxiously – just once, a split-second, sniffs trouble, not wrong – and charges off in the other direction.

'Give us a fuckin hand,' Sonny says as he reaches me, 'Standing there like some soppy cunt, fuckin watchin.'

'Nice to see ya, Sonny,' I say, 'You should get one of those porters to schlep it for ya.'

'I don't want 'em near it, the thieving cunts,' he says.

He's sweating buckets cos he's still dressed for windswept London, and it's thirty-two degrees in the shade. Morty and Roy arrive with their cases.

'It woulda cost ya three Bajan dollars,' I say to Sonny. ''Bout a quid.'

'Don't be smart with me, cunt, okay, just don't,' he replies. 'Where's the fuckin motor?'

I nod at the non-descript Chrysler parked in the tow-away zone.

'Fuckin hell! Is that it, Mort?' screams Sonny, 'Didn't ya tell this cunt to get a big car?'

Mort just shrugs, ain't worried either way. 'You jump in there with him,' he says to Sonny, 'Roy and me'll get a taxi. The driver'll know the hotel. You tail us in, okay.'

Morty summons a cab, and him and Roy manhandle their massive suitcases into the boot while Sonny pushes his onto the back seat of the rental. So I get lumbered with Sonny, who's now panting with the heat and furiously wiping his shaved head with an airline napkin. I would really like to be two-ed up with Morty so I could ask him what the fuck is going on but I follow Roy and Mort's cab at a leisurely pace, taking in the scenery. Luckily Sonny was never much of a conversationalist. He says nothing, just munches gum menacingly.

The hotel they're booked into is a collection of bungalows and three-storey blocks surrounding a lagoon-shaped swimming pool. It's been landscaped with neat, clipped lawns, meandering paths and palm trees. There's a quaint signpost made from pretend driftwood pointing to the reception – an open-air office with a counter, a veranda with chairs and sofas around bamboo tables.

As we park up, Morty and Roy are out of the cab and checking in. Sonny won't let porters near his case but hollers at Mort and Twitchy to come and *give him a fuckin hand – paira lazy cunts.* Bajans don't like people swearing in quiet conversation, let alone roaring across hotel lobbies. Other guests turn and give Sonny a funny look but he's oblivious, *telling* the receptionist he wants three rooms in a row, peeling battered American dollars off a fat roll and throwing them at her. She gathers up the banknotes – because it's a few weeks' wages – then derisively hands them their keycards, still looking offended as we walk away.

We all troop up to the rooms on the third floor with a view over the rolling Atlantic Ocean, but instead of the three of them going into their own rooms they all march into Sonny's. They haul the three suitcases onto the massive double bed. Sonny immediately takes off his Versace leather jacket and slings it into the corner, peels off his soaking sweatshirt and gym vest, then stands under the full-blast air con looking like a big, sweaty Buddha.

Morty sinks into a bamboo chair in the corner, lights a snout and opens some duty-free cognac, taking a long swig, straight from the bottle. Roy is trying to work out how the telly works with the remote control, pushing every button. Suddenly the room erupts with the deafening slapstick of cartoons. Royski is instantly captivated and enchanted. I feel spare.

'Can I ask a question?' I ask Sonny. 'Two questions, actually.'

'Go on,' says Sonny, borrowing Roy's twitch.

'First, what am I doing here?'

'You're here to give us a hand with something. Next question?' says Sonny, starting to laugh real sinister.

'What are you two doing here?'

'All in good time.'

'Sonny,' says Morty, a tiny wink in Sonny's direction, 'stop fuckin about and show the man. Let the dog see the rabbit.'

'Roy, fuck's sake,' says Sonny, suddenly playing the Don. 'Turn that fuckin racket off and show the geezer here the you-know-what.'

Roy gets up, flicks the telly off, goes over to the cases, and begins to tear off the shrink-wrap covering each case. Neither Morty nor Sonny goes to help or offer any encouragement. Every time he tries to dispose of a solid ball of plastic it won't leave his hands – it sticks, like it's meant to.

'It was your big idea, Roy,' says Sonny dryly.

Roy cracks on with his battle with the shrink-wrap. I go to help but Sonny motions me not to. Every time I go to speak Sonny places his finger silently over his lips – shut up.

Eventually Roy gets all the wrap off. The cases are lying neatly in a row on the bed. One by one he begins to feed in the combinations and flicks back the locks, leaving them shut. When they're all unlocked, Roy goes back to the first and – with a sense

of drama that I never imagined he had – walks along flicking each
one open in rapid succession to reveal bundles of fifty and twenty
pound notes, some in bank-wraps, some in elastic bands, crammed
into every corner, packed with care so all the Queen's heads are
pointing in the same direction. All the bundles have been
professionally vacuum-shrink-wrapped, like supermarket bacon,
to deter highly motivated sniffer dogs detecting massive amounts
of grubby currency making its way across the globe.

'How much is there?' I ask.

'Two million, seven hundred and forty thousand,' says Sonny
with a shrug, 'give or take a grand.'

'That's an awful lotta holiday money, chaps.'

Sonny's suddenly angry, across the room in three strides, right
in my face.

'You know what you are, don't ya?' he says with a pointy
finger under my nose. 'You're too smart for your own good.'

'Oi, Sonny,' says Morty, taking a swig on the brandy, 'behave
yourself, okay? Be nice.'

CHAPTER THREE

A DIFFERENT KINDA BANK JOB

'Don't get too cosy, you lot. We're a bit early,' says Sonny, tapping his watch. 'You know what? We shoulda told that cab to wait.'

'Ring the reception,' I suggest. 'They'll ring one local.'

'Don't talk 'bout it! Do it!' says Sonny, turning to them, pointing at me. 'Listen to this cunt, givin out his orders.'

I ring for a cab and ten minutes later we're on our way into Bridgetown, me and Sonny in the rental, Roy and Morty padded up together. I think maybe Morty's deliberately swerving me, but I don't know why.

It's three o'clock and the temperature's in the low nineties, hot for the time of the year, even by Barbados standards. Sonny wants all the windows open and the air con full on at the same time, won't let me explain that the windows need to be shut for the AC to work. Sweat runs down my face and into my eyes. In the rear-view mirror I can see Sonny's suitcase on the beat seat. It strikes me as bordering on reckless, checking in luggage to be fiddled about with at Heathrow, but then an enterprising gent like Sonny would have people straightened out all over. Sonny's suitcases, wrapped in their cocoon, would be the last thing to get loaded onto the plane before it took off.

Bridgetown is bustling when we arrive. I spent some time in Barbados a few years ago, before I landed in Curaçao. Today the main duty-free shopping street is crowded with affluent, retirement-age punters – sloppy Joes, emblazoned with 'Jamaica', 'St Lucia' – palm trees, parrots and sunsets. There's three cruise ships in the harbour and the tourists are ashore in swarms, dropping their dollars for luxury goods and services.

Sonny's told me to head for St George Street, over by the Lower Green bus station; he's clutching a moist, hand-drawn diagram. He told Mort and Roy, if they got lost, to meet us there, specifically by a set of Cable and Wireless phone booths, *four in a row*. As luck would have it, I find it straight away and there's a vacant parking space next to the phones.

'What's the time here?' says Sonny, tapping his watch, on London time, approaching seven p.m.

'About ten to three,' I reply.

'Good, we're early,' he says, getting out.

Only one of the four phones is occupied. Sonny stands, arms folded, in front of a booth where a young guy is parked up obviously talking to some lady friend – flirting, dancing, giggling and whispering – coaxing her knickers off. Sonny starts pacing in front of the guy's phone box but Romeo's oblivious, what with being all fired-up. I nod towards the other three phones but Sonny shakes his head. I work it out. Sonny isn't making a call; he's looking to receive one. He wants *that* phone booth, that number. Romeo puts the phone down and strolls off.

Sonny steps into the phone booth just as Mort and Roy pull up, pay the driver, haul their cases out the taxi and line them up next to the rental motor. Sonny's now got the receiver tucked under his chin. He gets out a cigarette packet and slings it over to Roy.

'Light us one of them, will ya?' says Sonny.

'What, someone chop yer hands off?' says Roy, indignant.

'I'm busy, ain't I?' says Sonny, nodding towards the receiver. He's got the button pushed down. I was right. Roy lights a snout for Sonny.

'Come on to fuck,' Sonny says to himself, looking at his watch again.

'What time you got, Sonny?' says Morty, leaning on the motor.

'Comin up to eight,' he replies, showing Morty his wafer-thin, platinum timepiece.

'If the guy said eight,' says Mort with a shrug, 'he means on the dot. You can set yer watch by these guys.'

The clock on the Anglican church starts to strike three o'clock. The phone rings exactly on the last chime. Sonny smiles, gives us a wink, lets it ring twice then picks it up. He has a short conversation, finishing with one final 'Okay Skip, over and out.'

He puts the phone down. He's grinning, rubbing his hands together like a racecourse bookie. He even gives me a playful slap on the shoulder.

'Right, we're all systems go. Royski, Mort, you know where you gotta be,' Sonny says, and hands Mister Mortimer the diagram. Then he turns to me.

'Give Roy them car keys, son.'

'No, I'll drive,' I say.

'No, Bullseye, you're on point with me.'

'But why? I don't understand—'

'I was *told* to bring you in there—'

'Where?'

'You'll see when you get there.' He gives me the pointy finger, 'You wanna consider it a privilege.'

'Don't worry, bro,' says Morty, 'you may have to do this on your own.'

Sonny shoots Mort a nasty, sideways look. Morty spots it.

'You okay, Sonny?' says Mort with a sarcastic wink. 'Feelin the heat?'

'Nah, nah, Mort, I just wanna get it done, have a shant. Go off-duty,' says Sonny. He takes off down the street. 'Leave the fuckin cases!' Sonny shouts over his shoulder. 'Follow me! And hurry up! Come on, we've got an appointment! You'd think we've got all day to fuck about, the way you behave!'

A minute later we arrive outside the Conciliated Bank of Barbados. Sonny spits his gum out on the steps, kisses the ends of his fingertips and lovingly pats the polished brass plaque, leaving grubby fingerprints. As we're about to go in he deliberately holds the door shut for a split-second, turns to me, winks, flicks his head, extremely cocky now. 'Look and learn, son,' says Sonny Fuckin King, a man I wouldn't ask to lick a stamp. 'Look and fucking learn.'

Inside, the bank is colonial, wood-panelled, marble-floored but very hi-tech on the business side of the counter. It's dark after the bright sunshine. The ceiling fans work overtime but are fighting a losing battle. A line of customers wait to be served – ladies with Sunday hats and battery-operated hand fans, gentlemen in short-sleeved shirts with string vests visible underneath, wiping sweat from the backs of their necks with neatly folded handkerchiefs. We stick out like a pair of snowmen.

'Can you see Customer Services?' he says, looking about.

'Over there, Sonny,' I point with a nod.

'Don't fuckin call me "Sonny",' he says outta the side of his mouth.

'You shoulda told me that before,' I whisper.

'I'm tellin ya now, ain't I, you cunt,' says Sonny, the church-like acoustics carrying his voice like he's singing opera. There is no known word for 'tact' in Sonny's vocabulary.

Half the queue – young and old alike – turn and look at us disapprovingly, shake their heads and pull lemon-sucking faces.

Sonny, oblivious, rings the bell by the Customer Service window. A few seconds later a young woman appears at the other side of the counter.

'I'm Mister Berkeley,' says Mister King, ludicrously pointing at himself, 'and I'm expected.'

'One second, Mister Berkeley, someone will attend to you shortly,' she says, then disappears.

A second woman, dressed like a head prefect in a sky-blue and white CBB blazer, comes to the window. 'I'll buzz you through,' she says. 'That one there.'

She points at a door with a wired-glass window and combination keypad where the keyhole should be. There's a long buzz. Sonny opens the door. We walk through. Now we're in a tiny room – I could touch both walls – like an airlock but with another windowed door. The inside door buzzes. Sonny tries to open it. But it doesn't respond. Through the glass the woman shakes her head, motions for him to be patient.

I've seen these set-ups before – all buzzes and blips, one door has to be shut before the next one opens – in banks and prison visiting wings. As soon as the weighted outside door clicks shut, the inside door releases and the woman opens it and welcomes us through. But she turns to talk to me. 'Good afternoon, Mister Berkeley,' she says, 'Mister Curtis will be along—' I hold up my hand, say nothing but nod towards Sonny, now AKA Mister Berkeley. She turns to Sonny. 'Oh, sorry, Mister Berkeley, I thought ... I'm terribly ... Please come this way.'

The woman, whose blazer badge tells me her name is Pearl and she's a Customer Relations Manager, leads us down a windowless corridor, a total contrast from the sedate, old world, public end of the operation. There's closed doors every ten feet. It's air con chilly. She stops at a door, punches in a combination number, opens it. We're in the airlock scenario again. We enter, like strangers in an elevator while we wait – an awkward shyness, thin smiles, shuffles and raised eyebrows.

When the inside door eventually buzzes Pearl motions us into a spacious room with no windows, furnished, at the far end, with comfy sofas and coffee tables with tasselled lamps. In contrast, at the end nearest the door, there are two metal office desks with an IBM computer terminal on each one. It has the air of plastic corporate hospitality, like it was ordered from an industrial furniture catalogue. On the walls there are repro paintings of boats being loaded with cargoes in Bridgetown's Carlisle Bay. Fanned out neatly on the coffee tables are upmarket investment and fashion magazines – US editions. It has the feel of a private doctor's waiting room.

'Mister Curtis will be right down,' says Pearl. 'Can I get you some coffee? Tea? Iced water?'

'No, no, we're all right,' says Sonny in a slightly posh voice. Mister Berkeley is nervous but covering it well, standing like a fidgety schoolboy, arms folded awkwardly across his chest.

Pearl gives me a cheeky smile, turns and goes through the rigmarole of getting out, leaving Sonny and me alone. He begins pacing the navy blue carpet with the CBB emblem woven through it in gold. I sit down, shuffle through the magazines and start reading an article in *Cosmopolitan* about plastic surgery addiction while Sonny tears up the carpet and huffs and puffs enough for two. But I'm getting more curious, working out what we're up to – suitcases crammed fulla readies, pre-arranged phone calls, synchronised watches, aliases, appointments at banks, red carpet treatment ...

I'm also starting to enjoy this. Something's woken up, and that something deep inside likes sitting in the inner sanctum of a bank, being offered cups of tea or coffee, being *welcomed* in, being *invited* to enter.

Q. Why?

A. Because for generations the likes of me were drilling through reinforced concrete walls during bank holiday weekends, bypassing security systems, coming down through ceilings, up from sewers, or using frontal assaults with sawn-off shotguns, trying to get the banknotes *out* of the bank. Nowadays the likes of me and Sonny are assembled here – locked *in* rather than locked *out* – one of us patiently reading in *Cosmo* about all-the-rage-in-Hollywood designer vaginas, the other wearing a hole in their monogrammed carpet, waiting for them to *accept*, with thanks, three suitcases full of plunder.

I hear the door buzz, look up and see a gent waving regally behind the glass. Another buzz and into the room steps a guy I take to be Mister Curtis. I'm pointing at Sonny to avoid any confusion and denting Sonny's ego.

'Mister Berkeley?' he says to Sonny, half question, half assumption, sticking out a hand. 'Rupert Curtis.'

'Yes, that's me. I'm Mister Berkeley,' says Sonny, shaking hands, trying to sound like a swell. 'Glad to make your acquaintance.'

I have to stop myself from laughing out loud. Sonny spots me grinning and snarls while Mister Curtis turns his attention to his paperwork. I get up to shake hands with Mister Curtis. Sonny – AKA Mister Berkeley – introduces me. 'This is my colleague, Mister Hunt.'

Someone's briefed Sonny on exactly what to say; the word 'colleague' is definitely not in his vocabulary. And someone has definitely got a sense of humour cos now we're Monsieurs Berkeley and Hunt ... AKA a right pair of Berkeley Hunts.

'It's good to put a face to a name, Mister Berkeley,' says Curtis. 'We always welcome meeting our valued clients face to face. And we are willing to accept cash ... on occasion, when necessary, from the favoured few. You do understand, don't you?'

This is flattery. Curtis would have your hand off if you walked in here with cash to deposit.

Mister Curtis is about my age, looks good – tanned face, sun-bleached hair, the sharp Caucasian features of a native of Stockholm or Oslo. His accent is pure Bajan – a well-preserved eighteenth-century West Country English. The white Bajans ruled the island for years – owned everything, the slaves and the sugar plantations – and they still occupy all the positions of power. They stick together and marry among themselves. I spot a long chain hanging from his belt, down almost to his knee and back into his front trouser pocket.

'Everything appears to be in order, Mister Berkeley,' says Mister Curtis, nonchalantly. 'Shall we get cracking? *Tempus fugit.*'

'Do what?' says Sonny, mystified.

'Time waits for no man,' replies Curtis.

He leads us through the two-door arrangement into the corridor. We follow him briskly round a corner and up to a double steel door. There's a very relaxed but very armed security guard sitting at a metal desk. Mister C greets him real friendly, first-name terms. They have a how's-the-wife-and-kids chat while Mister Curtis fills in a form on a steel clipboard. He looks up at a wall clock, writes down the exact time then hands it to the guard. He steps up to the door, takes a long thin key from the chain and unlocks first a top lock then a lower one. Then Curtis taps in the combination. A long buzz. Tumblers roll inside the door. Then using his weight he pulls the steel door open.

We step into yet another antechamber – larger than any of the previous, with an ominous CCTV camera tilted down at us, its red eye blinking – with a heavy steel door. I realise that they're giving us the new punter's tour, showing us the vault so we can sleep peacefully knowing all our funds are tucked up safe.

'This is a pain in the ... ' whispers Curtis, like he's said something naughty, 'but necessary.'

He does the whole number again – keys, locks, combos, buzzes – and then, with a flourish, he swings the door wide open.

I'm looking out into an empty car park, behind Bridgetown's main drag. I'm whacked by a surge of scorching heat, like I've stepped into a sauna. I'm squinting; have to shield my eyes from the intense late-afternoon sun. Through the haze I spot Mort with Twitchy Roy, leaning on the motor, bored, killing time, shades on, snout in one hand and the other shielding his eyes. The Samsonites are lined up, neat and tidy, straight as soldiers.

'Are those your other colleagues?' Mister Curtis asks. Sonny nods. 'Best we get weaving then, hadn't we, Mister Berkeley?'

CHAPTER FOUR

DROPPING OFF THE BAGWASH

Money laundering is basically getting the nasty, tainted cash cleaned up and into the money-go-round so it can be spent without attracting attention. It's getting it from being large chunks, or suitcases full, of paper into credit digits on a balance sheet. If you try to buy a property these days using cash, it can't be done without creating suspicion. You can't wander into estate agents with bags full of readies and select the Desirable Residence you want, although some whacked guys try. If you ain't got the agent and solicitor seriously Vale of Kent you can end up getting seriously nicked. You can't even pay off a large credit card bill in cash anymore. Bundles of cash ain't a lotta good, not in the amounts that people are making these days. If you turn up at a bank and try and deposit over ten gee, they're meant to inform the authorities, if they think its très suspect. Whether or not this happens depends on who you are, and who they are, what they have to gain by keeping quiet, and how corruptible or straight they are. If you've got good reason to be paying in cash – you own bars, nightclubs or a chain of dollar shops – fair enough. But increasingly everything – goods and services – is being bought and sold with plastic magic. In the future cash will no longer exist, wealth will only exist as credits on a database. Banknotes won't be worth the paper they're written on, but for the time being what you need is a 'sink', meaning quite literally somewhere you can sink your *schwarzgeld* into the system. When I was active, four years ago, I had shares in cash-heavy businesses – letting agencies, clothes shops, car washes, flower stalls – whose sole purpose was to spin the skull profits. If we did no trade that week, no problem; we'd still send a good few gee through the highly fictional accounts. I was paying income tax on drug earnings. I was a portfolio-maintaining, property-owning, role model.

If the law flop on you, kick the door off at six in the morning, cos they think, or they *know*, you're up to skullduggery cos you're living in a huge drum – six bedder, swimming pool, tennis courts

– and you can't show them where you got the funds, ze authorities can seize any assets they can find. Nowadays you gotta have a good, nod-and-a-wink accountant in the hedge as well as a canny lawyer on twenty-four-hour pager call.

It's a game. If Sonny King wants to buy a house, a car, Park Lane with a couple of hotels on it or a nightclub to sink even more funny money into, what you need is a Credit Transfer or Letters of Credit from your highly respected bank. If an up-and-coming sniff retailer wants to treat himself to a BMW rag-top, straight off the forecourt, he has to riddle out how to do it without giving the salesman a chunk of cash, cos he's obliged to drop the dime. The hard part nowadays is getting your loot *into* the system rather than getting it out.

When you start to make money in the telephone numbers category – and Sonny is evidently making money – it's handy if you can just tip up without any pretence about being legit and simply fire your soiled readies into the global bagwash. Finding an accommodating bank can be a lot harder than wholesaling vast amounts of drugs. Somebody obviously vouched for Mister Berkeley, so when we arrived it was simply a question of crossing tees and dotting eyes. It starts to become clear, judging by Mister Curtis' sycophantic attitude, that Sonny is already an account holder of some standing but I get the distinct impression that this is the first time he's dropped by *in person*.

Someone, most probably back in London, could have set up an electronic route around the like-minded establishments, so although Sonny's readies woulda physically stayed in the vault of the CBB, Sonny's credit balance would have been pin-balling around the global financial markets, never staying any longer than a few minutes in any location but leaving an impregnable maze to follow. You'd start off with crooked banks and slowly work your way towards the legit ones. If you're very smart, know your shallots, have the right connections, you can send monies flying at the click of a switch into the labyrinth. Every transfer makes it that little bit more legit but you'd still need to show the UK authorities how you earned your riches, *if* you decide to bring it home; you could leave it tucked up in beautifully anonymous Zurich, or start buying up real estate abroad.

Sonny can deposit his chunk in Barbados and seconds later it's landing in an account in Switzerland. If Sonny was to drop down dead here in the West Indies tonight – had the jammer up a ten-dollar hooker – nobody, not his relatives, business associates or British Old Bill could get those funds out of a Swiss bank. If you think about it, the peace-loving, neutral Swiss must be playing host to trillions or zillions of pounds, dollars, euros, francs and yen that's been squirrelled away by profiteering Nazis, global narco-crims, corrupt autocrats, shady arms dealers or African dictators who've met an abrupt end. All that being dead secretive can work both ways, if you end up secretly dead. You put your loot in, on the QT ...

'You don't come back? Vee get to keep, yah? Wunderbar! Wundervoll!'

Simple Swiss genius.

What's in it for the Conciliated Bank of Barbados? They will charge a handling fee, assessed on a percentage of the value of the transaction, depending if the money is to stay in their moneybox available for loans and investments, or the funds were just being landed; that is, sunk and moved on. If you're a bank you can never have too much cash splashing about; a basis principle of banking is that you hope that all your customers don't want to withdraw their money at the same time. Even at a commission of between two to ten percent it's a good afternoon's work. This trifling percentage might even be a secret contribution to Curtis' own personal pension fund.

It took almost two hours to count the money. Mister Curtis had two teams, each two-handed, sending the notes flying, taped up into bundles of ten and twenty grand, then cobbling into hundreds, then the hundreds went into millions, checked and signed for. The girls looked like they had a system going; teamwork was the key. Mister Curtis patrolled with a steel clipboard, writing down figures, running between the desks, tapping away at the computer terminals, punching numbers into a quaint old-fashioned adding machine, tearing the paper off the roll and handing it to Sonny.

Sonny kept the girls under surveillance the whole time. I think he was worried that they might stick a few notes down their panties, and he wasn't working all hours, day and night, to subsidise anyone. One of those bricks of notes represents a lifetime's labour – maybe they're too honest for their own good.

All the notes had been prepared in advance, all facing the right direction for feeding into counting machines. I was quite looking forward to watching the fit girls in their sky-blue and white CBB uniforms feeding the notes in. In its full glory, a counting machine in action is a sexy thing, whirling and clicking, but this outfit, the CBB, actually *weigh* the notes on seriously accurate electronic scales. It gives them a reading down to the fourth decimal point and they know, from experience, *exactly* how much ten thousand in Bank of England tens, twenties and fifties should come to. It's quite sedate. After a while I went and joined Morty and Twitchy on the sofas, drinking coffee and flicking through magazines. Only Sonny watched the whole show.

Roy and Mort both dozed off at different times. They'd had a long day and looked relieved as the count started to slow down. Blocks of money were put on a stainless steel handcart and wheeled away. A final figure was arrived at and both Sonny, signing awkwardly as Mister Berkeley, and Mister Curtis signed the receipt. Sonny was presented with a *belated* customer service pack like any new customer visiting the branch. *You never got one of these, did you, Mister Berkeley?*

Mister Curtis then disappeared for a few minutes and returned with fresh statements. He and Sonny went into a huddled conversation while me, Mort and Roy waited on the sofa. Sonny emerged rubbing his hands like they were about to catch fire. As he got up to leave he even went as far as to pat Curtis good-naturedly on the shoulder, said he'd pop back later for his suitcases.

The bank was shut as we left through the back entrance, walked across the car park, up the street and round the corner onto the harbour. It's six, dark, and cooler than it was. A shower of rain has fallen. As Sonny's walking he makes a call on his cell phone, probably back to London. Then he clenches his fists, crouches and starts rocking his torso backwards and forwards.

'Yes, yes, yes,' Sonny says over and over but he seems to be saying, *I've showed them cunts! I showed 'em!* Then Sonny sidles up beside me, calm now, puts his arm around my shoulder, opens the CBB ledger statement and holds it under my nose for me to read in the twilight.

'Read it and fuckin weep, bruv.'

The credit column is full, one after the other, of six-figure deposits, while the debit column is empty. I do a double-quick double-take. Sonny's ongoing balance at today's close of business is a smidgen over fifteen million dollars, about nine million pounds sterling.

It's my turn to be bewildered. How did a belligerent lunatic make that sorta money?

By the time we've walked around the quayside – full of yachts and catamarans bobbing on the gentle swell – and sat down in the Harbour Rendezvous bar, Sonny's a lot more with us but now my head is seriously spun.

The Rendezvous is about as trendy as it gets in Bridgetown, full of early evening drinkers, groovy Bajans, black and white, rich tourists, ex-pats and ocean-going sailors.

'Let's have champagne, but first I wanna large brandy,' says Sonny. 'What ya sayin, chaps?'

'Whatever,' says Roy, with a tired shrug.

'Fuckin 'ell, liven up, Mister Burns, you're on holiday now. That,' says Sonny, pointing back toward the bank, 'is mission accomplished.'

'Just a bit tired, mate,' says Roy, a low-grade twitch starting to appear.

'Okay, don't go on,' says Sonny. 'Am I a genius, or what?'

'That was a tidy bitta work,' says Mort, trying to get a waitress's attention. Without warning, Sonny's on his feet, clenched fists, screaming. 'Yeeessss!!!'

'Sonny, mate, sit down,' says Morty, firmly. People turn and look. It'd only take one disapproving glance for Sonny to be kicking off. Morty's pulling him back down into his seat.

'Keep it dark, Sonny,' I say, then regret it.

'Who are you, tellin me to keep quiet?' roars Sonny, standing up again, blocking the light.

'Sit down, Sonny,' says Mort. 'We don't want anyone gettin busy.'

I'm scared. I'd be mad if I wasn't. Inside Sonny's head there's a switch and if it's thrown, nobody is gonna stop him from tearing me apart. Once geezers like Sonny go they go. All the jails and punishment blocks in the world can't stop them. Morty coaxes him back down into his seat. Sonny's breathing heavy. What he's saying is now he's got money a cunt like me should respect him, whether I like it or not. And strangely enough, he has just shot up in my estimation. A waitress comes over. Mort orders four brandies and four beers.

'Later, Sonny, we'll have champagne,' says Mort, like he's reassuring a child. 'We'll have a nice shower and go somewhere nice to eat. How's that sound?' But Sonny's screwing me – eye-to-eye contact. Locked in.

Sonny, I'm thinking, you have to keep a low one over here. This isn't London. You can't just lose yourself. Everybody knows everybody's business. You gotta respect the way people go about their business. They don't fuckin curse and fucking swear every other cunting word. To them it's offensive. These Bajans are religious people; wait till you see them on Sunday, all dressed up, off to hallelujah-jump-up church. They're grafters in the old-fashioned sense. We have to blend in, camouflage ourselves. Flashing the cash brings attention. People talk; it's human nature. They ask questions. People start getting busy. And to be honest, I'm surprised a Bajan bank entertained a manoeuvre like that. If we were in the Caymans or Panama ... Sonny, you ain't the first to think of turning up here pretending to be a package-holiday punter. Half the dudes knocking around this marina are plainies, undercover operators, or registered informants having a sniff to see who's buddied-up with who. This is the Caribbean, the Wall Street of the narcotics business. Every government has got agents knocking about. Think about it. Bobbing and weaving are UK Old Bill, Crim Intel, National Crime Squad, MI5, MI6, British Navy, Customs and Excise, Special Boat Service sailors on special assignment, nosing about. Then you've got the DEA and CIA, TAF and the FBI in the mix. The United States government have got warships – billion-dollar listening posts – steaming non-stop from Port of Spain to the Gulf of Mexico, Miami to Panama, in one big circle, looking and listening. Mister King, it's *always* a good idea to keep a low profile. Out here you could be the one taking a fall – the law need bodies. You do heavy jail time while the local operators run riot. And, by the way, your two and three-quarter mill, Sonny, and your fifteen mill in dollars back over at the CBB, it might be a big deal – it impressed me – but it's chump-change to some of the outfits who do their laundry round here. And one more thing to think about – there's some naughty, seriously twisted geezers in this part of the world who'd make you suck their dick before they decapitate and dismember you.

'Does that sound like a plan, Sonny?' says Mister Mortimer.

'Yeah, okay, Mort,' says Sonny, turning to me, slapping my leg, bringing me round.

'You've gone quiet,' he says to me. 'Something on your mind?'

'No, no, Sonny,' I reply. 'I'm sweet.'

CHAPTER FIVE

MADHEADS, MELTS, MACKERELS AND HEADPECKERS

Now Sonny's got his champagne – at two hundred dollars a pop, in the best seafood restaurant on the West Coast – and he's as happy as a pig in shit. I got the best table, on the first-storey balcony, overhanging the sea, cos I dropped the headwaiter three hundred bucks. The waves break on rocks below us, sending up spray that doesn't quite reach us. Yellow-beak cranes fly over the swell and stingrays play kiss-chase in the floodlit water below.

Sonny wants a big basket of French fries, so we can all dig in, and two more bottles of champagne, *the fuckin best 'n' all*. Classy guy. Psycho-trash-with-narco-cash. I had the waiters bring a huge seafood platter for a starter, told Morty I'd have what he's having, then went for a mooch about. I needed a break from Sonny and Roy. Also needed a think. I reckon there's a drop of entrapment occurring here, but not by law enforcement. I'm being headhunted. But:

Q. If Sonny has a nightclub to flush the spoils, why the cases full of cash?

A. Fuck only knows.

Maybe they need a pointman over this side, to meet couriers off planes, but every time I go to manoeuvre Morty aside, he tells me he's tired and *we'll talk tomorrow ... but it's all good*.

The August night is balmy, the gentle warm breeze changes direction every second. The moon is almost full, there's fairy lights on the cruisers out to sea and the food is the best. With different company this could be paradise; as it is I'm edgy cos Sonny, I've realised, has only three moods – got-the-hump, hostile or mad ecstatic – under the emotional hide of a rhino. When I get back he's on me.

'You're from London, right?' Sonny's saying to me, his arms folded tight across his chest, adopting attack mode. 'So why you talkin like a cunt, some fuckin Yankee. *Cell phone, fire-truck, sidewalk*,' he loudly mimics a bad Californian accent. Half the diners here are Americans.

'You pick up the accent very—'

'Either that or some moody swell, some posh cunt, on yer *splendid holidays*. Is that who you think you are? Some fuckin lord or something?'

'Sonny, I had to have it on my toes outta London. All that talkin outta the side of your mouth like a ... '

Whoops.

'Like a fuckin what, pal?' Sonny's alight, leaning forward.

'It brings attention. And people don't understand what the fuck you're on about.'

'Talking like a fuckin what?' He isn't letting go. I ignore him.

'You gotta be a bit,' I say, turning to Mort, 'what's the word?

'Inconspicuous?' suggests Morty.

'Answer me question,' hisses Sonny, leaning further over, giving me a poke. 'Talkin like a what?' He pokes me again. I give him his answer.

'Talking like an obvious London villain. Okay?' Sonny locks his eyes into mine, he's spitting furious.

'Loose lips sink ships,' says Roy, saving me.

'Do what?' says Sonny, baffled. 'What the fuck, Roy?'

'Wassat yer sayin, Royski?' says Mort, suppressing a grin.

'Talk, it's how we get caught. We talk too much.'

'Royski ... listen to me, now, okay,' says Sonny. 'Shut the fuck up, okay?'

'Tell the boys that story,' says Mort. 'You know, the one ... 'bout Evey.'

'Nah,' says Sonny.

'Go on,' says Morty.

'Okay. Listen to this,' says Sonny, instantly persuaded. 'This'll make ya laugh. I starts seein this bird called Eve, about three stretch ago.' Three years ago. If it's the Eve I'm thinking of, Mort used to call her Eve the Mackerel or just Mad Evey. Said she was the kinda bird who came home paralytic with her knickers in her handbag.

'She was all moved in, as I remember. Wasn't she, Sonny?' says Roy.

'Yeah, yeah, fuckin chavvie 'n' all. Kid was a right horrible cunt. She's moved in and things are sweet but one time she'd been into the gear.'

'Brown?' I ask. Heroin. Not like Sonny at all.

'Oh, yes. The Camden Town. But this was long before I met her. The kid's old man was bang at it and she ended up getting a habit as well. The old man's been lumped-off, like fourteen years. Geezer's a melt, a one-man crime wave, doin building societies and petrol stations with a sawn-off, robbing bookmakers to feed a gambling habit.'

'Went from social security to maximum security,' says Morty.

'That's good ... I like that.' Sonny starts to laugh, warming up now. 'Anyways the geezer's no real talent.'

Morty told me that Eve's husband, the kid's dad, brought shame upon his family – a tidy family of housebreakers – by running off and joining the British Army, *wanted more from life*. He met *and* married Eve on leave. Big mistake. She soon started driving him mad so he started volunteering for tours of duty in South Armagh to get some peace.

'So she's cleaned her act up, right?' I ask as innocent as I can.

'Yeah. He's three years into his fourteen stretch. Eve's dropped him right out, not even a letter, just stopped goin to see him. He's had the scream, about the kid, sent his family round the gaff. When I starts going with her I had a word, and everything's sweet. At first.'

'What was the problem?' I ask.

'I see now I got a bit *too* fuckin cosy. She starts gettin sneaky, sniffin me personal uncut stuff in daylight. You know what I say, don't ya?' says Sonny, looking serious. 'Cocaine's like the stars; only comes out at night. I'm out chasing a pound note, comin home and she's pranged, but moodyin she's ain't.'

'That's when the trouble starts,' I say. 'When people start losing control.'

'You're dead right, bruv,' he says, upturned index finger. 'Cokeheads are liabilities,' pronounces Sonny King, extremely affluent cocaine wholesaler, all high and mighty. 'Dangerous! Madheads!'

'Yeah, liabilities,' echoes Royski, coke-rich professional sidekick, nodding his head.

'I like a drop of the oats meself,' says Sonny, 'but she's gone silly on it. In the end I've slung her and the kid out but I've let her come back cos she's ringin me up crying and beggin.'

'Good move?' I ask.

'No, not really. She got worse. It wasn't a giggle anymore. Some people really enjoy a row, a good scream. Evey's a bird who likes nothing better than a smack in the mouth on Christmas morning, all the presents goin up in the air. All this in and out has gone on for a year. Soon I'm gettin dragged in, sitting up nights sniffin, drinkin like a fish. She starts pipin, smoking stones. Crack! Can you believe it? After she's had the big use-up she's ... What's the word?'

'Remorseful,' says Morty.

'That's it,' says Sonny, 'remorseful. And every time's the last time.'

'Till the next time,' I say. 'It's no good.'

'You're dead right. I ain't payin attention to business. But when she's on nuffin she's a headpecker, drivin me mad to get her something to take the edge off. Mornin time, instead of being out graftin, I'm huntin down those DF 118s. You know the ones I mean?'

'I know 'em,' I say. 'Heavy-duty opiate painkiller.'

'Right. Bodysnatchers I call 'em. She's tryin to come down so she can get the chavvie to school and kip all day. I'd end up on missions – tried to bribe a chemist one time to get a few Temazepam.' He takes a long slug of champagne. 'Almost got nicked, they rang the law, it kicked off, gaff got wrecked. Crack whores ... Bad news.'

'So what'd you do?' I ask, genuinely interested. This is confessional and contradictory. Maybe the booze on top of the jetlag is going to his head.

'Then she's got back on the gear, the brown, for real, so I've slung her out. But it's the old story – she's swearing on bibles, the kid's life, her mother's life. I taken her back but she's got a habit. I had an idea. I've taken her and the kid down to Spain so she can do a detox. I've gone down there to see Ted Granger and his firm.' This is serious name-dropping. Ted 'Duppy' Granger is a major international drug smuggler based in Spain, a good pal of Morty's.

Duppy is a nickname he is not exactly happy with. A duppy is a ghost, a cruel spirit.

'So you've gone to see Ted?' I ask, half impressed.

'Turns out a few of Duppy's team are dabblin, using the brown but obviously keepin it dark. I've come home but I left Eve plenty of spends. But after a coupla weeks I'm gettin reports that Evey's taken up with some hound down there,' says Sonny, giving me a dose of eye-to-eye. 'First I'm ready to jump on the plane, go down there, get tooled up, and serve the cunt, but I started to tell Morty about it.'

'And what did Mister Mortimer say?'

Sonny leans over and gives Morty a playful slap on the shoulder.

'Well he's brutal, beautiful but brutal.' Sonny laughs his mad laugh, refills the champagne glasses till they overflow and make puddles on the tablecloth. 'Mort won't beat about the bush,' continues Sonny, 'or fuck about.'

'Or spare your feelings?' I say.

'Morty says I should send the geezer down a case of Scotch or a parcel of gear. He's done you a favour. Mort gives it, "I don't wanna be rude about your ladyfriend but if this yard-dog has taken her off your hands, he's got enough on his plate without you goin down there and serving him. You're capable, Sonny, but do you need the grief?"'

Good old Morty.

'Morty says, "Do you love this Evey?" I say, "I don't know, Mort." He says, "Do you even *like* this Evey?" I says, "I don't know that either." Mort says, "Do you wanna do life in a Spanish nick, or start some feud with Duppy's firm, over some bird that you don't even *like*, who you've been tryin to jettison for years? Well do you, Sonny?" See Mort's made me see the funny side of it.'

'He a very good consigliere, Mister Mortimer,' I say.

'Morty says I shoulda lozzed her out at the first sign of mischief,' says Sonny. 'First sign – out!' He takes a celebratory hit of his drink, nodding, convincing himself over again. 'Ain't got time to have people messin with me head. It's about priorities.'

'Sounds like sense,' I say, appeasing Sonny.

'Right. So anyways, this is the killer. One year later, eight in the mornin, phone goes and it's her, Eve, cryin and wailin. I can hear all that bing-bong, tannoys, announcements, flights numbers, so I figure she's in an airport.' Sonny impersonates Eve, '"Boo-hoo-hoo, I'm really sorry, Sonny, I really am. I love you Sonny. I had to do what I did to know. Maybe we can get back together." The kid's screamin in the background. She ain't got a deano. Her money's run out so I've rung her back.'

'She's in Spain, right?' I ask.

'Oh, no. She's at Gatwick. She's junk-sick, cluckin, can hear it in her voice. She's sayin "Sonny, can we come over? Please, I'm beggin yer, I really fuckin need your help right now." She's desperado. I says, "What happened to yer boyfriend?" She's given it, "It was a mistake Sonny, I'm sorry." She's givin it, "Can I get a cab over?" I says, "Have you got any money?" She says, "I've had to sell everything to pay for plane tickets, Sonny." She's fuckin potless. Ted's crew wouldn't talk to her. Turns out the geezer she took up with was a grass.'

'That's not *her* fault, Sonny.'

Sonny switches, points at me. I'm spoiling his story. 'You bein funny? You a pie and liquor?' Sonny says coldly to Roy and Morty. 'When did he become a priest?' Sonny turns back to me, stating the obvious, 'She's *contaminated*.'

'Wasn't Eve a good mate of Ted Granger's sister, Bridget?' pipes up Roy.

'Yeah, what of it?' snaps Sonny.

'I'm just saying ain't I,' says Roy, shrugging his shoulders.

'So what happened with you and Eve?' Morty interrupts, starting to pay more attention.

'I told ya before, Mort, a few times,' says Sonny.

'Ya did, Sonny, but tell me again,' says Mister Mortimer, very dry.

'I says "I'll come and get ya."' Sonny's pretending like he's talking into a phone. 'She says, "No, Sonny, I'll get a cab." I says, "No, Eve, we could miss one another, don't go wanderin about, stay by the phone. Now, tell me where you are. By the KLM check-in at Gatwick? You stay there, Evey babes, I'm comin down to get ya."'

Curious, I never booked Sonny as that forgiving.

'I can hear the chav screamin. Always hungry, that kid.'

'How old's the kid?' inquires Morty.

'Five, six. Fuck knows. I put the phone down, went in the bedroom, got the suitcase off the top of the wardrobe, packed for a week somewhere hot, got me credit cards, bitta cash and headed out to Heathrow.'

'Hang on,' I say. 'You said she was out at Gatwick—'

'She fuckin was!' says Sonny, exploding with laugher. 'That's the fuckin beauty of it, waitin by the KLM desk at Gatwick Airport, with the brat, not a fuckin deano to buy any grub, waitin for some mug, this mug, to turn up and rescue her. Musta been trippin, soppy tart.' Sonny's become a slobbering, psycho teddy bear.

'So where did you go, Sonny?' asks dozy Roy, completely missing the point.

'I always head off on my jack, mid to late February, get a bitta colour, two weeks offa the booze, come back sharp. I normally go down the Canaries, pop in to see the chaps on the Costa on the way back, but the law was gettin busy, drivin poor Duppy mad. Business was a bit quiet, always is, February – kipper season, nobody ventures out. Evey made my mind up for me.'

'So where did you end up?' I say.

'Tunisia,' he replies.

'And how was Tunisia?' I ask.

'Was okay but never again. Funny gaff, really. You could fuck little boys no probs, but tryin to punt for a bird was a major operation.'

'Wouldn't recommend it, no?' asks dozy Roy, knowing the answer already.

'It was too fuckin hot, sandstorm blowin everyday. I stayed in the room most of the time with a coupla hookers. I got 'em proper performing. They beg ya to give it to 'em up the shitshoot, they plead with ya.'

'And you obliged?' inquires Morty.

'When in Rome, I say,' shrugs Sonny, laughing. 'You coulda bought these two, I mean to keep – your property, to bring home – for a score each.'

'Any word of Eve?' I ask. 'She been spotted?'

'She could still be at fuckin Gatwick Airport for all I care. Fuck her. I told ya it was funny.'

'When was this, Sonny?' I ask.

'Coupla years ago,' he replies.

I don't say nothing, there's nothing to say, but I catch Morty giving Sonny a curious look, smiling thinly. You can sometimes hear the cogs in Morty's brain turning, thinking about the starving kid, waiting out at the airport. Mort spent his early life being the hungry kid, plotted up outside the boozer, munching crisps for Sunday dinner, waiting on the alkie mother or the father, the permanently skint betting shop benefactor.

'What was the kid's name, Sonny?' asks Mort, quietly.

'Rory. The kid's name was Rory. You've never asked before, Mort. Why now?' Mort just raises one eyebrow a smidgen. A snapshot of his cool expression stays with me. 'Anyway,' says Sonny, turning to me and Roy, big grin, 'she always was a nuisance, that bird. Drink up chaps, there's plenty more. We're celebrating.' He turns to Royski and slaps him on the shoulder. 'I told you it would be okay, Roy. Do you see anyone following you? You worry too much.'

The main course arrives. The waiter silently places a plate in front of me. 'The king fish for you, sir,' he whispers.

'What's that you're havin?' says Sonny, leaning over.

'King fish.'

'Do what, pal?' says Sonny, suddenly aggressive.

'Hang on, Sonny, it's actually called *king fish*.'

'I know it's fuckin fish, pal. What sorta fuckin fish?'

'King fish, Sonny – Kay, Eye, En, Gee.' Then Sonny's cracking up laughing, slapping the table. Other diners turn to look.

'I had ya goin then, admit it, I did,' he's pointing at me. '"*It's actually called king fish.*"' Sonny's slapping the tabletop. The waiters look concerned, even scared. Royski don't get it but Morty looks at Sonny like he's measuring him for a coffin. 'Whatta cunt! Fuckin king fish! I saw it on the menu. They named a fuckin fish after me.' Sonny's turning crimson, gone hysterical, 'I say it meself. I can be a funny cunt.'

'Yes, Sonny, you can be funny,' I agree, nodding my head.

Fuckin funny peculiar.

CHAPTER SIX

MORTY'S PITCH

Morty asked me to come by their hotel at eleven the next morning so here I am, by the swimming pool, like a prick, in a linen suit, catching looks from Sonny. Morty is half-asleep on a sunlounger but more interested in watching a pair of bottle-blond Geordie birds – who are deliberately frolicking in the water for his attention – than letting me know why I'm in Barbados. Sonny and Royski are fidgety. And Sonny just can't accept that I want to sit in the shade under a sun umbrella; I ain't got the proper sun protection but Sonny seems to think that factor fifteen is *for irons and girls*. Sonny is happy, in his primitive way, talking non-stop, telling stories about the celebrity punters he gets down his club, going on about how he ignores them, how they're just ordinary bods to him, trying to appear blasé and nonchalant but he reveals himself as a little gossip and starfucker. If you're consciously ignoring someone, stands to reason, you have to be aware of them in the first place.

'I let Dougie get all the publicity,' he laughs. 'No fuckin good to me, in my line of work.'

'Who's Dougie?' I ask, fishing.

'Dougie Nightingale, my partner. Swell, but not a bad lad when he behaves himself and leaves the oats alone. You'd bet yer bollocks he was an iron, bent as a nine-bob note.'

Morty opens his eyes. 'I wanna borrow my man here for a coupla hours,' he says, pointing at me, getting up. 'We need to go and have our little chat.' Sonny nods, but then says:

'You could do that here. Might save time later, Mort.'

'Nah,' says Morty, not entertaining any discussion, 'I'm gonna have a shower and then we're gonna have a mooch about. A spot of lunch, maybe.' And with that he gathers up his bits and pieces, heads out, leaving me alone with the terrible twins.

'Is this the bollocks or what, Roy?' Sonny asks Roy, ignoring me. 'Nobody giving ya a moment's grief. No reason to watch ya back.' Sonny goes for a dip but Roy stares into space, looking almost tranquil, his appearance belying his paranoid mindset. I knew Roy once upon a time, in the mid-nineties, when Twitchy Roy Burns was shifting kilos, making a good living but nothing spectacular. Not like the scale me and Mort were working. We would always give Roy a wide, wouldn't serve him if we could, because Morty always reckoned Roy got his rocks off on all the creeping about, playing secret squirrel, just being on the dark side. If Roy had come under scrutiny from any of the heavy-duty crime squads they would've assumed he was a bigger player than he actually was. He was completely obsessed with vigilance, kept up with all the latest innovations, read working manuals of various state police forces. Roy also read every spy book – fiction or non-fiction – gleaning procedural and technical data. At home Roy had devices wired into the phone that enabled him to tell whether anyone was listening in. All this input slowly fed his suspicion. *Even paranoids have enemies*, he would cryptically tell anyone who'd listen.

Roy spent a good deal of his profits on counter-surveillance equipment. If one day he got word that the kit he was using had been superseded he junked the lot and bought new. Imagine some hi-fi freak, gripping his missus' arm, telling her, 'It ain't the *sound* of music, luv, it's the sound *quality* of music that counts.'

Roy would drive round for hours, in circles, jumping reds, reversing up one-way streets, checking if he was being followed – even if he was only stepping out to rent a video – then wonder why Blockbusters was shut when he got there. Roy employed the same *attack imminent* precautions even if he was only popping over to see his dear ol' mum, who he worships, in County Kilburn for Sunday lunch. Roy electronically swept the motor and his slaughter daily for bugs, would *sweep yours* if ya liked. This was routine stuff for Roy.

When Roy had to go anywhere, he had an elaborate system for losing non-existent tails. This would involve jumping on the tube, waiting for the train doors to shut, then slipping off at the last second and doubling back in the direction he'd just come from. Roy would have different motors plotted up outside different tube stations so he could jump in, drive across town, park up, dive into the Underground, jump in another tube heading to fuck-knows-where. And Roy, straight-faced, would tell people he could smell plainies – undercover police officers – on the breeze.

I have to remember that Twitchy Roy is a wee bit dangerous and not to get carried away with the prevailing ambience of ridicule and mockery. Sonny and Morty might take a few libs but I'm not in the same category. I look at Royski's bony feet – basted with factor-two suntan lotion, smelling of chemical coconuts and fake bananas, white as a hospital bed sheet, in spite of him living in Spain – and imagine them stomping some unfortunate's skull.

After ten minutes of tranquillity, listening to the waves break on the coral reef, Sonny climbs out of the pool. He's obviously still highly offended by my outward serenity. He dries himself off. He's starting to go very red across the shoulders.

'You wanna watch that sun,' I tell Sonny. 'It's deceptive.'

'Oh, yeah?' says Roy, snapping out of his trance.

'You don't think it's hot, cos it's breezy, but it's roastin ya alive. It's the trade wind blowing off the Atlantic, it meets the wind coming from the Caribbean—'

'Cunt's a fuckin geography teacher now,' Sonny says to Roy. 'Take no notice.'

'You don't think it's hot but it is,' I tell them. 'Especially this time a day, this time a year—'

'I've sat in the sun all day, in fuckin Spain,' says Sonny, throwing a suntan lotion bottle at me. I dodge it. 'I tan easy. Just cos you wanna sit under a brolly. You're like someone's fuckin Nan—'

'And that lotion you're putting on is worse than useless. That sun isn't like Spain, it's lower in the sky. We're nearer the equator.'

'Look, mister school teacher, fuck right off!' says Sonny. Then he starts on Roy. 'Where's that suntan lotion, Roy?' he shouts. 'I'll do your back if you do mine, okay?'

I throw the lotion back to Sonny. He catches it. Roy gets up, bends over and Sonny starts squirting the sickly gunk over his back and neck. Sonny rubs it in roughly. Roy squeals. Morty reappears – as if by magic – all spruced-up after his pit stop.

'You know something?' says Mort, nodding towards Sonny

and Roy, without missing a beat, heading towards the car, 'In some civilisations you two would be married now.'

'You still here, Mister Mortimer?' says Sonny in mock civility. I follow Mort, wait till I get to the corner, then shout back. 'Watch that sun! Cook ya alive.' Then I jump outta sight.

This is good. At last an opportunity to talk to Morty alone, but Morty's not saying anything, puts his index finger across his lips and gently shakes his head. I know Morty well enough to know when he's gonna be receptive to light conversation – or the big Q and A – and when it's a lock-out. And this is a waste of time.

We drive away from the hotel. Morty tells me to drive towards Bridgetown. He looks out at the countryside, raw and rugged inland, at the tidy dwellings, at the people mooching about, at the tourists' duty-free shopping malls, the taxis, buses, cars and lorries honking their horns as they pass their pals, and at every tiny intersection. Morty's dead calm, absorbing every detail.

On the outskirts of town Morty tells me to take a turning into the Savannah Grounds, an exclusive part of Bridgetown. Once upon a time it was a parade ground but nowadays the outside is used as a racecourse. The inside of the track is laid out for both rugby and polo. A beautiful, leafy, shaded avenue runs around up to the spectator stands and paddocks.

We park up against some freshly painted white railings and get out. A short but heavy shower has fallen but the sun is out again. It's now midday and already in the nineties, but humid. There's a tiny breeze blowing through the tops of the trees but apart from that it's very quiet, very bright, and very white. I'm squinting, even with my sunglasses on. Sweat has broken out across Morty's forehead.

'Let's walk,' says Morty, leading the way. We stroll slowly and silently over towards the grandstand of the racecourse, through an unlocked gate and up, high into the stand itself. We sit down halfway up the seats.

A racecourse, like a funfair shut for the night or seaside promenade in deep mid-winter, has a melancholic, vacant air when it's off-duty, when all the cheery punters have wandered off home. A tote sign creaks in the breeze. The seat is warm under my arse. I can see a maintenance man through the haze, a hundred yards away, leisurely repainting more white railings. He looks up, spots us and waves. We salute back. Then he goes back to his graft. This is tranquil and I hate to break the spell.

'Why are you and Sonny and Roy Burns here, in Barbados, now, here, at this time?' I ask. 'They're just a coupla hounds, nil class—'

'Listen, comrade,' Mort interrupts, hand up. 'If you wanna gang up on Sonny and Roy, you're gonna have to do it on your own,' says the very mellow Mister Mortimer. 'Sonny's gonna help you get very rich all over again.'

He allows himself a grin and a wink in my direction then takes out a pack of English snout, Bensons, puts one in his mouth, lights it, takes a long drag and blows the smoke out. Morty's dying for me to ask what he means.

'How is the old tin can these days?' he asks belatedly.

'Coming back to life, Mort, getting better by the day. Maybe it's what I need, a bitta verbal with Sonny King.'

'Don't be sarcastic,' says Mort. 'You ever get homesick?'

'From time to time. There's a lot I *don't* miss about London.'

'Did you keep all your old contacts in one place?'

'No way. Be insane. I remembered figures, who owed who what, what we held, phone numbers. I taught myself, did memory exercises ... Why?'

'I'm curious,' he shrugs. '*People* are curious.'

'If you and me sat down for a while and kicked it about, I'm sure we could remember. A lot of them wouldn't be in circulation.'

'But a lot of them would.'

'I couldn't come back to London for good, my nerves wouldn't stand it.'

'No need. You commute. Think about it, all those dudes we used to serve, back in the day, some are big-hitters now. Four years is a long time. Some are missing in action or semi-retired, in Thailand. Some got careless or Old Bill got lucky. There's a total lack of sensible geezers back in London,' he says, looking straight ahead.

'Who'd be involved?' I ask. 'Not Sonny, not Roy.'

'Sonny's governor.'

'And who's that, Mort?'

'Sonny works, indirectly, for Ted Granger.'

'Duppy?'

'Correct,' says Morty. 'If you meet Ted don't call him Duppy, okay?'

'Ted looks after Sonny?'

Morty nods.

'I wouldn't have thought.'

'Well, he does. Things change ... Sonny makes him money and distributes his merch.'

'Since when has Ted been serving Sonny King?'

'I dunno,' he shrugs, 'last coupla years.' But something in that casual shrug says don't get busy, mate, please.

'Ted Granger brings in the white, and Sonny King breaks it down and gets it to where it needs to be. Ted doesn't like Sonny all that much, never did.'

'That doesn't take a lotta workin out.'

'Ted's attitude is, what has *liking* someone got to do with business. Bridget Granger – Ted's sister and junior partner – seems to have a pathological hatred of Sonny King but will concede that Sonny is very good at what he does.'

'Bridget?' I ask. Ted's twin sister, geezer-bird, hardcore. I'd rather fuck her than fight her.

'I know, I know, don't say it,' says Mort, reading my mind, 'we all *think* it but just don't. It ain't polite. Ted is never in the same place for long, Bridget dislikes Sonny even more than Ted does so they need a buffer. A go-between.'

'Go on.'

'And that's me, middled-up and up for none,' says Morty. 'Now Ted wants to open up a whole new front, wants to shift some serious weight. Needs a salesman. You negotiate on behalf of Ted. He's a smuggler not a salesman.'

'Who'd do the schlepping?'

'Sonny King. Well, Sonny's crew deliver *for a consideration*. Everything's *for a consideration*. Look, it's dead simple,' says Morty, 'Ted needs to shift tackle, needs a *closer*. You hit the ground running. Go back to London, meet up with Ted. He points you at all the leads you need, plus what you can drum up yourself.

You get a *commission* same as any salesman. You don't negotiate one-offs. You agree consignments to be delivered each month or week. Repeat business. You work on a sliding scale – more weight, better price. Less cash that needs spinning, the better the price. If they need bail ... You work out with Ted what they return. You work out the details with Ted. But he needs to know quick if you agree *in principle*.'

'I'm interested but—'

'It's a good move,' says Morty, slightly incredulous. 'You wanted me to put out feelers.'

'True, but I'm still a target with the law over there—'

'You'll never be near any tackle or readies. If they nick ya for *conspiracy* to supply you'll slip out of it.'

'Let's hope it never comes to that. Does Sonny know the reason you're here?' I ask.

''Course. And he's screwing. Ted wouldn't have it any other way. He's looking to create a drop of sibling rivalry. See, here's the thing, bruv, the wholesale price per kilo has dropped to twenty-three grand ... ' Was nearer to twenty-eight gee in my day. '*And* the quality is better. Twenty-three grand buys a top quality brick, sealed and stamped with a moody scorpion. There's an awful lotta powder out there that needs shifting.'

'It's interesting, Mort.'

'Nobody's going to trouble you if you're with Duppy, and I'll be making sure your whack gets to you. Any deals you make, contacts you develop, you get paid.' Morty's laying it well, perhaps *too* well. Mort always did *over*sell.

'If you're half-wanted, you'll wanna keep it dark. You only see who you gonna see. No welcome home parties. Nothing's changed over that side. Some of them ain't changed their underpants since you've been away. You fly in, do the business, then away. It's like corporate hospitality these days. You chase up all our old contacts—'

'I'm not sure why they're here.'

'Who?'

'Sonny and Roy. Who else?'

'They needed to get outta town, I needed to speak to you. I

didn't wanna go to Jamaica cos it's on top at the airports, too much law enforcement.'

'Why do they need to be outta London?'

'God knows, bruv. Probably gave someone a hiding. I didn't even know Royski was *in* London till a few days ago.'

'And what about the two-point-seven and change, where's that from?'

'You tell me, mate. They've *obviously* turned someone over.'

'And you ain't curious?'

'I am, but I don't want to get told lies,' he shrugs. 'They're *saying* it come from a *bitta freelance.*'

'They can't stay off the phone, ringing home every two minutes for the *sit-rep.*'

'You know what they're like,' says Morty, starting to laugh, 'Roy gets didgy, it gets contagious.'

'What was all that performance in the bank all about? Sonny showing off? Why's he bringing his poshes halfway round the world?'

'That money wasn't outta the business. That much I do know. It's not how it works.'

'Go on.'

'Don't underestimate Ted. He fills the warehouse. Buyer calls on the oats. Sonny delivers it from the warehouse. Everyone's sweet. The buyer *transfers* the agreed amount into an offshore account. Ted don't like to take cash payments anymore, too much paperwork.'

'He won't take cash for *drugs*? What's the world coming to?'

'He'll take it but he don't like it. You wanna pay cash the price goes *up* not down. Ain't like paying builders. Cash is a liability.'

'So Sonny buys a nightclub to rinse his money out?'

'It's an obvious move but Sonny's an obvious geezer. He buys a club, with Giles holding his hand, of course. Giles set up Sonny with that account in the CBB.'

'Back up a minute. Who is Giles?'

'Giles Urquhart. You'd like him, or be entertained by him. A proper toff.'

'But who is he?'

'Sonny's tricky lawyer.'

'Tricky?'

'Not particularly, but he's a swell. All tricksters – can't help themselves, can they? But Giles did fire Sonny onto an agreeable bank manager.'

'Curtis?'

Morty nods. 'Old school pal. Giles will wanna get you sorted with an account of your own.'

'Bit too cosy for me.'

'Yer man, Giles, *absolutely insisted* you meet his chum Rupert Curtis.'

'That was sweet of him,' I reply. 'You know Sonny showed me a balance statement coming outta that jug showing almost fifteen million dollars. That's nine million pounds ... How could that belligerent cunt accumulate that sorta money?'

'Pure hard work. More pies than fingers. Sonny's got your nut, ain't he?'

'His *bank balance* has seriously cracked my coconut.' Mort laughs. 'Does Ted know about Giles?' I ask.

'Who knows what Ted knows. Ask him when you meet him but I'll warn ya, Ted's not very forthcoming.'

'No?'

'You go into a restaurant with Ted, look at the menu, you ask Ted what he's having, he won't tell ya – tell ya you're being nosy.' Morty gets up, stretches. He looks tired. 'Well,' he asks. 'What are ya saying?'

It's what I need. I nod.

'Now,' says Mort, 'that charade out at the airport – coming in with the bucket and spade gang – was Roy's idea. No harm in it, but I'm outta here on a scheduled flight the day after tomorrow and I've got you the hardware to fly out tonight using that profile you ordered.'

'Tonight?'

'Yeah. I've got you a passport, flight ticket, the lot, back to London.'

'Did you say *tonight*?'

'Yeah, first class. Why hang about?' he says, lighting another snout. 'The sooner you get over there, the sooner you can have a sit-down with Duppy. Speed is of the essence.'

'It's just a bit sudden, Mort, I'm half wanted over that side.'

'Get on the plane, nice milky drink, get yer nut down and wake up at Gatwick. They took the liberty of booking you a hotel, over by the City. No curious eyes or big mouths chatting yer business. And you're on expenses. You just gotta sit tight and Ted'll be in touch. He has to pick his moment, just in case he's being spied upon by the odd lot. If it all goes to plan, you agree terms with Ted. Coupla week's time, you're back in Jamaica. You save up, buy out your partners on the QT, and scarper. You pop in and out of London to do a few deals. Get outta Jamaica, mate, it's not the smartest place to go AWOL.'

'Why didn't you mention it before?'

'I *assumed* you knew what you were doing.' Morty starts to walk back down the steps. 'Now, let's go and get a nice bitta lunch down in Bridgetown, leave those two nuggets to their own devices,' he says, rubbing his hands now. 'And don't worry, mate, it's gonna be cool.'

'You're asking me to have a bitta blind faith?'

Mister Mortimer stops, turns, winks, wisely nods his head.

'*All* faith is blind, brother – ain't no other sort.'

CHAPTER SEVEN

GOING BACKAYARD

Needless to say, when we get back to the hotel, Roy and Sonny are *severely* sunburnt; glowing and scorched even beneath layers of calamine lotion, sizzling red like Brick Lane chicken tikka masala. Serves 'em right, maybe they'll listen in future.

They're feverishly huddled in the shade by the breakfast buffet, arms folded across their chests and long, spanked faces on them. Sonny has a wet towel wrapped round his head and Royski, who's worse, is rocking like a rabbi at the Wailing Wall, with a pool towel across his shoulders, nose already blistered. The pair of them attract looks of concern from other guests but the normally inscrutable Bajan waitresses are having trouble repressing their delight. Sonny had been snapping his fingers at them before we left.

'You wanted to look like tourists,' I tell them, feeling brave. 'Now you do.'

'Fuckin watch yourself, pal!' says Sonny with the pointy finger. 'You're startin to give me the right hump.'

'Let's take a few beers up the room, Sonny,' says Morty. 'Have a little sit-rep.'

'Let's do that,' says Sonny, groaning melodramatically as he gets up. 'And Roy, bring that calamine lotion!'

Driving into Bridgetown from the racecourse earlier, I started to realise how much I miss London, how much I'd been in limbo. I don't miss the cold, the winter dark and the continuous moaning. What I really love about London is the energy and the sense that it really is the centre of the world. Back in Jamaica I would read every paper and magazine from back home I could lay my hands on. I would sit drinking four slow beers looking out onto the most spectacular sunsets you've ever seen in all your life – burnt oranges, awesome golds, fiery reds and violent yellows – getting nostalgic for driving around London in torrential rain, hypnotic windscreen wipers sending me into a stupor, paranoid about being tailed by the Odd Firm, the law. Crims, like everybody else, get nostalgic for a time or a place that never really existed.

And there's a Londoner's attitude that you never lose. One evening, I'm sitting on the hotel terrace, watching the sun disappearing into the sea, when I feel a presence behind me. Turning around there was this shit-kicker from Memphis, Tennessee stood there.

'That, sir ... ' said the Yank, pointing spellbound into the west, 'is the Good Lord's paint-box.'

'Fuck off, Elvis,' I said. 'This part of the hotel's private.'

In reality there's nothing stopping me from excusing myself, leave them waiting in Sonny's hotel room, driving to the airport, getting a hop-fight over to Jamaica, tidying up affairs there – there's two or three people I trust – and flying straight out again, maybe on to Australia via Honolulu, new places and people. But after Morty said I was going back, after four years exile, a green light came on.

Morty taps in the combination of Sonny's room safe. The tumblers roll and the door pops open. He reaches in, emerges with a plastic envelope and lobs it carefully over to me. I catch it. Inside are a flight ticket and a nicely aged British passport containing the photos I couriered to Morty last week. I look dangerous, but who looks good in a passport? Inside, at random, on the various pages are entry stamps and visas from other Caribbean counties, the US and – a nice touch – a ninety-day work visa for Australia.

'Hear you're goin on a trip,' says Sonny, lying back on his bed in discomfort. 'You should be flattered to be working with me.'

'Oh, I am,' I say.

'We've got you a ticket as well – this evenin's flight outta here,' he says. 'You'll be in Gatwick in the morning. A bit previous I know but ... there's no place like home. Royski, give him the thingy.' Roy digs in his pocket, brings out a tiny key and walks it over to me.

'What's this for?' I ask.

'Key to a safe deposit box,' says Sonny, trying to be cool, 'in the Deposit Box Centre, on Finchley Road.'

'What's in the box?' I ask.

'Coupla kilos, split into samples. Ain't been slapped.' Sonny points at the passport that's now lying innocuously on the bed. 'That name's been authorised – to get you in.'

Roy pipes up. 'You'll have to bottle the key when you go through the airport.' He's eating a banana, turning a deeper shade of red. Morty laughs.

'What's the problem?' Roy shrugs. 'You grease yer arse, bitta Vaseline, and slide it up. Won't get found.'

'That key's plastic,' says Sonny. 'Don't show up on X-rays.'

'It's an emergency key,' says Roy. 'Ain't meant to be used any more than a coupla times.'

'The proper metal one's in the deposit box already,' says Sonny. 'You open it with that,' he nods over, 'and get the metal key.'

'I'll put it on a keyring,' I say. 'They'll never think of looking there.'

'Don't be funny, pal,' says Sonny.

'Don't worry, Sonny, I'll get it back to London but I ain't sticking it up my arse.'

'Don't see your problem – it's what you do in nick all the time,' says Roy.

'You've never done any serious bird, have ya?' asks Sonny.

'Don't intend to either, Sonny.'

Royski's eating his sixth banana on the trot cos the waitresses told him, deliberately and erroneously, that they're good for sunburn. Morty's smirking. Sonny's stretching out on his cot, hands behind his head, looking up at the hypnotic fan, muttering to himself. 'I don't know what's the matter with ya, pal,' says Sonny King, a man I wouldn't ask to blow up a balloon. 'Your bottle ain't gone, has it?'

'No, Sonny, my bottle's gone nowhere but if I'm going, I better get moving.'

Things move fast. Sonny insisted that Roy, not Mort, drive me out to the airport. He's ringing it that it was his idea for Ted to get me back on the firm, hijacking the idea, and Morty, being Morty, is happy to allow him to do it. I was glad to get away in the end, glad to be getting on with it but now I'm tripping out, thinking about London and what I've got waiting when I land.

After my initial shock on the arrival of Mister Mortimer with Sonny and Roy in tow, after Morty's pitch and time to think it through, I've come to the conclusion that they're manna from heaven. If Ted's putting it together, Sonny and his merry men are doing the warehousing and distribution, and Mortimer is chasing down the paperwork I'd be silly to turn down a serious opportunity.

So three hours after Morty's suggestion that I go back to London, Roy's driving me out to the airport but driving me mad at the same time. He's been waffling on while I've been daydreaming and watching the parched countryside go by. The sugar cane is high in the fields and the rum distillery – looking like an oil refinery – is pumping hard, turning out its lethal, colourless liquor that could take the paint off the bonnet or send you permanently insane. Roy pulls up at an intersection, scratching his head and looking hard at his map. It beats me how he can lose a whole international airport but Royski is talented. I point him in the right direction and away we go.

I learnt long ago to tune people out if they started to become a pest, but now I begin to pay attention. Roy's onto his favourite specialist subject: surveillance.

I am, due to a spot of trouble back in spring ninety-seven, barred from the UK, have been told that if I even set foot on British soil, before I even get the chance to engage in any illegal behaviour, I'm getting nicked. I took my warning seriously. Now I'm about to get on a plane to London and land at Gatwick, a viper's nest of surveillance personnel. I could very easy get led away in chains. Roy started off ten minutes ago giving me the you-ain't-got-a-thing-to-worry-about speech, a morale-boosting pep talk. But soon he couldn't help himself – Twitchy Burns started banging out a familiar old riff:

'They've got spotters at the airport, lookin for anythin outta the ordinary, signs of stress, they can even *smell* if yer scared. I've been a fugitive myself, you know, travelling on a wrong 'un. Old Bill are clued-in, get on it if you're over-compensating, if you're tryin to be *too* cool, seeing if you avoid eye contact or seeing if you deliberately try and look straight at 'em, like you don't give a fuck. They reckon they've got this computer gadget now that recognises facial features. The CCTV's clockin ya and if your details are in the database and you get flagged-up – crash! You're fuckin nicked! Eye recognition's the next big one, yer fuckin iris! Think about that. Along with voice tone recognition, about one hundred times more unique than fingerprints is the human iris. You could lose your fingerprints but you couldn't lose your iris, not without goin blind. They'll have 'em all on one computer, pan-fuckin-continental, so they can cross-reference – Interpol, FBI, MI5, French or Spanish and Italian Old Bill, the fuckin lot. You come through an airport and you've got a bitta outstanding, bang! You're gone!' Roy considers this for a moment. 'Unless they let you run, they put a team on ya, let you go wandering but tailing you in, under obs – maybe a tiny GPS device tucked away in yer luggage or on yer person, seeing where you end up, who you meet up with. You think you've gone through the slips but you ain't! Little fucker's givin out a signal, beep-beep-beep, up to a fucking satellite. Global positioning systems! You're totally fucked! They're smart fuckers these Old Bill, customs – highly intelligent people. They've been to university, degreed-up. These ain't everyday plod. They're clever geezers. If they're droppin yer phone, they can set up the system so it recognises keywords, like names, your name, my name, or coke, or white, or oats – any malarkey, it alerts the controllers. It comes from the time of the Cold War. You know that MI5 are on everybody's fuckin case now back home. You know that, don't ya?'

'Why the lecture, Roy?'

'I'm markin yer card.'

'Roy. I'm on a final warnin back home. I can go to jail for trespass.'

'It's gonna turn out okay,' says Roy. 'Sonny knows what he's doin.'

'I'm going over to see Ted Granger.'

'Okay ... easy,' he says. 'Fuckin relax, pal.'

That's fuckin choice, coming from Twitchy Roy Burns.

When we arrive at the airport, Royski hangs about even after I've told him to trap back to the hotel. He's burnt fiery red, literally glowing. Living up to his name. The Bajans look at him like he's crazy. *Why do these extremely white folk lie out in the dangerous sun, getting fried?* Roy is totally oblivious.

It was only when I got the ticket and passport out of the envelope that I remembered I was travelling first class. Ted was obviously willing to pay the money to get me back to London alive and in one piece. The woman on the desk didn't mention my distinct lack of luggage, just directed me towards a first-class lounge, but Roy, talking out the side of his mouth, insisted we *bake-up*, sit tight, in the arrivals lounge where I'd met them yesterday.

Then it occurs to me that he's been *instructed* to hang about to make sure I don't go absconding off to Jamaica. He sits patiently drinking a warm Coca Cola and flicking through the Bajan newspaper. Eventually they call my flight over the Tannoy. I get up to go but Roy grabs my arm. 'Listen, one last thing,' he says, all business. 'Anyone asks you where me and Sonny are, you don't know, okay?'

'Roy, I doubt very much if anyone's—'

'But if they *do*, like, you don't know anything, okay?'

'But who's gonna—'

'I don't *fuckin* know, *anyone*, okay? You understand?' he says, getting irritated.

'Okay, so nobody's looking for you but if anyone asks I ain't seen ya, is that right?'

'You're taking the piss now,' he says, getting twitchy.

I move in close on Roy, then whisper in his blistered ear, 'Royski, I'm getting fuckin bored now. *Please*, let go of my arm, cos I need to get on my flight. I don't want these security bods getting fuckin lively, okay?'

Roy lets go of my arm.

CHAPTER EIGHT

HOME SWEET HOME

Gatwick Airport, London
Friday, 24th August 2001

It's five in the morning, London time, when I get off the plane. I sail through immigration without a hitch. The guy took a polite glance at my Jekyll passport and waved me through; someone had been bright enough to put a Barbados entry stamp in it. Also in the little parcel I was given back in Sonny's hotel room was the return half of a railway ticket. Sonny told me to get the train on to St Paul's station, not Victoria – *it's easier to see if you're being followed* – and the hotel is a short walk. I haven't been on British soil for over four years so I haven't felt cold in all that time. Waiting for the train, the cold bites. It's August, but early morning, and chilly for the time of year. Sonny volunteered Royski's prized but battered Aquascutum raincoat for me to commandeer – *he can't very well wear me or Mort's, can he now?* – but I already feel a shopping trip coming on.

The train arrives and pulls out slow. It soon starts to pick up speed through the English countryside. It's starting to get properly light, the sky crystal clear and ice blue, the early morning sun starting to poke over the horizon. The train slows, pulls into Croydon, and fills up with early morning commuters. Everyone has their head in a newspaper. Or they look incredibly bored. I feel a sudden twinge of melancholy. I'd be homesick if I knew where home was. Mundane days are starting. Traffic is starting to build up on the roads below. I spot my first red London bus. The train increases in speed. It rushes, without stopping, through suburban stations. No time to read the names. The sun is getting higher in the sky. I'm rushing. My heart's pounding. Hands getting clammy, mouth getting dry. I'm fidgety on my seat. It's half anticipation, half buzz. I'm feeling good to be back in the UK, in

London. Then Royski's words come back to me – *maybe they'll let ya run*. All the passengers, however unlikely, immediately look like plainies. I start checking faces, getting para. The train slows and stops at London Bridge. All the commuters I had down as definite suspects get off while new passengers scramble for seats.

Suddenly the train turns a corner and, in a flash, out across the river I can see St Paul's cathedral, massive and glorious, surrounded – guarded – by skyscrapers, constructed in concrete and black glass. The sun hits the water, like a river of molten gold. The grandiose bridges disappear into the distance, down to Canary Wharf in one direction and Battersea power station in the west. I see the London Wheel and the new Tate Gallery for the first time. I'm seriously impressed, get a sudden realisation of why people from all over the world wanna be here. To lots of people worldwide the streets of London *are* still paved with gold. Things happen here. Good things, bad things, strange things, hard things, simple things, illegal things, lawful things, inexplicable things, mysterious things, mad things. But mostly people come to see if they can't get a tiny slice of a very big pie. You can feel the power in the chilly morning air.

And me and London? I need to get in, do my business, and get out. I'm deep in thought as the train crawls into St Paul's station. Sonny-boy told me during my final briefing to book into the hotel in the City – someone's made a reservation in the moody name on my passport – and later someone will be in touch with details of a meet. Pretend you're a tourist or a businessman. Be a ghost in your own hometown. And *stay out of any of your old haunts*.

Sonny told me, in all seriousness, to go and find myself a friendly sauna and punt for the deluxe polish off a creamy brass, on expenses.

'Cheers, Sonny,' I said. 'Will you be needing a receipt?'

'You tryin to be fuckin funny, pal?' But I'd decided already, as he was droning monotonously on, defiance growing, that I wasn't gonna be sitting on my hands waiting till one of his whacked-out posse, or Ted even, decided to put in an appearance or make a call.

I find the hotel no sweat. It's new, twenty-eight floors and five stars. It looks like it's made entirely of glass. I walk in and silently place my passport on the reception desk. They immediately find my reservation. I'm staying one floor from the top, on the twenty-seventh. The bellboy shows me into the lift and pushes the button with a mischievous grin. The lift flies up the side of the building like a fairground ride, the pavements rushing away, then comes to an equally abrupt halt. The bellboy shows me to my room and it's the same as a million other hotel rooms worldwide, the same layout. The only difference is an awesome view looking west over London, so high up it looks like a map. I can pick out neighbourhoods, the bends in the Thames, and hills in the far distance.

I'm too wired to sleep so I have room service send up a pot of strong coffee. I sit and drink it overlooking the city, then decide I better pick up a few bits and pieces – I'm travelling too light. I get the lift back downstairs, thinking I'll get a taxi over to the West End. As I walk through the lobby the concierge calls me back.

'Excuse me, sir.' I turn around. 'We have a package for you,' he says, turning to the pigeonhole and producing a tape-sealed padded envelope, 'I was just about to buzz your room.'

'I've saved you a journey. Did it come by courier?' I ask.

'Oh, no, sir, it was hand-delivered,' he says, turning to the bellboy for confirmation. He nods awkwardly. Could be coincidence that it arrived just after I did, or it could be that I'm under surveillance. Someone knows I'm here but nobody's doing much to make me feel welcome.

I take the package. It looks innocent, no sense of skullduggery about it. My bogus name is typewritten on the front and something about it tells me it was prepared well in advance rather than hurriedly put together.

I walk towards the main entrance. The automatic doors sweep open and the bellboy runs ahead and opens a taxi door. I tell the driver to head into the West End – *just drive, I've been outta town*. I wait till we're underway and open the packet. Very curious. As soon as I open it a phone and a charger – the red light winking, all charged and ready – tumble into my lap. Then an unsigned gold American Express card in the same bogus name as my passport. Then two hundred pounds in sterling, like daily rations. Last out is a blank white card with only a magnetic strip running across the back, and a sealed envelope, like the ones PIN numbers arrive in, an elastic band holding them all together.

I've seen these anonymous cards before. Not even numbers embossed across the front. They're from discreet banks in Switzerland or the Caymans, basically an upmarket cash point card. As I'm replacing them all back in the packet I spot a smaller sealed envelope tucked right deep in the corner, like it went in first. I open it. A neatly typed message: '*Please be in your room tomorrow morning at 9 a.m., prompt, to receive further instructions. Thanking you.*'

'Please' and 'Thanking you' means it's not from any of Sonny's firm. This is no doubt from the geezer who rang Sonny in Bridgetown exactly on the chimes of the church clock. A poetic touch, punctuality being a gentleman's calling card. The stationery is superior quality, proper Bond Street issue. I'm getting more curious by the minute, but curiosity can get your nose bitten off. It don't seem like Duppy Granger's MO either.

The cab heads west, the driver chatting away like mad, a running commentary, blahdy-blahdy-blah all the while.

'Nice suntan you've got there, mate. You been on yer holidays?'

'No, I've been ... ' Meter clicking away nicely, click-click-click, up past the tenner mark in no time. We head along the river, then over the bridge, up through Soho, all the old haunts and memories, meter's up past the twenty – a nice little fare – heading into Old Bond Street.

I have the cab drop me off, then stroll till I scope out what I'm looking for, an ATM *inside* a bank. I go inside, remove the card from the envelope and put it carefully in the machine. I punch the PIN number in. I ask to withdraw cash. It asks me how much.

'How much?' I say to myself. 'Good question,' I reply. I punch in the figures – five, zero, zero – and hit the 'enter' button. Instantly I can hear money being counted automatically, a beautiful, whirling sound, same the world over. The screen shows those exquisite words, '*Please take your card and wait for your money*'. A thin but tidy wad of notes – five hundred sterling – slides out of the machine. The ATM is flashing, '*Do you require another service?*' Out of curiosity, I push the '*Account Balance*' button.

'Let's see how much yer holdin, bruv.' The balance instantly appears on the screen – £149,500.00p in credit. If that's what Mort meant by Ted putting *me on ex's*, that's generous. A very nice surprise.

I eat lunch then go and buy the bits and pieces. A salesman on Jermyn Street admired Roy's battered Aquascutum raincoat but suggested *reconditioning*. I laughed. I'm feeling surprisingly relaxed, like this whole set-up might be a bitta me – flying in and doing deals, with a hundred and fifty grand in my expense account to be getting on with, *to show good faith*.

I sit in Green Park till late afternoon, watching the world go by, then head back to the hotel. Now I'm tired and suddenly jetlagged. There's a red light blinking on the bedside phone. I'm pouring myself a brandy, a nightcap, from the mini-bar before I answer it when it starts to ring again. For some reason I'm thinking it's Morty ringing from over there. I let the phone ring three times before I answer it.

'Hello?'

'Hello there,' says a quiet, rasping Londoner's voice.

'Who is this?' I say, double cautious, but the caller completely ignores my question.

'See,' he says, 'I've been ringing you all day. I thought you were supposed to wait home indoors.'

'I got a note.'

Drag on snout. Small cough, 'Well, where was ya?'

'I went for a walk,' I say cautiously.

'Musta been a long fuckin walk. I ain't got time to fuck about.'

'I've got a cell phone, you coulda called me on that.'

'Work of the devil, them things.' Who the fuck is this? Is this Ted? I don't wanna ask him. I can hear him take another pull on a cigarette before he continues. 'Now lad, has your pal rung you yet? With the news ... '

'What news?'

'Bad news, I'm afraid.' Drag on snout. 'The fella they call *the ghost*—'At that very second the mobile in Roy's raincoat starts to ring.

'One second,' I say into the landline as I try to find the mobile, searching through all the pockets till I find it. It might be the elusive Ted himself. I answer the mobile, 'Hello?'

'Listen, I ain't got long,' says Morty, breathless, feeding coins into a payphone, 'I'm in the airport, in Barbados, trying to get an earlier flight. Gonna be tight but ... What time is it there?'

'Seven at night,' I tell him.

'I'll see you there at nine tomorrow morning. We're going to a funeral.'

'Who's died?'

'Ted Granger,' says Mort.

'Ted's dead?'

'He better be – they're burying him tomorrow.'

'That ain't fuckin funny.'

'Well, that's the best I can do at the moment,' says Morty. 'I'm a bit ... He was a mate.'

'This fucks everything.'

'Not on the phone, pal,' he half-whispers into the receiver, like it would make a difference.

'This fucks—'

'That's selfish, that is.' I guess it is. Morty goes quiet. I can hear the bing-bong of the PA in Barbados Airport.

'You got money?' he asks. 'You better pop out and buy some funeral clothes.'

'Morty, it's seven at night. All the shops are shut.'

'You'll have to go as you are.'

'Funerals! I'm meant to be keeping a low.'

'You gotta pay yer respects, bruv.'

'This fucks everything,' I say. 'Am I right?'

'No,' Morty replies defensively, 'but you're not wrong either. It's gonna need a rethink.'

I realise I've still got the landline receiver in my other hand. 'One second, Mort,' I say, 'I've got some joker on the other line. Give me two seconds.'

'Hello?' I say into the receiver, 'You still there, buddy?'

'Yeah, I'm still here. And I heard all that,' says the voice.

'Heard what?'

'The bit about the funeral,' he says, 'and the bit about *some fuckin joker*—'

'Oh, yeah? I didn't say *fucking* joker—'

'Whatever. Lotta business gets done at funerals, son,' he

interrupts then pulls on his snout again. 'Listen, I'll see you tomorrow, okay.'

'Hang on, pal, one second,' I say. 'Why did you ring exactly?'

'To tell ya the bad news. About Ted. But it seems ... Till tomorrow, son,' he says, and the line goes dead. I go back to Morty.

'Who the fuck was that?' I ask Morty. 'Ringing me here?'

'How the fuck would I know?' he replies. 'Listen, they've found me a flight. Gonna rush, but get up early, go and buy some kit, you know what I mean.' A silly hat and big divvy glasses. 'And maybe buy a proper raincoat. I've seen the weather forecast and it looks like rain.'

'Anything else ya wanna tell me?'

'I'm gonna love ya and leave ya,' he says. 'See you at nine sharp, tomorrow.'

I'm left with dead phones in both hands and a severely spun nut. I play the earlier message back. The same smoky, phlegmy voice I spoke to a minute ago. It's short and sweet. 'Where the fuck are ya?' Don't recognise the voice, and the gent neglected to leave a name.

CHAPTER NINE

LOVELY DAY FOR IT

Ted Granger was big school. In the age of *Time* magazine exposures about multi-national plutocrims, villains whose sole aim is simply to acquire more and more capital using the latest technological advances, utilising the internet, making satellite-phone calls from the inaccessible jungle or inhospitable desert, operating like powerful business school executives but in reality groomed in nefarious criminal finishing school, operating over continents, using diplomacy, tact and trickster lawyers to cement alliances between organised illegal groupings, from Japan to Columbia, Zagreb to Bangkok, Ted – 'Duppy' as he was fondly known – Granger was like a whiff of over-boiled cabbage bringing everybody back to Earth. Ted was more artful dodger than Don of Dons. If that sounds like an obituary from The Criminal Gazette, so be it.

The late Ted Granger was legend in the fraternity. He was an international drug trafficker but his reasons for being in the business were not as straightforward as the serious top-end money-makers. Ted was a gambler, addicted to drug trafficking the same way as a crackhead is welded to his cherry. What made it all the more bizarre was Ted's lifestyle.

Lifestyles of the rich and famous it was not. He had more money than he could count but didn't know how to spend it. He didn't look like a deadbeat, cos every bitta clothing was boil-washed and steam-pressed – always wore a vest, even in mid summer, and the mail-order, ex-RAF, special-purchase shoes were spit-polished. Ted looked like he got kitted-out in the army surplus store but he shaved every morning, and once a week he got whoever was on hand to use the hair clippers up the back and sides so he looked like a squaddie off to batter insurgents down in Malaya. Even pensioners thought Ted was a throwback. Ted was the most unlikely master criminal there ever was.

At forty-five he had energy but looked world-weary. If someone

asked you to guess his age you'd say mid-fifties cos jails had
nicked years they were never going to give back. Ted had gone
through approved school, borstal training, then heavier stretches
for highly organised burglaries and robberies. Ted did a four and
a six. He was, like Twitchy Roy Burns, someone you
underestimated at your peril. Rumours said he was responsible for
possibly three murders – he was heavily implicated in the fatal
stabbing of a Palestinian terrorist in Parkhurst. The prison
authorities couldn't prove anything, but Ted was ghosted up to
Durham, the other end of the country. This is a guy who looks like
a whistling milkman – *extra pinta, missus?* Somewhere along the
line he picked up the moniker 'Duppy' from black prisoners:
Duppy meaning ghost or spirit. Nobody could work out if it was
a compliment or an insult but it stuck. Maybe because Ted was so
glow-white, translucent from too much birdlime, too little
sunlight, looked like he could see through walls; always knew
what was going on in the jail, in the prison system, in your head.

How did Ted get up there? There was a time when dealing in
drugs was considered below the dignity of the British criminal.
Ted had got nicked, got a seven, of which he did almost four.
Morty and Ted ended up with adjoining cells in Wandsworth and
soon become allies in the constant battle of wits with the screws.
Ted would be lecturing Morty about the cancerous effects of drugs
on the fraternity – the end of everything he stood for. Morty had
no such scruples. Morty thought Ted was a man born in the wrong
era. But, Ted being Ted, he was soon on his feet again after
getting out, working meticulously as a burglar on an industrial
scale, stealing computer equipment, jewellery, watches and
perfumes, antiques, family heirlooms from long-term storage
facilities, spares for high performance cars, official documentation
from remote sub-post offices. Anything, in fact, that was sellable,
cos Ted liked his punt on the gee-gees.

Ted's well-executed robberies become his trademark. He had
teams of experts – alarm specialists, drivers – but most
importantly Ted had eyes and ears all over the Home Counties
who got a bunce if any work they put up paid off.

But the problem with having a recognisable criminal trademark
is that it brings attention. He had to lose a tail every morning

before he could *go to work*. The Regional Crime Squad was tailing him in shifts, baked-up outside his drum. They even put him under observation when he took his extended family down to Tenerife for some winter sun. It was as much about *them* topping up their tans as watching Ted. He was no longer flattered. When the law has to justify the expense of plane tickets, hotels and subsistence allowance, you know you're looking at a long stretch.

One night about a decade ago, nineteen ninety-one, Ted came away from a burglary in Brighton with a Chinese cabinet over five hundred years old. It had a secret compartment; he found four kilos of pure flake inside. When an acquaintance told Ted what it would fetch *wholesale* – in the region of one hundred and twenty grand – Ted decided he was in the wrong profession. All the incredibly dated criminal morality went straight out the window and Ted jumped full-blast into the drug importation business. He entered the world of hopefully *unreported*, supposedly *victimless* crime, away from alarm bells, flashing blue lights or wailing sirens. Ted entered a world where his organisational skills, criminal pedigree and ability to hold his own under questioning all went in his favour. Into a world where, for Ted Granger at least, anonymity was paramount.

Ted was an amateur smuggler who became an international trafficker, who became so big he never saw any tackle. He became a glorified haulier. Ted went from hiding merchandise in juggernauts criss-crossing the North Sea to delivering sealed containers via shipping brokers in only four or five years. Promotion comes rapid in the drugs game; there's a lot of natural wastage. Smuggling is the ultimate gambling experience. You win some, you lose some. The law *knew* he was at it but they couldn't *prove* it – the tricky part. Duppy was more schooled in police and legal procedure than most cozzers. He loved the cat-and-mouse – the surveillance, the meets in dark places, the ready-eyes, the codes, the phone taps, the bugs, the bribes, the odds – but I guess what Ted Granger liked most was the adrenaline. Loving it didn't stop him from having a persecution complex, cos the authorities wouldn't leave him alone to break international law on an industrial scale. He believed he was being systematically hounded, was a businessman who'd done his birdlime and grafted hard. *They* were jealous.

Ted Duppy Granger started working outta London till it got warm, so he decamped over to The Dam. Some days he had four surveillance teams on him. So he uprooted himself once more, down to Southern Spain, Costa del Sol. He thought that some of the chaps down there were loudmouths, so he relocated to Costa del Azahar, near Valencia, where the address of a house could be a map reference, the entrance a narrow track up a mountain, and that suited Ted. Even up there, up among the goats, he had to keep moving, but he's at the top of his game, got his funds all spun and spendable, smart lawyers and accountants to keep the heat off. He could easily have stayed home and watched the horse racing.

What does Edward Albert Granger do? According to Mister Mortimer, he's up early, six or half past. Old lag's thing that, always up early, does an exercise routine devised in a punishment block, the HMP Segregation Unit workout. *Don't need equipment! Simply bags of motivation!* Consists of hundreds of press-ups, sit-ups, star-jumps and running on the spot in thirty-bob plimsolls and baggy Y-fronts. *Keep those fuckin knees up!*

Then Ted has a stripped-to-the-waist wash, his shave, a coupla boiled eggs and a gallon of strong diesel tea made with long-life milk. Then at about eight thirty he goes off on his rounds, out to meet his team up and down the coast, in churches, railway stations, on golf courses, in gas station washrooms or boats out on the Med. They rendezvous on building sites, luxury villas tucked in the hills, flitting in and out back doors, and on crowded beaches, all because every single thing Ted the Duppy Granger needs to tell his crew, he needs to tell them face to face. It then becomes the job of the *capos* to track back to shipping agents, enforcers, boat captains, loaders and suppliers. All to keep the buzz going. And he rose to dizzy heights. But now he's dead. *Adios amigo*.

But he got the perfect weather for a funeral – unseasonable cold snap, ten degrees centigrade under the norm for the time of year, persistent, driving rain. Ted would have approved. Once upon a time Morty would have avoided the funeral because these things can turn into a gathering of the clans for both the fraternity and the law enforcement élite, but he's full of surprises these days. Old Bill will – no doubt about it – be lurking about, smudging up the proceedings with a long lens.

Morty was insistent that I come along. And what a gathering of faces it is, the real boat show outside the crematorium chapel, waiting for the festivities to begin. We have the up-and-coming and the semi-retired, the dabblers and very active, liggers who love a scoundrel and the dear-departed's kith and kin – the Granger family.

Four brothers, not counting Ted who's in the box, one other missing, away up the country for a double-figures gig, and four sisters, bruisers with very hard, sharp faces, and Missus Granger the senior, going on eighty, with a lit Capstan Full Strength wedged in her mouth like a Canning Town docker. She's coughing and spluttering, rattling her dentures, looks frail as a brittle twig but going strong, fuelled by non-tipped snout and milk stout. Her hair is stained nicotine yellow above her right eye. I catch her eye, or more to the point she catches mine. She looks straight into me, fearless. I look away quick. I realise she's made from high-carbon steel. Unbreakable.

The younger gelhead members of the Granger clan had been transplanted out to the more gentle pastures of leafy Hendon and sedate Edgware courtesy of Uncle Ted's charitable foundation but they're still joined by an umbilical cord to the old toil-and-trouble neighbourhood. They can never really let go because their neighbours out in the bland suburbs view them with creeping distrust – neighbourhood watch *generalissimos* taking photos of the new-installed pikies.

Ma Granger and all Ted's brothers and sisters have that malnourished look, the legacy of rickets and scurvy, that takes generations of pease pudding and good living to shift – the high cheek bones and the wiry, double-jointed physique. They could easily handle a raging smack habit but regular doses of vitamins and fruit would have them keeling over. Their systems couldn't handle it. They've all got the same darting eyes and pronounced frown. They're all snouted-up as well, lighting one off the other, but it ain't the constant fags that's given them the seriously caned complexion, it's year after fuckin year of stress and anxiety.

The Granger Family don't look quite right in their funeral garbs either. Some guys can wear formal clobber, and these guys can't. The collars on the shirts are too big, making them look

scrawnier still, all red razor rash and protruding Adam's apples.
The suits are baggy on the shoulders, the shoes almost brand new,
only getting out to weddings, funerals and court appearances. The
sisters, wives and girlfriends have obviously had an outing to
Bondo Strasse to get togged out but it still doesn't look right.
Santa Versace and Giorgio A's best black creations weren't meant
to grace a damp crematorium in windswept Cricklewood. A
couple of women wear inappropriate, sodden satin shoes that are
now ruined, but even in their grief they couldn't give up the
desperate need to impress. This is where Holloway meets
Hollywood, California meets Caledonian Road.

Upsetting Sister-Number-One Bridget could be fatal, get the
face ripped off your head. Bridget looks like a female bodybuilder
– hard boat, drag queen calves. She's greeting people she likes by
calling them a cunt, as a term of endearment – *all right, ya cunt,
glad ya could make it, ya cunt*. She's definitely in charge of
today's proceedings, as she's the dear-departed's twin. I get the
distinct feeling that some of the congregation have had a massive
sniff of white to get them up and on parade. I also get a whiff of
cut-one-and-we-all-bleed camaraderie, closely aligned with
vicious jealousies and bitter sibling rivalry. They can have their
disputes between themselves, but woe betide any poor fucker who
attacks any of them.

Morty in his funeral garb looks like the dignified Third World
Head of State at Ascot – the charismatic Brigadier General who
staged the *coup d'état*. All he's short of is a silk top hat. He's got
a barrister look thing going on – black jacket and waistcoat, with
pinstripe strides, white shirt, black tie, obviously, shiny brogues,
with an ankle-length, waxed moleskin topcoat from a swell's
shooting-and-fishing outfitters. He's got a black golf umbrella
that's about six foot across. When you're that well prepared you
don't really give a fuck about a full-blast monsoon. Morty's
holding black leather gloves, soft as fuckin silk. Now I'm jealous.

I've got Roy's borrowed Aquascutum raincoat that turns out to
be no good in driving rain and a telescopic umbrella that's worse
than useless, a heavy gust of wind will soon send it inside out.
Morty's got me wearing a pair of ridiculous, tinted spectacles and
a deerstalker hat as a lame disguise. I feel damp, dishevelled,

jet-lagged and I've got a feeling I'm having the piss ripped out of me by General Mortimer. I also feel like a criminal starfucker, cos I never knew Ted 'Duppy' Granger personally. Looking round there's guys here who are legends in their own imaginations – *do you know who I think I am?* They're here to pay their respects to a guy worthy of that twisted respect the chaps bestow upon each other.

The hearse arrives with a wreath saying 'ADIOS BROTHER', picked out in pink and white carnations, leaning against the side of the coffin. I suppress an urge to laugh, put it down to nerves. The whole hearse is packed solid with flowers from well-wishers. It's surreal; bright, vibrant colours in a drab, wet crematorium. The drilled undertakers load up four of the brothers with the casket containing Ted and they make their way slowly into the chapel of rest. It occurs to me that it's all being done in complete silence. No blubbering, no wet hankies or hysterical, fainting mourners. I can hear the gravel underfoot and my own breathing.

Ted's *kinda* in the box. The term 'remains' in this case is appropriate and accurate. There wasn't a great deal left of Ted to send home, and cremating him *again* seems pointless. An eyewitness reported seeing Ted's powerful car go skidding off the road and into a gorge. They watched it, horrified, sailing through the air, till it bounced a few times before exploding in a fireball at the bottom. Ted had been driving very fast, heading towards the main road that heads towards the south of Spain. He'd been spotted in a petrol station twenty minutes before the accident; told the kid pumping the gas that he was in a rush, kept asking him, in bad Spanish, if he could *hurry up, por favor*. He still had the kid clean the windscreen, check the oil and fill the radiator with water. Ted tipped him five euros, so he remembered him, the serious-looking English gentleman. Ted also had the petrol tank filled right up. All the signs were that he was heading off on a lengthy journey, but the irony was that the full tank made the carnage all the more destructive.

Ted's scorched and singed personal effects that had been found in the car had, strangely, followed the body home in plastic bags, meticulously labelled and documented by Spanish plod. They thought Edward Granger was a tourist because it was a hired motor, and contacted the British Consulate straight away. The consulate Johnnie had the dental records faxed through from the UK, the only available records being kept in the Prison Service database. They were out-of-date but held enough information to determine that the charred remains were in fact Duppy. There was a loud whisper that British Old Bill asked their Spanish counterparts to double-check everything but a senior detective in the Guardia Civil sent though a report saying they were convinced that the remains were Edward Granger. They were treating it as a road traffic accident.

Mister Mortimer and me slip into the last row of pews. The damp seems to have followed us in. A couple of heavy looking dudes, the kind who have turrets instead of heads, show out to Mort with a wink or a nod of the head. One guy gives Morty a pat on the shoulder in passing. As Mort turns they give one another a wry smile and a there-but-for-the-grace-of-God shrug. Another lively dude, a bitova face, a big dealer, passes by, whispers something in Mort's ear and jogs on without waiting for an answer. Morty turns to me and gives me the same stoic shrug.

A large photo of Ted has been placed in a gilded frame on a stand surrounded by vases of white lilies. Ted obviously didn't like having his picture taken so he glares out into the chapel with a hostile expression. He's got the most razor-sharp widow's peak you've ever seen, and the camera's bleached-out flash, plus a drop of red-eye, gives the deceased Duppy an ironically demonic appearance.

The coffin is placed in front of the altar. The crowd settles. The piped organ music begins to fade. Suddenly two gents come walking swiftly, trotting, up the aisle of the chapel looking like they're holding hands. Their hands swing in unison but one is dragging the other along. They march to the front and squeeze into the family pew. Members of the family reach over, shake hands and kiss cheeks with one of the late arrivals but the other one just stares straight ahead. I cotton on. The two guys are handcuffed together, one a con, one a screw. Mort turns slowly backwards towards the door. I turn as well. Behind us, stood in the door, is a guy with 'Prison Officer' written all over him, chewing gum in pure defiance and brushing drops of rainwater off a waxed anorak. The screw gives us a smile that's unadulterated sarcasm.

The prisoner in the ringside seat has the definite stamp of the Granger Clan about him, with added buried-deep-then-dug-up concrete complexion – the Seg Block suntan. Now with all ten kids together, dead Ted tucked up cosy in his coffin, Ma Granger's offspring are reunited under the one roof. She looks nonchalant, like she's waiting for the bingo to start. *Eyes down for a full house*. There's not a blubber from anyone in the whole church, more a tangible sniff of impatience, wanting to get the whole thing done and dusted and a few slurps of firewater inside them.

The service is short and sweet – no Sinatra, just a bitta bible-blahdy from some threadbare chaplain. It's all wrapped up in minutes and away goes Ted 'The Duppy' Granger, multi-millionaire career criminal par excellence, through the tasselled scarlet velvet to rendezvous with the equalising flames of the gas furnace and the ultimate bewigged sentencing judge, sitting on the high bench of the Great Central Criminal Court in the sky. Ted had simply, on this last occasion, run out of final grounds for appeal.

But where does that leave me?

CHAPTER TEN

NUT DOWN IN CHELSEA

For guys like me or Mister Mortimer to travel five miles we have to drive ten. Doing U-turns back to where we just come from and going round roundabouts twice becomes second nature. We left Ted's wake in the upstairs room of the boozer in full swing. After the toasts with Scotch to wash down the ham and mustard sandwiches, we ghosted away quiet. Morty slipped off at one point and was having a word with Bridget, but nodding across at me, like my ears should be burning. Mort also had a few confabs with some seriously connected guys – some with battered, stoved-in faces, some tanned and handsome – plenty of whispering and double-handed handshakes, a few brief bear-hugs and several knowing nods in my direction. These are heavy guys, but beneath the enamel – among their own, at funerals and weddings – their sentimental nature comes lapping over the sides. A couple of these guys, obviously business associates of the late Mister Granger, turned to me and without any introduction ...

'Hello there, son,' little wink, nod. 'Nice to see you back over this side.'

Then they'd carry on talking to the rest of the company without missing a beat. They knew who and what I was. I didn't know if that was a good or bad thing. Part of me would dearly like to remain anonymous but another, less rational, part of me quietly loves the recognition of these headmen and elders. We all wanna be one of the chaps.

'Chop, chop, you're in a fuckin daydream, you tart, hurry up!'

Morty, as is his habit, breaks the spell. We're half-trotting down the wet pavement, like old days.

We've eventually parked up in Chelsea, just off the King's Road, a select neighbourhood. It's still relentlessly pissing down. I got wet crossing the pavement to the car, got rain running down the back of my neck and I'm cold to the marrow. It's no use suggesting we hole up somewhere till it stops, cos it ain't stopping. English summer weather.

'Why you pulling the face?' says Mort. 'The lemon face?'

'Sorry, General, I didn't realise I—'

'You'll feel a bit more at home round this neck of the woods,' says Mort, 'bit more upmarket.'

'Have you sorted me a gaff over here?'

'Oh no, pal, we're just visiting. There's someone I want you to meet,' says Mister Mortimer, with a hint of smile. 'Last place you'd look for *this* geezer.'

'Is it much further? Only I'm getting soaked here.'

He stops dead in his tracks.

'You've never done any heavy bird, have ya?' he says.

We've had this conversation a million times.

'No, Mister Mortimer,' I reply. 'And you already know—'

'I want you, pal,' he says, giving me the pointy finger, 'to take that insubordinate tone outta your voice. I know a lotta guys who are in-car-sir-rated who'd love to be out in the rain.'

'Point taken,' I say wearily, as rain drips off my nose.

'Anyway, it's only a shower,' says Mort, with a morale-boosting but unconvincing smile. 'Let's go. Wouldn't want you catchin a nasty head cold.'

I can hear rolling thunder in the distance, the piss-yellow streetlights are on at two-thirty and I can see sheet lightning over the rooftops.

'Who are we going to see?' I ask, knowing I won't get an answer.

'You'll know in a minute, little chum. Keep up.' Morty's scanning the street. 'Chop-chop, this is bandit country.'

You're not wrong there, Mister M. All the large gaffs are noticeably belled-up, sinister red lights blinking on discreet CCTV cameras, neighbourhood watch signs on every lamppost. If one of the gentlefolk rang the local constabulary to say a couple of chaps were trotting along – *one white boy, soaked to the skin, one big and coloured, acting suspicious* – the cavalry would actually turn up, blue light flashing.

We walk round the block. We do a sharp right, then another one, the same theory as the car journey. We arrive at a house in a short but leafy cul-de-sac, like a country cottage, very outta place. There's wild roses growing around the door, ivy racing up the walls and oak beams on the outside walls. An upmarket mock Tudor. Out front there's an overgrown privet hedge and the chequered windowpanes are daubed with whitener so busy neighbours can't be nosing in.

We step up to the door. Morty's looking up and down the street but nothing's moving. He ignores the bell and taps out a pre-arranged knock – a code – on the ornate knocker. We wait a few seconds. The rain gets even harder, sweeps across the pavement in waves. I hear a shuffling about inside.

'Mort?' says a grumpy voice through the door.

'Right first time,' says Mort.

'Don't be funny,' says the guy as he fiddles with the catch.

He opens the door and leaves it to fall open. Me and Mort step inside. The guy is already strolling back down the hall. Inside it's heated like an orchid farm hothouse.

'Make sure you shut it properly,' shouts Grumpy, over his shoulder, as he disappears into a back room. 'And, Mort, put the fuckin catch back on – okay?'

I know the voice from somewhere ... The house appears to be empty, no carpets, no furniture, bare floorboards; his voice bounces and echoes. Mort shuts the door, replaces the catch, takes off his coat and hangs it on the banisters, then motions me to follow him. I can smell recently fried sausages and hear booming, over-excited horseracing commentary.

'I wanna see the end of this race, Mort,' says the guy as we enter. 'Won't be long.'

In the back room – which somehow reminds me of a neat cell – there's a camp bed, very tidily made-up with hospital corners, a telly sat on the box it came out of the shop in, a kettle, fridge, tabloid newspapers folded neatly open at today's runners and riders page and a couple of chairs that look like they were salvaged from a skip.

And sitting on a stripy garden chair with an old Embassy Regal ashtray on his lap, very possessive, like he won't share, smoking a pencil-thin liquorice paper rollie, intently but silently watching the gee-gees, is a gentleman who could win a Ted 'Duppy'

Granger look-alike contest hands-down, no fuckin contest. The same hollow, scrawny, edgy face. The same mean and lean physique. Same salt 'n' pepper spear-point cropped tight against his bony skull. The race finishes; his grim expression tells me he didn't have the winner.

'Work of the devil,' says the guy, turning to me as he mutes the sound.

'Horse racing?' I ask, nodding at the screen.

'Nah, them phones,' he says, pointing at my mobile. The same voice that was on the phone last night.

'Oh, right, yeah,' I say, agreeing.

'Unnecessary. Makes things easy for Old Bill.' He shakes his head and turns to Mort. 'Well, how did it go? Any problems?'

'No, no,' says Mort, lighting a salmon. 'It was fine.'

'Good turn-out?' he asks.

''Bout hundred and fifty.'

'Any Old Bill sniffin 'bout?'

'None that I could see, don't meant to say—'

'I know,' he says, raising his hand to silence Mister Mortimer. 'How was Mum?'

We're getting warm. Could still be a long-lost brother ...

'Hard to tell. She's bulletproof, your old mum.'

'Shame I can't ... you know ... ' he says, his voice trailing off. We're getting warmer.

'What? Let Mum know?' says Morty, the sympathetic voice of an agony aunt. 'Maybe, in the fullness of time, Ted ... '

Ted. I was right. I've just been to your funeral, never having met you in my life, or *your* life either. Your wake is just getting going across town. The customary brawl isn't scheduled for hours. But I'm curious – if Ted's plotted watching the ponies from Kempton, who got incinerated at Cricklewood Crem?

'Your mate got a lovely send off,' says Mort. 'Always said he'd do anything for ya. Never 'ave got hundred and fifty bodies at his own funeral.

'Nah,' agrees Ted, shaking his head. 'Was a cab driver ... Do they have a lotta mates?'

Ted's genuinely inquisitive.

'*Acquaintances* rather than mates,' says Mort, shrugging.

'They have lots of *acquaintances*. Mates, acquaintances ... it's different, like.'

'Sad, really,' says Ted, rolling his eyes, shaking his head, 'wanted to be one of the chaps ... worst kind – pisshead plastic gangster. Took a bitta bottle, though.'

'Sonny King sent a wreath,' says Mort. 'Signed it *The Big Fella*.'

' *"The Big Fella?"* Could be anyone.'

'Had the florist draw a little crown on the card.'

'What a fuckin ... ' says Ted, shaking his head, 'Where's he now?'

'They're on their way back.'

'From Barbados?'

'Yeah.'

'Who's *they*?'

'Told ya. Sonny and Roy Burns.'

'Oh, right. Twitchy, bless 'im.'

'Should be back later.'

'Did the undertaker take the cards off the flowers? Wouldn't want Old Bill nosing—'

'They always do, Ted, to show the relatives.'

'Do they?' asks Ted, 'Give 'em to Bridget, did they?'

'I suppose so, Ted,' says Morty. 'Anyways, the thing is, it's too late for an inquest now.'

They both chuckle like kids. Ted suddenly stops. He rounds on me.

'What you got to say for yourself?' he asks.

'Not a lot,' I reply.

'Are you takin your fuckin coat off or what, pal?' says Ted, pointing under my chair, 'Only you're makin a puddle on me floor.'

I look down, but of course there's no puddle. Ted's checking me out the whole time, staring intently, smoking his skinny snout, seeing how I shape. I look back without getting combative. Mort says nothing. I enjoy the silence while Ted smokes his snout down so he has to use his nicotine-stained fingernails to get a last drag. He drops it into the ashtray to burn itself out. Morty breaks the silence.

'My pal here,' says Morty, nodding at me, 'is in the Sonny King fan club.'

They laugh at their private joke.

'Is that right?' says Ted, still staring intently at me. 'Good pals with Sonny, are ya?'

'He's all right, is Sonny,' I say diplomatically. 'Got his funny little ways.'

'Oh, right. That's good, *got his little funny ways*,' says Ted. 'That's one way of putting it.'

'I take it, Ted, you don't like the geezer,' I say.

'What makes you think that?' says Ted with mock surprise.

'Instinct, intuition – take your pick, Mister Granger,' I say with a shrug.

Ted leans forward, points his stained finger at the tip of my nose. A switch has been flicked.

'Hold up, don't get smart with me,' he says, leaning forward, his natural frown getting tighter. 'I was payin cunts when you was in short trousers. I put 'em in the ground, so don't be givin it.'

Morty leans forward, hands up to pacify him. 'Ted, listen to me—'

'Don't ever forget it, pal,' says Ted, eyes locked into mine. He spits out imaginary tobacco.

These geezers think they're soldiers. And you're contemptible if you don't hold your corner.

'Ted ... ' I say as slowly as I can, 'let's not waste each other's time. You got me here, and the sooner you let me know what's required, the sooner I'll be able to tell ya if I can help. If I can't ... I'll go back where I came from.'

Ted just screws me like he's got all the time in the world. Ted Granger instinctively knows that silence is more powerful than ranting, something Sonny will never understand. Ted opens his baccy tin and takes out another roll-up without taking his eyes off me. The tin is full to bursting with rows of identical ready-rolled fags. Up close the eyes that were red in the photo are icy-blue and drilling into me.

'You don't like Sonny King, do you?' I say to break the silence. He waits a long time before answering.

'No ... I don't,' he says with a tic, 'but then again, I've never met the man.' I look to Mort but he's pure deadpan.

'That don't make sense, after that night in Barbados ... You do business together ... ' I look back to Ted. 'He said he knew you ... went to see you in Spain ... ' Back to Ted. He's searching for a match. 'But I was given to understand, Mister Granger,' I say, 'by Sonny King, I might add, that you two were buddies ... '

Ted lights his roll-up. 'You know something, pal,' he says, puffing hard to get it going, 'you talk like proper Old Bill, CID. And I've only know ya two minutes. Straight up, I'd think you were a gavver. All that *I have reason to believe*, and *I might add, I was given to believe*, like you was in the witness box, reading a statement.' He mimics a cozzer, '*May I refer to my notes, me lord.*'

He doesn't laugh. Neither do I. He instinctively waits. Then, 'If you hadn't come in here with Mortimer ... ' He points over at Mort but keeps his mincers locked on, 'And he said you was sweet, let me know yer previous I woulda booked ya as a nailed-on plainie.'

Ted fidgets in his seat, breathes hard but shallow. The oxygen in the room has rapidly evaporated. I wait, listening to the rain hitting the window, the hum of the fridge. I watch the colourful jockeys assembling for the next race.

'You know something, Mister Granger,' I say, eventually. 'I've often thought that myself – people must think I'm Old Bill, but you know what?'

'Wassat?' he snaps.

'I'd be too obvious to be a cozzer. You know what I am, don't ya?'

'No,' says Duppy.

'I'll tell ya ... ' I say slow. My turn to keep *him* waiting. 'Like I was trying to tell Sonny King, but *he* couldn't get his nut round it—'

'You're what, pal?' says Ted. 'Tell me!'

'I'm an undercover criminal.'

'I like that,' says Ted, starting to grin slowly.

'And it would appear – from what I can see these days – there's only a few of us left. Tried explaining it to Sonny ... '

Ted smiles wider. Then he starts to laugh. Then he starts coughing, just like his dear old mum. He starts rocking, pounding his own chest, going red in the face, eyes watering. Ted takes a long drag on the snout – fuzzy logic, that – but starts to cough and laugh harder.

'Let's have a cuppa tea. You wanna cuppa tea, son?' he says through the hacks, walking over to the kettle and flicking the switch.

'That'd be nice,' I say, winking at Mort. 'A *proper* cuppa tea.'

'An undercover criminal, I like that,' he turns back to face us. 'And Sonny didn't get it?'

'Totally spun him out, Ted. Confused him,' I say.

'He's one big stupid cunt, that Sonny,' says Ted, shaking his head, about the guy he's never laid eyes on. He goes in the fridge and fishes out a carton of pasteurised milk.

'He likes ya,' whispers Morty, nodding in Ted's direction.

Then suddenly Mort snaps his fingers, sits bolt upright. He's forgotten something important. 'By the way,' he says. 'Sorry, I've gotta ask. Your ashes – where would you like them scattered?'

Ted raises his eyebrows, his tongue poking out. Thinking hard, massaging the back of his neck. Then, a revelation. He clicks his fingers – a dry snap.

'Scotland Yard!' says Ted with a double straight face. 'Scatter 'em at Scotland Yard.'

CHAPTER ELEVEN

YOU LIKE RIDDLES?

'When did you die?' I ask.

'Three days ago. Wednesday, late evening, just as everyone was going off-duty,' says Ted with an ironic smile. 'And buried today. Couldn't have had it sooner, not without booking the undertaker in advance.'

'That woulda been suspect,' says Mort.

'I was flown in yesterday morning, kept on ice, a sealed casket,' says Ted, 'too burnt up for anyone to see.' Then, like it's been bothering him, 'So Sonny didn't show at the crem? Coulda made the effort. You did.'

'So Sonny knows you're alive?' I ask.

Ted shakes his head. 'Don't you be worrying about Sonny ... And don't be telling him either.' Then with the eyes, 'And you better be nice to Sonny. Okay, mate?'

'And what about Bridget? Does she know?'

Ted looks to Morty before answering, 'Yeah,' he says with a small nod. He points at me but talks to Mort. 'How much does he know?'

'How much you gonna tell him?' replies Mort, pokerfaced.

Kevin the Cab went over the side. He turned up in Spain just before last Easter and *begged* Ted to help him kill himself. Assisted suicide. He was dying from an AIDS-related illness. Picked it up in Thailand, fucking too many bar girls. Few years ago he'd had the stopover holiday on the way to Oz. Bad move. Once he got a taste he was trying to make up for a lifetime of going without. *Could never nick a bird. If Kevin the Cab fell in a barrel of tits he'd climb out sucking his thumb.* So he filled his boots in Thailand and Vietnam. Ted knew him from when they were juniors. The disgrace would have killed him – and his family – along with the AIDS.

It's a funny one, ain't it, neighbourhood morality? Round

where I grew up, you can be a psychopath, drug dealer or a dangerous lunatic who sticks broken glasses in people's throats, but for God's sake don't do anything bizarre like become a born-again Christian, a spit-and-polished reformed alcoholic *or* go catching AIDS.

Ted thinks he did him a favour. It's that debatable fuzzy logic.

Kevin, I suspect, walked into a scheme that was already being hatched. Kevin will end up on the missing persons list; his family thinks he's MIA in South East Asia. The 'witness' who reported seeing Ted's car going into the deep gorge – after the driver had been driving *muy rápidamente* around the tight hairpin bends towards the tollroad – is a Spanish builder who was paid by Ted for his complete fabrication. The builder forgot to mention that Ted had intensively coached him. What he'd *really* witnessed was Ted getting *out* of the car and a paralytic drunk Kevin getting *in* – *Kevin the Cab could handle a motor, drunk or sober.*

It gets better ... Ted also had a senior detective in the Guardia Civil *straightened right out.*

Ted's Spanish cozzer was put in charge of the accident investigation after the English started asking questions. He was the one who sent back the report saying they were convinced that the charred remains were those of Edward Granger, Spanish resident, one-time fugitive but *not wanted or under any indictment.* The Spanish indignantly informed the British that they had checked the deceased's dental records. The British police – smelling a toasted rat *and* corruption – worked without overtime pay to investigate, went over the head of the Civil Guard detective, and asked that the dental records from Mister Granger's Spanish dentist and the dental chart of the charred skull be sent up to the UK to be checked with the ones they held. They thought they were being smart. This was what Ted wanted – this was his *coup de maître* – his masterstroke.

The dental records were faxed through to the detectives in the UK and immediately checked with the records held by Her Majesty's Prison Service. They thought they had an ace in the hole. They *must* be conclusive, if a little out of date. But the records had been exchanged by a trustee prisoner who was doing life-meaning-life and was going nowhere-meaning-nowhere. The lifer got a few quid in his canteen account, paid in by an anonymous benefactor. When the records got sent over, they corresponded *exactly* with the charred remains because Kevin had been sént to see a malleable Spanish dentist who filled out a genuine HMP dental chart. The Spanish coroner who examined the charred remains thought the British were overly suspicious.

'How long had you been planning something like this?' I ask Ted.

'All my life,' Ted replies with a sip of tea.

'But why do you need to be dead?'

'Why not?'

It's a good criminal career move, to be dead. Will the police stamp his file 'deceased'? Who knows with the law? They've seen it all before, go to college to learn how to be sceptical.

Ted hands me an original copy of a Spanish death certificate – *Certificado de Defunción* – folded neatly in four, like it's been steam-pressed. For something that was only issued by a Spanish civil servant yesterday morning it looks incredibly worn.

I read aloud, '*La causa de la muerte – lesiones múltiples.*'

Cause of death – multiple injuries.

'Don't be starting with all that Spanish bollocks,' says Ted. 'I won't miss the fuckin lingo.'

'You never learnt Spanish?' I ask Ted.

'Never had to,' he replies defensively.

'It's easy, really. All those languages derive from Latin.'

'Do you know how mad that sounds ... ? *All those languages derive from Latin?* Where the fuck did Morty find you? I suppose you speak Spanish?' he asks.

'I lived in Costa Rica for a while. *Nobody* spoke English. It was learn or starve. You pick it up listening to football on the radio, talking to people in bars.'

'Birds, you mean? I can see you're a lover not a fighter.'

'What's the beef between you and Sonny?' I ask, curious now. 'You've never met him.'

'What's that got to do with anything?'

'Quite a lot, I woulda thought.'

'Now you're sounding like the counsel for the prosecution. I trust him to get the gear to where it's meant to be ... Listen, Sonny's a good moneygetter. We need him.'

'But you don't like Sonny?'

'I *thought* I'd made that clear, pal,' says Ted with an edge.

We sit in silence, watching Ted thinking hard. Suddenly he's alight again.

'Sonny was always turnin up in Spain, sniffin about, lookin for a move. He knew a few geezers I had on the firm. I had no reason to talk to him. He was flash – drew attention, slinging money around. I couldn't have eejits round me. I was making moves with geezers from all over *the world*. I didn't need some slipkid. It was Bridget who said he'd come in useful.'

But it was Morty who first piped up he could work with him, two years ago. Sonny can move a lotta product and do the distribution for Ted's tackle. Any business is all about distribution. Sonny needed coaching in how to behave, needed the *really* rough edges smoothing. What we've got now is the refined version of Sonny King, the one who's been to finishing school.

'But he still ain't proper ... ' shrugs Ted, 'but I know he ain't a grass. Some of these fellas nowadays ... They'd go QE like that.' He clicks his fingers. The dry sound echoes. 'Sonny always likes to knock about with the top geezers.' He nods at Morty as if presenting exhibit A. 'Thought something would rub off on him ... '

'Likes a toff, does our Sonny,' adds Morty.

Ted turns to Mort, slaps his arm, 'Tell him that story about Evey and the chavvie stranded at the airport.'

'He's heard it, from the man himself,' says Morty.

'What a dog-move, aye?' Ted says to me, looking for me to agree.

'Was she okay?' I ask, 'Eve?'

'Don't worry about Evey. Born survivor. Just loves a wrong 'un ... '

Ted gets out a folded piece of paper and hands it to me. The paper is quality – powder blue, watermarked and flecked – again, like the death certificate, folded *exactly* into four quarters. I open it up. It has a fourteen-digit phone number, an American bank sort code, account number, bank membership number and Personal Identity Number, printed on separate rows.

'Call that an advance, a sign of goodwill. There's just shy of a hundred and fifty grand in that account. Ring that number. It's automatic, those numbers take you through security, and then you tell the bird in the call centre where it's going.'

'Where's the call centre?'

'Fuck knows. Timbuktu. Atlanta, Georgia. It's not important.'

'Won't they want clearance with that amount?'

'Joking, ain't ya? One-fifty, ain't a big deal. It's how we do business – bank-to-bank transfer. Put it somewhere safe, it's yours to keep,' he says like an insincere game show host. 'Call it expenses, but there'll be plenty more when we start shifting weight.'

'Do I need some samples?' I ask. 'Sonny said there was some raw in a deposit box.'

'Samples is for kids, but keep that key safe,' he says. 'It's all Brahma gear, quality product. If buyers wanna smash the granny outta it, that's up to them. I'll return, to you, two grand on every kilo *shipped* on any deal you negotiate, whether you're around or not—'

'But what's to stop you just—'

'Swindling ya? I want you happy. I'll account to Mortimer. Two gee a key is a generous deal. I want you workin.'

Then Ted Duppy Granger goes into a sales pitch worthy of a Miami condominium salesman, full of key words, catchphrases and blue-sky thinking.

Big plans. Broad strokes, creating dynasties. Expansion and growth rates. Spun readies are better than mountains of cash. Need digits on a balance sheet somewhere. Money up front. Future's in commodities. Bold speculation. Bulk buying. Raising capital. Reinvestment. Criminal hedge funds. Black money and grey money. Business is too lucrative to be left to criminals. Quick returns on capital investment. Returning a good dividend on the outlay. Speculation. Venture capital. Quick turnover. Cash injection into an ongoing concern. Lucrative returns, not shares – shares mean shareholders, and shareholders mean guaranteed headfuck.

Anyone who believes this geezer's a throwback is a fool.

'Any bods with money, that are looking to invest, you reel them in, send them to me. Here's a word for ya,' says Ted, by way of grand finale, 'symbiotic – sym-bi-otic.'

'Meaning?'

'We – me and Sonny, me and you, you and Sonny – need one another, like the bees need the flowers and the flowers need the bees. And you know what bees make?'

'Honey?'

'And you know what *we* make?'

'Money?'

'Lots of it. How much do you think you can shift?'

'You tell me, Ted,' I say with a shrug and a laugh. 'How much you got?'

'See, if you could place a couple of tons, it would *really* be helping me right out.'

'A couple of *tons*!' My voice shooting up an octave. 'Fuckin *tons*!'

'You're in the wrong key, son,' says Ted, dry as a twig. 'Why do you think we got you back here? Half those geezers back there are potential punters.'

'Back where?' I ask.

'Fuck's sake, son!' He rolls his eyes. 'Why'd you think we had a funeral? Coulda been cremated in Spain.'

'Do *they* know you're not dead?'

'Fuckin 'course not. But how else was I gonna get all those people in one room?'

'What about Roy Burns?' I ask. 'What's his role in all this?'

'What, silly-bollocks-secret-squirrel Roy? You tell me.' Ted shakes his head, shrugs. 'Roy's a turn – a tonic for the troops. Roy's a one-man radar station. The only cozzer Roy won't spot is the one who strolls up and nicks him.'

That's the trouble with crims – they love a crank.

Ted gets up, flicks the kettle on again, puts a teabag in just the one cup. 'I wanna know why Sonny and Roy are running around like Rottweilers with their tails tied together, but in the meantime be nice to Sonny but *don't* be giving him my regards when you see him, okay?'

'Just for the record,' I say, feeling bold, 'I'm beginning to feel like I've been brought here on false pretences.'

'You're right,' says Mort, nodding. 'Dead fuckin right.'

'Thank you, Mister Mortimer,' I say, feeling vindicated.

'I was *actually* talking to Ted,' says Morty. 'You're right; he *does* talk like a cozzer. *Brought here under false—*'

'I told ya, didn't I, Mort?' says Ted, feeling vindicated himself.

Morty and me get up to leave but Ted sits back down, hitches up his strides, like old geezers do – so their trousers don't crease – then leans forward. 'You like riddles?' he says.

'Not especially, no.'

'Here's one for ya,' he says, ignoring my answer. 'Why do people go to prison? Think about it.'

'Dunno.'

'Try harder,' he insists straight away. 'Why do people go to prison?'

'For committing crime?' I say.

'No, no,' he says, shaking his head, pretending to be disappointed. 'Think again. You'll kick yourself ... It's not for *committin'* crime.'

'Oh, I get ya. It's for gettin' *caught.*'

'Now you've got it, son. I knew you was a bright kid. It's for gettin *caught* committing crime. So be lucky.'

'Very good,' I say with a weak smile. Morty nods indulgently.

Ted laughs, slapping his leg. He's cracked himself right up. 'Riddles are easy ... when you know the answers.'

CHAPTER TWELVE

UPTOWN BELLY BUMPING

I thought I might pop back to the hotel room, have a kip for a couple of hours, but the phone was ringing as I entered. It's Sonny in a public phone box.

'You're back?' I ask. 'I thought you were away for a week.'

'So did I, mate, so did I.'

'So what happened?'

'We come back. Twitchy's a laugh but you have to have a third party or he starts to become hard work. I don't know who fills his head with magic. We got on to the holiday firm, told 'em he's been burnt half to death with sunburn, told 'em it was a medical emergency. We had that rep bird terrorised – couldn't wait to see the back of us! Just goes to show, don't it?'

'Yeah, it just goes to show,' I agree.

Funny – Sonny's being nice as pie. Morty's obviously told him to behave.

'Now,' says Sonny, all business, 'we need to have a chat, one on one. You get it? I've been thinking. Long flight home. We need to straighten a few things out ... ' He pauses, as if referring to notes. 'Let's be amicable. Is that the word? Amicable? Let's be friends, mate—'

'You sure you're okay, Sonny?'

'You can fuck off, pal,' he says, instantly losing his new found amicability. 'I fuckin tried. You come to my club at ten. Okay?'

The phone goes dead without Sonny waiting for his reply.

With a name like the Monarch Sonny's club could be a shithole boozer in some backwater, full of dusty coffin-dodgers; instead, it's a cool bijou nightclub tucked in a dead-end turning over by Piccadilly. I had the cab drive past so I could get my bearings. It had a small entrance – just red ropes and a black gloss-painted front door – with the name picked out in tasteful neon. It appeared surprisingly classy and sophisticated, like it was trying to be the groovy boutique spot rather than the mega-rave club, aiming for quality rather than quantity. I was quietly impressed by Sonny's set-up; even a tad jealous, if I'm honest.

I had the cab drop me up the street then walked back. Rented white stretch limos were causing gridlock along the street, and there's a couple of big 'roided-up geezers, who don't sniff like cozzers, sat in a BMW X5 checking out everyone, up and down the street. I caught one of them looking straight at me, then making a call on his cell – reporting my arrival to person or persons unknown.

The door seems to have a siege mentality. Very unwelcoming, like it's some concrete bunker in an Estuary town. The door crew frisk everybody, subjecting them to heavy manners and metal detectors. Nobody escapes the self-important security – not the toffs or the hip, young Japanese tourists. It's busy and pleasantly chaotic but bouncers just opened the red rope as I approached, nodded in recognition, and ushered me in.

One of the bouncers followed me up the tight staircase. 'Mister King asked that you be shown up to the office,' he says, like he'd rehearsed the line.

He walks me past the cash desk and even more bouncers but this little firm of heavyweights are trying to look inconspicuous. He leads me into the club, motions above the loud music for me to follow him around the side of the dance floor. He pushes open a concealed door made of smoked glass with his considerable shoulder and leads me up a flight of steep, winding stairs. The bouncer leads me along a corridor filled to the ceiling with boxes of booze and into a small, dimly lit office. The only light is from a banker's lamp that floods the desk with an intense glow.

'If ya want a drink ... ' he says, pointing at a glass-fronted fridge filled with premium imported beers and dinky quarter-bottles of champagne, 'help yerself.' He turns to leave.

'Good luck,' he says.

And then Sonny purposely leaves me sitting like a prize prick, on a battered leather Chesterfield, listening to thump-thump-thump-bass-bass-bass, nursing a Japanese beer, to await my audience. When he called me earlier and said he wanted me to come by the club to talk, I could hear something in his voice – an anxiety to impress. He doesn't actually like me, but he desperately wants to impress me.

After a few minutes the door at the bottom of the stairs opens. The music gets louder for a couple of seconds, and then goes back to the muffled thump. Here comes Sonny. But then I unexpectedly hear giggling and laughter. The door flies open and a man and woman come stumbling into the room, kissing one another passionately, pulling at each other's clothes, oblivious to me. She's got her legs wrapped tight around his waist – he's half carrying her. He kicks the door shut with his heel and plants her on the office desk. She's holding a champagne bottle by the neck, strangling it. She puts it down with a great deal of care but a moment later it gets knocked over in the frenzy and rolls off the table.

He's reefing her up already – his hand is deep in her knickers – her short skirt is pushed up around her waist. Her eyes are rolling back in her head but she's also laughing like a banshee. He retrieves his hand for a split-second, expertly licks the ends of his own fingertips and slips his hand back down her knickers. She groans and hurriedly drags her own sequined top off, over her head and flings it behind her. She's skinny but very fit, very fuckable; her tits seem bigger than they should be. She's dragging him out of his shirt, pulling the buttons off to get it undone. Now she's desperately trying to undo his strides. Suddenly they drop round his knees. Not very elegant. The whole scene is somewhere between erotic and slapstick.

He's talking to her the whole time in a posh but slightly camp accent. You'd think he was a nailed-on gaylord if he wasn't trying to fuck a fit bird on the tabletop. He momentarily stops and grabs at his shirt pocket, pulling out a small silver gadget. He holds it up to her nose – concentrating really hard – so she can snort some cha-cha and get charvered at the same time. She's snorting and coughing but going back for more, pulling the gadget against her nose and inhaling deeply.

He's pulling her knickers off now with animal-like fumbling and grunting. She's helping him by wriggling out of them. He pulls them down past her knees until she desperately, anxiously, pulls one leg out. She opens her legs wide and leans back. The discarded black lacy knickers are dangling, swaying off one pointy-toed high-heeled shoe. She lays back.

He's kissing her tits, crudely biting and sucking at her nipples. She's groaning. Then he's licking and kissing down her stomach, then into her navel, then he holds up one leg and runs his tongue in one flowing moment up the inside of her thigh. But now he's pulling at the catches on her skirt, desperate to get her totally naked.

'Leave it,' she groans, rolling her eyes in the twilight. 'Just fuck me, you bastard.'

He drags her forward on the desktop. He leans forward – fumbling, impatient, desperate to get his dick in.

'Wait ... ' she says quietly, but then shouts, 'for fuck's sake, wait!'

The guy stops, completely still, for a moment. She carefully guides him into her and they both let out a simultaneous, ecstatic moan. Then he starts to fuck her roughly. She grabs his back, tearing and ripping at it with her long nails. Her top lip curls upward. She's shaking her head so her hair flies in all directions. She bites hard on her own bottom lip. He's hitting a bitta rhythm. They're in a world of their own.

All of a sudden he starts talking to her brutally, in a weird, gruff caricature of a cockney accent – 'You dirty bitch. You love it, don't ya? Cressida, what kinda name is that? Yer a dirty cunt. What are ya?'

They instantly both go hysterical, weeping – like it's a running joke.

'Stop it, Dougie, just fuck me properly, *yer dirty cunt*,' she screams in her jolly-hockey-sticks accent. Always sounds dead horny – well-bred gals *begging* to get fucked.

So this is Dougie. He doesn't look like a fruit to me. His heart's in the right place, or his dick is. She pulls herself up – kissing him – her arms around his neck while he pumps away.

'You're tense, Dougie,' she says.

'I know. Sonny's gone weird.' Dougie don't exactly look tense; he's hitting his stride now. 'Metal detectors, roughnecks everywhere. Bad for business. Does that 'urt? Why ain't you screaming then, you dirty bitch?' Dougie says in his hissing mock cockney. He whispers right in her ear, laughing the whole time, 'Tell me it 'urts, you posh cunt. You love it, don't ya, ya dirty bitch! Don't give it if ya can't take it, I told 'em, the cunts!'

He's giggling so much now and crying with laughter that he can't catch his breath. It's bizarre. I work it out – it's Dougie's impression of Sonny doing his mucky business.

'You love it, you posh birds. You're all the same, love a big fat cock up ya, don't ya? I'll flip ya over and do ya up the shitshoot if ya don't shut up.'

'Stop it, Dougie, stop.' She's telling him to stop but screaming with laughter. 'Stop talking like that! Fuck me properly!' But she don't want him to stop fucking her – she *is* really loving it. And I wouldn't spoil anyone's fun by interrupting. She's throwing herself around and he's pulling and moving her about on the tabletop.

'I'll do ya up the shitter. It's my thing, ain't it,' Dougie growls. 'You love it up the dirtbox, you posh slags!'

'Don't go off-road now, Dougie, whatever you do!' She's laughing like mad.

He stops for an instant. 'Ask nicely,' he teases.

'*Please*, please, please, fuck me,' she squeals. He starts fucking her again, hitting a rhythm again.

'Do it! Say it!' he says. 'Come on, *please*,' like it's his turn to beg.

'No!'

'Please!' he insists.

'No!'

'*Please!*'

'Fuck's sake,' she says and then in her best pikey voice, 'come on, you nasty cunt, call that fucking! Oi, mate, that's nice. You dirty ... Fuck me properly, you grubby roughneck cunt!'

I can hear him groaning and giggling and pumping like mad, all at the same time.

'Fuck me,' she laughs. 'Come on! You've only got a little knob!'

Dougie stops dead; a freeze-frame moment. 'Steady on, girl ... ' Dead serious all of a sudden. Then Dougie hits his stride again. And he's back to his impression of Sonny. 'I wanna see ya getting fucked by me pals! Like seeing the missus getting chopped, don't I!'

'Dougie, Dougie!' she screams. 'You're possessed!'

'Ain't I!' he screams with a manic laugh. And then he goes into an insane mantra – 'I'm a dustman, a dirty, dirty dustman! I'm a dustman, a dirty, dirty dustman!'

Her knickers swing, gathering speed. Dougie howls like a wolf. 'You're a dirty whore! And I'm a dirty dustman!'

Then he carries on till the desk is creaking under the weight. Suddenly Cressida's looking over Dougie's shoulder, straight at me, eye-to-eye contact, but she doesn't say anything for a good five seconds. Should I give her a little wave? Maybe she'd get off on it. Dougie pumps away, groaning, starting to hit the vinegar strokes, getting to where he wants to be.

'Dougie, there's a man in the corner,' she says, calm, like she was admiring a lampshade. 'He's watching.'

The Dougie cat is trying to ignore this bit of information, to carry on regardless.

'Stop, Dougie, I'm serious. There's a man. Look!'

He stops, white arse motionless. I can hear him breathing heavy. He turns, in slow motion, his eyes all mad and angry.

'Who the fuck are you?' he snarls, squinting to focus.

'I'm a friend of Sonny's,' I say. 'That's a spot-on impression.'

Suddenly Dougie isn't so intoxicated by the booze, gak and pussy.

'Am I in trouble?' He asks, half serious, half childlike.

The girl goes into a fit of hysterical giggles. 'Oh, Dougie,' she screams, 'you are funny. *Am I in trouble?* You're not in school!'

'Shut up!' he tells her. 'Just shut fucking up!'

The more she tries to suppress her laughter the more she laughs.

'Sonny's meant to be meeting me here,' I tell Dougie.

'In the club?' he shrieks.

'In this office.'

'Oh, fuck!' shrieks Dougie.

He pulls his trousers up and starts frantically buttoning up his shirt, but some of the buttons are missing. It panics him. The girl meanwhile has jumped off the table, pulled her knickers up, found

her top in semi-darkness, pulled it back on, straightened herself –
and her skirt – out and is respectable again in seconds, calmly
smoothing out her hair and rubbing some mislaid coke into her
gums. The mere mention of Sonny turned the arrogant dude
upside-down, turned him into a thumb-sucking imbecile – putting
the right buttons in the wrong buttonholes.

The girl starts to drag Dougie out the door without another
word. No goodbye. Dougie's face as he leaves is half naughty
schoolboy, half sweaty ziphead. He slams the door and hurries
down the corridor. I hear the door at the bottom of the stairs open
– thump-thump-thump-bass-bass-bass – then a muffled
conversation. Then someone approaching.

The door swings opens and Sonny walks in with Royski
trailing behind. He turns the lights on, dazzling me. 'See him, that
geezer,' says Sonny, pointing with his thumb, 'I don't know how,
but he can't half nick a bird ... '

'Who's that?' I ask.

'Oh, right, you didn't meet him,' says Sonny, bewildered,
pondering the unfathomable. 'You woulda thought he was a dot
on the card gaylord.'

'Who we talkin about, Sonny?' I ask. 'I'm lost.'

'Don't matter, pal,' he says, shaking his head.

Sonny leans on the front of the desk facing me – arms folded,
dead envious – where two minutes before Dougie was chopping
double-horny Cressida, suggesting *he'll do her up the dirtbox ...*

'You all right?' Sonny asks.

'I'm sweet,' I reply. 'You okay?'

Sonny ignores the question but just one look tells me that
they're a pair of troubled souls, but both trying hard to appear
relaxed. Roy is swivelling round and round in an office chair –
like he ain't got a care in the world – stopping only to drum out a
nervous tell-tale tattoo.

'What do you need to talk to me about, Sonny?' I say at last.

'I just wanted you to drop by, to have a word. See, I was
thinking ... You being here in London is all fine and dandy, but I
might need to go under myself, so now might not be the best time
for your state visit, you understand?'

'No, I don't understand,' I say, truthfully. 'You might need to explain ... ' They look at me like I'm mad. I start again, 'If this is about Ted, it's business as usual. Bridget was more involved than—'

'Bridget don't like me – never did,' snaps Sonny.

I could tell him that Ted never liked him either but that wouldn't be diplomatic. Instead I say, 'I don't see, Sonny, how that matters.'

Sonny pushes himself off the tabletop so he's standing up now, suddenly angry. 'Don't be fuckin telling ... ' his voice peters out. He rolls up his fist in frustration, like he'd love to punch me in the mouth. I don't feel danger; if Sonny wanted me shuffled to the bottom of the pack, I'd be gone already. He leans back on the desktop, picks his words with care.

'You fuck me over – make me look a cunt in front of Morty *or* Bridget Granger – I'll kill ya. Don't make me an enemy—'

'Listen, Sonny, I'm here cos Ted Granger wanted me—'

'You're a right smart cunt. Always got something to say—'

'I ain't got time to fuck about.'

'And you think I have?' says Sonny. 'You don't know the half of it. I've got naughty people wanting to do me and him ... ' he nods at Roy, ' ... damage.'

Roy snaps to attention, twitch breaking out.

'Sonny,' I ask, actually curious, 'who wants to do you damage?'

Sonny gets up, strides three short paces over to the wall and punches the plasterboard partition, hard enough to leave a crumbling dent. He doesn't seem bothered by physical pain, might as well be patting a balloon.

'I'm confused,' I say. 'You think that people want to do you damage?'

'Listen, don't ask *me* questions. Disregard everything I've just said. And don't be telling Morty about anything either.' Then, as an afterthought, he adds, 'Or Bridget either. They don't need to know!'

'Know fuckin *what*, Sonny?' I'm getting the zig now.

'Nuffin, they don't need to know nuffin, okay? You understand?'

'No, I don't. I'm confused if I'm honest—'

'This conversation never happened,' he says, suddenly exhausted. 'There's something about you I don't like. I ain't worked out what it is yet ... '

'*You* asked *me* to come over here for what, exactly?'

'To tell you to fuckin behave yourself—'

'And now, Sonny, you're talking in riddles – *don't tell Morty about you-know-what or Bridget Granger either*—'

'Don't get fuckin smart with me!' screams Sonny, pushing off the table, eyes locked in. 'I ain't impressed with you!' he says, his face getting red. 'I'd just as easy bury you. Don't think I wouldn't, pal, cos I'd fuckin enjoy it! Maybe I will, you cunt!'

Sonny steps in closer, then stops dead. He's spotted something on the carpet.

'Wassat?' he says, pointing down.

'What is it, Sonny?' Roy is out of the seat, on red alert. 'What ya found?'

'Easy, Royski,' says Sonny, the calm one now, 'nice and easy ...' Sonny bends down, picks up something delicate, studies it intensely then holds it up to the light. 'It's a button,' he says, 'a fuckin pearly button. See that ... ' He shows it to me, tiny in the palm of his hand. 'What the fuck's that doin here?'

'Fuck knows, Sonny,' I reply.

It captures his imagination for a few seconds before he flicks it away, shrugs with a worried forehead, then he's back on me. Lost his thread but regained his temper. 'Anyway, you behave yourself, shift some weight, we'll get along famously.'

Sonny moves towards the door, happy again. 'Come on you two – lively! Let's go downstairs, have a little sherb. Now you're here, pal,' he says to me, 'I want you to meet someone.'

Sonny King, I'm thinking, following him out, is more scared of Sister Bridget than he is of Mister Mortimer *or* the ghost of Duppy Ted.

Once we get downstairs I can see why a gentleman like Sonny would want a share in a Mayfair nightspot, one like the Monarch Club. Apart from the obvious bagwash opportunities – and the incredibly good chances of indulging in belly-bumping sessions with extremely fit upper-class women – the whole gaff is one gigantic ego-fest for Sonny. The VIP area especially is a microcosm where criminal heavyweights and bemused aristocracy come to give each other a jolly good backslapping. It's that curiously strange but perfectly understandable mix of off-duty villains and never-*on*-duty aristocrats who get along famously. Who else doesn't have to get up for work at seven on a cold and frosty morning? Who else has easy-come-easy-go money burning a hole in their pockets, begging to be squandered? Who else regards morality, timekeeping and good manners as purely optional? Who else have what psychology books would call a '*sociopathic sense of entitlement*'?

Everybody loves a gangster – till they meet one. Everyone loves a toff – till they meet one.

Sonny, of course, is in his element. Everyone's showing great respect or laughing till they weep at his war stories. In many respects Sonny's a basher but he's grafted, through hard work and ruthlessness, to be the owner of a not insubstantial piece of upmarket property. He might not attain the so-called class of these debonair swell dudes – all hanging-out, poncing off each other, piking-out when the bill arrives – but this is a geezer who's escaped a kennel in Kilburn, who could buy and sell a lot of these cunts who look down their nose at him.

Money is flying. International clientele – the so-called Eurotrash, who don't have anything trashy about them and increasingly don't have anything Euro about them – have colonised the tables surrounding the dance floor where the minimum spend is a grand. There's plenty of Dom Perignon and sniff going round but with admirable caution – discreet waiters handing over wraps in matchcovers, diplomatic sorties to the powder room, polite notices advising against drug use. But most of the clientele are charged-up, well pleased with themselves. You could get to thinking that sniffing coke is a bit old, not a lot of imagination involved.

Sonny wants to park me up in the VIP and feed me champagne and caviar on toast. He formally introduces me to Dougie. In a less forgiving light, Doug is a disaster area – a sweaty cokehead, not pretty. You get the sense that Douglas Nightingale is from a different era – that peculiar mix of ultra-perceptive, seen-it-all-before, and at the same time naïve, childishly stupid, too trusting for this cruel life.

'I thought your paths might have crossed somewhere along the line,' says Sonny.

'Oh no,' I say, shaking Dougie's clammy hand, 'this is the first time we've met, isn't it?'

Dougie nods with hostile eyes. Sonny disappears. Dougie – like a half-fucked dog – is transfixed by a girl dancing provocatively in front of him. Then, without a word, Dougie wanders off, leaves me standing like a plum.

The club is full to bursting now but I don't really feel in the party spirit, I feel jet-lagged and spun-out. I was at a funeral and then had my head mangled by the deceased. It's time to go. Then I feel a big slap on the back.

I turn round to see Sonny with a huge cigar stuck between his teeth. He's with a well-dressed swell who's grinning like he's had a noseful.

'This is my man Giles,' Sonny shouts above the music. 'If ya ever wanna buy a Picasso, or a nightclub, then he's yer boy. A *proper* lawyer,' says Sonny with a wink to Giles.

They both laugh. Giles has a girl on each arm, like some handsome, foppish playboy wastrel who's escaped from a Broadway musical, but looking at me like he knows something I don't. I lean in close on Sonny, 'I was just cutting out, Sonny.'

'And?' he shrugs, dead dry. 'That's up to you. Shame you two couldn't have a little chinwag.'

Sonny gets distracted by some passing admirers. He drags them over to the bar, snapping his fingers for champagne.

'Another time, another place, perhaps,' I say turning to shake Giles' hand. 'It's hello and goodbye at the same time, I'm afraid.'

'Yes, yes,' says Giles, shaking my hand, nodding his head, looking absorbed, like he's scheming. He carries on shaking my hand.

'Can I have my hand back, mate?' I ask.

'Oh, sorry!' Giles says. The girls laugh and so does Giles, good-naturedly.

'Actually, Giles, I've had a long day. I hope you're not offended – or Sonny – but I'm just off.'

'Offend our Sonny?' he says. 'I didn't believe that was possible, old buddy.'

Again the girls laugh like it's the funniest thing ever.

'We'll meet again, sir,' says Giles, very loaded, with a small nod.

'Sure, sure,' I say, suddenly desperately wanting to get gone. 'Till next time.'

'You're not wrong, pal,' says Giles the Toff with a wink and a smidgen of Cockney accent.

CHAPTER THIRTEEN

CHA - CHA WITH THE DEVIL YOU KNOW

Sometimes life is about sitting tight. Right now it's about waiting on Ted Granger. I slept on it and it's a good deal – two grand a kilo shipped *on any deal negotiated*. Nobody's being greedy. Ted or Bridget need to build in as many buffers as possible. I started getting ideas, working out where we could place product. But, after I left Sonny's Monarch Club, I got a distinct feeling of being watched. I couldn't see anyone but, as Ted would say, that don't mean they ain't there.

This morning Morty rang – told me to *stand down, it's Sunday* – and suggested a trip out to a restaurant on the river in Berkshire, one of his new haunts. I dodged around on the tube and met Mort outside Baker Street station, by the flower stand. Morty's old habit – rental motors. My old habit – jumping around on the Underground. Soon we were heading out towards the Home Counties.

And it was just like old times – all the stories, good food, people on boats, waving as they chugged by; swans, ducks and moorhens – Mort feeding 'em bread. Then he talks bits of business – jogging my memory – old connections for new supplies.

But talking shop is dangerous. Customs and Excise, or the law, will nowadays try and prosecute using the *conspiracy* laws rather than possession with intent to supply. They'll keep an eye on geezers they *suspect* of being involved with import and supply of powders. If they get a hint of skull-business they can move in and nick them for conspiracy. Years ago to get a conviction the defendants had to be caught red-handed with the gear. But now juries only have to be convinced that these guys *conspired* with the aim of committing a criminal action – the *planning* was the crime, not the execution. Guys are getting sent away without the customs seizing product. If the law fancy you're at it they target you, and your life becomes very difficult.

I ask Morty what his plans are, but Morty's plans are, as usual, a lazy shrug of the shoulders. He's happy to mooch around in the countryside, reminiscing. He's good company until the sun goes down and we decide to head back into town, Morty gets in the motor and switches, becomes a boy racer.

I must have spent years of my life in a motor with Mort but I never felt comfortable in the passenger's seat. I remember how fast Morty drives. As we hit the motorway I remind him I'm still a man who the police would like to help them with their enquiries. We drive real fast for ten or fifteen minutes as it gets dark.

'One second ... ' says Mort, holding up a gloved hand, looking in the rear-view mirror more than the road ahead. Now he's increasing his speed again, to a hundred miles an hour.

'Do ya wanna slow down a bit, Mort?'

But he ain't listening. He's got on something in the rear-view and checking the wing mirrors – taking quick looks, left and right, in case someone's sneaking up on us.

Without warning, but double calculated, Mort jerks the wheel down hard to the left and sends the motor hurtling across three lanes, from the inside to the outside. We're travelling diagonally across the road, tyres screeching, two wheels off the tarmac.

'What the fuck!' I'm shouting, hanging on tight.

Morty's heading for the slip road off the dual carriageway but he's overshot it. He swings the motor around hard. We're travelling fast *towards* the oncoming traffic, dazzled by headlights! Mort then brakes hard. The back of the motor skids round. Mort jerks the wheel down hard to the right – hits the gas – sending us accelerating up the slip road, pushing me back in my seat. I can hear car horns shrieking, braking, skidding of tyres back on the carriageway below. There are traffic lights at the top of the slip – showing red – but Morty speeds over them, maybe didn't see them. Luckily there's nothing coming. We hit a large roundabout. Mort opts for an unlit road heading off. And hits the gas.

'Someone was following us,' says Mort, still checking the rear-view.

'How do you know?'

'I just fuckin *know*,' he shrugs.

'How can you tell, it's just one straight road? Everyone's travelling in the same direction.'

'Just believe me, I know.'

'Who is it? The law?'

'Don't think it is.'

'How can you tell?'

'Law don't rent motors. Can tell a rental with my eyes shut.'

Morty pushes our rental through another roundabout. Immediately we're on a dark road in the middle of nowhere, heading nowhere, with only cat's eyes to guide us. I turn in my seat to see if anything is following but the road is empty.

'What car was he driving?' I ask.

'Couldn't tell.'

'So how the fuck do you know we're—'

'Trust me,' says Mort.

'So where is he? Ain't putting up much of an effort.'

'That's the problem. It's like he's letting us run.'

'You've turned into Roy.'

'Shut it, okay! Ain't funny!'

'Okay, Mort, do ya wanna slow down a bit, let him catch us up?'

Morty slows right down – to sixty.

'Fuck Ted ... And fuck Sonny ... ' says Mort, almost to himself. 'Fuck 'em all.'

The motor skids a little, back and forth across the white line. There hasn't been a car in either direction for miles but he's still caning it. Morty is muttering to himself, spitting angry. I wasn't spooked before when he was throwing it around at a hundred miles an hour, the wrong way up a dual carriageway. Maybe I shoulda been. I'm thinking we're gonna end doing a somersault into a fuckin ditch; some farmer's gonna find us dead at dawn. We're hurtling down an unlit and curvy country road.

'What's the fuckin hurry?' I ask. 'Pull over! We'll see if anyone's on us!'

Morty's either ignoring me or he doesn't hear me. Then he abruptly pulls over into a lay-by. In one swift movement he pulls on the handbrake, throws open the door and jumps out into the chilly night air. He walks round the motor, through the skinny pampas grass, towards a wooden fence. I get out but don't walk towards him. I lean against the car and wait. It's almost completely silent except for some crows shrieking. In the tranquil countryside there appears to be a million stars in the cloudless sky. Morty is using all his energy to restrain his temper but his breathing is long and deep.

'So, Mister Mortimer ... ' I ask after a while, 'where are we?'

'I'm not sure ... ' he says. And then he starts chuckling to himself. 'In fact, I ain't got a clue.'

We found our way back, eventually, onto the dual carriageway. We drove a few miles south and stopped at the services. Morty completely ignored – like only Mister Morty can – my inquiries about his furious episode. Instead he said he wanted to check something out. But he's alight, scanning the huge car park for anyone who could have us under surveillance. He's got paranoid, double-quick.

'Go in there and buy a torch. Don't be a schnorrer, spend a few quid,' says Morty, as I start walking towards the petrol station. 'And don't forget the fuckin batteries,' he hollers after me.

In the service station shop I find a big yellow plastic torch with a massive, reflective dish armed with a mean-looking halogen bulb. Could blind a man. It doubles up as a warning light, with a red dome that flashes to alert motorists in the case of traffic accidents. It's a bargain at nineteen pounds and ninety-nine pence. I buy my flashlight and *fuckin batteries* and head back out to Morty. He's still scanning the car park for our phantom pursuers. I hand the flashlight to Morty but he doesn't take it.

'Put it together, bruv,' he tuts, 'don't be a lazybones.'

I eventually pull the plastic packaging apart while Morty stands, studying the back end of the motor, concentrating hard, pacing backwards and forwards, dead pensive. 'I think I saw two geezers sniffing around ... back at the restaurant. Didn't look like Old Bill ... '

'So what *did* they look like?' I ask.

'Like a coupla waiters, Spanish or Italian, but like *heavy* waiters.'

When the torch is assembled I hand it to Morty. He turns it on.

'Fuckin 'ell!' says Morty, dazzled by the intensity of the beam.

Straightaway, Mort's down on one knee, searching under the back of the motor.

Next thing he's unceremoniously on his back, crawling under the car, rolling around in all his dandy finery, on oil-stained tarmac, disappearing under the rear wheels, shining the light up into nooks and crannies. His Armani leather is ruined, torn by the gravel. I stand and watch. The torch throws out weird shadows and spooky shapes.

'Naughty-naughty,' I hear him say, like he's spotted something untoward. Then he's reaching in, stretching, trying to grab something with his fingertips, making grunting noises.

'Oi! Here! Take this! Quick!' Morty's shouting. 'Take the fuckin thing. Quick!'

I take the object from him. It's a tiny, two inches by three, heavy black plastic box with a tiny green light blinking slowly. The bottom is basically a magnet. It appears to be brand new. If he'd handed me a snake I couldn't have been more concerned cos I know what it is straight away – a global positioning device – a tracker. Morty emerges squinting, trying to adjust to the car park floodlights.

'Straight question,' I say. 'Who's put this on the motor?'

'Keep it dark, bruv, outta sight,' he says, ludicrously lowering his voice.

'There's nobody fuckin here, Mort! Answer the question! Who?'

'I dunno,' he says, going to take the tracker but I hold it outta reach.

'It's Old Bill! Gotta be! You can drop me back at the airport! I'm gone!'

I've got the serious zig now. A GPS tracker can deliver the exact whereabouts of a vehicle, a container or a human being onto a cell phone or laptop anywhere, gives the exact location, or map reference even, of where the target is. And that's what we are, all of a sudden. Targets. Morty's gone straight into defensive denial mode. He looks upon being followed as part of the game, is used to having the law on his arse.

Mort and me are now instinctively covering our mouths with our hands. Old habits die hard. The customs and Old Bill have got directional microphones that can eavesdrop conversations from miles away. Are we being smudged up with a telephoto lens as we speak? Are we gonna end up in evidence booklets, with time and date captions neatly stuck in the bottom corner?

Morty's pacing when I came outta the petrol station shop was him working out how they placed the device. Whoever put it there crept up while we was eating.

'You know what, Mort?' I say. 'He's here, our new mate, somewhere out there.' I nod at the colossal car park. 'Watching us right now ... '

'You wanna go for a little walk?' asks Mort. 'See who's about?'

'Be pointless ... unless you need the exercise.'

I hand the tracker to Morty. He studies the device then he starts wiping it with a silk hanky, removing sticky fingerprints. He's still polishing – about to fling it – as we go to get into the motor, but then walks over to a smelly lorry that's got a massive cartoon of an upright dancing fish, smiling manically, like it can't wait to have its head lopped off and dive into the deep fat fryer. It has the name of a Lowestoft fish wholesaler emblazoned on the side. It's meandering, manoeuvring at walking pace. Morty coolly – using the pink silk hanky as protection – holds the device high in the air between his forefinger and thumb so anyone watching can see it. Then he swivels and places the tracker on the side of the metal container. Then Mort walks back towards our motor. The lorry starts to gather speed out of the car park.

Morty gets in and is about to start the engine when my phone rings. I don't recognise the number. I'm reluctant to answer it. Morty shrugs, pulls a quizzical face. The phone stops but immediately starts ringing again. I answer it.

'Hello?' I say.

'Hello.' It's Sonny.

'Now's not a good time, mate,' I tell him. 'We might have problems—'

'Start again, bruv.'

'There was an extra on our motor,' I say. 'To keep an eye ... on our movements.'

'You telling me you've found a tracker on your motor?'

'Not saying anything.'

'Listen, where's it now?'

'On a fish lorry.'

'How did it get there?'

'Got repositioned.'

'Right, well go and get it,' says Sonny, calm as ya like.

'What?'

'What don't ya understand?' he hisses. 'The device, you stupid cunt, go and get it!'

'Don't talk to me like I'm a cunt!'

'So stop talkin like one. Go and get it.'

'Why? What the fuck—'

'Don't ask why. Just do as I say. Stop arguing. Go and get it. I need that kit.'

'It's gone already.'

'Well, follow it! It's a big fuckin lorry!'

'Is it yours?'

'Do you know how stupid that is?' screams Sonny. 'I can use it to work out—'

'Use it?'

'Do *you* know who put it there?' he asks.

'No—'

'Exactly. Do you think it will be in our interests to find out?'

'Yeah—'

'Be a big clue, *having* the device,' sneers Sonny in pure sarcasm. 'I don't know shit about trackers but you know who *will* know? Our twitchy friend ... '

'But the tracker will still be transmitting. I don't wanna go near it.'

'Follow this fuckin fish lorry, get the kit off it—'

'Are you fuckin mad?'

'I ain't mad,' he says dryly. 'First sign of madness, you know that, don't ya, calling people mad? Do as I say. You understand? And sling that trom – I'll get you another one.'

He's gone. I put my phone away and give myself a quick *situation report*. Sonny wants the tracker, for his scrutiny, so he can narrow down who would be electronically following Morty and me. Morty's lit a fag. 'What was all that about?' he asks a bit too calmly.

'We need to follow that lorry and get that tracker—'

'You fuckin mad?' says Morty, incredulously.

'First sign of madness, apparently, calling people mad.'

After a mad dash to start with, we followed the lorry at a leisurely pace into London. It's a hard thing to lose, a smelly juggernaut. We hung back, wanted to see if anyone else was following the lorry. Morty concluded – everyone's a surveillance expert – that information was being relayed back, via satellite, to a static position, to some cat sat in front of a computer. No one was *physically* following the lorry down to the fish market, 'cept us. Once Morty had given them the slip back on the motorway, they have confidently – *over*-confidently as it had turned out – thought they could rely on the tracker to produce the information they wanted without risk of *further compromising their cover*. But all this idle chat about imagined tail cars and real electronic trackers was feeding a pull to Heathrow and a flight to Jamaica. Things had gone bandaloo very quickly.

We pulled up behind the fish lorry at a set of traffic lights in Baron's Court. There was nobody about, not a fuckin sòul. I got out the motor, strolled up to the wagon and pulled off the tracker. It took quite a tug to get it off. I got swiftly back in the motor and put it in the plastic folder the rental documents came in. When the traffic light changed to green we did a right while the lorry headed straight on.

We parked up by some secluded lock-up garages off the main road, then got the box spanner out of the spare-wheel kit. Morty hit the tracker a few times until the green light disappeared, then we headed for home.

Morty held his index finger across his lips; we didn't know if the motor was bugged. He tuned the radio to a classical music station – Bach and Chopin up real loud. It took hours of detours but nobody was following us. I studied the tracker all the way home, was worried that the tracking device looked *too* dead, that it was still pumping out its snide signal in spite of being apparently deaded. What little writing there was on the plastic casing was in Spanish but the product itself was, like my brand new flashlight, *Hecho en China* – Made in China. Why the fuck would anyone bother to import a Chinese-made GPS tracker from

sunny Spain? It didn't look like standard-issue British police
equipment.

As I'm getting out round the back of my hotel I ask Morty
where he picked up the motor.

'I didn't,' he replies, but something in his voice suggests he's
being evasive. 'It's one of Sonny's. Rents 'em by the dozen.
Wouldn't worry about it, mate.'

CHAPTER FOURTEEN

LUNCH AT SONNY'S HIDEAWAY

When Roy heard about the tracker, he went directly to Condition Red – a heady mixture of vindication and *clear and present danger*. He began thinking *I was right all along – they,* whoever the fuck *they* are, *are* out to get us.

This morning Roy wouldn't talk on the hotel hotline just arranged a meet in a primitive code – *one click north of the fish tank, ASAP* – the next station north from Bank station as soon as possible – then rang off.

Before I went anywhere I rang the number that Ted gave me, chatted the bird up and ascertained that she was talking to me from a call centre just outside of Antwerp, Belgium – talking English with a slight Flemish accent – but per-fect-ly pro-noun-cing eve-ry syl-la-ble of eve-ry word.

After going through a vigorous security procedure I transferred the funds to an account I hold in Jamaica, me looking out across London and the woman in a cubicle like a million and one others. If I'm shipping out, now's the time to put the money beyond reach; let them ask for it back. Then I headed out to give Royski the tackle.

The bad news is Morty is being evasive, rung to say *it'll only take one of us to deliver the thingy.* I could hear a woman giggling in the background, then Morty started laughing as well. His delivery got a bit breathless. He clicked off abruptly. Then I riddled it out – he was getting huffy and puffy from an early morning blowjob. The next time I speak to Morty it might be to bid him *adios* from the airport.

In contrast to Royski, Morty and Sonny don't appear to be that fussed about the device – *tracker, maraca*, is their attitude. But Roy's a different mindset, constantly on the lookout for something to spin out about. Sonny is, apparently, referring to Roy in phone calls as *The Chief of Police*.

Overnight I'd hid the dead tracker in a carrier bag in a small park not far from the hotel. I wanted to swiftly hand it over to Roy when he came to meet me at Moorgate station, but he insisted I get in the motor and come with him to meet with Sonny.

'He wants you to go over to his place and have some lunch with him, hang out.'

'Hang out?' I asked. 'Are you sure about this, Roy?'

'Yeah,' he says. 'Like hang out ... '

Someone has told Sonny to make the effort to be nice to me whether he *fuckin likes it or not*. Maybe Ted gave him the same *symbiotic* spiel before he died.

Roy tells me, when I get in the motor, that *it's safe to talk, bruv* – he's swept it with a scanner that detects radio signals. He double-checks that I left the trombone at the hotel. I tell him I no longer possess a mobile phone, that I ditched it in a lay-by out near the M4 under direct orders from Sonny. Roy walks to the boot of the rental car, opens it, and hands me a brand new, but as yet unactivated one, from a collection.

'The number's on the box, okay,' he points. 'Don't turn it on till later, okay?'

'Okay, Roy. You wanna see this bitta kit?'

'In a minute,' he says, checking the skyline for snipers, covering his mouth. 'Keep it dark.'

We drove north for a while, then west. When Roy's curiosity couldn't stand it anymore we pulled into an underground car park in Russell Square and Roy gets to have a good look at the tracker. His expression registered relief but then he immediately got all pensive, worried again straight away. The relief was from the fact that it *wasn't, definitely not*, UK Old Bill issue. When I suggest the lettering on the casing was in Spanish and this might have something to do with Ted – *maybe the Spanish police are following me? Maybe this is something Bridget needs to know* – Roy got all stroppy and twitchy.

'She ain't to fuckin know, you get it? It's all about containment.'

'About what?'

'Yeah, containment, need-to-know ... ' he says, embarrassed, twitch level rising.

Then he goes strangely and *overly* calm. That's spooky – Roy attempting to be some chilled-out individual when this development has clearly rattled him. Much as Royski tried to disguise it I was left with the impression that he didn't want, under any circumstances, for reasons of his own, to let Auntie Bee know about the tracker. Roy's attempted cover-up makes me think that he *knows* – or has a good idea – where the tracker came from. Any probing questions will send Twitchy over his tipping point. So I ignore the definite friction in the air, as Roy drives northwards to Sonny's bijou slaughter.

If a kid from our part of town makes a tub-full of money, legally or not, they decamp out to the far-flung suburbs where London peters out or into the countryside proper – Maidenhead or Chalfont St Giles – or they camouflage themselves in Marylebone or Hampstead. Sonny has gone for the Hampstead option. Royski is taking the long route and is, as ever, over-alert to surveillance, busy concentrating on who's behind us. My concern is that he spends more time looking backwards than where he's going.

As we travel through Islington traffic police are marshalling cars past an accident. Roy's twitch begins to activate at the sight of law enforcement. It doesn't calm down again until we approach genteel Hampstead, the neighbourhoods becoming more gentrified and leafier. We skirt around the Heath, a few thousand acres of untouched parkland.

Hampstead is what Americans think England should be like – a quaint village with tight streets and coaching inns. We pass through the village, up a hill, over a small roundabout, and down a leafy lane. Roy takes a last look in the rear-view then pulls off into an almost hidden road. After twenty yards we stop at a gatehouse in front of a large set of black gates. The uniformed security guard flicks open a window.

'Good afternoon, sir,' he says politely. 'Can I help?'

'Could you let Mister Berkeley know I'm here?'

'And you are?'

'Mister Johns,' says Mister Burns. 'And this is Mister Hunt,' he says indicating me.

The guard has already picked up a telephone and buzzed through to Sonny, now AKA Mister Berkeley again. The gates open. The guard salutes as we drive through into the courtyard of a modern apartment block, an updated version of Art Deco with curved glass windows, rounded corners, painted brilliant white and pistachio. Like a hotel from South Beach, Miami, transposed to old world Hampstead.

Royski drives around the back of the building and parks up in a space set aside for visitors. We walk over to the entrance of the block. Roy buzzes the intercom, looks up and winks at a CCTV camera positioned above the door. The door buzzes. Roy pulls it open.

Inside, the block is incredibly quiet. From an entrance hall – huge, light and airy – four wings split off, not unlike a penitentiary. Discreet uplighters wired into the varnished brickwork throw up subtle light. Cameras sit unobtrusively – no doubt reassuringly – at corners and angles, their red lights blinking silently. We come to an elevator next to a staircase.

'Lift or stairs?' asks Roy.

'Why have a dog and growl yourself?'

We get in the elevator, made from industrially-toughened glass, with shiny new steel cogs, cables, pulleys and counterweights exposed. Roy pushes the button for the top floor.

As the elevator door opens, Sonny – chewing gum like a piston, brand new Nike tracksuit, bare feet, smelling of eye-stinging aftershave – is out in the hall, waiting to meet us.

'It's like fuckin Fort Knox in here, this gaff,' he says as he gestures us inside.

As we step into the spacious hallway, Sonny playfully slaps Royski on the back as he passes. I notice a bank of monitors by the front door showing the outside of the building and atrium downstairs. Nothing stirs on any of the screens. Sonny points down the hall and I follow Roy into his living room.

It's strikingly big, surprisingly classy and immaculately clean. Spotless. It's also simple – parquet flooring and extremely tasteful furniture – more accurately, *pieces* – white sofas, huge rugs, coffee tables heaped with photographic books, and on the walls still-life photographs and ironic thirties advertisements framed in brushed aluminium. On some shelving units there's a discreet music system and, on display, antique toys, sailboats and aeroplanes, vintage metal robots painted in primary colours.

Tucked around the corner at one end there's a pristine, open-plan kitchen and at the other end of the room a huge flat-screen television set has been suspended on the wall. It's switched on but with the sound muted, showing an old western – Arizona mountain ranges, rock piles, dry dusty riverbeds and hordes of Red Indians appearing over the top of a ridge. John Wayne pulls his famous grimace. The silent movie only increases the spooky, muffled vibe. Except Sonny's his usual boisterous self, happy I'm impressed.

'Do you wanna see this gadget, Sonny?' I ask, holding up the plastic bag.

'In a minute, pal. What's the big rush? You got to be someplace?' asks Sonny, suddenly sounding stressed and preoccupied; no good at disguising his emotions, is Sonny. He's swerving it in the hope that it will go away.

'What did this cost you, Sonny?' I ask. 'A couple of mill?'

'I didn't buy it, not yet. I *rent* it. I was *told* to rent it ... by the money man.'

That makes sense. The living room has the air of a luxury rental – the sorta place they let to high-flying business executives – which is what Sonny has become, I guess.

Sonny and Roy seem to be communicating in primitive sign language on my blindside – nods and winks and shakes of heads, index fingers over tightly closed lips. I pretend to be distracted by the fixtures and fittings. Sonny's reading matter gets my attention – a chunky biography of Napoleon on the coffee table. It's a thousand pages but Sonny's only managed to battle through the first ten. Inside, on the title page, is a written dedication – *To Sonny. Enjoy. Remember the battle is won by the most persevering* – signed *From your 'Swell Mob' Pal*. Underneath is a squiggle. I think it says *Giles*, the smooth lawyer from the Monarch Club. That would make sense – the patronising dedication and illegible signature.

Sonny pushes open two of the sliding glass doors that lead out onto a huge sun deck and beckons me outside to admire the stunning view. The decking is the size of a large London apartment, shaped like the bow of an ocean-going liner, and the view is spectacular – acres of lush and green woods with the towers of the City of London beyond.

'Good cover for surveillance,' suggests Royski, like an expert in field craft. 'Difficult to overlook the property in winter – no cover – but, now in summer ... '

I realise I'm still schlepping the tracker around in the service station bag. I'm tempted to lob it over the side. Sonny has set up, on a precision-engineered tripod, a gigantic pair of high-powered binoculars. I go to look through them but it's all a green blur. I look for the viewfinder.

'How do I focus these, Sonny?'

He shrugs his shoulders. 'They ain't mine, pal. Come with the gaff.'

'You use them?'

'There's nothing to see, is there? Only a few fuckin trees.'

'That,' I say with a nod into the haze, 'is maybe the greatest city in the world.'

'Is that right?' says Sonny, rolling his eyes. 'Like I say, they ain't my binoculars.'

Sonny spits his gum over the side, and motions for Roy and me to follow him. In the far, shaded corner of the deck someone has laid out a dining table and chairs, with four set places, complete with a linen table cloth, crisp white rolled napkins in holders, silver cutlery, wine and water glasses. Sonny has had some food delivered from a local delicatessen and laid out. Under film, in dainty serving bowls, prepared and ready to go, are chicken breasts cooked with artichoke, olives, garlic and rosemary breads and an assortment of Italian delicacies. A bottle of dry white wine has been uncorked and left to sit in an ice bucket by the side of the table. The wine is a good one. A small bar arrangement, with beer, water and a basket of fruit, has been set up in a solid brick barbecue that's been built into the edge of the balcony.

'Four places, Sonny?'

'Giles might drop by,' he says with a wink.

I knew Sonny had an ulterior motive. He pulls the film off one of the bowls and starts munching a handful of marinated garlic cloves dripping in olive oil. Sonny is looking straight at me with a hint of unspoken defiance in his eyes – *this is a bit of class, bruv, right or wrong? You can't fuckin deny it.* 'Fuckin handsome,' he says eventually, as he pushes another handful of garlic cloves into his mouth. 'An army marches on its stomach. Napoleon said that. Victory belongs to the most persevering.'

'Meaning?' I ask.

'It isn't the most talented; it's the most *persistent*, who wins the day. Last man standing gets the prize.'

I get the vibe that Sonny's discourse about Napoleon – the well-worn gangster cliché – is something he's repeating parrot fashion. And the guy who said it – probably Giles – said it with more panache.

'What do you need to talk to me about?' I ask, trying not to sound curious but coming across as irritated.

'Don't be like that, mate. No rush, we got all day. Look at London down there – fucking great ain't it?'

'Yeah, great.'

Sonny peels the film off the rest of the prepared dishes, one by one, rolls it up carefully, into one ball, and then slings it over the side.

'Try this,' he says, pointing to one bowl, 'baby squid, marinated, fuckin lovely.'

Sonny sticks a handful of squid into his mouth, dripping oil onto the cloth. He spots the mess, laughs and bends over to pick up another handful of garlic. Roy is making himself a ham sandwich.

'This is nice, ain't it? Have some chicken, it's lovely. You want anything?' he asks. 'You comfortable?'

'I'm okay. I'll just pick if that's okay, Sonny.'

I pick up the tracker in its battered bag. 'You wanna talk about this?'

They both ignore it. This is a turn-up. Royski, sparky at the best of times, seeing imaginary threats everywhere, is trying to discount a real-live tracker removed from a vehicle on hire to Sonny.

'See, Sonny,' I say, 'I'm curious about that two point seven mill. Remember, Barbados, Curtis, the CBB?'

'It's nunna your fuckin business,' snaps Sonny.

'I'm going to wash my hands,' I shrug. 'Where is it?'

Sonny points. 'Back where you came in,' he says with his mouth full.

I go and wash my hands but the bathroom window is open to allow a breeze in. I can hear Sonny hissing at Roy. Sonny can shout in a whisper. I can only make out a few words here and there – *pretend – getting back – I don't know, Roy – you think of something.*

When I go back out on the decking they've both got the most innocent expressions on their faces. I'm obviously getting grafted here. Sonny cockily shovels more baby squid and garlic cloves in his month while Roy intently studies the bag containing the tracker.

'See ... ' says Roy. 'This could be industrial espionage ... rivals and that ... '

'Really, Roy?' I say. Sonny's eyebrows go skywards.

'See,' continues Roy, 'Sonny's competitors could be looking to find out what he's up to ... '

'Or it could be the Serious Crime Squad getting busy now that Ted is dead. Creates what is called in police circles a *power vacuum.* Don't play me for a cunt, okay? Givin me bollocks about industrial espionage.'

Sonny looks angry but suppresses it. Roy starts to get twitchy. Bridget Granger is the key.

'It's all the more reason,' I tell them, 'to let Bridget Granger know ... if Morty hasn't already.' They consider this with long faces. 'I'm considering my options,' I add.

'Meaning?' asks Sonny, frown appearing.

'Have I got to spell it out? I ain't done anything illegal ... I'm jumping about on a snide passport. No big deal ... I might just bail—'

'But Ted brought you over special,' says Roy.

'Fuckin shut it, Roy,' barks Sonny. 'Do you know how ridiculous you sound sometimes?'

Roy's twitch upgrades. He nibbles his bottom lip.

'Listen, mate, I told ya,' says Sonny, 'Bridget don't need to know. Why bother her? Her brother's just died.'

'Cos she needs to know,' I say, returning Sonny's glare. 'Forewarned is forearmed—'

'What kinda bollocks is that?' snaps Sonny.

'Read yer fuckin history book,' I say.

'Have you told Bridget Granger?' Sonny asks me. 'Yes or no?'

'No,' I reply. 'But why's it such a big deal if she knows or not?'

'It ain't ... ' says Sonny shrugging, 'It's just ... '

'Fuckin sounds like it is, gents,' I say. 'Listen, if me and Morty have got a tracker on the motor, it's game over and I'm back to where I came from.'

'Give us that fuckin tracker here!' says Sonny, clicking his fingers.

I hand Sonny the tracker. He tips it out onto the table. In daylight it looks very dead. Roy and Sonny crouch down, studying a nondescript, plastic box.

'Are you two sure that thing's deactivated?' I ask.

Roy rolls his eyes and fetches a scanner. He places it next to the tracker. *No signal, see, not a peep.* They eventually conclude that the law *definitely didn't put that on that motor.*

'How can you be sure?' I shrug. 'Someone put it there—'

'Fuck off, smartarse,' snaps Sonny. Then he crouches even closer, studying the tracker, starts to slowly shake his head. Then he says, half to himself, half to Roy. 'This is all your fuckin fault, Royski ... '

Roy explodes. 'Bollocks, you cunt! Who dragged me back from Spain? You did!'

'Fuck off, Roy!' snaps Sonny.

'Don't talk to me like I'm a cunt, Sonny,' roars Roy. He steps in close to Sonny's chest, twitch going full blast, face red. Sonny pushes him backwards. Roy looks instinctively for a weapon. But suddenly a large flock of wood pigeons fly out of a tree. They break cover like they've been startled.

'Wassat?' says Roy, turning his head, like a gun dog. Alarmed face. The pigeons circle aimlessly overhead.

'Maybe someone's walking their dog, Roy,' I say. 'You two wanna calm down.'

'Fuckin ain't,' says Roy, like it's an absolute certainty. 'Someone's out there!'

It's a freeze-frame moment, nobody moves, and then Roy starts moving in slow motion, pure concentration on his face. Another bird flies from the tree. Roy suddenly grabs my arm.

'Get down! Fuckin get down!' he says, spilling my drink. Roy grabs Sonny by the arm and pulls him downwards. Roy's studying the trees, twitch going mad. Their argument is forgotten.

'What can you see, Roy?' whispers Sonny.

'Nothing,' replies Roy, 'but I can *feel* something's out there.'

I go to stand up. 'There's nothing out there.'

Their conciliatory mood has evaporated. 'Get down, you cunt!' hisses Sonny.

'I ain't burying you if you get shot!' agrees Roy, studying the trees intently. 'Could always be gavvers, Sonny, creeping up.'

'You might be *praying* its gavvers, Roy, if it's the other firm.'

'Who the fuck's out there?' I whisper.

'Fuck! If you hadn't ... ' hisses Sonny at Roy.

'Well, I did, didn't I?' replies Roy. 'It was *your* fuckin idea—'

'Fuck off, Roy, I didn't tell ya to—'

There's a rustling in the trees, could be the wind or another pigeon or a squirrel.

'Let's get inside,' says Roy. 'I don't like it.'

'Me neither, Roy,' says Sonny. Then he turns to me and whispers. 'What do you think?'

'That you two know something I don't.'

'Let's move,' says Roy. He suddenly, like some deranged bodyguard, pulls me from the decking and propels me through the open sliding door. At the very same time Sonny runs towards the door but he slips, knocks over the table, sending chicken breasts and squid, baskets of breads, flying everywhere. Next thing he slides over on a chicken breast, lands with a thud, bounces up again and scurries inside.

Now we sit tight, listening hard. Mundane sounds suddenly sound threatening. I crouch behind a solid wall and catch what they've got. Paranoia is contagious. Meanwhile, on the back wall, on the television, in the silent western John Wayne has organised the wagons into a circle and is shooting Apaches off horses.

'Do we have tools here, Sonny?' asks Roy. They're mates again.

'In the attic, bruv,' replies Sonny. 'Sling the you-know down, just in case we gotta trap.'

Roy creeps out the living room, keeping low, looking for cover.

Sonny and me wait, still watching the trees. Roy's only gone seconds before he returns with a heavy holdall. He dives into the bag and pulls out a pair of driving gloves. He pulls them on, pulls out another pair and throws them to Sonny. Sonny catches them and puts them on. Next out of the magic bag is a sturdy-looking matte-black pistol with tape around the handle and the trigger.

'Careful, mate, safety's on,' Roy whispers. Roy tosses the pistol over to Sonny, who catches it with both hands. Sonny undoes the safety catch. I realise that Sonny isn't humouring Roy, when Sonny starts to roll back onto the decking, keeping out of range of snipers. Sonny slowly looks around the corner of the wall like he's behind enemy lines.

Roy goes into the bag and pulls out a small submachine gun. He starts to crawl back outside onto the decking, studying the tree line, alert to every sound. Roy Burns has gone operational.

Roy and Sonny are communicating with hand signals, creeping across the decking. The woods are deathly quiet again but the pigeons have landed on the roof of the building, gently cooing. This seems to spook Roy – coming under attack from the Hampstead wildlife. The table that Sonny clattered is lying on its side. It don't look right. The ice bucket is on its side. Food is scattered across the deck – chicken breasts trodden on, baby squid and olive oil in puddles. Slowly birds begin to land and begin nibbling and picking, tearing at the scattered bread till it quickly becomes a feeding frenzy, in complete contrast to the silence coming from the woods – all the birds are over here. We wait and wait, but nothing happens.

'Roy,' Sonny whispers over to Roy, 'let's get out of here.'

'You're right. We're sitting ducks here, Sonny.'

'Hit the road. Roy?' asks Sonny.

Roy nods gently. He's holding the machine gun tight to his chest. Then he sprints back inside. Sonny crawls back inside, jumps up and pushes the sliding doors shut. Now Sonny is hurrying Roy along, clicking his fingers. Sonny wants to *get the fuck out*. They march into the hallway and motion for me to follow them.

Lying in the middle of the hallway is a brand new – or seldom used – Gucci executive briefcase that's been dropped from a height. Directly above it is an access panel that has been pushed up to expose an opening to the loft space. Sonny snatches up the briefcase and holds it across his chest, like some designer religious relic. Roy is checking out the monitors. Not a soul moving.

'There's no one out there,' says Sonny over his shoulder.

'No, Sonny, you can't *see* anyone out there,' replies Roy, 'don't meant to say—'

'Yeah, I know, whatever. Here, put this on,' says Sonny, snatching a raincoat off a peg and throwing it over to Roy who pulls it on. It totally engulfs Roy. It's huge and comical but it gives him cover for the machine gun. But it still doesn't look right. It's midday – the temperatures are soaring into the thirties. Sonny unlocks the front door then grabs the first thing he can get his hands on – an anorak with a fur hood. He pulls it on, sticks his pistol in one of the front pockets, pokes his head around the door and checks the landing. All clear.

We head out of the flat. Sonny slams the door shut. They're both hiding their guns under their coats or in pockets the whole time. They don't seem worried about the law – the law ain't gonna shoot them dead, and they wouldn't get tooled up for the law.

We half-trot down the hall, turn a corner and bump – *fuck it* – straight into one of Sonny's neighbours, a little old lady. She's seriously freighted-up with bags from shops and delis. Roy spins around, startled, pulls his gun out, and almost shoots her. Luckily she picks that moment to reach down to scoop up her lapdog. She doesn't notice the gun being waved around. Me and Sonny silently scream at Roy to put it away. She appears too preoccupied with her own trials and tribulations.

Sonny goes to dodge past her but she blocks him off. She wants to chat, chat, chat, to Sonny, her new neighbour – complain, really – about the *sudden change in the weather*. Sonny tries to edge round her but she's taken him hostage, wants to talk. Sonny nods but he's sweating profusely; poor boy's melting before her eyes. She looks at him strange. He's wearing a padded anorak *and* complaining about the heat. She's blocking our exit. Sonny's looking like he *wishes* Roy *had* given her a quick spray with his machine pistol. Roy's getting impatient – barely holding the coat and the tricky head together – sweating because he's carrying a bag of guns and ammunition.

I break left while Roy breaks right and we dodge past. Sonny tails us out, leaving her in mid-sentence. We trot down the stairs, two at a time, hit the ground floor, march across the lobby in long strides. As we get outside Sonny hugs the Gucci briefcase even closer to his chest, like it's chained to his wrist.

'So, what's in the case, Sonny?' I ask. 'Anything important?'

'Mind that,' he says, tapping his nose. 'You wouldn't wanna lose it.'

Answers my question.

CHAPTER FIFTEEN

NO MUM - DOG EAT MUM

Roy has the stripes now, definitely in charge. He marches towards Sonny's Range Rover, checking the locale, walking backwards, shooter tucked under his arm, snatching the keys. 'I better drive – know a few back-doubles.'

Roy unlocks the doors. Sonny's clutching his Gucci briefcase close to his heart. I grab the scanner that's sitting on the top of Roy's box of tricks.

I turn it on, walk to the rear of the Range Rover and hold it against the boot. It starts beeping – beep-beep-beep. This is getting worse.

'We'll leave it here. Quick, in that one, it's clean,' says Roy, nodding at the rental.

Roy opens the door, pushes the holdall under the driver's seat, jumps in, and motions for us to *hurry the fuck up*. Soon as we get in Roy pulls away with a wheel spin. The gatekeeper has seen us coming and opened the gate. Roy pushes the motor into traffic. The car behind us beeps his horn. Roy is oblivious. He's straining to see if any cars are pulling out to follow us. He drives fast for a hundred yards then cuts across oncoming traffic to slip into a narrow turning. He hits the gas, pushing me back in my seat. I look out the back window. Nothing, and nobody, is following us.

We rush past rows of grand houses – coach drives and pillars and no change outta five million. If a police car was to trundle up, Roy'd be getting his collar felt for dangerous driving. Wouldn't wanna end up in a situation where Roy feels no choice but to use the shooter.

'There's nothing behind,' I say, cautiously. 'You might wanna come off the gas.'

Roy ignores me, blocking everything out, but seems to know where he's going. Roy must have his head crammed full of emergency contingency plans and exits. He appears to be zigzagging west towards his old manor of Kilburn, racing down forgotten streets, throwing the motor round corners, accelerating then braking hard at junctions. Roy's doing textbook U-turns, working the power steering. I'm getting slung about in the back.

I notice something about Roy. When the threat is real, attack imminent, and Roy gets to mobilise his crisis planning – no twitch. But when the threat is only *perceived*, Roy starts twitching like mad. These guys didn't get where they are today by being spooked by pigeons. Someone *is* looking for a fight. Roy's got a bag of automatic weapons under his seat – serious jailtime. These ain't trigger-happy youngsters. I've never seen Roy so happy – been proved right. This is *not* an exercise.

Roy's giving us a whistle-stop tour of north west London's suburbs, past golf courses and cemeteries, avenues of sycamore trees along the Underground track, through Golders Green, Hendon then Cricklewood. Fair play to him, he's got us back to the reservation. He begins to slow down to thirty. Roy's odyssey has only lasted ten minutes but we can safely say there's nobody up our arse.

'Where we headed to, Roy?' Sonny asks.

'Me mum's. I'm starving.'

Roy does a sharp left down a short road with a 'No Through Road' sign at the top and an Underground line at the bottom. He pulls the motor up in front of a galvanised metal fence topped with ugly spikes, cuts off the engine, jumps out, walks around the back, scanning the area. Then he strolls back to the driver's door, opens it again, pulls out the tool bag. He slings it over his shoulder. As Sonny and me get out I notice there's a footbridge going up and over the railway. A train is approaching fast. As it rushes by Roy instinctively turns his face away, locks the motor and starts climbing the metal steps.

'We'll leave that one here for the time being,' says Roy. 'Now let's go and see Mum.'

The bridge is the classic armed robbers' paradise – rob the jug, jump in the motor, skid up at the bridge, ditch motor, over the tracks, pick up stolen motor parked on the other side, leaving any pursuers scratching their heads.

Roy's buzzing, adrenalined-up. Sonny doesn't like this shift in power. We trot over the bridge, down a pissy alleyway and emerge out in a quiet street, walk to the end and come out into a small post-war housing estate – four-storey blocks built around a courtyard. There's a plaque, a crest in the brickwork – 'Built by the London County Council – 1948'.

Roy leads us into the courtyard. There's a gaggle of teenage kids – boys and girls, black and white, smoking and play-fighting around the entrance to a block. They see Royski approaching and instantly fall silent. The kids nod and stare with big eyes, almost genuflecting, at Twitchy Roy Burns, and some even dare to snatch a glance at the legendary Sonny King. They clear a path to let us through – pure *Apocalypse Now*.

Roy leads us up two flights of concrete stairs, and half-trots down to the end of a landing. He stops at a front door with a grilled security cage. Roy pushes the bell in some primitive recognition code. After a few seconds we hear a deadlock being turned. Then the door opens slowly a smidgen and a frail, wrinkled face peeks suspiciously around the door. Missus Burns, Roy's mum, is about five foot and a fag paper tall and would weigh about six stone in hobnail boots. She smiles – loose dentures in her shrunken head – and opens the door wide.

She invites us in with an accent so thick it never left the West of Ireland. The small, immaculately tidy council flat smells musty – of snout, fried food, bleach and, sadly, old people's smell. She obviously knows Sonny, and although Roy tells her my name, I can tell she's instantly forgotten it.

'What you got there, Roy?' she asks hopefully, nodding at Roy's bag. 'Washing?'

'Tools, Mum,' he replies truthfully.

'We was doing a bit of maintenance at one of my properties,' Sonny lies.

'That's good,' says Missus Burns. 'You'll save yourself a good few pounds, doing it yourself.'

'That's my policy, Missus Bee – hands-on.'

Missus Bee shepherds us into the front room. There's too much furniture; it's cluttered and cramped. She's fond of swirly carpet and a crocheted lace arm covering or ten on her velveteen sofas. There's no Catholic trinkets or icons, no pictures of His Holiness the Pope or glow-in-the-dark Sacred Hearts but I spot a collection of funeral Mass cards tucked into the frame of an embroidered map of the Auld Country.

There's a shrine to Santa Royski – school photos of Roy – a chubby-faced boy who certainly looks capable of pushing up the pecking order to become number one school bully and terrorising the teachers. There's mistrust and suspicion in his scowl, a studied air of *what you looking at, cunt?* If it wasn't for the stripy school tie it would be a prototype mugshot. There's a scattering of polished pewter amateur boxing trophies and yellowing photos of a triumphant teenage Roy, his arm being held aloft by a red-faced and sweaty – no doubt a sex case – priest who appears to be acting as referee. The other kid in the photo – Roy's battered opponent – looks dazed and confused, face pummelled into jam, eyes swollen.

Sat perched on top of a glass-fronted display cabinet, crammed full to bursting with china plates and crystal glasses, there's a portable television with an indoor aerial. On the shelves there's a few tattered books, mostly counter-espionage textbooks. I assume they're part of Roy's reference library; I can't see Missus Bee needing a surveillance evasion handbook to go down the newsagent to pick up her *Galway Advertiser*.

'You hungry, lads?' asks Roy's mum.

'We skipped luncheon, Missus Bee,' says Sonny, in his swell's voice, and winking at Roy.

'I'm not sure I've got much in, boys,' she says, disappointed. 'If I knew you were coming I'd have got something nice.'

'We're starving, mum,' says Roy. 'A fry-up'll be fine.'

'That's no problem, lads. I've got bits in the freezer.'

We sit down as Missus Burns goes into the kitchen next door. Almost immediately we hear the sound of slabs of lard hitting a white-hot frying pan. Sonny places his briefcase carefully down the side of the sofa. With Missus Burns out of the room I lean forward.

'Sonny ... ' I ask, trying really hard to remove all trace of confrontation, 'who do you and Roy believe to be pursuing you?'

But Sonny slowly and unhurriedly places his index finger across his lips.

'It's bad manners, pal,' says Sonny King, that relentless defender of civility and propriety, nodding towards the kitchen. Then Roy and Sonny look at one another, shake their heads, like it would be a total breach of etiquette to be discussing such events in the sanctuary of Missus Burns' humble abode.

'So those are alright, are they?' I say, pointing at Roy's bag of weapons nestling between his feet. 'Mum's not gonna have a problem with those?'

Sonny gives me the pointy finger and shut-the-fuck-up eyes.

Mum is certainly a relic from a bygone age, seventy if she's a day. One of a generation parachuted in from Ireland in the austere fifties, looking for work, tipped up in Kilburn, stayed but never felt like they belonged, always talked about *going back home*. Nowadays it's all Polish and Russian kids on Kill-and-burn High Road. The Irish immigrants are disappearing fast. There's still a few drinking Guinness, getting sentimental, melancholic or homesick, getting busy on their own funeral circuit, but another Great British Tradition – the Irish colonising Kilburn – is dead.

We sit in silence, listening to the activity next door – whistling kettles, can openers hitting tins, *chunk-chunk-chunk*, fridges and freezers opening and shutting, eggs breaking, bacon beginning to sizzle, sausages being hacked off a frozen block. She fusses between the kitchen and front room, wearing her favourite apron, bringing tea and setting up fold-up tables while a strangely comforting smell creeps down the hall. Missus Burns has gone operational.

In truth you can't beat a full English – or Irish – if you're well hungover, it's February, there's black ice on the pavements, and you need the grease. You need the heart attack on a plate – overcooked bacon, exploding sausages, baked beans, slice after slice of buttery holy ghost, eggs rock hard in the middle, burnt to a frazzled crisp around the edges, and fried bread to soak up some of the fat, all served in a slippery layer of lard – and Missus Burns does not disappoint. She even smokes snout while we eat – which I always believe to be essential, the smell of burning tobacco enhancing the taste – sat on the sofa, with tea towels over our laps, because Missus Bee insisted. *You don't want to be getting your nice clothes dirty.* Missus Bee says nothing about the fact that Sonny has a long streak of oil up his jogging pants.

'Will I put the television on for you, boys?'

'Yeah, go on, Missus Bee,' says Sonny, between mouthfuls.

'Roy wanted to buy me a new set but I said no ... there's not much on worth watching these days. Save your money, I said.' She switches on the small portable and, would you believe it, it's John Wayne riding into the sunset. 'There's so much violence on the television these days, it's on the news and everywhere,' Missus Bee says, shaking her head. 'Wasn't there a boy killed up in Willesden for his mobile phone only last week? It's got very dangerous up there ... and Harlesden too. You boys be careful. You hear me?'

'Oh, yes, Missus Bee. I will be,' nods Sonny, licking his knife.

'And you too,' she says turning to me and pulling hard on her snout.

'I will be,' I say, nodding my head.

'You don't say much, do you?'

'No, Missus Burns.'

'These boys get led astray. My father used to say, God rest his soul ... ' she quickly blesses herself, 'you are the company you keep.'

'That's so very true, Missus Burns,' I say, winking at Sonny and catching a homicidal look.

'It's all those drugs,' she continues without pausing for breath. 'It was on the *News at Ten* only the other day. There's drugs everywhere. They send people mad – this crack and that cocaine. It's not safe to go out anymore at night. Missus Cassidy down the landing doesn't even go out during the day. And gangsters! And they've got guns! It's got terrible. You don't feel safe in your own home!'

Roy, the fuckin lunatic, is nodding along in agreement.

'I said I'd buy ya a dog,' he says. 'Get ya a big bastard—'

'Roy! I've told you. Don't swear,' she scolds him. 'You've got a God-given vocabulary.'

'Train him up, Mum; anyone comes in the gaff, bite their nuts off—'

'Roy!' says Missus Bee, pulling a harsh face, like she's never heard the like. Sonny laughs.

'Seriously,' says Roy, 'I'll get ya a dog—'

'And who's going to feed him?' she asks. 'Take him for walks?'

'I'd take him for a walk,' says Roy, 'over the Heath.'

'Let me think about it. The company might be nice,' she says, putting out one snout and lighting another.

'A nice Staffie, a puppy ... ' says Sonny, nodding, 'or a Doberman.'

'Oh, no, only a small one,' says Missus Bee, shaking her head.

'Doberman would suit you, Missus Bee, a couple maybe,' says Sonny, grinning now.

'You're teasing now, Sonny.'

'Oh, no. I'd contribute, put a few quid in,' says Sonny. 'Be a pleasure, get pedigree papers.'

'I couldn't have a big dog, council wouldn't allow it.'

'Fuck the council,' Sonny says with a dismissive wave of his fork.

Missus Burns looks at Sonny quizzically, then sideways at Roy, but Sonny trundles on regardless, oblivious.

'You don't need to worry about *anyone*, Missus Burns,' he says, waving his knife around to emphasise the point. 'Anyone gives you any grief, Missus Bee, you let Roy, or me, if Roy's away down in Spain, know. Straight away, get on the phone. You get any trouble ring me or Roy and we'll come over and sort it out for ya.'

'You're a good boy, Sonny, but I never get any trouble,' she says, still perplexed. 'All the coloured boys who sit down in the porch offer to carry my shopping up if the lift's broken, and it breaks down a lot ... '

'Maybe, Sonny,' I say in spite of myself, 'you should have a word with the lift repairman.'

'Fuckin shut it, you!' snaps Sonny, leaning forward, pointing now with his knife. 'We don't need your fuckin sarcasm!'

Missus Bee looks bewildered, her snout, with its long ash, hovering inches from her mouth.

'Sonny, language! Me Mum,' says Royski, nodding towards his puzzled mother.

'Oh, I'm terribly sorry, Missus Burns,' says Sonny, in his

money laundering voice, 'I forgot my manners for a moment then. I'm very sorry indeed.'

Sonny zeroes in on me, giving me the narrow eyes. 'Can I have a little word?' he says sarcastically over-polite, nodding out the door. 'In the hallway, perhaps?'

Here comes trouble ... But Sonny is all sweetness and light. Sonny suggests as nicely as possible that perhaps it's not such a good idea to mention this *slight overreaction of Roy's* to Mister Mortimer. 'You know how he worries about your welfare. Wouldn't want you mixed up in something that could get you ...'

Sonny realises – too late – he's said the wrong thing.

'Killed, Sonny?' I ask. 'Killed by who?'

'Oh, you know ... anyone,' he says, shrugging calmly, spitting out a smidgen of bacon. 'You know what our Morty's like ... '

You never know with Sonny. When he's trying to be pleasant he comes across as supremely manipulative, sounds more sinister than when he's blatantly intimidating.

'It would be quite a major omission,' I say.

'Mort don't need to know—'

'But it ain't an issue anymore—'

'Do what?' he asks with a grimace.

'I'm shipping out. You just made my mind up for me.'

'Whaddya mean?'

'It's simple, this conversation is the final straw. I'll ring Mort and tell him—'

'Tell him what?'

'I'm going back to Jamaica.'

'You can't just fuck off—'

'Just fuckin watch me. Everyone's didgy, there's trackers on motors, people telling me *don't tell this one that, don't tell that one this.*'

'Mort'll blame me—'

'And he'll be right.'

'It ain't the law who put that tracker on the motor ... '

'Tells me nothing. Mort'll be disappointed,' I tell him, 'but he'll get over it.'

'What do you need to know?' asks Sonny, uncharacteristically desperate.

'A few answers,' I tell him.

'I need a word with Roy. This is about him ... ' he says, getting angry. 'It's more about Roy than it is about me.'

'Drop me at the tube, Sonny. I'll make my own way out to the airport.'

'I think ... ' he says, 'you're overreacting.'

'There's a lot of it about.'

When we return to the front room Missus Burns has laid out slabs of Battenberg cake on a Wedgewood dining plate. Roy is preoccupied with tuning in the scanner, checking police activity. Missus Burns doesn't seem to be at all put out by this.

'Have a wee bit of cake, boys,' says Missus Burns. 'I'll put some hot water in the pot ... '

'We better be going, Missus Bee,' says Sonny, rolling his eyes towards the door, back in control now. 'Roy, we've got to tell our chum here ... that story ... '

'The *whole* story?' asks Roy.

'Yeah, the *whole* story,' nods Sonny.

'Oh, right, yeah,' says Roy getting up. He goes in his kick, pulls out a chunk of notes, peels some off, and puts them behind the clock on the mantelpiece. 'Here, Mum,' he says. 'Can't have you, a pensioner, feeding us working men.'

'You're never a pensioner, Missus Burns!' jokes Sonny, full of mock surprise, 'I'm not having that!'

'You're making fun now, Sonny,' she laughs, enjoying the flattery. She takes the notes from behind the clock as Roy picks up his tool bag, 'Roy gives me money every time he comes, posts it back from Spain, but I put it in a post office account for him.'

'Very wise, Missus Bee,' says Sonny. 'Thinking of the future.'

Missus Bee walks us to the front door, fag in hand, cardigan pulled tight against imaginary cold. It's still bright sunshine but she looks cautiously along the landing.

'You boys be careful ... ' she says lovingly, 'and remember it's the braver man who walks *away* from the argument. No matter how tough you think you are, there's always someone tougher.'

'I like that, Missus Bee. Come on you two!' says Sonny as he takes off down the landing. '*A brave man walks away from the fight*. Let me know about that dog, Missus Bee,' he shouts over his shoulder, 'I know a fella who's got some Ridgeback puppies.'

Roy shifts his heavy bag from shoulder to shoulder as we trot down the stairs, Sonny taking point with me and Roy behind. I stop, almost causing a pile-up.

'Sonny, you left ya briefcase in Roy's mum's,' I say. 'You musta forgotten it—'

'Didn't *forget* anything.' he replies with a snarl. 'Told yer before, mind yer business—'

They stop at the bottom of the stairs. Roy burrows about in his bag, pulls out a pistol, stuffs it in the raincoat pocket then pokes his head round the corner into the courtyard.

'Are you two in some kinda trouble?' I ask, aware it's a stupid question. Sonny and Roy look at one another. A quick shrug and a manic chuckle.

'Are we in *some kinda trouble*, Roy?' says Sonny, pondering the question. 'We *kinda* could be.'

We retrace our steps to the motor, drive to the park, sit in the café and drink tins of Coke, watching the sun go down. I spend an enlightening couple of hours, the extended Q and A, head-in-hands stuff for them, *full disclosure or it's next stop Heathrow for me, gentlemen!* I wish I'd given them the ultimatum earlier.

Sitting in the cab back into town, I was still alone, digesting their confession and Missus Burns' breakfast, doing some day-dreaming of my own. When I was a kid around the flats, about ten years of age, there was an urban myth that used to do the rounds ... A guy walks into a Chinese restaurant with a Fucking Big Alsatian. He wants to eat dinner but he realises that he can't keep his dog in the restaurant so he asks the inscrutable Chinaman to take the dog to the kitchen, maybe give the thirsty hound a drink of water, whilst he eats. The Chinaman nods, bows low, and in a mixture of Chinese and English tells the customer – *no problem, sir.*

The Chinaman takes the dog away as the customer sits down. Nobody comes to take his order or give him a menu. Every time a waiter or waitress walks past they just nod enigmatically and smile thinly. The man is just about to leave when, as if by magic, waiters descend on his table with an emperor's feast – five different dishes, steaming and looking delicious. Being famished, and not wanting to get into the hassle of explaining he has yet to order, the man tucks in. He eats till he's fit to burst. The food is scrumptious; he clears the plates, leaves not a morsel. He's licking his fingers one by one, loosening his belt and patting his belly.

The Chinaman who owns the restaurant is no longer inscrutable but beaming with pride at his customer's contentment. He presents the bill. The customer pays, leaves a huge tip, compliments his host, and tells him he will be returning very soon, bringing all his friends. He gets up and asks for the return of his dog. This is where the trouble starts.

'No-no,' says the Chinaman, waving a finger, shaking his head. 'No dog. You eat dog.'

Even squatting in a school playground, being told the tale, I knew Big Fucking Alsatian wasn't coming outta that kitchen, not alive. I didn't believe it, but a lotta kids did. I knew that the lesson of the story had nothing to do with stir-fried Shih Tzu or sautéed Chihuahua. It was a good example of people believing what they *want to* believe. They *wanted* to believe that the guy ate his dog.

Missus Burns and a fully grown Rhodesian Ridgeback, twice her bodyweight, is an awesome combination – handy for the lion hunt down Kilburn High Road – until one day she's not nippy enough with his dinner or the tin opener snaps on impact, *chunk-chunk-chunk-ping* – and the dog eats Mum. No Mum – Dog Eat Mum.

Sonny and Roy *want* believe that if we all keep quiet about certain developments everything will go back to normal – shifting loads of drugs without a care. Sonny and Roy want me to play the inscrutable Chinaman, but we cut a deal.

So as soon as I get back to the hotel I call Morty from a payphone. He doesn't answer so I leave a message – *need a meet, Condition Rojo* – and wait for him to ring. An hour later, as I'm eating – not Chinese – my phone rings. It's Morty.

'I hope this is important,' he said.

'Trust me,' I replied.

I arrange to meet Morty over by the Festival Hall. I jump on the tube for a while – till I'm back at Bank station – then slip out and get a taxi to London Bridge. I walk along the river. There's nobody about, just some skateboarders doing tricks under a bridge. I sit on a bench in the dark till Morty noiselessly appears behind me holding two polystyrene cups – a real Morty manoeuvre.

'I bought you a cup of coffee, young sir.' He hands it to me. 'What's happening?'

'Sonny and Roy have been withholding information.'

'You got me here to tell me that squirrels like nuts?'

'The trackers – plural,' I tell him, 'are not *yours*, or *mine,* they are *theirs*, Sonny and Roy's, and it's not the law who's on their haystack.'

'Knew it wasn't Old Bill,' he says. 'Didn't smell right.'

'There's terms and conditions involved,' I say. He pulls his curious face. 'The deal I done—'

'Never make promises you can't keep, mate—'

' ... is that I tell you, out of courtesy—'

'*Or* make promises on my behalf—'

'But Bridget Granger doesn't need to know.'

'We'll see about that ... ' says Mort. '*I've* not promised anybody anything. Now, what's the story?'

CHAPTER SIXTEEN

JESUS - HAS - OOZE -
AKA GOLDEN GOOSE

Approximately two weeks ago a courier arrived in London from Miami to collect a parcel. His name was Jesus, as in Little Baby Jesus – but pronounced *Has-oose* – rhymes with golden goose. And his surname was Zambrano – simply pronounced *Zam-bra-no*.

Q. What South American country *was* Jesus from?

Clue. This country is often overshadowed by its more illustrious, headline-grabbing and *apropiado loco* – proper crazy – neighbour, Columbia.

A. Venezuela. Jesus *was* a Venezuelan.

Jesus was meant to fly into London from Miami, scratch about in a five-star hotel, wait for the parcel to be dropped off and, on delivery, ship out to mainland Europe and a less security-conscious airport than the London ones and fly west, back to the hacienda and the welcoming committee. But Jesus went off-reservation ...

Sonny and Roy, doing things arse-about-face, as per their usual operating procedure, decided to *really* check him out, using all their nefarious contacts, *after* he became a problem. Jesus the Courier, it transpired, was the livewire nephew in a notorious Venezuelan outfit working out of Caracas but with branch offices in Florida. He's creeping towards his mid-thirties but everyone treats him like a junior. The leader of the clan – his uncle, commuting between Biscayne Bay and his villa high above his home city – did good business arranging trades with European and American smugglers. They'd also shrewdly purchased a string of legit businesses to hide cosily behind.

I've met some Venezuelan criminals working over in the Caribbean – going to collect money, work out a transportation problem or sort out disputes – and they'd grill you and eat you for a bet, or shoot someone in the temple to test a firearm. They were a heady mixture of psychopathic and hideously wealthy. A few settled in Jamaica but it's strictly business. I don't think they liked Jamaicans very much. And the Jamaicans hated them. They believed that the English police *and* criminals are a soft touch. The British crims have no mandatory shooters, are not ruthless enough, and simply can't get law enforcement straightened out, try as they might.

The Venezuelans believed the Anglos had lost all contact with the street. *Nunca pierda el olor del barrio* – never lose the smell of the street. Anyone who's got any sense is scared of Venezuelan crims. They're wired in all that macho shit. It's not simply about making readies and living the *vita bella*, it's far too much about face and reputation – shit that'll get you killed for zero profit.

What the Venezuelans did like was their home-from-home – Miami, Florida. Every single thing about it; they were made for one another. The other inhabitants of that region call them *Demedos* – meaning quite literally, *bring me two*. It started with the rich oil folk but spread to mean *all* Venezuelans. Soon after they started exploiting the oil reserves the whole country was flush with money. They'd think nothing of organising weekend shopping trips to Miami via private jet, importing gold-plated Rolls Royces, swagging every designer label. They got unapologetically flash. They *wouldn't* buy something if it was *too* cheap. Then they started doing that thing that the newly rich do – despising the poor.

Imagine a country that's corrupted by petroleum *and* cocaine – Texas meets Medellin, traffickers and miners, smugglers and wildcatters, crooked politicos and the powerless masses. There's lots of cowboys yahooing down there, working the oil and gas fields. And lots of black gold and *schwarzgeld* floating around, plus literally lorryloads of coke, crossing the porous borders with Columbia and Brazil. There's huge profits to be made by getting product into profitable territories like the States or Europe.

And these traffickers are capable of sinister but artful murders. Organisations would leave bodies hanging off bridges at intersections – the populace seemed to appreciate their flair. They'd get reviews in newspapers, complete with photos. Folks got blasé; crucifixions only made page seven. Kidnapping – both of other criminals and law-abiding individuals – was popular. Ransoms get paid out; foreign companies buy insurance policies to protect themselves. There was a big craze for insuring the mother-in-law, then having her murdered. It's a real big *status symbol* to have bodyguards. Always thought it was bad policy to employ lunatics with an obsession with firearms to protect you from lunatics with firearms. One look at these bodyguards told you they were duplicitous, kidnapping their own charges.

So Jesus, *número uno demedos*, arrives in London during a heatwave and Jesus knows best. No sitting around in a sterile hotel room. He checks into the Inn on the Park but doesn't like it – full of rich but wrinkled Yanks on whirlwind tours of Europe, and dull businessmen, so he slips the bellboy a hundred bucks and asks him where the action is – *the beautiful people, you know what I mean?* He tells him he should be at the hipper-than-hip Cosmopolitan Hotel, a hundred yards down the road. A cab drops Jesus at the Cosmo P.

Jesus keeps the cab waiting outside while he checks in, and then it takes him to Bond Street. He goes and gets all dressed up – *God bless Johnnie Versace, the Dee and the Gee and the Goo-chee.* Jesus Zambrano – a proper shitkicker born in the arse-end of Caracas, who upgraded to the more salubrious suburbs, via troubled stints in fee-paying private schools, via spells in Biscayne Bay, Miami and Caracas, then a drop of jailtime in Tallahassee, Florida, for pistol-whipping some poor fucker – found his El Dorado in New Bond Street. Can't decide which colour silk suit he prefers? White or gold? *Demedos! Give me both!* Shoes to go with the new silk suit? Croc or snake? What's the magic word? *Demedos! Demedos! Demedos!*

Back at the Cosmopolitan Hotel he's meant to be inconspicuous. He's thinking of ringing an escort agency to get them to send a girl, or two – *demedos!* But as he admires himself in the mirror he decides it's a crying shame to get all dressed up and sit about a hotel room.

So he heads out. He wants to experience the jolly old nightclubs of Mayfair and by some mischievous synchronicity, he asks the junior concierge where the local hotspot is. Sonny's crew have this Portuguese kid, Flavio, straightened right out with top quality cha-cha and a few quid. He's a corruptible chap who gives them the heads-up on who's staying at the hotel – makes his *proper money* by being wired in with gaffs like the Monarch, lap dancing clubs, paparazzi, grand-an-hour hookers, room creepers and dial-an-ounce gak dealers.

So Flavio sticks Jesus the Courier in a taxi to the Monarch Club and then – this is where fate plays its hand – texts his connection to let them know they've got *ripe punter on way – gold suit – look after – DEFINITELY not short of £$£$*. When Jesus arrives the bouncers welcome him through the red rope and point him up the stairs. In the hustle and bustle Jesus collides with some fella who appears to be drunk – swaying, barely keeping his drink in his glass. Jesus delivers a Venezuelan version of *Do you want a fat lip?* Followed by that evergreen chestnut – *Do you know who I am?*

The drunk who literally bumped into Jesus gets bounced straight out. *And don't fuckin come back* ... But it's a get-up. The gent was an acquaintance of Mister Sonny. Jesus gets given a humble apology and comped-up with a real, not fake, bottle of Veuve Clicquot. Jesus is getting grafted by Sonny's Uptown Crew ...

He's meant to be keeping a low but it's becoming a struggle. The ego is roaring. Instead of sitting in a corner booth being unobtrusive he totally grasses himself off. He's dropping the girl running the VIP – minimum spend a grand – mucho casho to sort him out a booth – then clicking his fingers, calling on more champagne, waving and calling across to posses of girls to come over. *Have a little drink! Help me drink this bottle! Pleeeeese, ladies!*

A few ladies, who like a chap who slings his money around, join Jesus. He leaves his credit card behind the bar – gold American Express – impressive if that's your intention; looking for trouble, some might say. Sonny's firm knew he was bona fide – not a joker – but it did occur to them, *what's he doing in London, on his Jack Jones, a long way from home?* Sonny – getting more *interested* by the minute and with the instincts of a hyena downwind of a fresh carcass – had the punters in the next booth to Jesus bounced out. He then slipped a couple in, snogging each other's faces off – no talking but plenty *listening* – next to Jesus. Maybe Jesus had a few lines of gak before he left the Cosmo – he's chatting like a monkey ...

Miami – All expenses paid – Consignments – Acquaintances – Me? – Jesus! – Zam! Bra! No! – Paris! – Cargo! – Delivery! – Schedule! – Uncles! Mother! Fuckers! More champagne, ladies? Waitress! Demedos!

This Jesus guy is the criminal equivalent of the poor little rich kid – one generation removed from the gents who had the meteoric rise from the barras to the gated mansion. Jesus is the spoilt kid walking into the family business who can't think why his folks can't just send money. But there's a charisma about a kid who can land in London, alone, and be embedded in the VIP, arms around a couple of posh slaps come nightfall, after almost starting a fight. It suggests that Jesus was fearless to the point of reckless. Both Sonny and Roy agree that *he was not right in the canister* – and, coming from those legends, I get the impression that Jesus was bordering on insane. Transpires that Jesus had done his jailtime, and maybe a killing or two – the ritualistic welcome to the clan – so Junior knows the feeling of getting a splash of blood on his boots.

While Jesus was chatting his business in the VIP area at the Monarch, getting on famously with his stable of up-for-it birds, who *loved* his sexy accent and gold suit, members of Sonny's team, with the cooperation of Flavio the Concierge – who can get duplicate key cards and slip in after the housekeepers turn over the top sheet – spun his room at the Cosmo P.

Try as they might they couldn't get the room safe open so they called in a specialist who happened to be in the area. This guy could open a safe as easy as most people can open up the Sunday paper. In the safe they found three passports – one Venezuelan, one Spanish, one US of A – same smudge but different names, bundles of cashish – pounds, euros and dollars – plus train and air tickets outta London by half a dozen routes. They're just cleaning him out when timing plays its hand. Sonny gets the *situation report* from his couple in the next booth – in London *picking up a parcel*? Interesting; we like the sound of *Jee-zuss*.

So Sonny rings the firm in Jesus' hotel room and tells them –

hold yer horses. We're missing a trick. They replace everything in the safe and lock it again. Sonny has decided – *we're gonna sit on this cunt, see how this goes down.* Sonny's such a cunning fucker, a good example of someone who's undeniably intelligent in his own stratum of society but in some respects is ridiculously reckless and unable to comprehend the consequences of his actions. Sounds like the prison psychiatrist's assessment, but it's also true. A money-spinning nightclub, a thriving drug business and transportation franchise isn't enough for Sonny; at the sniff of easy readies he reverts to being a greedy junior with his snout in the trough. Sonny decides he wants Jesus watched *day and night.*

Q. Who's the expert in the black arts of surveillance and countersurveillance?

A. Roy 'Twitchy' Burns: One-man sleeper cell.

Location: Marbella, Southern Spain.

'Ring, ring,' said Roy's mobile phone. Roy eyed it suspiciously, a noticeable twitch beginning to appear above his right eyebrow.

No answer. One of Sonny's team flew down to Malaga the morning after Jesus' appearance in the Monarch, drove to Marbella, explained the coup to Roy. He was recruited and was landing at Stansted Airport in time for a late luncheon and full tactical briefing with Sonny King. Roy had been waiting for his opportunity to dazzle. He's put inconspicuous guys in the lobby to liaise with Flavio, and in motors around the hotel. The concierge is texting Sonny's crew with up-to-the minute updates, *sit-reps*, and photos from one of those camera phones. The afternoon after his arrival Jesus had a short meeting in the Cosmopolitan with a smooth South American gent. They drank tea, talked with their heads a foot apart, and then parted. It looked and smelt nice and dodgy.

Either it was Jesus' original plan to steal the parcel or somewhere he did a mental shift of gears, started thinking – *fuck this, peddling over to London like the hired help? What am I? A gofer? Do you know who ...*

Something suggested he was going to abscond with the consignment. He's got plane and train tickets and three passports, not including the one that's been left at reception. Maybe he was now planning something treacherous. Roy's crew are following him everywhere. He's gone down to the British Airways office on Piccadilly and bought *another four* open airline tickets – Miami to Heathrow. Bringing in reinforcements? Plus a single ticket to – *fuck me, Paris to Zurich*, paying cash. Now he's got a *collection* of airline and rail tickets. Zurich really made Sonny's ears prick up because Switzerland is famous for ... ?

'Clocks and watches?' says one of the crew.

'And?' says Sonny.

'Skiing and mountains?'

'No, you cunts! Banks! Switzerland is famous for fuckin banks!'

Maybe Jesus was heading out to do a freelance *geldwäsche* of his own but meanwhile he's a fixture in the Monarch Club every night. Ain't exactly doing the open-top bus tour. Jesus is living in a five hundred yard radius of the Cosmo P. Hotel, Bond Street, and he's down the Monarch more than Dougie Nightingale, doing serious readies on his gold-to-match-his-suit Mummy-and-Daddy card. Sonny had the bar manager ring American Express to see if the card was stolen – *not a problem, not been used much lately but ... thanks for your call, sir.* Roy, meanwhile, is researching the Zambrano Clan, utilising the Internet, and getting a tingling in his testicles.

Flavio – who's well webbed up by now – rings one day to report that ...

A. He has just ascertained from the off-duty night porter that Jesus Federal-Expressed an envelope to a post office box address in Miami the previous evening.

B. Mister Jesus has just met up with the same South American-looking gentleman as before. They had coffee and a bun. Then Jesus swings by the front desk to ask if it's okay for his *colleague* to park his rental motor downstairs in the underground car park. Jesus is gonna be using the car himself and needs a parking spot, *stick it on the bill*. The South American splits but *leaves* the rental motor with Jesus. The mystery man gets a taxi outside, tells the driver *Paddington Station*. West outta London? To the airport? A little later Jesus, watched by Flavio at a distance, hauls three large Samsonite cases, with built-in wheels and telescopic handles, from the rental and moves them, in convoy, up to his room, locks the door and ain't seen again till morning, by which time he's made arrangements with the front desk to check out. At ten to nine the next morning he gets in the pre-booked taxi and that was the last known *public* sighting of him.

In reality Jesus got into the *first* taxi to arrive to take him to Waterloo Station. Another one, the legit one that the reception had called, tipped up five minutes later, and found no Jesus. Meanwhile the first taxi trundled towards Waterloo, with Jesus in the back, whistling a happy tune. The taxi driver tells him he's gonna take *an Irish short cut – it's longer but it's quicker*. He sails due south through Victoria, detouring away from highly protected and police-patrolled Westminster, over Vauxhall Bridge and slings a left up Kennington Road, into darkest Lambeth – Apache country.

Jesus has stopped whistling now. He's starting to think this is très fish, starts tapping on the glass partition but gets no response. Instead the driver accelerates, does a sharp left and left again. The taxi is now bouncing up a cobbled street, garages and warehouse entrances on both sides. A couple of cars and an ominous white van are parked up on the pavement. The cab driver skids to a halt. Jesus goes tumbling off his seat into an unruly pile on the floor, screaming and cursing in Spanish – *Hijo de puta!*

The driver gets out, walks coolly to a parked car that has just started its engine, leaving Jesus baffled but catching on *rápidamente.*

The car skids away. Jesus realises that he's surrounded by four men, with either sawn-off shotguns or ugly automatic pistols with homemade silencers pointing at his head, all wearing paper coveralls, motorcycle gloves and ski masks. They grab the struggling Jesus – fighting all the way, it must be said – secure his hands and feet with cable ties, slap duct tape over his mouth and eyes, pull a sack over his head and manhandle him into the builder's van. They speed away, leaving the stolen taxi, doors wide open, meter ticking over.

The plan was to take him out into the countryside and leave him there, naked, at nightfall – not a very well-thought-out manoeuvre. They didn't wanna kill him stone dead, thought it would take him a couple of days to find his way back to London, by which time they'd have gone under. Roy would be back down in Spain, without anybody having noticed that he'd been gone. Sonny and his firm still didn't know what was in the heavy suitcases but they had a very good idea that he hadn't flown round the world to pick up a dirty book collection.

Sonny the Mastermind – in time-honoured tradition – was waiting at the Hideout, an associate's farm. They got the cases out of the van but left Jesus rolling on the floor. They jiggled open the combination locks – *piece-a-piss* – popped open the cases and – *fuckin result!* Sonny's done the scheming, put the two and two together and got three million pounds in used notes, neatly vacuum-packed, high dominations, '100k' handwritten in felt-tip pen on the outside of each mini-parcel.

Sonny is pleased with the result ... for a split-second. Now he thinks there may be more where this came from, and it would be a shame to release Jesus to start his schlep back to London. Sonny tells Royski to give him a few slaps to see if he can find anything out – *use some of those interrogation techniques, Roy, the Special Forces ones ...*

They drag Jesus into one of the outhouses. They remove the blindfold and tape and start slapping Jesus. He starts telling them they could *fuck off* if they thought he was going to tell them where *it* was. When they told him they had *it* already, the cash, Jesus laughs in their faces – *I'd wipe my arse on that!* They couldn't riddle out what Jesus meant. After a while they worked out that he thought *he* had something *they* wanted apart from the three mill, but they didn't know what *it* was. *Jesus* thought he was holding out. The bit of a slap turned into torture with a car battery and buckets of water, turned into smashing the geezer half to death. Jesus doesn't realise he's a busted flush. He kept laughing at them; the more they hit him, juiced him up and stuck his head under freezing water, the more manically he laughed. He's the comic book villain, growing stronger with every kick, every jolt.

Jesus keeps telling them he's gonna take a shit on them – *I shit on you! Queers! Me cago en ustedes putas! Maricones!*

Royski knows a little Spanish but now he's getting the crash course in Venezuelan curses. Jesus is cunting and dogging him non-stop – *Pendejos! Maricones! Mama güevos! Hijos de putas!* Cunts! Faggots! Eunuchs! Thieves! Fuck you, you faggots!

Jesus turns the screw on Royski, flips it back on him. Who's torturing who? Roy's still in his ski mask – on a balmy August evening – sweating like a pig. No longer in control. Jesus is.

Then Jesus suddenly, abruptly, tells them all to be quiet – *please, please, sirs, señors.* He has something to say, sounds very conciliatory. Everything goes quiet. He beckons Royski closer. Jesus locks onto, and then talks to, the eyes in the ski mask. 'Okay, you got me, I do you deal ... You get them but I keep it ... ' says Jesus gently. Roy smiles. 'But when all this is over ... ' continues Jesus, spiteful now, 'I'm gonna find your mother ... You queer fucker, you have no wife, no children, never will, no balls, you faggot *maricón*. I tie Mama up, I beat her, bend Mama over, pull down her drawers and fuck her ... right in the arse.'

Roy shoots Jesus dead.

CHAPTER SEVENTEEN

CONSEQUENCES

Roy *obliterates* the golden goose with the Czech-made Skorpion automatic −. three second burst, full clip. Twelve bullets punch through the walls, seven bullets hit Jesus in the chest, four in the stomach, two in the canister and two through the neck. Blood sprays everywhere.

The geezer wouldn't shut up. Roy don't like being laughed at, and seriously don't like people insulting his old dear. Sonny told himself that Jesus was killed *due to his belligerent attitude.* Jesus had told Sonny's crew *non-fuckin-stop* that they were lightweights who wouldn't have the bottle to actually serve him; must have been on some death wish because there's a time to speak and a time to keep it zipped.

And so to business. Sonny's team buried the body out on the acquaintance's farmland, after knocking out the teeth with a mallet, cutting the fingers and toes off, removing some tattoos − skulls and eagles − and stripping off Jesus' designer clobber to be burnt with diesel. They dug a narrow but deep trench along a tree line with a mini bulldozer, slung a few bags of lime into it, fired Jesus in, backfilled and flattened the area, slung leaves, twigs and stones around the hole so nobody would know that the clay had been disturbed. Then went back and hosed down the outhouse but *those farms are all covered in blood and shit, anyway.*

After getting the prize, none of Sonny's firm had the smarts to riddle out that maybe Jesus thought they were after something else. Jesus didn't think that they were *only* after the three million; he thought he had some power in the negotiation. But all that got forgotten about in the excitement of getting the loot and digging the hole. Sonny was thinking Jesus was in town to collect a parcel of Rolexes or Patek Philippes or firearms − *always come in handy* − or jewels, cut or uncut, but not pure cash. Now he's giving out orders and divvying up money − working on the King Principle;

instinctively calculating the *exact* amount he can get away with giving them without provoking a mutiny.

He splits two hundred and thirty gee between the crew – with the promise of more to come – *when*, exactly, nobody's got the bottle to ask.

Sonny schleps back to London, the remaining readies are sat round, getting his nut, making him para. He knows it must belong to someone naughty. He's his normal hostile self, but part of him knows there'll be consequences. It's making him suspicious – he could get turned over. He also knows at some point he has to negotiate a share with Roy. Sonny doesn't trust his own firm, knows he's sold them a line. He doesn't fear a *coup d'état* but being a greedy cunt has its disadvantages. So after consulting with Royski – probably not the best person to give sound counsel – and getting spooked, he decides to *completely* change his routine and living accommodation, hence a skippy exodus to Hampstead, rented with a few grand out of one of the magic suitcases. The paranoia is festering. Roy's uptight – torturing, killing and burying Jesus wasn't enough, the insult to his old dear preys on his mind ...

Q. What would you have done?

A. Exactly the same, Roy.

A couple of days after the killing Roy was recuperating, watching television in the Hampstead apartment, antennas out, periscope up. He's sweeping the airwaves for something to get comfortably twitchy about. And he's found it on a rolling news channel. Be careful what you pray for ...

A Venezuelan national, surprisingly anonymous, an importer of exotic woods, who lived in a picturesque village in Berkshire, had turned up dead sixty miles away in a burnt-out car in rural Wiltshire. No witnesses were coming forward in spite of police appeals and assurances of anonymity. Sweeping through the news channels, Roy found out that the dead man had been garrotted – almost decapitated – and afterwards set on fire.

Roy started applying lashings of Burns Logic, twitching like a fried egg, and thinking like a detective – *if you wanna know why someone died, examine how they lived.* The murder was *obviously* a public announcement from some dangerous people, a message to any of their associates who might be *thinking* of stealing from them.

Roy headed out to the Internet café and continued his investigation. The police traced the car back to a rental company. They had identified the charred remains but were putting off naming the victim until they had informed his next of kin. Unfortunately, they couldn't find her. The police, and Roy, both agreed that the body *was intended to be found* – it was *deliberately* messy. Roy guessed that this was the geezer who delivered the money to Jesus. The police didn't know about Jesus Zambrano. Roy wasn't going to tell them.

Roy's theory was that someone had to take the rap for the disappearance of the Jesus fella and the victim was the nearest thing to a guilty party. As far as the killers were concerned he was the last person to see their courier alive. They had no way of knowing he had delivered their readies. It was guilt by association. The dead Venezuelan's financial records were meticulously kept and the police couldn't find anything incriminating. The guy was a genuine clean skin – no record, either side of the Atlantic.

Sonny wasn't answering his phone but Flavio down the Cosmo was. Roy told Flavio to *go and check if that rental motor is downstairs*. Meanwhile Roy went home and flicked through the news channels. There was some breaking news ... The Somerset and Avon Police were ready to name the victim in the Wiltshire murder. Samuel Laniado. Who?

Sonny arrived home. Roy pointed at the telly, briefed Sonny on the developing situation. Sonny fell in straight away. Flavio rang back. The car was gone. *Why's it important?* Flavio asked. *No reason,* replied Roy, *just curious.*

Sonny then makes a smart move but takes a few liberties. Ted Granger – before his demise – had informed Mister King that Mister Mortimer was heading out to Jamaica or Miami to recruit me into the sales team. For some reason Sonny didn't fancy Miami and Morty didn't like flying into Jamaica, too much airport action. Why not go to *Bar-fuckin-bados?* Sonny sold Morty on the idea of a meeting with me on neutral territory, and then declared he'd tag along – with the skanked money – convincing Morty that it was *freelance spoils*. Sonny wanted Morty incriminated in the

Jesus robbery – an extra insurance policy. Going over on a charter flight was Roy's idea. Morty thought it was a youth club jolly that didn't offer the right degree of flexibility if they had to vacate. Morty had his own return ticket and snide passport metaphorically tucked down his figurative underpants. Morty, Mister Amicability, agreed to roll a Samsonite suitcase, containing pure readies, out of Grantley Adams Airport, if Sonny could get it on the plane *without a scream-up*.

Sonny got Giles to ask Mister Curtis to accept the chunk of cash into his *own* account. Sonny tells Morty he can introduce me to Mister Curtis who at this stage Sonny hadn't met himself. Sonny goes to work on Roy and persuades him to come out to Barbados rather than dee-dee to Spain; he'll wash up his cash and transfer it back later. Sonny promises Roy a job for life, second in command, tells Roy he needs sensible heads, loyal allies. Roy is flattered and agrees – one of nature's right-hand men.

Obviously Jesus wasn't reported to the police as a missing person. The Cosmopolitan started getting calls – plural – looking for Mister Zambrano. The callers were annoyed to be told that the gentleman had checked out a couple of days previous. Another call was made to confirm this, to double-check that the account was paid up and closed. People were looking for Jesus. Sonny and Roy mistakenly thought that Jesus Zambrano could go missing without anyone sending up a flare. This was the sign that they needed to pull the trigger on the Barbados extraction plan. They'd sit tight over there till things settled down.

So the three wise men ship out. I was right – Sonny did have people in Heathrow who could bypass customs and load the cases straight onto the plane. They arrived and banked the money but on the second day they were there, a few days after Jesus went missing, back in London a couple of discreet, well-dressed Venezuelan guys turned up at the Cosmopolitan Hotel, asking questions and laying money with the receptionists to find answers. They found out that *Mister Jesus Zambrano* had checked out. *Where did he go?*

Mister Jesus Zambrano had ordered a taxi to take him to Waterloo. *Must have been catching the train to Paris. Mister Jesus Zambrano* did get in the taxi – with three large suitcases –

and then completely disappeared. In fact, the receptionist told the Venezuelans – *funny, really* – that morning *two* taxis had shown up at the hotel to take Mister Zambrano. The Venezuelans smelt something très fish – a set-up perhaps?

So while Sonny and Royski were relaxing in sun-drenched Barbados, getting toasted to a crisp, they started getting calls – from Dougie the Nightingale, Flavio the Concierge, from members of Sonny's close crew. The gist was that a pair of smooth but heavy dudes – *Venezuelan for fuck's sake* – had turned up, first at the Cosmo P. Hotel, then at the Monarch, looking for any information about *some kid called Jesus*. They're dropping readies, wanting to search the room, looking for phone bills and copies of his itemised hotel bills. The hotel manager won't play ball, threatens police. So they go *back* to the Monarch and collar Dougie in a nice, flattering way and quiz him. Dougie, being a coke-addled ziphead don't remember *anything*, let alone some dude in a golden silk suit – *called what, darling? Buying bottles of sha-sha? For everyone? Happens all the time, darling*. Douglas tells them he *seriously can't remember, darling*. Dougie has the memory of a goldfish but the Venezuelans think he's being dismissive. The numero uno Venezuelan doesn't like being called *darling* but he lets it go ... for the time being, *Dougie, darling*.

Sonny and Roy are getting *real-time sit-reps*, five hours behind London time. They're preoccupied, forgetting to reapply their sun tan lotion. This possible crisis in London, as well Roy's severe case of sunburn, gets them heading for home – *couldn't leave it to Dougie, could fuck up boiling a kettle*.

Sonny, diplomatic as ever, goes to find the holiday rep, dragging Red Roy along as evidence, Exhibit A. They track her down at Cobbler's Rock where she's overseeing the Buccaneers' Banquet and Barbecue. Ironically, all the mums, dads, god-forbids and holiday reps were dressed up as ruffians, pirates and ne'er-do-wells. Sonny loudly demands repatriation to the UK *on the grounds of Mister Roy Burns' life-threatening sunburn*. She tells them, politely but assertively, that *to cover this kind of eventuality* they *should have bought holiday insurance*. Sonny tells her *fuck yer holiday insurance!* The optional *yer bollocks! Don't talk to me like I'm some 'obbit!* She asks him where the third member of their party is. Morty had left and was attending Duppy's funeral. Sonny tells the holiday rep *he's black! How the fuck is he gonna get sunburnt? That's fuckin racist, that is! I wanna make a complaint!*

They flew them home *pure freebie*, swagged them out of there quicker than you could say public relations disaster. This is a geezer who's just deposited two-point-seven million plus for *overseeing* a glorified street robbery, screaming and shouting about a couple of airfares.

The day they arrived back Flavio was straight on the phone, panicking. He'd spotted another posse of Venezuelan guys – all false smiles, shades and raincoats, trying to look inconspicuous – hanging around the hotel, trying to bribe the chambermaids to be let into Jesus' old room. The advance guard had got no joy so the Air Cavalry had arrived. Flavio was awaiting orders. Sonny, totally ignoring Flavio's protestations, told him to offer to help them in exchange for money, *otherwise they won't trust you.* Control the situation, and see what they're about.

Flavio the Concierge worked out who the point man was – only he's not Venezuelan but some slick American. *You're Flavio, is that right? You wanna speak English or Spanish? My Portuguese is rusty.* Any illusions Flavio had about controlling the situation vanished; the Yank was running the show. Flavio was just the conduit between Slick and the hotel staff. The Yank, with a small team of Americans *and* Venezuelans, paid to secretly, but systematically, search Jesus' room – in the back of the television, behind bathroom panels, up in the false ceiling – but only got frustrated when they found nothing. Flavio's reported everything back to Sonny. Roy's twitching, Sonny's pacing – thinking overtime ... And he's riddled something out – they wouldn't be trying to find a hundredweight of banknotes *stuck down the back of one of those flat-screen televisions.* Or under the carpet. *What the fuck are they looking for?*

Flavio's soon back on the mobile – *they're dismantling the fucking room! With electric screwdrivers! Removing light fittings! The phones by the bed! Unscrewing bathroom panels!* Someone on Sonny's crew – Benny the Ball, Brains or Choo-Choo – has a brainwave. Why don't we get Flavio to *ask them nicely* what they're looking for? Tell them, maybe it's down lost property. Not a bad idea ...

The Yank listens to Flavio's suggestion – *maybe someone found it, the thing you're looking for ... and took it home. This here's a minimum wage environment ...*

Yank thinks for a second, weighs things up, hands Flavio two hundred quid – *have some of these monkey English dollars ... Now go look in the lost property ...*

Transpires they're looking for a memory stick, a digital storage device, with *a few files, personal pictures – could be compromising, you understand? No sentimental value but its disappearance could be embarrassing to the family I work for ...* Then, menacingly – *Do you have family, Flavio?*

Flavio reports this development back to Sonny – very curious now.

Q. Whatssa memory stick?

A. You put it in the back of a computer, you click on the information you wanna save and it zaps it up – now everything's on the memory stick. You wanna read what's on the memory stick? Put it in a computer, *anywhere in the world*, and, hey presto, it's back. Fuckin magic! *Fuck me, what will they think of next?*

But Sonny starts to feel mugged-off. It's grown to a feeling of being obviously *blatantly swindled* with *only* three million in sterling. *They ain't mentioned the cash, only this gadget. Like they've written it off ... Do they think I'm some sorta cunt? We're gonna find this thing, you fuckin hear? Before any other cunt!*

CHAPTER EIGHTEEN

SPECULATION

Back on the South Bank, Morty is clinically, meticulously pulling his polystyrene cup to pieces.

'We're in ... ' I tell him, 'whether we like it or not. These Venezuelans are sticking trackers on motors, ready-eying us. They've worked out that Sonny's got something to do with Jesus, and we're with Sonny ... '

Morty flicks his snout away. Sonny, I've realised, being pragmatic, is letting *me* tell Morty rather than doing it himself, now it's become inevitable. Morty's not as annoyed as I thought. Think he saw something like this coming.

'The Jesus fella was definitely on the rob,' he says, looking out over the river. 'You don't come to London to collect three mill on your own ... Not unless you're skanking someone, or you're mad, or both.'

'Sounds mad – was gonna cut *them* a deal ... tied to a chair, shooters at his head. So ... ' I ask, 'what do you think? Do Bridget and Ted need to know?'

'Not for the time being,' says Mort, shaking his head. 'Ted'd go spare. Three mill is chicken feed to what they're dealing with ... ' He lights another snout. 'Ted would want that memory stick as compensation.'

'Compensation?' I ask. 'For what?'

'Venezuelans ... ' says Mort, shaking his head. 'Why can't they rob Japs or Yanks like everybody else?' We walk back towards London Bridge. 'The memory stick would be about how big?' he asks. 'Smaller than a pack of chewing gum?' I nod. 'And he's travelling across borders, through airports, past metal detectors?' He stops walking. 'If you had something small but valuable, you wanted to keep safe, you're about to get on a Eurostar train, where would you hide it about your person?'

'I'd bottle it,' I say.

'Exactly,' says Mort. 'You'd stick it up your arse. I think he's flown into Heathrow with this gadget up there and it was going out the same way.' Then he claps his hands and breathes in deep. 'Someone's got a nasty job to do. I'm wide awake now—'

'You're electric, Mort.'

'And I think that memory stick is half ours, through default,' he shrugs. 'Sonny shouldn't be such a deceitful cunt.'

'Shall we go and find Sonny and Roy?' I ask. 'Let them know your theory?'

'No rush,' Mort shrugs. 'The Jesus kid's down his hole. He's going nowhere.'

I couldn't sleep last night. I got back to the hotel late after Mort and me had a mooch about a few bars. My insomnia might have been connected to Mort's coffee or rampant speculation.

Q. Speculation?

A. A conclusion, theory or opinion based on incomplete information or evidence.

What could be on that memory stick?

First thing this morning Morty rung to say he's made a meet with Sonny and Roy but not told them the reason. Let their heads do a number on them. An hour later I cut out of the hotel, did my usual ducking and diving on the tube, then Morty picked me up from around the back of Finchley Road station. Sonny wanted the meet in the same place as we came yesterday for the big confessional – a café right in the middle of a park – the kinda gaff you can get sandwiches and cakes, nothing fancy, but you can see anyone approaching because there's precious few trees and little cover. It was, originally, Royski's choice of venue.

Me and Mort take a leisurely walk across the park; it's not us who has the guilty conscience. Sonny and Roy are waiting when we arrive, sitting at a corner table, both facing the door. Sonny's demolishing a sausage sandwich but Roy looks vacant, picking rather than eating. The café is quiet, mostly dog-walkers. Morty orders two cups of coffee from the waitress without asking me what I want. We both sit. Morty has his raincoat buttoned up and driving gloves still on.

'To business, gents,' says Morty. 'I think you've been greedy and brought trouble down on us at a difficult time. You thought it would be simple, easy readies, but it's turned out to be more complicated. Now, in an atmosphere of mutual forgiveness, *we*, my colleague and I,' he nods at me, 'are prepared to let you know where the memory stick is.'

'You know where it is?' blurts out Roy as Sonny leans forward.

'You *think* or you *know*?' asks Sonny.

'We know,' says Morty firmly. 'Listen, Sonny, you ain't out of the woods so don't be acting the smart cunt. *I'm* going to tell you where to find it and *you're* going to go and get it, okay? And we're in this thing four ways.'

'How do you work that out?' asks Sonny with a shrug.

'Because you seriously fucked me, and him, about with all that malarkey over in Bridgetown,' says Mort. 'I was led to believe that money was something to do with the thing we do ... ' Sonny nods. He's taking it on the chin. 'I didn't know it was some robbery.'

'But I still don't think that's right,' says Sonny.

'Sonny,' interrupts Morty, 'I don't fuckin care what you think. You've made a mess. You're in danger of dragging us all down.'

Sonny's wishing he'd stayed in bed, knows he's getting overrun. Morty looks around – there's nobody there – before carrying on.

'When Bridget asks me where that two point seven four million suddenly fuckin appeared from, what the fuck am I meant to say? *I don't know, Bridget? Are they swindling me, Mort? Dunno Bridget.* Well I *do* fuckin know and I don't like lying.'

Morty's eyes are alight, zeroed in on Sonny. Sonny's stopped eating his sandwich. Roy's observing Sonny's rucking in a detached way until ...

'And you, Roy,' says Morty, turning to Roy, 'what the fuck was you thinking of, shooting people just cos they say nasty things about your old dear? You need to grow up a bit.'

Roy looks reprimanded, bashful. The pair of them are off-balance. Morty marches on. 'This is the story,' Morty tells them, '*we* own that memory stick four ways, *or* we carve that two point seven.'

'What?' splutters Sonny, hadn't seen that coming. Neither had I.

'It's easy. Either *we* own half the gadget *or* half the money you swagged off this Jesus.'

Morty pronounces 'Jesus' like *Jesus Christ*. Sonny leans forward, elbows on the table, palms together in front of his nose, like he's sending up a prayer. Sonny certainly doesn't like what he's hearing, doesn't wanna give up a cent. His meanness is playing havoc ...

'Win or lose,' says Mort, 'you're already well ahead. If all that's on that gadget is a few embarrassing smudges you get to keep the money. Some might say that *I* should be looking to claim a bigger whack ... I'm entitled—'

'Okay,' says Sonny, holding a hand up for Morty to stop, 'we agree. You tell us where it is, we go and get it. It's a deal, okay?'

'Okay,' says Morty.

'So?' says Sonny, 'Where is it?'

'The memory stick got buried with Jesus.'

'What?' says Sonny, shaking his head. 'Couldn't have, didn't have a stitch on ... '

Morty leans forward, beckoning them ever closer. 'I know,' says Mort, 'it was up his arse.'

Sonny gets it straight away. Now it's obvious. He rubs both temples. Roy starts nodding, the realisation sinking in. Sonny slowly turns to Roy and looks at him like he should have known. Sonny whispers to Roy, 'You didn't check his bottle?'

Roy shrugs his shoulders, palms up, puzzled expression on his face. Then Sonny goes into a bizarre whispered rant at Roy, like it's standard procedure to be hunting around up someone's rectum after you've killed them. Roy, in his madness, is trying to *justify* the omission. The conversation is becoming weird, Sonny prosecuting his argument and Roy desperately trying to defend himself against the million to one chance of burying someone – after first tearing them apart – with a valuable computer accessory secreted up ... Roy stands accused of negligence. Morty brings them down with a bump.

'You realise that someone's going to have to go and dig him up ... if you want that memory stick. If you're gonna hold up your side of the bargain ... if you wanna keep the readies.'

'This is all speculation,' snarls Sonny. 'What if it's not up there ... or down there?'

'You get to keep the funny money, Sonny,' shrugs Morty, stating the obvious.

'How long ago did you bury him?' I ask.

''Bout ten days ago,' replies Sonny.

'I think you're gonna be all right. I don't think he woulda decomposed.'

'So you're volunteering to give us a hand?' Sonny asks me. I shrug. 'Oh, right, leave the dirty work to us—'

'We did a deal, Sonny,' says Mort, 'two minutes ago.' Sonny grimaces and shrugs. 'You two didn't riddle out where the gadget was.'

'We would have,' says Sonny, 'eventually.'

'When the body was a putrid mess,' says Mort, leaning across the table. Everyone else has cleared out of the café leaving us conspiratorially in the corner. Morty gestures to the waitress, with a smile, for two more coffees; the first are untouched.

'We want that memory chip,' says Morty with an edge. 'I suggest tonight you get your merry men together, you tell Old McDonald you're coming back down his farm, and get digging.'

'Then when we get him up again,' says Roy with a growing frown, 'someone's got to go poking around to get the memory stick—'

'This is all theory,' says Sonny. 'He might have had a safe deposit box somewhere—'

'Then everybody's seriously fucked,' I tell Sonny. 'Whatever's on that thing is worth these Venezuelans coming over here, breaking cover, risking getting nicked, or killed. And they're a man down already.'

'If you've got a problem,' says Sonny, with a fuck-off smile, 'go see the welfare officer.'

'They believe that *we're* somehow involved,' I tell him. 'We could claim a finder's fee but that could be tricky. Depends on how much they liked their cousin.'

'Jesus is as dead as Elvis,' says Roy, half to himself.

'Very droll, Roy,' says Morty, bemused.

'We're ahead of you,' says Sonny using his posh voice, 'we already have a financial infrastructure in place to exploit to the maximum any resources contained on that piece of hardware.'

Sonny is repeating parrot-fashion something he's been told, maybe by Giles. He's run this by someone with some financial expertise.

'Sonny,' replies Morty, annoyed, 'what the fuck do you think I do with my money, put it in a piggy bank? You only have *financial facilities* because of that toff lawyer—'

'Whatever, but it's *obviously* financial data ... ' says Sonny, still in his posh voice. 'What else is there to fall out over?' he adds, again repeating someone verbatim.

'True,' I say to Sonny. 'Very true.'

Sonny's getting his swagger back. He leans back in his plastic chair, puts both hands behind his head and says to me, 'You know, as much as you get on my nerves, most of the time, you're a good skin to have on the firm.' This is what passes for a compliment. Then Sonny turns to Roy and beckons him closer. 'Now listen, Roy. You got us into this – no one told you to shoot the cunt – so you better start thinking about how you're gonna get us out of it.'

Roy doesn't say anything but he blows out hard. He's fucked and he knows it, stuck with the messy job. Sonny gives Roy a look – *you fuckin got us into this ...* No appeals will be heard.

'One thing, gents,' says Morty, 'I don't want that memory stick going missing. I wouldn't want you to dig him up and *deliberately* find nothing.'

Sonny looks affronted. 'Mort,' he says, 'what do you take me for?'

'Roy,' says Morty, 'I want you to swear on your mother's life.'

'Are you taking the piss, Mort?' says Sonny, leaning forward. His chair hits the floor, hands slap the tabletop.

'Yeah, Mort, mate,' asks Roy, 'is this some kinda joke?'

'Would make me feel a lot better,' says Morty, dryly, 'if you swore on your mother's life.'

'Swore on me mother's life?' asks Roy.

'Yeah, Roy,' says Morty, impatiently. 'Swear on your mother's life.'

'Okay,' says Roy flippantly, 'I swear on my mother's life.'

'No, Roy,' says Morty. 'Say it properly.'

'This is bollocks, Mort,' says Sonny like he can't believe it.

Morty turns to Sonny threateningly, 'Shut the fuck up, Sonny.'

Then he turns back to Roy. 'I ain't fuckin joking. Say, I swear on my mother's life I will bring back the memory stick if it's there to be brought back. Repeat that.'

Roy repeats it, slowly, word for word, like it's the most solemn oath he's ever taken. Morty nods sternly along. Now Roy's spooked. Morty looks suddenly like he could go over the table and obliterate Sonny. The waitress brings the two cups of coffee just as Morty gets up to leave. He nods at me to follow.

'Don't you want these now?' asks the waitress.

'No worries, honey, my associates will pay for them.' he says to her, then turning to Sonny, 'Take it outta my whack, mate. Give me a shout when you've got ... ' Morty gives Sonny a wink, not a friendly one. 'See yous two later.'

We walk out the café and across the park. Morty doesn't say anything, just marches on. He got angry with Sonny for no reason. I don't pry. I speculate. It's all this talk of mothers.

CHAPTER NINETEEN

MADE IN CHINA

'I was right,' says Mort, looking out at the slow-moving Wednesday morning traffic. 'Knew I was.'

Last night the memory stick had been retrieved. Morty's speculation about its whereabouts proved correct. 'Don't fuckin bear thinking about,' continues Morty, 'down a hole, dead of night ... don't bear thinking about. I told them, the dynamic duo, do not, under any circumstances, do anything without us.'

'And how were they with that?' I ask.

'Not best pleased.'

'How are you so certain they ain't switched it?' I ask.

'I know ... Trust me on this one.' Then he shakes his head again, repeats his mantra. 'Don't bear thinking about.'

'Could Giles come in handy?' I ask.

'All in good time,' he says. 'Let's see what's on the magic gadget first.'

Sonny and Roy have *temporarily relocated* their slaughter to genteel Highgate, a large five-bedroom house up a long concealed driveway with privet hedges on either side. Morty drives by the address, finds a spike, *borrows* all my change, pays for two hours, and we walk back. Those two can't do inconspicuous if they tried but Sonny's Range Rover appears to be in dry dock.

When we arrive neither of them look good but Roy especially looks paler than ghost's shit. He's got dark bags under his eyes like he's been on the brandy; there's a bottle of five-star sitting on the coffee table. The house is sparsely furnished, giving Sonny and his close crew the appearance of squatters. The chaps have taken on a siege mentality. Looks like they've been up all night hitting the booze and having a council of war. The whole gaff stinks of smoke and is scattered with full ashtrays – half full Marlboro Red packets are slung around.

Sonny asks us, quite surreally, while pulling hard on a snout, if we'd like a *slice of pizza*. He leads us to the fridge but his phone begins to ring in the next room and he goes to answer it. The fridge is full of booze and pizza boxes, stacked one on top of the other. They've had dozens delivered but hardly any have been eaten. Morty opens a box, tears off two slices of congealed pizza and hands me one, along with a napkin from a pile that are, oddly, stacked in the fridge. I have a couple of bites of pizza while Morty fishes around trying to find the makings of a cup of tea.

When I go to throw away the remains of the pizza in the pedal bin I spot a strange telltale sign. A whole giant-sized, thin-crust pizza – Roy's favourite, olive and anchovy – has been discarded with only a single mouthful out of it, leaving a crescent of teeth marks. And a ball of what looks like chewed pizza spat on top of it. It's like someone sat down to eat it, chewed and chewed at the first bite but couldn't bring themselves to swallow it. It looks like modern art. I nod into the bin; Morty looks but fails to see any relevance. He shrugs with indifference.

In the living room the memory stick sits ceremonially on the mantelpiece, clean as a whistle, with nothing to betray its recent hiding place – a stainless steel rectangle an inch and a half long, covered in a chunky plastic that snaps apart to reveal a computer input, nothing written on it to betray its importance except *128MB* and *Hecho en China* – Made in China.

'So?' says Morty.

'So, you was right, Mort,' says Sonny, drinking a bottle of beer.

'Sorry, Sonny,' says Morty, 'come again, only I'm a bit hard of hearing—'

'Fuck off,' says Sonny with a contented smile.

Morty picks up the memory stick, 'Is this what all the fuss has been about then?'

Sonny shrugs, 'Mad, ain't it?'

It transpires that Sonny had volunteered his crew to return to the scene of the interment, in the dead of night, with Roy, full moon high in the clear sky, owls howling. They managed to find the hole again and started digging down. Roy's gone dressed for the job – full protective clothing, charcoal masks, latex gloves, like a proper scenes of crime officer but no doubt massively fortified by a bottle of Napoleon brandy. *It doesn't bear thinking about*. He's got to physically start poking around inside a corpse, a dead guy. It's not like he's simply got to retrieve the gadget outta Jesus' shirt pocket. He's got some seriously macabre messing around to do down that hole. Sonny's crew dig and they finally come across Jesus, covered in lime and stinking worse than a sack of dead rats.

Sonny's crew left Roy down the hole to do his thing. But one by one they got weirded and fled. Roy, having finally found what he came for, but alone, realised he couldn't leave Jesus uninterred. In fact it was the reburial that *really* done his head in because he was doing it all by himself ... except for Jesus, the geezer he's murdered. Proper Edgar Allan Poe routine. Seems Roy's getting the karmic consequences for killing the *flash cunt* sooner than he thought, and Royski believes all that cosmic retribution shit. No wonder Roy looks drained. Sonny was smart enough to delegate, wasn't down that hole in any show of solidarity with Roy Very Twitchy Burns.

To stop Roy from battering them – for *running away like little girls* – Sonny has sent two of his crew to buy two computers as soon as the shops open. Roy wants *clean kit* so briefed them to buy both a Mac and a PC, but to buy them from different shops. Roy told them to buy the upgraded operating system, the one with the most programs *preinstalled*. The new slaughter has been selected because it has a modem and high-speed Internet connection. Sonny explains that he's already sent for an expert in the field all the way from Brighton *just in case Roy gets stuck* – little wink – *this Smiler kiddie is the nuts*.

The two guys arrive back with the computer gear. Sonny sends them next door, out of the way – *help yourself to pizza*. The two guys don't like it but they go. Roy sets up the laptops while Sonny paces impatiently, telling him to hurry up, *open the fuckin memory stick*, but Roy plods along. *This will save us a lot of time later, Sonny.* He connects the laptop up to the modem, plugs in a mouse and installs a printer. Seems strange that Roy, a certified nutcase, would know the ins and outs but it's his field – cyberspace, where dark arts and conspiracy theories dwell. Sonny would have strolled into a cyber café and opened up the memory stick but Roy has counselled Sonny that it's far more *professional* to open it in laboratory conditions, we have no idea what electronic sorcery could be unleashed from that innocent-looking device.

When he's ready Roy places the memory stick in the back of the laptop. Three folders appear on the screen. Roy clicks on the first folder and two unnamed files appear. Roy's face is now like a wide-eyed boy opening presents at Christmas, *delaying* the gratification. He clicks on the first file but it won't open.

A dialogue box keeps jumping up to tell him that he doesn't have the correct software installed. Maybe the program has been written especially for the client. Sonny starts kicking empty boxes, frustrated because there's resistance, but Roy is calm. 'I half expected that,' he says. 'That's why we've got Smiler on the way up. Be patient, Sonny.'

Morty laughs at the absurdity of Roy's request while Roy tries the second file. No joy – won't open. Sonny's shaking his head. It's a *fuckin waste of time.*

Roy clicks on the second folder but it requires a password. He shrugs, double-clicks on the third and last folder. This time things begin to happen – a photography program opens but with one file on it. 'This file has been added later,' says Roy pointing at the *file created* date. A digital contact sheet of photographs appears on screen. He immediately clicks on the 'slideshow' feature and the pictures begin appearing, one after the one other, a couple of seconds on each.

The first photographs – some would say they were pornographic – show a very fit, tanned Latino girl, about twenty-one or two, giving her blonde boyfriend, an athletic, Americano-looking, surfer dude, a first-class blow job. He's almost doing a crab in one shot – *who's a lucky boy?* – arching his back. In the next couple she's grinning up at her spent, exhausted lover. Then there's some shots of them tumbling and turning, him on top, then her on top. Then some shots of them laughing because they're performing for each other in front of a hotel mirror – him sat behind her cupping her beautiful tits with large erect bullet nipples in both his hands and kissing her neck while she melts. The breasts are the real thing – no surgery, no taut skin exposing the rib cage – not veined sacks or absurd balloons.

The photos are a memento of a particularly energetic session, but you get the impression that they weren't intended for happy reminiscence. The sex appears to be incredibly consensual but the pictures don't. Neither of them has had a go with the camera. All the pictures are taken from the same place, as if a tiny device has been placed in a corner of the room. There's a date stamp in the corner of the photos – a little over two months ago. These aren't porn photos; they look like they're genuinely having a good time. Porn stars look bored or overact like mad.

She ain't no hooker either. Guys don't, as a rule, slide two pillows under hookers' arses and go down on them. If this is blackmail material, *she's* the mark. All the photos show her face full on wherever possible. In some of the shots the guy's face is half-obscured or his head is completely cut off. Some of the photos have been blown up to show her face more clearly, giving them a pixellated effect. There could be no denying who the lovers were – they're certainly up to the job of compromising the woman.

It's definitely a hotel in an upmarket resort – white towelling bathrobes, reading lights on the headboard, stationery on the writing table, designer phones on both nightstands, huge bed, room service menu. I'm trying to work out where it would be. My hunch would be Miami or the Keys. Looking hard, I work out that there's a wrap of coke open on the bedside table. In the later pictures I'm proved right – she's sitting cross-legged on the bed, sniffing a line of zip off a CD cover. A line after the main event, a post-charver pick-me-up. The shots click on. They share a cigarette, she laughs, her head thrown backwards. She's very attractive, more attractive when she laughs, but who isn't?

Why would the pictures of her sniffing cocaine be on the memory stick unless she was some important woman? Someone's thinking of blackmail?

Q. Her perceived crime?

A. Doing drugs and fucking.

Worse. Fucking with expertise.

Does anyone care about drugs these days? Could cause you problems if your position depended on having a lily-white image. It would be problematic for anyone connected with politics, law enforcement, religion or sport.

Roy says that you could easily buy a pinhole camera, invisible to the naked eye, to take the photos. You'd just need to slip into the room, set it up, and have a room nearby. I ask Roy if that's Jesus in the photos. He shakes his head.

'Any idea who it might be?'

Roy shrugs.

'Know something?' I say to nobody in particular. 'It got personal between this bird and Jesus.'

'How do you know?' asks Roy.

My turn to shrug. 'I don't. Just a feeling ... '

I think Jesus had an extremely dark side and he was very in touch with it.

The slideshow finishes. I sit down and click on the first photo, zoom in, so it almost becomes pixellated. There's a hotel crest and name on the menu that I'm trying to move into position so I can read it. Sonny thinks I'm just having a perv.

'What a fuckin slag,' says Sonny, nodding at the screen.

I feel strangely protective of her. Sonny doesn't like her – she's out of his league and he knows it. I ask Roy to print the photos.

'Why's that then?' Sonny asks. 'You gonna knock one out later?'

The photos begin tumbling out of the printer.

'What do we do now?' asks Sonny, getting bored.

Roy shrugs. 'We wait for Smiler to open those files.'

'I hope this whole fuckabout wasn't just about some dirty pictures,' says Sonny. He rubs his hands together. 'You know what, I'm a bit peckish. Anyone hungry?' he asks.

'There's plenty of pizza,' says Roy.

'Fuck pizza!' says Sonny, rolling his eyes. 'I'm gonna order a curry. From Edgware Road, for everyone. Get them to stick it in a cab.'

'It's still morning,' says Roy hopefully. 'They won't be open.'

'Oh, yes, they fuckin will,' replies Sonny.

Half an hour later enough curry arrives to feed an infantry regiment. Sonny – in some officers-serving-the-enlisted-men-at-Christmas way – dishes up large potions for everyone, whether they want curry for breakfast or not. Roy sits by the coffee table, lights yet another snout, with a heaving plate full of lamb Madras, rice and peshawari naan in front of him. But he can't eat, seems revolted by the smell, looks about to dry heave. He's got a trainer wedged against the table leg, pulsating with nervous energy. And he can't, through strength of will or prayer, make it stop. But he doesn't want anyone to see, either.

Sonny can eat though, enough for ten, shovelling king prawn vindaloo curry, rice and Bombay potato like a stoker and swigging vodka and coke, pausing only to catch his breath, his nose beginning to drip. 'Where's that soppy cunt, Smiler?' he says between mouthfuls.

Sonny picks up his phone and pushes the speed dial number for the driver they've sent to collect the computer expert. He puts it on loudspeaker and then carries on eating. The driver answers – *the geezer won't stop moaning*, keeps *insisting* on stopping for food and cups of tea. *Subsistence*, he calls it. Sonny asks the driver *where is Smiler right fuckin now?*

'In some bushes, having a gypsy's kiss. Reckons he's got a weak bladder.'

'Stop giving him tea,' snaps Sonny. 'Won't need to be pissing, will he? No more tea!'

Sonny tells the driver to *put the Smiler fella on the trombone when he gets back*. There's a pause. Sonny carries on eating. We can hear traffic. Smiler comes on the phone.

'Alright, Sonny?' says the voice of doom. 'It's me, Smiler.'

Sonny wipes his mouth with the back of his hand and says *hello, Mister Smiler, how-ya-doing, you sweet?* But without waiting for an answer he threatens to break his fingers with a club hammer if he's not here in *one hour. No tea.*

'That should liven him up,' says Sonny. Then he abruptly jumps up and marches across the room, bearing down on Roy. Roy looks up, frightened.

'You eating that bitta tucker, Roy?' says Sonny. 'Only, be a shame to waste it.'

CHAPTER TWENTY

READING BETWEEN THE LINES

Another forty minutes later and enter the legendary Smiler who never smiles, the Internet crim par-excellence, who makes his money stealing from bank accounts, jamming the servers of gambling sites, using everyday computers as zombies, unknowingly pumping out spam. It's a game to Smiler, a world of spyware and phishing; emails demanding bank details to deposit winnings from Spanish lotteries, addressed to bods who don't own passports. In another life Smiler used to procure the best counterfeit documentation but now finds fiddling about on the net much more lucrative.

Smiler's day: sits in front of his battalion of computers, tucked away in Brighton, looking out on the Channel from his Regency apartment, acquiring more wealth, getting more cynical, complaining about *grockles* staggering drunkenly down the front. Now Sonny's summoned him to assist on a special mission but Smiler would do well to remember that around volatile people it's like playing a pinball machine – one nudge too many ... tilt ... game over.

When the driver walks in behind Smiler you can tell he's taken an ear-bashing all the way up. Smiler – a pale, stringy grimace on legs, mid-forties but looks older, millions squirrelled away but dressed like a schlepper – runs the sceptical rule over the set-up that Roy has put together and begrudgingly nods his approval. No intros for me or Morty, who's sitting reading the paper on the sofa, smoking and drinking coffee. Roy begins to give Smiler a sit-rep – *can't get these two folders open. We've tried getting ...*

Smiler holds up his hand to silence Roy. He sits down, starts typing, cutting and pasting, downloading software, opening up accountancy files. He's swearing under his breath, writing down passwords on manuals, cursor flying round the screen, a dozen programs open at once. Smiler is airborne.

Morty meanwhile flicks off his shoes, manoeuvres himself

horizontal, shuffles the pillows and goes to sleep. Roy and Sonny
look at one another with raised eyebrows. Smiler looks over his
shoulder. 'Excitement must be too much,' he says sardonically.

Sonny tells Smiler to try and get into the untouched folder
straight away.

Smiler ambles into the folder, goes through the security system
like a knife through butter – like it wasn't there – using a
password-busting program. The screen fills with files –
fifty-seven files in all – *nice odd number*, as Smiler puts it. Most
of the files are systematically dated and titled. Always two names,
always one called Miguel – *Miguel y General, Miguel y Victor*.
Miguel and General, Miguel and Victor. *Miguel y Jenna, Miguel
y Raul*. Always the date of the recording. There's a few scattered,
unnamed files at the end.

'These are audio files – MP3s,' says Smiler to Roy.

'Recordings?' asks Roy. 'Not documents?'

'Compressed digital recordings,' says Smiler.

He downloads yet another program and waits patiently for it to
install itself. When it's ready Smiler clicks to play the first file,
'Here we go,' he says. The three of us lean into the laptop screen.
Two voices are talking in Spanish.

'They're talking Spanish,' says Smiler.

'I can fuckin hear that, Smiler,' screams Sonny, 'I ain't fuckin
stupid.'

'Next question,' says Smiler. 'Do you want me to translate it?'

'You speak Spanish?' asks Sonny, impressed.

'No, I'll send it to a translation service.'

'I speak a bit of Spanish,' I say, 'but I think it's a dialect. Play
it for a minute, Smiler, see what we've got.'

Smiler shrugs and lets the recording play. It's some gadget. He
can drag the conversation along, fast-forward it or stop it dead
with the mouse. Then Smiler starts jumping around – in and out
of different conversations, different files – with five or six open at
any one time or parked-up at the bottom of the screen. All the
conversations feature one voice that's consistently in all the
recordings – Miguel. His name is in every conversation. Smiler
finds a conversation in English – *Miguel y Banquero* – Miguel and
Banker. They talk about the *bank in the Caymans* – *simple*

schemes are the best – for us it's a bridge-burning exercise. The essence of the deal is putting distance between us ... Miguel's telling the Banker *don't try to be to too clever with these people, they will not appreciate it. They might be wealthy but around money most of them are dumb as farm boys.*

But who is Miguel? Seems young but *really* assertive, telling people exactly what he wants. It isn't Slick from the Cosmo; he's not American.

Smiler gives us the whirlwind tour. Some of the recordings are telephone conversations, some meetings in restaurants. *All* of them are clandestine, *none* consensual. All sound conspiratorial, talking in analogies and the third person; like guys aware of conspiracy laws, planning high-level *projects, schemes, undertakings and endeavours.* No doubt they were recorded with concealed listening devices.

Smiler clicks a random file. Two voices are speaking in Spanish – Miguel and some slightly camp, but somehow disturbed dude. I get a gentle slap on the arm from Roy. 'That ... ' he says, 'is the Jesus fella ... '

Roy is spooked. Jesus' voice echoes around the room, with shrieking seagulls and Latino hip-hop in the background, like the recording was done in Miami. We listen for a while, but you wouldn't need to understand Spanish to grasp what's going on.

Jesus is trying to skunk out Miguel, trying to get him to reveal information and incriminate himself. But it's Miguel who's leading Jesus into an ambush – the conversation sounds like a Q and A. Jesus asking plenty of leading Qs but getting no satisfactory As. Miguel is charming but telling nobody nothing, blatantly denying knowing people or being in certain locations.

Roy asks what they're saying. 'They're talking plenty,' I tell him, 'but saying nothing.'

Their conversation ends abruptly, with Miguel trying to embrace Jesus – *cousin, let me hug you.* Jesus resists the attempt to check if he's wearing a wire. Miguel knows he's being recorded. Jesus knows Miguel knows. Jesus knows he's fucked.

Miguel has tumbled that Jesus is, or has been, recording him. There's a rustling – someone grabbing the microphone – then an exchange of Spanish insults. Miguel yells at Jesus *No debería*

*haber hecho caso a mi padre, debería haberte acabado contigo
hace años!* – roughly translated: *I shouldn't have listened to
Father, I should have finished you years ago!* Then the recording
stops dead. End of story. Seems the whacked, neurotic Jesus was
running a vendetta against the calm, unruffled Miguel.

'What I'm going to do,' says Smiler, 'is run them in real-time,
one-by-one, but send them through *transcription* software, then
send the transcript to a *translation* service. Then you'll have a
transcript of the conversations. They may take a bit of deciphering
– the program won't know who's talking – but you'll know
enough to work it out.'

'Let's print it up and drive it over to them,' says Sonny,
rubbing his hands.

Smiler laughs, a bit fearless now. 'We send it over *the net*,
Sonny,' he says, pointing at the computer screen. 'The Internet. I
click a button and it's gone.'

'Comes back when? Tomorrow?'

'About a minute.'

'A minute!' says Sonny, clapping his hands, doing a dance.
'Brilliant. Right, let's get going!'

Smiler starts typing in search engines, finds his way into a
translation site then runs the recording. It begins to appear, in
English, on the computer screen.

About a minute later he clicks on the print button and a
transcript starts tumbling out the printer. There's a lot of spelling
mistakes, underlined in red like a schoolteacher's biro.

'Keep 'em coming,' says Sonny.

Smiler keeps them coming all afternoon, feeding Roy and me
more riddles and puzzles to be worked out. While we exchange
transcripts, Sonny paces, Smiler fiddles with the final unopened
folder and Morty sleeps on.

The first transcript, the one entitled Miguel and Papa Victor, a
conversation between Miguel and his father, reads like gossip from
the inner sanctum – two guys cosied-up in a study. Deals, offers,
bargaining and negotiations. There's talk of backhanders, politicos,
high-ranking soldiers, who's a greedy bastard, lawyers working as
bag-men, corrupt bankers, even a cardinal providing false alibis.

There's a character constantly referred to as the 'dark one' – *el oscuro.* It's meant as ridicule and half as a warning. They're referring to Jesus, name-checked as the Little Devil – *El Pequeño Diablo* and *El Niño Diablo* – the Child Devil. I knew he'd be putting in more than a cameo. Miguel is spitting angry and I think, reading between the lines, that Miguel wants to kill the devil. Something *El Niño Diablo* has done has genuinely shocked Miguel and his father, gents who accept murder and corruption as a business model. The father goes into a long rant about nepotism and fratricide, voodoo, and insanity, goes on for five pages. The *dark one's* repulsive scheme will *ruin everything.* Throughout the transcripts Miguel is telling anyone who'll listen not to tell that prick Jesus *anything, nada – he's up to something.*

On another one Miguel and his father, Papa Victor, are talking about an incident at the University of Miami, someone getting killed. Jenna, Miguel's sister, Victor's daughter, is taking flak. Victor is *asking* Miguel *as a favour* to give Jesus, his younger brother's wayward child, *one last chance.* Miguel isn't keen, says it could jeopardise the *big picture.* The campus police are getting busy and the Miami police department have opened a missing persons file. The Zambrano's name is getting bounced about. Miguel decides to move Jenna to Columbia – *it will be safer there. We can keep an eye.* And double her bodyguard. Safer in Columbia?

There are snide insults about powerful people, nicknames and in-jokes. Miguel's side of the family, the sane side, led by the patriarch Papa Victor, is fiddling about in the neighbourhood where criminality bleeds into government. Jesus' side are just fiddling about. Miguel calls them *the deadwood.*

I tell Smiler – who's busy trying to open the third folder but getting frustrated – to print off a copy of the original Spanish transcript. Immediately it comes tumbling out of the printer.

Next instalment is interesting. This scheme involves the army, the Venezuelan one I guess, and a diplomatic bag operation into the States via various sleepy Caribbean islands. Maybe Jesus was shifting weight, moving his tackle, in a D-bag. The guy talking with Miguel – Raul, some kinda enforcer – says the people they work with in America, Switzerland, Uruguay and Argentina would be sickened by this ungodly behaviour – *vendiendo corazones a los Americanos ricos* – selling centres to rich Americans – obviously a mistranslation. Shopping malls?

Miguel appears pragmatic, nonchalant, about the long history of misdemeanours his clan has been involved with but is now worried that something Jesus is up to would finish them off, like there's a limit to what even highly corruptible people will turn a blind eye to. Nothing must threaten *the plan*, he says repeatedly but doesn't care to elaborate on what *the plan* might be. Raul and Miguel speculate about killing Jesus *accidentally* – without Papa's permission. Raul laughs. Miguel doesn't.

There are obviously a lot of references to *Perico* – literally parrot, cocaine, because of the brainless, repetitive chatter it induces. *The parrot went via Cuba. They got paid. The government seized their parrot and sold it to us. Perico disappeared. We knew our friend The General wouldn't let us down. He kept the parrot safe.* It's full of riddles – *the circus won't be coming to town. The funds we received from the parrot went straight to Zurich.* They appear to be pragmatic about any law enforcement they can't buy off or kill, like it's a game.

It would be a major embarrassment to Miguel if the contents of the memory stick were exposed because it's all information that only an insider would know – times, places, tax havens, banks, accounts, frivolous gossip, who's got multiple mistresses, including a general with a tits-and-dick transsexual tucked away. The source would be easy to prove. The information concerning payments to military personnel could get you killed. The files are a complete blackmail package, assembled by someone with more than a grudge – a seething, slow-burn resentment – but also access to the family hacienda.

Maybe Jesus *and* this Miguel fella are both dead. Jesus was a blackmailer, blackmailing his own family, but never got the chance to spend the loot before Roy tore him in half. Alive or dead, there's not a lot of love for Jesus. I think the three million Sonny and his merry men intercepted was the pay-off ... *or* the first instalment.

After reading the transcripts it becomes apparent that Roy and Sonny were holding out. Surprise, surprise. The Zambrano Family aren't *some nutty South American firm* but a powerful organisation. Roy gives Sonny an outline of what's on the recordings.

'Could we sell this back to them?' asks Sonny.

'Could be tricky,' says Roy.

'Extremely fuckin dangerous,' I say. 'What exactly was you expecting, Sonny?'

'Something better than chit-chat and dirty pictures.'

'This information is extremely valuable. They've written off three million pounds.'

'All these folders are connected,' says Roy calmly.

'Here ya go,' says Smiler. He stands up, punches the air. 'Cracked it!'

The screen is full – top to bottom, left to right – of neat columns, figures and numbers, squiggles and hieroglyphics. Smiler scrolls down the page. It's endless.

'What the fuck is that?' asks Sonny, pointing.

'The last folder – financial accounts, two sets, shadow accounts,' says Smiler. 'Two of everything – ledgers, credit and debit.'

'You can tell just by looking?' asks Sonny.

'Trust me – that's the cumshot,' says Smiler. 'Those columns are figures. This is bespoke kit, designed to be impenetrable.'

'Can you encrypt it?' asks Roy.

'You mean *de*crypt it,' says Smiler smugly. 'Given time. It's like code-breaking.'

'How long?' asks Sonny.

'Fuck knows,' replies Smiler. 'This program could have tripwires. Work it out – if someone gets a unique bit of software, they're gonna make sure it's protected. There are different levels of encryption. I can tell it's hardcore. Actually, it might be mad but ... ' Smiler reaches around the back of the laptop and tugs at the memory stick. The figures disappear.

'You ain't lost it, have ya?' says Sonny taking a step nearer to Smiler.

Smiler shakes his head then pushes the stick back in. The program reappears. He clicks to save it but a dialogue box appears saying the action is not permitted. Smiler is beguiled and impressed. 'Half the information is on the stick and half is on the net. The memory stick, Sonny, is the modern day equivalent of a treasure map ... But one *half* of the treasure map.'

'Where's the rest?' asks Sonny.

Smiler takes a deep breath and exhales. 'Somewhere,' he says at last. 'Somewhere out in cyberspace is the other half of the program, its twin ... It's a file-sharing program, nicking bits of other programs and creating a new facilitating host. But some extremely clever data burnt deep into that gadget pulls it all together and allows you access to the prize. You want a piece of advice, gents? I'd say keep that memory stick where the sun don't shine.'

Roy lunges at Smiler, 'You trying to be funny, you cunt!' Sonny jumps in between them. Roy tries to get at Smiler, to seriously hurt him. Sonny holds him back, tells Roy to calm down.

Morty wakes up, sits bolt upright. 'What's with the fuckin noise?' he roars. 'Can't a man get his head down without you cunts screaming?'

Sonny and Roy immediately come under manners, stop pushing and shoving. Smiler is startled. He'd forgotten all about Morty.

Sonny turns to Smiler, 'Well?'

'There's nothing I can do, not right now,' he says awkwardly. 'I need time, and equipment.'

'Have I got this right?' says Sonny, 'That stick is a one-and-only?'

'Correct. I mean, yes.' Smiler's nodding his head off.

'I need you to stay here,' says Sonny, 'and work on this, for as long as it takes.'

Sonny pulls out a brick of notes that's broken into thousand-pound chunks. He peels off three and slings them on the table. 'Now, here's an advance, for services rendered, not bad for an afternoon's work. I'll be very generous if that ... ' he nods at the computer, 'turns up trumps.'

Smiler nods and takes the money. 'Now I need a chat with my colleagues ... ' Sonny points at the door.

Smiler goes to leave, then something occurs to Sonny. 'Oi! Smiler, I'd be upset if I thought you were chatting my business. You gonna keep quiet?' Smiler nods his head and slips out the door. The very next moment Sonny's phone rings. He looks at it and decides to answer it. 'Hello, Flavio, how goes it?'

I can make out someone telling Sonny some bad news in a high-pitched voice. 'Calm down, Flavio, for fuck's sake! Flavio, stop screaming! When was this?'

An anxious look passes between Sonny and Roy. 'How many?' Sonny asks, looking concerned. 'Whaddya mean, not the first lot? Where are you now? Are you sure they didn't follow you? Stay there. No, meet me at Dollis Hill tube. Fuck's sake! Just get on a train! Duck about! Lose them! Give me twenty minutes!'

Sonny puts his phone away, kicks a box, and looks perplexed. 'We gotta go see someone.'

'What's happening, Sonny?' asks Morty, getting up, lighting a snout.

'There's been a ... ' says Sonny, 'strange devolvement.'

CHAPTER TWENTY-ONE

STRANGE DEVOLVEMENT

Missus Burns would suggest that the phone call from Flavio about *some Venezuelans turning up* at the Cosmo was *God paying you back, for being wicked to that nice Mister Smiler*. And Twitchy would agree with Mum that there's a funny karmic thing going on.

Roy's driving along the North Circular Road to find *Young Flavio*, as Sonny calls him, with me, Morty and Sonny, all buckled up and trying to look inconspicuous. The sit-rep is as follows – Flavio the Concierge has told Sonny that *another* group of Venezuelans, unbeknown to the *first* group of Venezuelans, arrived at his place of work, the Cosmopolitan Hotel, this afternoon, asked some questions, didn't like the answers they received and got *very* hostile. Flavio left via a fire escape and phoned Sonny in a panic. Sonny has arranged to link with Flavio outside Dollis Hill tube station.

'Why Dollis Hill, Sonny?' asks Morty. 'Couldn't you just meet him in some boozer?'

'Trust me on this one, Mort,' replies Sonny, animal instincts alight.

We arrive at Dollis Hill station, after getting lost coming off the dual carriageway. Flavio's been waiting, feeling exposed. It shows in his face. We swag him away. Now it's a tight squeeze with three of us in the back.

Flavio's a good-looking kid of about twenty. He's still dressed in his black suit jacket but wearing brand new jeans that don't look right – too big. His shirt and tie, both black, are in disarray. He has the aura of a geezer who's strayed too far from the paddling pool. I think the reason he's wearing new jeans, instead of his suit trousers, is that he's either pissed or shit himself or both. And right on cue Sonny pulls a face ...

'Can you smell shit?' asks Sonny. 'There's a smell of shit, right?'

'No, there isn't,' says Roy categorically. He means, *you're crucifying the kid*, but Sonny don't get it.

'Maybe someone's stood in dogshit,' says Sonny.

'Forget it, Sonny,' says Mort. 'Okay?'

Flavio looks uncomfortable, while I feel embarrassed, because there is a naughty whiff coming off him.

'Where are we headed for?' Morty asks Sonny, 'Flavio here could use a wash and brush up.'

'Let's head for the AKQ,' says Sonny.

AKQ club is a clubhouse for desperados and loons housed in a corner shop in Cricklewood – all the usual fixtures, blacked-out windows, basement card-schools, hidden back rooms where a fugitive might get his head down, CCTV cameras above the door, banks of monitors over the jump. The owner lives in a barricaded flat on the top floor, comes and goes via a fire escape at the back. There were rumours of secret escape passages, and the club was regularly checked for bugging devices, just to keep the paranoia levels nicely bubbling.

Roy parks the rental up in the alley that runs the length of the row of shops and Sonny leads us into the club. As we enter it's a spaghetti western moment – the clientele look up slowly from their evening breakfasts or papers to see who's coming through the door. Most of them look like they haven't slept for days; they're pranged or pinned, edgy and paranoid.

The ground floor is, as always, furnished with worn lino and Formica tables, sells kebabs, sandwiches and bottled beer. Upstairs, card games go on non-stop, night and day, including Christmas Day. I hadn't popped in for years but I know the only thing that's changed is the light bulbs. It's a total contrast to Flavio's Cosmo P. The AKQ was minimalist in a different way – no Japanese spas in the basement or ylang-ylang scented candles. A few guys stood round a one-armed bandit nod over to Sonny and Roy. Sonny winks, tells them, 'Just got a little sorting to do. Catch ya in a minute, gents.'

He asks the guy behind the ramp, slow, stoned and fearless, 'Can I borrow a room? Need a chat with these gents.'

Without a word he beckons us to follow him. We pass through a narrow corridor and the guy opens a locked door. He gestures for us to enter while he stays outside. Sonny peels five twenty-pound notes off his brick and gives them to the guy. 'Can we get a few beers and a bottle of brandy?' he asks, then sticks a couple of twenties in his shirt pocket. 'A good bottle, yeah?' The barman nods. Not employed for his conversation skills.

Inside is a bare room, with a green baize card table, surrounded by six well-worn office chairs; the ideal place for a marathon card game, or an interrogation. The overhead light throws out a spooky glow. The barred window has been blacked out and an air conditioning unit hums and rattles. Flavio starts getting unnerved again.

'These men, these *Venezuelanos putos*, they were going to kill me,' he blurts out.

'One second,' says Sonny, holding up a hand, 'let me think ...' He's calculating whether it would be better if Flavio skipped town, or if he stayed put. It could look suspect if Flavio suddenly went missing – the hotel security manager might ring his CID contact down West End Central ... Don't wanna even *think* about ...

There's a knock on the door. Roy opens it. The guy is back with a battered tray – six bottles of beer, the brandy, glasses, no ice, no smile, no change.

'Sit down, Flavio,' says Roy, Sonny's unofficial head of security, 'make yourself comfortable.'

It would be impossible for Flavio to get comfortable but he sits. Roy sits opposite.

'Is there anything you'd like?' asks Roy, being so polite it's chilling. It's been a long and emotional twenty-four hours for Roy, what with all that digging.

Then Roy questions Flavio, gets him repeating the story, over and over, for the next half hour.

'Again, from the beginning,' says Roy, standing, his face in the shadows.

So Flavio relates the tale once again. The Venezuelans arrived, said they were *acquaintances* of Jesus. Flavio thought it was the first lot, or *associates* of the first lot, returning to ask more question so he managed to get them away from the reception area and swerve them into the bar. Flavio didn't want management finding out that they'd already paid money to search Jesus' room. Flavio told the Venezuelans he'd looked after Jesus while he was in town and he'd do the same for them. Then they asked to see Jesus' old room. In the room they began asking questions about Jesus, *exactly* the same questions as the first group. It soon developed into the classic scenario – *I told your colleagues everything I know, señor.*

'Excuse me, *señor*, I mean, sir,' replied one of the group politely, 'but what *colleagues*? Who are you referring to, please?'

Flavio told them that he'd told *their colleagues* everything he knew only a few days before. Flavio asked them if this was *a joke, no*? They asked for an explanation so Flavio gave them one – a team of Venezuelans came here last week, *paid a consideration*, and searched the room from *top to bottom*. When Flavio finished the Venezuelans started speaking *Espanhol muito rapidamente* – Spanish very fast – amongst themselves. They asked Flavio if he knew anything he wasn't letting on ...

Flavio tried to get cute. He shrugged his shoulders, pulled a charming, innocent cherub face, sensed another *consideration* could be forthcoming but unfortunately ...

Without warning one of the Venezuelans delivered a short, sharp punch to his diaphragm, deliberately knocking him breathless, doubling him over. They exploded into a well-rehearsed routine, grabbed Flavio by the hair, dragged him screaming into an enclosed shower stall, forced a plastic freezer bag over his head, pulled it taut around his neck and began suffocating him. The more Flavio struggled, the harder he breathed, the faster his oxygen got exhausted till he started to slip out of consciousness. My theory about his soiled strides was correct. Through the plastic, which was stuck to his face like skin, they told him that they were going to kill him if he didn't answer their questions – *don't be cute*. But Flavio couldn't breathe *or* speak so they contented themselves with bouncing his head off the tiles. The fact that there was another team of their compatriots asking questions about Jesus was a problem. It was only the intervention of the urbane and aloof head of the group, who up to that point in the interrogation had hovered like an observer, that stopped them from killing Flavio. He apologised for their conduct on their behalf. They left in an orderly fashion after giving Flavio five hundred pounds and asking him – with mucho menace – to keep quiet about their visit.

'What did this lot look like?' asks Roy. 'Were they different from the first mob?'

'They wore suits, but like bad suits, ill-fitting ... didn't look right, like a band on a cruise ship,' says Flavio, bitching. 'But the leader, man, he was dressed like an English gent ... *muito* strange. Like he had bought his clothes on Jermyn Street – tweeds and gingham shirts.'

'Did they ask about the memory stick?' asks Roy.

'Again and again! They asked about your club, Sonny,' blurts out Flavio.

'Oh, yeah, before or after they tried to suffocate you?' asks Sonny, selfishly concerned.

'During,' says Flavio.

'Did they ... did they ask about me?' asks Sonny like it was an innocuous question.

'They asked if I *knew* you,' replies Flavio. 'I said I was sometimes paid to send customers to the Monarch – rich guests, with money, I could get them into the VIP.'

'Why tell them anything?' asks Sonny.

'They had this Jesus Zambrano's American Express statements! They showed them to me!' Sonny shakes his head, disappointed. 'They were going to *kill* me!' screams Flavio. 'I shouldn't have got involved! I didn't have to make the call to you, Mister King! I could have got on a plane, gone to Portugal!'

Sonny looks hurt, bottom lip sticking out, 'And left me in the shit? That's not nice, is it?' He gives Flavio the burning eyes. Flavio looks straight down, ashamed and scared. Flavio begins to talk but can't. He begins to melt. He gets a folded piece of hotel stationary out of the top pocket of his jacket and places it on the tabletop. 'He told me ... ' says Flavio in a whisper, 'to give you this ... '

'Who?' snaps Sonny.

'The leader, the Venezuelan gentleman ... '

Flavio goes to hand the paper to Sonny. 'What the fuck is it?' asks Sonny.

'I haven't looked, Sonny ... it was meant for you.'

'Why'd you only mention this now, you Portuguese cunt?' growls Sonny.

'I was ... ' stammers Flavio. 'I was scared.'

Sonny leaps forward, quick as a snake, his face in Flavio's. 'What the fuck,' he roars, 'have you got to be scared of?'

'Nothing,' replies Flavio, hoping it's the right answer.

Sonny taps the paper. 'Have a look now,' he says, eyes drilling into Flavio.

He opens up the paper. 'It's a phone number, Mister King.'

'Any name?' Morty asks Flavio.

'Santos ... ' replies Flavio, looking like he's gonna cry. 'And he wants you to call him.'

Flavio places the folded paper down and pushes it across the table. Roy picks up the paper, and reads aloud.

'Mister King, please could you call me, AYC, on blah, blah, blah – that's a UK pay as you go number. Yours faithfully, Santos de Lucia.'

'What's this AYC bollocks?' asks Sonny, confused.

'At your convenience,' says Flavio. 'It's etiquette.'

'*Etiquette?*' hisses Sonny. 'This is a new one ... Fuckin *etiquette*!'

Sonny turns to Roy, issues an order, 'Stick Flavio in a cab, park him up, we might need him to ready-eye this Santos later.' Sonny turns to Flavio and pulls out cash. 'You done well, son. Call in sick to work, call in everyday. Stay away from the Cosmopolitan, but stay in touch with Roy.'

He hands Flavio a neatly folded grand. Flavio's having the worst day of his life but the most lucrative – fifteen hundred quid in his new jeans. Roy ushers him out while Sonny pours two brandies and places them in front of me and Morty.

'We need a strategy,' says Sonny when Flavio and Roy are gone.

'I don't want that kid hurt,' says Morty, pointing out the door.

'Thought never crossed my mind, Mort,' says Sonny, the picture of innocence. 'I've put you two in whatever's on that memory thingy but I'm gonna need a bitta help ... ' Neither of us says anything. 'We need to get this Santos off my 'ay.'

Morty drums his fingers on the tabletop but says nothing. 'This is the plan of action,' continues Sonny, getting desperate. 'It's simple, okay? Smiler cracks the codes. We get the info on those accounts. We talk to Giles. Move the operation to Barbados. Put Curtis on the payroll. We clear out the Venezuelans' accounts, bust up and go our separate ways. There's money on that thing – we just gotta get to it!'

Morty and me say nothing. Sonny's selling us best-case scenario. He needs us; you'd be lucky to get a dirty look off Sonny if he didn't have an ulterior motive.

'The situation is different ... ' says Mort. 'It's what Roy would call *fluid*.'

We pretend not to be convinced. It's deceptive front. Sonny is pacing now, circling the table.

'What's Giles got to do with this?' I ask.

'I'll level with ya,' he says. 'We have Giles right straightened out. He's a school pal of Curtis'. And Curtis does what Giles tells him ... It's how these swells operate. But, first things first, we need to get these Venezuelans away from us.'

'Not *us*, Sonny,' I tell him. 'It's *you* they wanna talk to.'

Morty laughs, claps. Throws back his head, slaps Sonny's shoulder.

'It's funny, Sonny,' says Mort. 'You gotta admit it.'

'I never admit anything,' says Sonny, deadly serious. 'Nothing. Never. Not my style, mate.'

CHAPTER TWENTY-TWO

BAD TO WORSE

Sonny can be the most awkward cunt ... Five minutes after agreeing *it's the only way*, to meet with *this Santos geezer*, straighten out *this misunderstanding* ... he's changed his mind. He's switched and decided that he doesn't wanna meet *this cunt* after all. I suggest that Sonny should have a sit-down with the South Americans somewhere public, where they would both feel safe. He started getting defiant.

'Can you believe this geezer?' Sonny asks Morty. 'Is he winding me up? He seriously wants me to sit down with this cunt.'

'He's right,' shrugs Mort, 'it makes sense. It's *deflecting* suspicion. You ain't on trial—'

'Fuckin right, I ain't!'

'It's not *me* you gotta convince. And he's right,' says Mort, meaning me, 'you're a sitting target, what with that club. If they wanna do a wet job on ya, they've only gotta plot up ... Try and convince them on the phone they're wasting their time.'

'Could be good,' says Sonny, seeing possibilities.

'If there are two teams operating,' says Morty, 'we could use the intel. You could sniff them out, Sonny.'

'Dead right ... ' nods Sonny, 'then straighten it out.'

'So, you'll meet them?' asks Morty.

'No! No fuckin way!' snaps Sonny, like it's a stupid question.

'Sonny, if they were going to kill you,' says Mort, 'they'd have done it by now.'

'You're very reassuring, do you know that?' says Sonny sarcastically, pouring himself a brandy, realising he's in a corner, 'This is all that cunt Jesus' fault,' he mutters, straight-faced.

The Venezuelans wanna ask him a few questions on behalf of the family back home, but the more Sonny evades them the more convinced they'll become that he's involved. And they'll have criminal connections that can easily find out Sonny King's pedigree.

Straight Q. – Is this Sonny King character a gentleman who could organise the robbing, and possible murder, of *our* courier carrying *our* dough back to *our* hacienda?

Straight A. – This Sonny King character could rob his own mother in her sleep. In *his* sleep.

Meanwhile Sonny's pacing again, muttering about *that cunt Jesus* ...

'There's *obviously*,' I say to Sonny, '*two* teams of Venezuelans in London looking for that memory stick.'

Sonny sits down, drags his fingers through his hair, shakes his canister. I could almost feel sorry for him. 'Two?' he says at last. 'Just what I fuckin don't need.'

'You need to think seriously,' says Mort, 'about getting these geezers to believe that Jesus shipped out to Paris.'

Sonny is only half convinced. 'Why should I sit down with them?'

'Because they might kill you if you don't,' Morty tells him.

'They can't fuckin kill everyone,' says Sonny.

'Oh, yes, they fuckin can,' Morty replies. 'They know you have a nightclub. If you leave London, where are you gonna go? You wanna be involved in a vendetta with a firm of South Americans?'

'I know what I'll do,' says Sonny. 'I'll send Roy in there. Roy killed the cunt. I'll let Roy sort it out.'

Morty pipes up. 'Roy could get us *all* served-up, Sonny. I don't think Roy's all that tickety-boo at the moment, not since, you know ... ' Morty mimes digging a hole.

'You're right, Mort, dead right ... ' Sonny does a brutal impression of Roy, twitching and winking. 'We should drop him out.'

'So you'll go on your own?' I ask, trying to conceal my hope.

'Fuck off! Don't try and be funny!' says Sonny, giving me the eyes. 'You and Morty are comin with! If ya want a bit of what's on that thing!'

'We're all talking,' I say, 'like there's a prize on that stick.'

'Trust me,' says Sonny, tapping his nose. 'I knew when they was fiddling about in that room at the Cosmo there was more to this – fuckin *knew*.'

'So,' says Morty, locking onto Sonny and downing his brandy, 'you need to make the call.'

Sonny doesn't want to make the call to Santos. You can tell that he's gonna need another drink, and another one after that. The purpose of the operation is to pacify them into believing that we – and especially the extremely guilty-looking Sonny King – are complete innocents. I wouldn't wanna end up in a situation where they decide to kill us all anyway because Sonny has incensed them or in what Roy would call an *information containment exercise.*

'Ring that fuckin number, Sonny,' says Morty, maybe enjoying his discomfort.

Sonny drums his fingers on his phone, frowning, like he's thinking hard. 'You know what, I'll ring him tomorrow,' he says. 'It's like ringing a bird, you don't wanna appear too keen.'

Morty lets go a disappointed sigh. Sonny bursts out laughing, slapping the tabletop. 'Look at his little face,' says Sonny, pointing at Mort.

'Fuckin ring it, Sonny,' says Morty. 'And remember, best innocent voice.'

Sonny King feeds the number into his phone and pushes the green button.

No answer. Sonny appears relieved. The number rings off the hook. Don't mean we're off the hook.

Sonny keeps asking Morty where Roy is – *where the fuck is Roy, Mort?* Just at the point where Morty's about to tell Sonny to fuck off, in strolls Roy like he's been to feed a meter.

'Roy,' says Sonny, 'where you been? We thought the Apaches had got ya. I rung that number, no answer. Do you think I should ring it again?'

'Definitely,' replies Roy, dry as a bone.

'I'm disappointed in ya, Roy. If I get killed, I'm coming back to haunt you.'

'If they were going to kill you, Sonny,' says Roy, 'they'd have done it by now.'

'We've had this conversation,' says Sonny.

'If you get given lemons,' says Roy, 'you make lemonade.'

'What the fuck you on about?' asks Sonny.

'You don't get it, do you, Sonny?' says Roy, annoyed. 'This is manna from heaven.'

Roy is now in his element. 'We start listening in to that

number, same as what the cozzers would do. We can track it, find out where they are at any given time, day or night. Smiler'll know how to do it. I think he's underestimated us, this Santos geezer, giving us that number.'

'Underestimated *you*, Roy,' says Sonny, slapping Roy on the back.

'In the meantime,' says Roy, 'we bug that number and Smiler can translate what they say.'

'Does this Santos have your number, Sonny?' asks Morty.

'I asked Flavio,' says Roy. 'Santos missed a trick – didn't get yer number off his phone.'

Sonny grabs Roy and pinches a big handful of his cheek. 'Look at that face,' he's saying, looking relieved, 'got a face only a mother could love ... '

'He should have checked the call history,' says Roy, 'to see if Flavio was calling you. We give Santos' mobile number to Smiler, see what he can come up with, who this Santos rings.'

'Fuckin brilliant, Roy,' says Sonny, rubbing his hands together. 'Blinding. I feel better now. You know what, Roy? You've just earned yourself a whole page in my memoirs.'

Sonny roars at his joke. Roy looks hurt as he turns to speak to me.

'When we go to meet these guys, *they're* gonna speak Spanish. We don't, at least *they* think *we* don't, so when *they* ask *us* if any of *us* speaks Es-pan-yola, *we* say no. What's "do you speak Spanish?" in Spanish?'

'Habla usted español?' I say.

'There you go. *You* do speak Spanish. We shrug our shoulders and say *no*. So then when *they* speak amongst themselves, *we*, or more precisely, *you*,' he says, nodding at me, 'will understand them. Understand?'

'Kinda,' I say.

'They'll say stuff they don't want us to know, so when we get there—'

'The thing is, Roy,' says Sonny, interrupting, 'we was having a chat ... See what I was thinking was to ask this Santos over to the club.'

'That's good,' says Roy, nodding, 'plenty of bods around. When, tonight?'

'No, in the morning, ten-ish,' says Sonny. 'But we was thinking that just me and Mort, and yer man here, would go on the meet.'

'Why's that then?' asks Roy, like he's upset.

'Roy, brother, you ain't in there because you're watching my back.'

Any sane person would be relieved but Roy's not any sane person. Sonny spots it, he opens his arms wide and gives Roy a bear hug, giving Mort a wink on Roy's blindside. 'I need someone I can trust making sure everything's sweet,' says Sonny.

And before Roy has time to think Sonny's out the door, leading us up the tight corridor, towards a fire door. He pushes it open and steps out into the street, motioning us *to hurry the fuck up*.

Morty whispers to me, sounding ominous, 'One day Sonny's gonna take the piss outta Roy once too often.'

'Dot on the fuckin card, Mort.'

Roy drives us back along the North Circular. I want them to drop me at a tube station, wanna get back to the hotel. I fancy a bath, a large brandy and a read of the transcripts. But then Sonny's phone rings with its *Another One Bites the Dust* ringtone. Sonny looks at the call display, rolls his eyes, answers and listens to a high-pitched voice at the other end, nodding his head slowly.

'Why didn't you call me earlier?' he asks after a minute.

The caller goes off into a long explanation until Sonny interrupts.

'Where's that tosser Dougie?'

You get the impression that things are not hunky dory down the Monarch. Eventually Sonny snaps the phone shut.

'That was the *Acting* Head of Security at the Monarch Club ... '

A bouncer, by any other name. This is a real-time situation report. The Head of Security had left the back door open so the bar staff, bouncers and various members of Sonny's crew could slip in without going through the front door. Suddenly, amongst the hustle and bustle that precedes opening time, the Head of Security turned around and four well-dressed geezers had appeared outta nowhere, and were stood in a neat line in front of the bar, with the lump he'd left guarding the back door under heavy manners. The bouncer tells them that the club isn't open for another couple of hours, but one of them – young, almost a boy – replies in perfect but accented English *they are aware of that*. The bouncer thinks he's maybe *Spanish or some fuckin thing* but then he works out he's with some of the Venezuelans who came by before. They ask for Sonny – no joy. Then ask some questions about *the Jesus geezer*, who had apparently gone missing after spending a few nights down the Monarch. They told the *Acting* Head of Security that *Jesus never got that train to Paris, 'cause they went and checked ...*

Ironically, it was the one time that Dougie the Nightingale had turned up early for work, part a of no-booze-no-drugs, new-leaf-turned-over offensive suggested by a life coach cum eastern mystic – eastern, as in Aldgate East. As Dougie enters he bumps straight into the four dudes stood in their neat row. He thinks it might be some hoods trying to muscle in on his lucrative gig, so he does his ex-public school routine that works so well for repelling bullies and cads – gets high and mighty, pompous and lispy. They don't understand him but they start laughing.

When they stop laughing, the young guy asks him if he remembers anything about Jesus, who was a customer a couple of weeks ago but has since gone AWOL. He's *extremely* courteous, apologising for the rude laughter. Nobody gets half-suffocated with plastic bags or feels it necessary to shit themselves. But Dougie does not consider these gentlemen worthy of his time. He orders a gaggle of the bouncers who are loitering nearby to show these gents out. *Pleasure, boss.* As the bouncers push their chests out and pull out baseball bats, one of these dudes has the downright audacity and dreadful manners to pull out an Uzi submachine gun. He nonchalantly locks and loads; points it, quite casually, at the ceiling.

'Mister Nightingale, can we start this conversation again ... ?' asks the young pup, 'And could you remember your manners, *please*? Let me tell you ... In my country I am also a chief ... '

The Venezuelans chuckle at this witty repartee but Dougie is now shaking like a park bench alkie. All the bouncers instinctively raise their hands and look to Mister Nightingale. Dougie's no longer listening. He knows one thing for sure – he won't be turning up early for work again in a hurry ... And he's gonna shoot that fuckin life coach stone fuckin dead.

Suddenly Dougie, true to form, bolts – across the dance floor and out through the back door, like a fox with hounds up its arse. They can hear him clattering and tumbling down the back stairs. Dougie, according to the *Acting* Head of Security, is now, as we speak, incommunicado – not answering either mobile or landline. The speculation is that he's barricaded himself into his Marylebone apartment with an ounce of zip and his latest highly neurotic girlfriend.

Meanwhile, back at the hacienda, the Venezuelans work out that Dougie isn't their man; he's a drip who couldn't hold up a wet handkerchief, let alone a deranged mummyfucker like Jesus Zambrano. But they do spot, wandering out of their VIP enclosure to see what *all the fuckin noise* is about, members of Sonny's Uptown Crew. Their eyes meet across an empty dance floor. Each recognises the other crew as big trouble.

They're here because they've done their homework on Mister Sonny and know *instinctively* that Señor King, and his collection of ne'er-do-wells, are *somehow* involved ...

They also know they're outnumbered, and possibly outgunned. They know that slaughtering everybody gets you nowhere, so they slowly, keeping their smiling faces pointed to the front and their backs to where they're headed, slip out the back door. As they disappear the *Acting* Head of Security walks behind the bar, hits the brandy optic. Treats himself to a quadruple.

Now Sonny's puzzled. Who the fuck were they? Which fuckin lot?

Morty turns to Sonny, 'You gotta sort this out, now. Damage limitation, Sonny. It's got out of hand. You'll have no club left ...'

Sonny reluctantly gets his phone back out.

'Try and find out,' says Roy, 'without being obvious, who they were.'

'I fuckin know that!' snaps Sonny.

But Roy is relentless. 'This Santos is gonna want an answer about Jesus—'

'I'll tell him *you* killed him, will I, Roy? Send him round your house?'

'That's not funny, Sonny,' says Roy, starting to twitch.

Morty loads the pressure on, 'He needs to be satisfied that you know *nothing*.'

'Oh, right, it's that fuckin easy, is it?' says Sonny, getting sarcastic. 'Let's hope he's a bit backward, shall we?'

'Sonny, mate,' says Morty, rolling his eyes, 'let's cut the chat and make the call.'

'Pull the motor over, Roy!' screams Sonny. 'For fuck's sake, pull over!'

Roy spots a convenient turning, turns hard left off the dual carriageway, hits the gas, up a hill, does a right, pulls over and stops. Deep in pebbledash country.

'You wanna calm down, pal,' says Roy, screwing Sonny hard.

'Don't fuckin call me *pal*, okay?' snaps Sonny.

'Okay! Enough!' shouts Morty, occupying the space between the two front seats, 'Now, Sonny, don't be talking to this fella with an angry head.'

'Okay, Morty ... ' says Sonny.

'Been a long day ... ' says Mort, pacifying now. 'Make the call, put it on speakerphone, so everybody ... nice and quiet ... '

The phone is answered on the third ring.

'*Hola, buenas noches,*' says a sharp voice.

'Hello. Good evening. Am I speaking to Santos?'

Sonny, alas, is using his posh voice – trying to sound classy but sounding deranged.

'Yes, it is,' says Santos, dryly.

'This is Mister King. I received your message. Bit heavy-handed, your method of delivery, if I may say so, *and* I've just received a rather alarming telephone call from my club.'

'Oh, yes, Mister King? Tell me all about it ... *please*,' says a polite and curious voice with a South American accent.

'Yes,' continues Sonny, 'a little disappointing it was, to be honest ... '

Sonny trails off – Morty has gently tapped him on the forearm. Mort is shaking his head, placed an index finger over his lips. Sonny beckons him close; Morty talks in his ear.

'Hello? Are you still there, Mister King ... ?' says Santos. 'Is there a problem?'

'Don't mention the geezers at the club,' Morty whispers to Sonny. 'Just make the meet.'

'Are you there? Mister King ... ?' asks Santos.

'Yeah, yeah, I'm very fuckin here, pal,' says Sonny, returning to snappy voice, giving Morty a wink. 'We had a burst pipe. That's why I didn't ring you ... till now ... '

'I'm *awfully* glad you did, Mister King. I was beginning to wonder ... ' Santos spits *Mister King* like it's a lesson in patronising.

'I think the best thing to do, *Mister* Santos ... ' says Sonny, rising to the bait, 'This *is* Santos isn't it?'

'That's correct, sir,' says Santos firmly, 'Santos *de Lucia*.'

'The best thing to do, to clear up these misunderstandings, is for us to meet up at the Monarch Club, my club, tomorrow morning, about ten? Do you know—'

'I'm sure I can find it again,' snaps Santos derisively. 'Thank you for getting back to me, *Mister* King.'

'You've been there before?' asks Sonny.

'A few days since, but I believe you were out of the country, on business.'

Mort was right – it wasn't this guy who was in the Monarch earlier.

'I'm not sure I can help you, sir,' says Sonny, warming up. 'I believe this is something—'

Santos interrupts, blunt as a club. 'Let's talk in the a.m., Mister King ... Thank you for your *precious* time,' he adds patronisingly.

There's a click from the other end; the line is dead. Sonny looks at his phone murderously, like he's about to crush it. 'Let's make one,' he says to Roy, then to nobody in particular, more to himself, 'got a feeling I ain't gonna like this Santos cunt.'

Roy starts the engine.

'It wasn't this Santos at your club earlier,' says Morty. 'There *are* two firms ... '

Nobody says anything. We don't move. 'Now, Roy,' Sonny says at last, 'are we gonna make a move, or are we gonna sit here like cunts all night?'

Roy pulls away, slow-burn twitch building. We hit the dual carriageway again. Sonny gazes out the window. I can hear him

breathing heavy through his nostrils. We get two minutes up the
road. Suddenly Sonny slaps his hand down hard on the dashboard.

'That cunt Jesus! Dead or alive, he's a jinx!'

Sonny's found himself in that horrible place of having nobody
to blame for his predicament but himself. It was meant to be easy;
it's a mess. He's wishing he could just blame the dead cunt.

CHAPTER TWENTY-THREE

SONNY - SANTOS - SANTOS - SONNY

I hardly get any sleep anymore. This speculation business is a killer. Tossing and turning, eyes tightly shut but electric under the eyelids, imagination chugg-chugg-chugging, flying off in a dozen different directions, till you're telling your own head to *shut the fuck up!*

Last night I fell asleep in an armchair, for ten minutes, with the transcript on my chest, so I got up and went to bed. That's when all the speculation business *really* started.

Not being able to sleep, I got the transcript out yet again. It's a comically bad translation, pages missing or untouched, leaving chunks of gibberish where they drop into dialect. It confused me. I flicked through to see if I could find anyone called Santos. Everyone seemed to have either codes names or pseudonyms. I was looking for any indication of what could be on the other file, the one that, hopefully, Smiler was prising open.

Seems there's an internecine struggle within the Zambrano Clan – brothers and uncles falling out. It's getting in the way of the serious shit – industrial-scale drug trafficking, corrupting high-level officials and making money. There's a patchy recording of a family council, hosted by Papa Victor, and beginning with a tirade against *El Niño del Diablo* – his lack of morals and his effortless ability to *commit sin without conscience* – by his *own father*. Another uncle expresses disgust at the *conducta* of Jesus – *Me da asco su conducta!* I am disgusted by his behaviour! He argues they must sacrifice Jesus to save the family. Jesus is the tipping point for men who have lived immersed in criminality all their lives. After a vote the patriarchs refuse permission to *erase the disgrace.*

In another transcript, back in the study, Miguel is haranguing his father – *Talk to them; get them to deal with their envy, but we need to keep this project from them. They are nothing to me! Nothing!* Miguel tells Papa – *The Plan and Jenna are our*

*salvation ... Do you understand what I'm trying to do? We must
be bold! Your grandchildren will be royalty! Never talk to me of
sacrifice, don't dare! This is a vision, Papa. I love this country but
it's wayward!*

Enough to get a chap curious, so this morning I overslept –
speculation mixed with brandy.

There's a lot of things I'd rather be doing right now than
chasing across town and sitting down with this Santos, but Sonny
made it clear that if we wanted to be in at the *bust-up* we had to
provide immoral support. Sonny has told Santos to come by the
club at ten. I woke up at nine. Sonny told me to meet him there at
quarter past *to sort the gaff out* ... I had a shower and slipped the
porter a twenty to jump the cab queue. I hate to give Sonny reason
to moan.

In the cab, the driver had talk radio on – *you may experience
delays.* Lecture from driver – *horse and carts were quicker.*

We pull up outside the Monarch. I pay the driver, slip through
the back exit, up the stairs, through the double doors at the top and
out into the club. My host greets me.

'Where the fuck you been?' says Sonny, never missing an
opportunity. 'This ain't a fuckabout, a bitta community service.'

Instinct tells me that Sonny's only looking for respite from
Roy's over-elaborate briefing. Roy – who wasn't supposed to be
here – is stood in front of Sonny with his index finger in mid-air
– like someone's pressed the pause button. Sonny is sat, *seemingly*
relaxed, in a booth in the VIP surrounded by cups of takeaway
coffee and half-eaten bacon sandwiches. Angled frosted mirrors
and lashing of crimson velvet enhance the regal themes that run
throughout the recently refurbished Monarch, but the gaff stinks
of snout, disinfectant and stale booze.

Morty sits next to Sonny like he hasn't got a care in the world,
flicking through newspapers. Ominously, cleaning gear and vacuum cleaners have been abandoned, in mid-sweep or wipe, no doubt
after the cleaners received a hollered order from Mister Sonny to
vacate – *fuck off for an hour! Go to the park! Comprehendi?*

Sonny suddenly looks at Roy like he's just noticed him,
puzzled by Roy's finger pointing into space. 'What was you
saying, Roy? Before this one turned up, fuckin late ... '

The pause button is released. 'Listen, Sonny,' says Roy, 'it's gonna be alright. When you're talking to this Santos guy, keep looking straight ahead. If yer lying you'll look off up into the corners of the room. If he asks ya something, pick a spot between his eyes and zero in on it, don't lift yer hands to cover yer face or mouth, that's body language for lying like fuck – deceit, basically.'

'Okay, I get it,' nods Sonny.

'He'll be on it straight away, know you're lying, but he won't *know* how he knows, but he will, it's *instinctive*, so relax, convince *yourself* that you're telling the truth. Consider yourself lucky that you ain't pumped full of sodium pentothal, then we'd be *really* fucked.' Sonny is massaging his temples. 'Maybe try and sow the seeds of doubt, like a decoy, a parallel theory, to where Jesus may have got to—'

'Roy ... ' Sonny interrupts, head in his hands, 'could you *please* stop talking?'

Roy looks offended. Morty looks over his newspaper, takes up the slack. 'Your job, Sonny,' says Mort, 'is to convince them that we know nothing, okay? Don't get flash. And *don't* let it get personal.'

Sonny peels the top off a coffee – it looks like brake fluid – just as his phone, lying on the table, rings twice then stops. 'Showtime,' he says. 'Royski, you need to disappear, son.'

Roy gives Sonny a wounded look and strolls, like a defiant kid, behind some drapes.

'You,' Sonny says to me, 'sit down next to Mort.'

We sit in silence. A minute later one of Sonny's crew appears at the door. Behind him, four guys, Venezuelans, stroll in. They all look very smart, Flavio was right. Three of them are suited and booted like body builders dressed for a wedding. The remaining one – the guv'nor, Mister Santos de Lucia, I assume – is doing a South American Englishman number; light tweeds, gingham shirt, tartan necktie and heavy brogues. He's a couple of years either side of forty, typical Latino, greased-back hair, so the attire looks at odds ... He's beefy rather than muscular and has the pinched nose of someone permanently encountering an unpleasant smell. Santos looks around, eyes adjusting to the light, assessing his surroundings.

'Oh, good, you found us okay,' shouts Sonny across the club. 'Please, come in.'

Santos and his three *amigos* walk over.

'Please, sit down,' says Sonny, offering them a seat in the booth.

'We'd prefer to stand, if it's all the same to you,' replies Santos on their behalf.

'Whatever,' says Sonny. Neither moves to shake hands. 'Can I get you something to eat?' asks Sonny, nodding at the debris of breakfast.

'We've eaten already, Mister King,' says the Santos fella dryly.

Santos looks towards me and Morty as if to say *who are these two? Don't look like bodyguards, lounging around* ... Sonny nods at us. 'Couple of associates, hope you don't mind.' Santos shrugs. He does mind but isn't gonna make it an issue.

'My counsellor,' Sonny says, nodding towards Morty, 'and *his* counsellor,' he says, nodding at me. 'You wanted to ask a few questions? I hope I don't need a lawyer.' Sonny laughs but Santos doesn't.

'That will not be necessary, my friend,' he says, none too friendly.

'I don't know why,' says Sonny, 'you're so insistent that I meet with you ... ' Santos goes to interrupt, 'But here we are, Santos, so fire away, sir, be my guest, ask me anything ... '

'Do you mind if my associate has a look round?' asks Santos.

'Well, I *do* actually ... ' says Sonny, leaning forward, lighting a cigarette. 'What do you think you're gonna find?'

'One never knows, does one?' says Santos, like he was dropping a killer line.

'Whatever it is, buddy,' says Sonny, impatiently, 'hurry up and find it cos I've got places to go, people to see.'

Santos nods to one of the three *amigos*, then points at the area around us. I think Santos de Lucia fancies himself as a bit of a strategist. Sonny watches carefully as the guy takes off and has a cursory look behind the curtain that our Roy just disappeared behind. After walking the length of the bar, nutting into a few booths, and not finding anything, he nods back to Santos. Sonny watches all this. 'You a happy boy, now?' he asks Santos. Santos nods.

'I hope you don't mind but ... ' says Sonny. He winks at the firm member stood by the stairs who approaches Santos and the *amigos* with a handheld metal detector – *please, raise your arms.* He runs it over them, finishing with Santos, who appears to be mightily indignant. The crew member nods to Sonny then disappears.

'So, tell me, firstly, who are you?' asks Sonny, 'And, secondly, what's all this fuss about?'

'Who I am is not the issue,' says Santos arrogantly. 'But to answer your second question, we're making inquires into the disappearance of Jesus Zambrano—'

Sonny interrupts him immediately, holds up his hand, 'I don't wish to be rude, pal, but you're barking up the wrong tree.'

'Are you deliberately trying to confuse me, Mister King,' says Santos, 'with your use of colloquial English?'

'Hang on,' says Sonny bluntly. 'What's *colloquial*?'

'Would you speak correct Queen's English, Mister King?' says Santos, rolling his eyes.

'I think you're being fuckin rude now,' says Sonny, genuinely angry, 'telling *me* how to talk in my own club.'

'Your club?' asks Santos, like he's scored a point.

'I'm a sleeping partner,' says Sonny. 'It's an investment.'

'A plaything, perhaps, Mister King?' asks Santos.

Sonny takes a breath before continuing, 'Look, I don't know what's happened between you and this Jesus geezer but I just own this club. If you have a beef with Jesus, it's none of my business, same as if Jesus came to me about you ... Jesus will turn up, these guys always do. I know nothing about where he went after leaving here.' He holds a hand over his heart, 'I swear on the lives of my children ... '

'In ancient Rome ... ' says Santos, checking his manicure, 'to *testify* would mean to swear an oath on your testicles.'

'Oh, yeah ... ?' enquires Sonny. 'And if you got caught out lying?'

'Well, Mister King, you work it out.'

'Ouch!' says Sonny, laughing.

'Now,' says Santos, 'you were telling me about Jesus.'

'Was I?' says Sonny with a shrug. 'There's not much to tell.

Try being here at three in the morning when we chuck out. It's chaos, everyone outta their nut, shitfaced. Jesus meets a girl; they end up moving on to somewhere else. They go home with a few grams of malarkey, turn the phones off. Modern romance.'

Santos can't work out if he's having the piss taken outta him. Sonny's getting hotted-up, his liar's imagination kicking in ... He's thinking – *this is going well, better than expected* ...

Sonny continues, moving forward in his seat. 'Maybe yer man Jesus *really* lucked out, got lucky. Might be on a private jet, off to somewhere *real cool*, Ibiza or Monte Carlo, *two* girls in the back cabin! And he's got them *performing* ... for his pleasure. You know *exactly* what I mean. I can tell you do.'

Morty is sitting up, taking notice now. Santos *does* understand, but only just – he's an *hombre del mundo*. But Sonny's one-man show is confusing *Los Amigos*. Sonny gives Santos a man-to-man wink. 'Maybe your buddy Jesus has got the Isley Brothers playing on the sound system.' Sonny starts singing *Who's That Lady*. 'And Jesus is *swaying* to the music, watching the girl-on-girl go down. You know the score?' Now Sonny's buzzing on his imaginary scenario. 'You know something? I'm jealous. When did your friend go missing?'

'Eleven days since!' snaps Santos, 'I told you!'

'No, you didn't, but *if* you did, tell me again,' says Sonny, taken aback. 'And watch your manners. I'm helping you out here. If I wasn't such a nice guy, I'd be telling you, and yer band ... ' he nods at the three *amigos*, 'to fuck off.'

Santos has hatred in his eyes; he'd really like to go to town on Sonny. Sonny spots this – *this could go either way*. He puts his hands up in mock surrender.

'Okay, let's start again,' Sonny says, 'I'm *really* sorry if I've offended you. I came here today to help. I think your friend will turn up but in the meantime ... ' Sonny leans back, arms across the booth, 'if you fancy a night out – on the house – let me know.'

Santos seems unimpressed, even insulted, with Sonny's offer. 'Jesus was a regular here, then he disappeared.'

'What is your point exactly, Santos?' Sonny pulls a bemused face. 'Maybe he was mugged. London's getting dangerous. A lot of people don't feel safe walking the streets. I wish I could help but we're running a nightclub, not an orphanage. I don't know where he went after he left the club. People get into all sorts of mischief ...'

'You *personally* saw Jesus in your club?' asks Santos, dryly.

'Yes. Briefly. Here, in the VIP.'

'And was Jesus having a good time?'

'Was like a paedophile at a funfair,' Sonny replies real droll, then bursts out laughing. Sonny's in danger of fuckin this up. Santos ain't laughing. He steps forward, zeroes in on Sonny.

'What do you know about other Venezuelan gentlemen inquiring about Jesus?' he asks.

'Only what people tell me ... like the kid you scared half to death,' says Sonny, locking on, eyeball-to-eyeball. 'That was unnecessary. You're a guest in this country ... ' Santos won't break eye contact but Sonny, remembering his brief, lights another cigarette. He takes a long drag. 'What do *you* think happened to your friend Jesus?' he asks innocently.

'We believe he was kidnapped.'

'Kidnapped! In London? It's not a very London thing, kidnapping. Where in London?'

'Outside his hotel, in a trick taxi cab.'

'So why are you *here*, quizzing me?' asks Sonny. 'Why don't you call the police?'

Masterful, Sonny. Santos looks like he wants to spit out a nasty taste.

'Has anyone else come here,' he asks instead, 'to your club, to enquire about Jesus?'

'Maybe,' says Sonny with a big shrug, 'I ain't here every night. You mean these *other* Venezuelan gentlemen?'

Santos nods, knows he has to give a little to get a little. Sonny, as nonchalant as his nature will allow, asks, 'Why, are these guys friends of yours?'

'Acquaintances,' Santos replies wryly, then aping Sonny, 'they're *fuckin* acquaintances.'

Sonny don't have time to be angry because Santos then turns to his companions and adds sarcastically, '*Amigos ausentes.*' Absent friends. And then, full of contempt, '*Los mercenarios de Miguel.*' Miguel's mercenaries. 'Miguel's Coca Cola cowboys,' sneers Santos. No translation necessary.

His *amigos* laugh at Santos' wee jest. Sonny pretends to be more confused that he is, shaking his head, looking from Santos to his three pals, to me, to Mort.

'And Jesus Zambrano,' asks Sonny innocently, genuinely curious, 'is he just a friend, or someone you work with? You're *obviously* concerned ... '

'Jesus?' says Santos with a sardonic smile, half over his shoulder, '*Es una mierda ... una mierda difunta debo suponer.*' Jesus is a piece of shit ... a dead piece of shit, we can assume. We all look confused while Santos' crew laugh.

'Sorry?' says Sonny, 'I didn't comprehendo – no understando la Spanish.'

'I'm sorry too,' says Santos with a snide wink at Sonny. 'My turn to apologise.'

'I hope you're not making fun of us, gentlemen,' says Sonny. 'That would be rude.'

'Sorry, Mister King, it's just a joke at the expense of an absent friend.'

Santos appears to have tickled himself. But what they seem to be saying is that they don't *really* give a fuck. And they know Jesus is dead. But how? He would not have abandoned his mission unless he was dead? It strikes me that this lot are very blasé about their fallen comrade. They're not exactly grief-stricken and weeping; in fact, Santos is still grinning.

'I have a proposition for you, Mister King,' he says at last.

'Oh, good,' says Sonny, rubbing his hands, sensing the beginning of the end of the Q. and A., 'we all like a proposition. Fire away, Mister Santos.'

'I will give you one million dollars ... today, cash, after one hour's notice ... ' says Santos, like a melodramatic game show host, holding up his index finger. 'And all I want ... in return ... ' he's smiling at Sonny totally insincerely, 'is that piece of computer equipment that Zambrano was travelling with ... or information as to where I might find it.'

Sonny looks quite taken aback, silenced for once. Was expecting hostility.

Santos continues his pitch. 'If cash is a problem, I can authorise the funds to be transferred into an account anywhere. I assume you have offshore accounts, being in the *precarious* business you're in. And I don't mean your nocturnal diversion ... ' Santos gives a regal wave, indicating the Monarch. 'The distraction that every successful Englishman must have ... '

Mister de Lucia is marking Mister King's card that he knows what he gets up to when he isn't lording it in the VIP area. Sonny pulls a quizzical expression, eyes narrowing. He turns to Mister Mortimer, shrugs, and says silently *a million dollars*. Then turns to me, and does the same, *one million dollars* ...

'I have,' Santos announces, 'absolutely no concern for how you came by the equipment or whether Jesus Zambrano is alive or dead ... '

There's a long pause while Sonny appears to thinking hard. Sonny might go for the bait but I know, *ipso facto*, that once these Venezuelans know that we definitely know the whereabouts of that memory stick we'd be signing our own death warrants. They'll torture us till they get what they want, because under all of Santos' urbane delivery there's a strong odour of condescension and contempt. He wouldn't part with ten bucks if he could get the same results by sending the Three *Amigos* to work. He thinks Sonny is a *pedazo de mierda*.

And all the time I've got the translation and the full set of photos tucked in my inside pocket. I've got a sneaky that if they knew, there'd be carnage; they wouldn't stop until they'd killed everyone who was *contaminated*, and the gadget was returned to South America.

And Santos hovers and watches, like a snake. His eyes flick from Sonny to Morty, to me, back to Sonny, looking for a clue.

'A million dollars?' asks Sonny. 'Nice ... Best offer I've had today.'

Sonny steps forward with his hand out, like he's going to shake Santos' hand, but instead he slaps Santos on the shoulder and bursts out laughing. It unnerves Santos.

'I would *dearly* love to take your money,' says Sonny. 'Fuck me, would I? A million dollars for a two-bob gadget!' Sonny turns to me and Morty, still laughing. 'You hear that? A million fuckin dollars! Let's start looking! Right now!'

'I do not like to be laughed at, Mister King,' says Santos, leaking indignity.

'Who fuckin does, pal?' snaps Sonny, not laughing, dead serious.

'Thank you for your *precious time*, Mister King,' says Santos, with a click of the heels. Then after a nod from Santos, he and the Three *Amigos* file out without a sound.

Sonny shouts after them, grinning like a mad thing, 'But, hey, Santos, I'm gonna keep my ear to the ground. I've got yer number! Maybe claim the reward!' And then an afterthought, 'Oh, yeah, I hope you find your *acquaintance, Mister Jesus!*'

'That went well,' Morty says dryly to me.

Well played, Sonny. I don't think they believed you. A smidgen more sympathy and offers of assistance might have taken the day. The second Santos is off the premises, Sonny switches. He marches over to me, waving his finger under my nose.

'I'm putting you in charge, okay?' he says with an insane look. 'Get Smiler working day and night! A million? As an opening punt! What do they think I am? Some pikey cunt?'

Sonny kicks a chair. It tumbles across the floor. Then he begins raging, 'I'll bury him, the slimy cunt! I'll put him down the hole with his bum chum! Think I've never seen a million?'

It got personal. We couldn't give them back their memory stick even if we wanted to, not if we wanted to stay alive. It's funny how you can take an intense dislike to someone. For once me and Sonny agree. Sonny *was* being diplomatic – for Sonny. He kept his temper in check; otherwise Santos and his pals could have ended up getting reunited with Jesus.

Roy casually appears, Sunday stroll style, trailing three cold-eyed soldiers. He's calmly pointing his Skorpion submachine gun at the ceiling, its ugly silencer bigger than the weapon. Never be in the same room as a murder weapon. Roy and his pals begin to peel away handguns that had been taped under the tables – unbeknown to me – *in case of grief*. They were prepared for a battle. Is there a 'borrowed' freezer lorry driving in circles, around Mayfair, waiting for a call? Roy's contingency plan in case it all went bandaloo?

'Thought you played it well,' Roy tells Sonny.

'Cheers, Roy ... ' says Sonny, acknowledging his praise. 'Means a lot ... '

What's Santos next move? Basically he's got a million choices – go to war, serve everybody, kidnap someone, send body parts to the Monarch, start looking for Sonny's nonexistent kids to use as hostages, indulge in proxy torture, inflict terror on Sonny's nearest and dearest but risk cutting off the only existing, and realistic, chance of getting the memory stick back.

Q. What would I do?

A. First thing – I'd find out who the big, black fella was. And who the mute observer was – the consigliere's counsellor, indeed – sitting there, smug, wrapped in his raincoat, saying nothing, only moving his eyes backwards and forwards, like he was watching ping-pong.

CHAPTER TWENTY-FOUR

SOME GOOD NEWS ...

'What's stopping us giving them a snide memory stick?' says
Sonny, pacing.

'Forget about giving them *any* memory stick, Sonny,' says
Morty. 'You'll get a bullet in the nut.'

'Yer man, Santos,' says Sonny, 'has just told us what it's
worth.'

'Yeah, a lot more than one mill,' says Mort. 'For all his airs,
he's a schnorrer.'

'What do you think, Roy?' says Sonny, looking for an ally.

Roy is sweeping the VIP area for *invisible micro-bugs*. 'I
think ... ' Roy says, preoccupied, 'we let Smiler crack on.'

Roy – *no lie-in for him* – has got himself up and out early to
the spy equipment store, buying countersurveillance kit using
counterfeit credentials. He now has an eavesdropping device to
monitor phone calls within a fifty-yard radius, meaning he can
listen in to Santos' calls – if he can find him. He issues me and
Mort with a device designed to detect minute surveillance devices.
They can make bugs the *size of a pinhead*, Roy tells us.

I get Roy's gents to accompany me to the tube, do my habitual
routine of jumping about underground, then head out to
Shepherd's Bush. My charge, Smiler, has been relocated.
Meanwhile Sonny is trying to find *Miguel's Coca Cola Cowboys*,
the firm who *did* turn up at the Monarch last night. Roy's firm are
trying, without much success, to follow Santos on his fruitless
hunt for Jesus. And Morty has gone to parlay with Bridget
Granger.

Roy's Allocated Code Name for Smiler? *Grimboat One*. My
ACN? – *The Raincoat*. I need to be away from Sonny and Royski;
forty-eight hours hanging with the Weird Sisters, letting their
paranoia seep into my bones, has got me twitchier than I should be.

I don't mind being detailed to look after Smiler – Smiler I can deal with. I find him in a faceless building on an Acton industrial estate. I have a vague recollection of being in this neck of the woods – I was getting rid of a shooter and some clothing – but I can't for the life of me remember why. Outside the building I ring Smiler's phone. One of Sonny's firm appears and lets me into the building, checking the street as he does. It turns out that Smiler's got a couple of geezers effectively keeping him under house arrest. Sonny doesn't want him fuckin off with the memory stick and he's under orders not to start fiddling about with the data – just *get it decrypted*.

Sonny's guy leads me up the stairs, to the second floor and into a large, empty office. The premises used to be a call centre; there's power points and telephone plugs everywhere. The low ceiling gives the room a claustrophobic effect but luckily there's English air conditioning – broken windows. Bedding is rolled up in the corner along with a camp bed. There's a kitchen area with tea-making facilities and a brand new microwave. It's basic indoor camping but Smiler doesn't appear to mind; he's probing on the New Frontier of this computer lark, deep in uncharted wilderness.

Smiler salutes when he sees me, appears happy that I'm on my Jack, without the dynamic duo. He leads me into a room in the far corner where his laboratory is set up. Smiler's new server is a beast – humming and blinking, the size of a door, *the firepower of a million home computers* and fans running to keep it cool. *You could run a city with that*. It's plumbed in, ready for action but Smiler still has rows of laptops with leads running away to junction boxes then into the mighty server. There's a smell of electronic equipment burning in, a comforting bouquet of warm copper connection.

'I see you've made the place your own ... ' I tell Smiler. 'Done a bit of decorating.'

'It's a lonely life, comrade,' giggles Smiler, with a pervy leer, 'being here on me own.'

Above his work space Smiler has stuck onto an *employee of the week* noticeboard printouts of the couple in the Florida hotel room, enough to make an impressive collage – some photos clipped then blown up so big that they've pixellated into arty porn or pornographic art. A bit Warhol. He's opted for multiple, identical shots of the fit woman with half an erect penis in her mouth.

'That, Smiler ... ' I say, pointing up, 'ain't fuckin right.'

Smiler chuckles then points out, like a proud father, his number one computer. Fragments – small random blocks of pixels – of something are beginning to appear, like a microscopic jigsaw puzzle slowly taking shape. Smiler punches some keys and the pixels become so magnified they blur. He zooms in on an indecipherable letterhead.

'It's definitely a file-sharing program ... ' says Smiler, impressed. 'Checking through websites, downloading what it needs, and using it to decipher the information on the stick.'

'Is that how it's meant to work?' I ask.

'To be honest ... I don't know.' He shakes his head. 'There's obviously a key to this – a site that operates as a combination lock.'

'How long till we get something worthwhile?'

'I can't say it's *ever* going to work,' shrugs Smiler.

'You sure this is the solution?' I ask.

'If you've got a better one,' says Smiler, 'let me know.'

'So, what shall I tell Sonny?'

'As little as poss,' he replies.

I sit him down with a cup of strong diesel and a few chocolate digestives – *I'll make sure you get paid, Smiler. Trust me. No harm will come to you ... We are allies, you and me.*

Flavio telling Sonny that the Venezuelans wanted Jesus' phone records got me thinking. I got Smiler to obtain the list of calls made, *or received*, by him. Smiler reckons hacking into a hotel mainframe is as easy as a gentleman jewel thief breaking into a garden shed.

Smiler gets to work – a little man-management works wonders. He hacks into an online reverse directory using a restricted code and then wires a Spanish translation program in, then some billing software. All in about a minute. He nods at more translated transcripts piled in an in-tray. I sit down on an old armchair to read but doze off with the sun on my face.

Smiler's red-hot laser printer wakes me up. I look at my watch.

I've been asleep for fifteen minutes. Smiler has left a stack of new paperwork. I find phone numbers and the identity of the destination ... notes in Smiler's spidery writing ... subscribers ... calls made to numbers he's identified as disposable mobile phones ... airport lounge payphones ... bars and private homes in Miami and Caracas ... airlines and embassies ... the Venezuelan embassy in Paris ... the ambassador or chargé d'affaires in Haiti ... calls to remote islands in the Carib ... timings in EST and GMT ... Jesus' old phone bills ... Smiler's scrawled note ... *subscriber allocated new number* red ringed ... *new number restricted*! Smiler is alight, eyes like a mad scientist.

'Would you say you were obsessive, Smiler?' I ask.

'About certain things, yes,' he says.

Smiler beckons me over; 'Have a look at this.' I go over to his monitor. He taps the screen with his chewed-up biro. 'Jesus calls a payphone in Heathrow Airport arrivals lounge at exactly nineteen minutes past eight in the morning. He talks for twenty-seven minutes, ends the call ... Then, *one minute later*, he signs off the hotel bill, leaves the Cosmo ... ' Smiler shrugs. 'Maybe he left to meet someone at Heathrow?'

I nod, but knowing Jesus' modus operandi it's more likely he thought it would be hilarious to have someone, maybe Santos, meet him at the Cosmopolitan at the exact moment the Eurostar train – departing London, Waterloo, bound for Paris – was going underground, entering the Channel Tunnel, at Ashford, Kent, not far from where he's buried. Jesus was meant to be having the champagne breakfast when Twitchy was abducting him.

One number leaps out of the printout because it's been called repeatedly. The calls are always short, between ten and fifteen seconds – in batches, at three or four in the morning London time, BST, night after night. Smiler sits me down.

'Let me show you something ... ' Smiler points at the first call, connected for only five seconds. 'That is someone receiving a call, accepting it, and straight away pushing the red button to reject it after answering to see who it is. They don't wanna talk to the caller.'

Smiler points with his ballpoint at the second call in the batch. It's comparatively long – one minute, thirty seconds. 'The second one is the caller ringing again and leaving a *long* message – the maximum length you can leave.'

I nod, taking in Smiler's analysis. 'And the rest, the others, are the caller ringing *again and again* and the person they've called pushing the reject button ... *or* they've turned off the phone so they *can't* leave a message.'

'You know that just by looking?'

'You never been in love?' asks Smiler.

'We talking being in love or stalking?'

'Never had yer heart broken?' asks Smiler.

'So tell me, Romeo, who's getting all the calls from Jesus? Who is the object of his desire?'

'A party by the name of Jenna Zambrano,' says Smiler, real smug.

'Jenna Zambrano ... ? Like on the recordings?'

Smiler gently nods; the cat that got the canary.

'*And*, I bet you a pound to a paper hat,' says Smiler, pointing up towards his montage, 'that *she* is Jenna Zambrano, the bird Jesus was ringing from the Cosmo. You wanna bet?'

Smiler starts hunting around on his messy desk under piles of papers and food wrappers, getting impatient. He finds what he's looking for – Sonny's three gee – wrapped in an elastic band.

'Here,' he says, waving the money under my nose, 'I'll bet you three grand ... that if you ring that number ... ' he taps the phone bill with his pen, '*she* ... ' he points up at his collage, 'answers. Three grand, okay? You on?'

'*You* ring it, Smiler,' I say. 'Tell her about your artistic tribute.'

'See, I don't give a monkey's, either way,' shrugs Smiler unconvincingly.

'How can you be so certain Jesus was ringing pin-up girl?'

'It's a hunch,' says Smiler. 'We having a flutter, or what? I'll dial the number for ya. You'll then know that the bird in the photos was the same one that was rung a million times by this Jesus kid.'

'You know what I think? You wanna get some proxy thrill by getting me to ring her.'

'We on or what?' he asks, dead droll.

'It's eight in the morning on the East Coast. She'll still be asleep.'

'Exactly!' says Smiler, clicking his fingers, like it's a *fait accompli*, 'She'll be unawares! You speak the lingo, a drop of the old Spanish. Chat her up a bit ... '

'So what are you suggesting?' I ask. 'I ring her up and do *what* exactly?'

'Establish my theory about the missing dude ringing this bird from the Cosmopolitan Hotel. I ring the number – she, Jenna, answers, and we're in business. If it ain't her, you take the money ... '

'Could be *any* woman answering ... don't necessarily mean it's this Jenna woman.'

'No, no,' he says. 'You say "good morning, Jenna" – in Spanish of course – and if she says, "you've got the wrong number, no Jenna here," you win. But if she says ... ' Smiler adopts a beyond-fuckin-bizarre sexy accent, '"*Hiya, Jenna here. Who's that?*" I win. You understand the wager?'

It's all the more perverse because while Smiler's talking I'm absent-mindedly studying his homemade collage.

'Look,' says Smiler, 'if it's being traced you're worried about, I can fix it so she won't know what *continent* you're on.'

Smiler is tapping digits – international exit and entry codes – into his cell phone while he clutches his biro, like a pirate's cutlass, between his teeth. He hits the speakerphone button. It begins to ring – a flat American tone. Smiler hands me the receiver. A woman – young, sleepy, yawning, stretching, still in bed – answers. This is gonna be easy.

'*Hola*,' she says. '*Quién es? Eres tú, Miguel? Quién es?*'

Hello. Who's that? Is that you, Miguel? Who is this?

'*Hablo con Jenna?*' I say, as innocently as I can, '*Jenna Zambrano?*'

Is that Jenna – Jenna Zambrano?

'*De qué se trata? Qué hora es?*'

What's this about? What time is it? She suddenly gets a bit angry, '*Mierda*,' – like she's just realised the time.

'*Estoy tratando de rastrear un huésped que estuvo en nuestro hotel,*' I say, '*dejó algunas cosas sin pagar.*'

I'm trying to trace a guest who was staying at our hotel – they left without paying for certain items.

'*Oh, sí, quién podría ser entonces esté?*' she says, the first bit of suspicion entering her voice.

Oh, yes, who would that be then?

I'm about to answer when she asks, '*Preferiría hablar Inglés si no hay inconveniente?*'

I would prefer to speak English – is that acceptable?

'Are you English?' she asks.

'Yes,' I say.

'I thought it was an English accent,' she says. 'Am I right?'

'Yes,' I say, a knot tightening in my stomach.

'Is this Jenna Zambrano?' I ask.

'Where did you say you were calling from?' she asks, swerving the question.

'The Cosmopolitan Hotel, London.'

'Be easy enough to check,' she says inoffensively, with a laugh. 'What did you say your name was?'

'Call her Jenna,' whispers Smiler. I say nothing but now she's laughing, catching on fast.

'I don't think you're from the Cosmopolitan Hotel at all,' she says, 'oh, but what a nice English accent – a London one I'd go as far as to say.' She does a very good impression of a swell's accent, '*I had to go home ... I ran out of Cologne.*' I laugh but I say nothing. 'You think that's funny, don't you?' she says, 'I can hear you laughing ... ' She's keeping me on the phone – trying to trace, or tape, the call. 'But, you know what? ... Are you still there?' she asks.

'Yeah,' I reply.

'I think you've spent time in the Caribbean – just a hunch – but you're *bloody blue collar*. What's your name?' she asks double-quick, trying to catch me out. She does her posh accent again, '*What's the matter? Is it raining cats and dogs in London?*' She returns to her normal voice, 'If you're not going to tell me, I'll call you Mister English ... after where you're from.'

'If ya like,' I say, then regret it. This is dangerous – charged.

I hear the static and echo off the satellite. I could finish the call, hit the red but ...

'What is it with you English guys?' she says, 'You can *look* at all the pretty girls but you just can't bring yourself to talk to us, can you? You going to tell me your real name?' she waits a few seconds. 'Give me a name, any name ... '

Smiler is drawing his finger across his throat. 'Kill it,' he hisses. 'You mad?'

'I think this was a mistake,' I say, 'I better be off.'

I go to hit the red when she says, 'I thought you'd rung to claim your bounty.'

'Bounty?'

'Oh, yes,' she says, but her voice has dropped an octave, deep and sexy, 'don't play the innocent, Mister English. The reward. Shame to let it go to waste ... ' She's purring. It should sound ridiculous but it's incredibly seductive. 'We could blow it together, in a big puff of smoke ... Good times, Mister English ... '

'What's the reward for, Jenna?'

She laughs. 'Come on, English, it's too early to get smart. Is it morning where you are? Where are you? London?'

'Could be for a couple of things, Jenna, who knows?' I say.

'Let me get this straight ... Jesus Zambrano was last reported in London and now I've got a Londoner, with a dash of Americano, who speaks a *poco español* ringing me from an untraceable line at eight in the morning, like he's trying to catch me cold. And now he's acting the innocent ... ' She waits again. Then, to provoke me, 'or real fucking dumb ... '

I say nothing. A hint of menace enters her voice, 'Mister English, you've gone all quiet, but will you answer one question for me?'

'Maybe.' I cringe like a teenager.

'Is Jesus Zambrano alive or dead?' she asks, extremely seriously.

She waits patiently; I can hear her breathing. Five long seconds tick by ...

'That's not an answer ... ' she says. 'You won't be hard to find. Now if you're not going to talk to me ... ' She laughs; a mixture of sexy and sinister. '*Adios.*' The line goes dead.

I hand the phone to Smiler. I realise I've fucked up and I've got a tug in my pants.

'I'll have to owe you that three grand, Smiler, I ain't got it on me right now.'

'It's not a problem ... ' he replies, awkwardly holding the

phone, like's it's evidence. 'Don't worry about it, actually ...
Forget it ... '

We sit in silence for a half minute – pondering, feeling naïve,
the worst possible crime around here.

'Smiler, you used to get hold of those quality passports.'

'Yeah?' he says, rolling his chair over to me.

'Can you still get them?' I ask.

'Should think so,' says Smiler with one eye on Sonny's sentry.
'Do you need one?'

I nod.

'I'd need to make a call, and I'll need a photo,' says Smiler.
'Maybe I can get a price on two,' he adds.

'I won't need two,' I say.

'No, but I might need one.'

I get up to leave, suppress the urge to clip Smiler round the ear,
and collect the next instalment from the in-tray. I stop at the door.

'Smiler, next time you have a hunch ... Do us both a favour –
keep it to yourself.'

CHAPTER TWENTY-FIVE

AND SOME BAD NEWS ...

I get to have a proper read of the next instalment on the rattler to Liverpool Street. This one is as crisp and clear as the daylight. The extended Zambrano Clan is split over the proposed marriage of convenience of Jenna Zambrano to the idiot son of a high-ranking Brigadier General in the Venezuelan army. Everyone has political ambitions for junior; he's being groomed for the senate. This arrangement would be a serious coup for the family, making them invincible, giving them a large degree of respectability both in Venezuela and abroad. Politically they would be untouchable. With the vast amounts of money the Zambrano family have acquired, together with the apparent respectability of the General's family – who can trace their lineage back to Spain – it would launch them into orbit. They could still be flying their gear around on military aircraft, using diplomatic channels, but they wouldn't have to worry about falling foul of the authorities. They would *be* the authorities. In South America they put the poor thief in prison and make the rich thief El Presidente.

It's the same the world over – crims ultimately want respectability. A lot depends on the marriage; they can't afford any scandal. Papa Victor is canvassing opinions. And Miguel totally disregarding them. Jesus must have been planning to use the photos to blackmail Jenna's family. Are Santos and his firm in London to retrieve the memory stick for Miguel? Trying to retrieve the bone for their master?

The next few pages answer the question – Miguel and Santos are adversaries, although Santos is not in the same arena. There are snide references to that prick Santos – *Nuestro dizque Inglés* or Our Pretend Englishman and *Comandante Churchill*. Transpires he's a devoted ally of Jesus, collaborating with him in drug trafficking and his other *repulsive antics*.

There's a solitary sheet of paper among the lengthy exchanges

– a short, terse telephone conversation between Miguel and some security operator who works for him. The Yank from the Cosmo maybe? The transcript has a scrawled note from Smiler in the margin – *In English*.

Is the boy dead? asks Miguel and the other guy replies that he is. Miguel is cursing, in English, *this is very bad, that fucking Austrian mother will want blood*. The other dude replies simply, *Give them Jesus ... It's overdue ... If they listened to you, boss ...* Miguel again: *this could have bad implications*. The security op again: *they found everything, in the sea, but no head* – he laughs – *funny, he was paid for his head*. Miguel: *I'm not in the mood for funny right now. Buenas noches*.

The episode ends abruptly – cliffhanging stuff.

Next up – a conversation between Miguel and his father Papa Victor. Miguel is getting infuriated with Jesus. Jesus is the man in the middle, agitating, but ultimately, as Miguel points out *only out for himself*. Miguel wants to *terminate* Jesus, but the council's edict won't allow it. Miguel could actually be in big trouble if Jesus was to disappear. Pure Venezuelan Shakespeare.

When I get out of Liverpool Street Station I've got a text from Smiler – *rng lndln ASAP*. I find a payphone and ring him at the call centre in Acton. 'Come back and bring the big fella back with you, if that's okay,' says Smiler. 'He's been here, the twitch, gone weird.' Smiler's didgy as fuck, 'It's not just ... I'll explain, when I see you, not on the hambone,' he says, panicking, ending the call.

I ring Morty. He can't see why I can't pop over to see *the queer fella on yer own* but I arrange to meet him at Shepherd's Bush. Morty will be driving – don't like the Underground – like a lot of old cons, prefers *to stay above ground*. I jump on the tube and head *back* out to Acton.

I meet Morty up a sidestreet. We drive in circles till we're both dizzy, then he parks up in a quiet leafy street. He commandeers all my loose change for the meter. We trot over a railway bridge and the atmosphere changes instantly from genteel residential to light industrial. Morty's been waiting to have his say, ranting as we march, that if *something don't break in two days* he's letting Ted the Dead and Miss B know about this *bollocks*. *What the fuck is Roy on about? Elvis has left the wigwam? Grimboat One is in situ? Who is Grimboat and what the fuck is 'in situ'? The Raincoat is travelling west? You're the Raincoat, right? Pure madness. The Raincoat has gone west? I said, dead? No, he says, gone to Acton. Roy's talking in fuckin riddles, in fuckin tongues. His own mother wouldn't understand him. He rung me earlier, chatting pure bollocks. Think he was talking about the Jesus fella but he didn't make sense. Think you're getting carried away, talking telephone numbers and seeing ghosts. You're in London on serious business, not to go on manoeuvres with these two nuggets.*

Morty has an ability to rewrite history, be smart in retrospect. One minute he's rubbing his hands in anticipation of the tidy pension and the next blowing the enterprise out of the water. I decided not to tell Morty or Sonny or Royski about the telephone conversation I had with the Jenna woman. I'll need to pick my moment.

I ring the number of the guy who's keeping dog on the premises and keeping Smiler under manners. He appears, on the first ring, and shows us in through a side entrance. Me and Mort are climbing the stairs when my phone rings. I don't recognise the number – number withheld. I let it ring.

'Who the fuck is that, now?' asks Morty, fuelling his bad temper.

'Dunno,' I reply truthfully. My phone bleeps; someone's left a message.

Morty continues his tirade as we climb – *If you get yourself killed by this Santos' little firm where the fuck does that leave me? Fucked – that's where – trying to explain this fuckabout to Bridget. God help us all if she finds out about this. You think these mugs Sonny's got on the firm can keep their mouths ˙ shut? You were recruited for your level head, not cos you're another fuckin idiot ... And what's this useless cunt Smiler getting a nosebleed about?*

When we reach the second floor Mister Mortimer suddenly goes hysterical ... with laughter. Smiler is self-consciously wearing a brand new white laboratory coat.

'It's not funny,' says Smiler. When Morty has calmed down,

Smiler explains that Roy turned up with the lab coat and insisted that he wear it *at all times whilst on duty.*

'He came over here. Not long after you left.' Smiler asks a leading question, 'Is Roy okay?'

'Combat fatigue,' says Mort with a wink. 'Keep that under yer hat.'

Smiler salutes. Nuff said. 'Next item ... ' he says, 'Small problem ... before we get to the big—'

'A problem with Mister Burns?' asks Mort.

Smiler nods. Roy has asked Smiler, *as a favour,* to find him something on the Internet. Roy wants *sourced* the *exact same memory stick,* with Spanish writing, *identical* make and size.

'Smart move,' says Morty. 'Could come in handy.'

'Exactly – *could come in handy.*' parrots Smiler. 'But he's getting me to order *two dozen gross,*' says Smiler.

Morty whistles, looks baffled.

'How many is that, exactly?' I ask.

'*Exactly?*' says Smiler. 'Three thousand, four hundred and fifty-six.'

'That's a lot. Did he say why he wanted them?' I ask.

'To use as *decoys,* Roy said. *Decoys? I said.* He says *can you fuckin get them or not?* Started shouting. I can get 'em. Comes to over seven grand. Do I need a purchase order? I explained to Roy that the Spanish wholesaler wasn't holding that amount in stock – they'd have to order them from the manufacturer in China. Roy told me to get on to the manufacturers *direct* and order from them, tell them they were for him, *Mister Roy Burns.*'

'Was he fuckin about?' asks Morty.

'No, perfectly straight face,' says Smiler.

'What did you do?' I ask.

'Told him I'd get on it,' says Smiler, pulling a resigned face. 'Don't wanna fall out with Roy ... '

'Three and half thousand of these memory sticks ... ?' says Morty, with a frown. 'Identical? It's either genius or madness ... '

'Between ourselves ... ' says Smiler, checking to make sure no one's listening, 'I think its madness.'

'Is that why you got us up here?' asks Morty. 'To tell us that Roy's gone heavy with the stationery order?'

'I wish, mate ... ' says Smiler, shaking his head, 'but it's rather bad news I'm afraid ... '

As Smiler leads us over to his playpen I play back the message on my phone. It's from Duppy, breaking criminal tradition and the habit of a lifetime by using the *work of the devil* to leave me a short but not sweet message – *You was told to wait where we could fuckin find ya. Where the fuck are ya?* I'm hoping Morty doesn't ask who's on the phone. Luckily Mort's distracted – he shakes his head at Smiler's montage of Jenna giving her boyfriend one.

'That's someone's daughter,' he says, looking at Smiler with narrow eyes.

'I didn't want to talk on the phone,' says Smiler. 'The reason will become obvious. If we're eavesdropping *them* ... *they* could be just as easily eavesdropping us.'

'What's happening, Smiler?' I ask.

'We've used the numbers on the hotel bill and the number you gave me, the Santos chap, and in spite of it being a non-contract, disposable phone, it's a *Judas* phone. It *betrays* the people you're talking to. I've used a program to identify frequently used numbers to build up a pattern. The program, developed for covert security agencies, automatically identifies configurations.'

'Meaning?' I ask, not liking the sound of it.

'The program *infiltrates* the telecommunications network; a number rang from the Judas device automatically gets checked out. If I'm under surveillance, I ring you. The program checks your telecommunications history and reports any corresponding numbers. It builds up a spider's web of data, a viral network.'

'I didn't come here for a lecture,' says Morty, lighting a snout.

'It's very bad news,' says Smiler. 'We intercepted the numbers they ring. The Venezuelans keep ringing the same number, like they were checking in. I can't listen in because they've got a scrambler on the system.'

'The point is ... ?' I say, getting irritated. 'Get to the fuckin point.'

'They ring the married quarters on a military base,' says Smiler sheepishly. 'Santos' guys are military personnel.'

'Military?' says Morty. 'Fuckin soldiers!'

'And it gets worse ... We combined the numbers, the base, area codes and approximate location. We *eventually* got a name for the base ... doesn't *officially* exist ... Then we came up with the name of a unit ... It kept popping up ... on the websites of civil rights watch groups.'

'Who are they, Smiler, this outfit?' I ask, not wanting to know the answer.

Smiler makes quotation marks, '*military intelligence* ... heavyweights. If these civil rights people are to be believed ... they're an operational death squad.'

I feel out of my depth. I let go a nervous laugh. Morty rounds on me.

'Don't fuckin laugh! We've got enough going on without this!'

'Will you promise not to hit me?' asks Smiler, 'Cos there's more ... '

'Bad news?' I ask.

'Just real weird shit,' shrugs Smiler.

CHAPTER TWENTY-SIX

WORRIED BOYS

There's no good way to deliver bad news about death squads but Sonny and Roy appear indifferent – almost doped-off – shrugging shoulders, blowing smoke rings and chewing gum without missing a beat. They both sit with their feet up on the office desk at the Monarch, seemingly unworried, but this is just a diversionary tactic. The major telltale sign that betrays their *internal conflict* is the fact that they're wearing bulky, box-fresh, Kevlar bulletproof vests. The care labels gently swing as they move, not that they move much.

Sonny knows he can't scream too much about Santos' extracurricular activities cos it was *his* moonlighting that brought this mess down on everyone's heads. Without Sonny getting busy we'd be quietly working Ted's product, Roy would still be home in Spain, Jesus would be a million miles away and there'd be no sociopaths scouting around London, looking for dead chaps, ready to start hostilities when they can't find them or their valuable cargo. Morty, without telling him, has *barred* Roy from receiving any more information about Jesus ... especially Smiler's last little postscript.

'And, Roy, what's all this business with Smiler,' asks Mort. 'Why are ya getting him wearing overalls and ordering lorryloads of memory sticks?'

'Thought he should look smart,' says Roy. 'He's a paraffin lamp, is Smiler.'

Morty takes a step closer to Roy. 'Why do you want seven grand's worth of memory sticks?'

Sonny's eyes go wide. Roy says nothing but taps his temple with the tip of his index finger, his expression inscrutable.

'You have a plan?' Morty asks Roy. 'You wanna tell us about it?'

Roy doesn't reply but he shrugs – an exaggerated grimace –

seems to be saying *could have, Mister Mortimer ... marinating nicely ... You wouldn't rush a surgeon ...*

'Roy ... ' says Morty, gently, 'try not to get us all fuckin killed, okay, son?'

'Do *you* have a plan, Mort?' asks Sonny, his feet dropping to the floor, suddenly serious.

'I think,' says Morty, 'we need to find Santos de Lucia, take no chances, but find out what he's all about. Let the hounds go if necessary.'

'You make it sound easy, Mort,' says Sonny.

'Listen, Sonny, whatever magic is on that memory stick has caused eruptions ... ' Sonny nods. 'And ... ' Morty continues, 'it's all your fault. If you had kept your greedy fuckin paws off the Jesus fella and his cases, we'd be getting our heads into Ted's thing. As it is I'm lying to Bridget, and she thinks I'm mugging her off, talking to her like a cunt. And she's still in mourning. Maybe I'd better have a spin over and answer a few of her questions. Questions like why everyone's suddenly gone fuckin mad.'

Sonny looks suitably chastised but Roy is staring off into space.

'Roy ... ' asks Morty, 'are you listening to a fuckin word I'm saying?'

Roy snaps out of his trance. 'Yeah, Mort. I'm just thinking ...'

'Thinking,' replies Morty, 'is what got you two in trouble in the first place.'

'I was thinking,' says Roy, 'that maybe we should go and see a spiritualist and try and—'

'A what?' interrupts Morty. 'A fuckin spiritualist? Are you taking the fuckin piss outta me, Roy?'

Sonny slowly runs his hand down his face, willing Roy to shut up, looking tired.

'Listen, Roy,' says Mort, regaining his composure, 'it's not a fuckabout. A joke's a fuckin joke ... '

'I was just thinking,' says Roy, 'that we could—'

'Listen, Roy,' says Morty, interrupting him again, 'you gotta work this Jesus thing out ... go and have a holler at the moon, get lagging drunk. It's gone inside yer nut and it needs to get out – quick ... '

Roy gently nods his head, digesting what's just been said to him, and then, 'See, I was thinking of going to see a psychic, to get in touch—'

'Fuck's sake, Roy!' says Mort, rolling his eyes. 'Do you fuckin listen to a word anyone says to you?'

'It's you who ain't listening, Morty,' says Roy, like Mort's the loon. 'It's *you* who's not open-minded enough to accept the existence of forces beyond our understanding.'

'Okay,' says Mort, 'who exactly did you wanna contact, over the other side? Don't fuckin tell me ... '

'This Jee-zuss guy.'

'Fuckin hell. This is too fuckin weird.'

'To ask for forgiveness. He'll be a restless spirit.'

'Listen, Roy, you'll be getting fuckin well nicked if you start telling some old trout down the funfair you've been murdering people and now you wanna ask their forgiveness.' Morty turns to Sonny. 'Who fills his head with magic, Sonny? Any ideas? Be ouija boards next!'

Sonny maintains a diplomatic silence. Roy looks benevolently at Mort but says nothing.

'This finishes here,' says Mort, with a sweep of the hand, 'right now, okay, Roy? Maybe you wanna start thinking about dee-deeing back down to Spain. Let Sonny keep an eye on things.'

'You're gonna have to explain that to me, Mort,' says Roy, looking at Morty intensely. Roy suspects the early rumbling of a swindle by his most trusted pals. To anyone else it would make sense to go under, but Roy can put two and two together and get a giraffe.

'There's too many cooks, Roy,' says Mort. 'You've already done stuff ... over and above the call of duty—'

'I'm going nowhere, Mort,' says Roy, almost hurt. 'I'm in this thing. I don't wanna be down in Spain. I've got a share in this bitta work and I intend to hang around.' Roy lights a snout and takes a long drag. 'To be honest, I think it's a lib to be even *asking* me to jog.'

Roy gets up, picks up a brand new, extra large sweatshirt, pulls off the labels and pulls it over his head. He now looks like a bulked-up bodybuilder who's done too much bench pressing. 'I'm going for a stroll,' he says. 'Feel a bit mugged off, as it goes.'

And with that he slides out the door.

'Take someone with ya, Roy,' Sonny shouts after him but Roy doesn't respond. Sonny puts a finger over his lips. He opens the door to check that the corridor is empty. Without a word Sonny sits back down, head in hands. 'Fuckin hell ... ' he says. 'Didn't see that coming.'

'So what do ya think?' asks Morty.

'I think yer right, Mort,' replies Sonny, 'he'd be better off back down in Spain, but *you* try and convince him. Roy lives for all this creeping about.'

'Well, Sonny, you better keep a beady on him, every moment of the day. Damage limitation, you get it?'

Sonny King knows he's got a dilemma – fucked if you do, fucked if you don't. Can't get Roy back in his box. 'Roy just needs a couple of days,' he tells Mort, 'to sort his head out.'

'This, Sonny,' says Mort, getting up to leave, 'is getting serious ... deadly fuckin serious.'

CHAPTER TWENTY-SEVEN

TAKE ME TO YOUR LEADER

Last night, after I left Mister Mortimer in a drinking club in Paddington, I went home to read the latest instalment of the Zambrano Papers. Things were hotting up. Transpires Jesus had taken to recording himself killing unidentified individuals when business negotiations got out of hand or a bit shouty. Earlier Smiler had played Morty and me the original MP3 recordings, and I wish he hadn't. And *Roy's not to know – it'll send him properly 'round the bend*. Back in my hotel room the transcripts became scripts to old radio plays. I'd heard the scuffles and curses, in Spanish and English, screams and choking sounds of life expiring, disregarded pleas for life, furniture getting wrecked. Jesus was placing the recordings on the memory stick for posterity, to relive at a later stage. Jesus had the ego and a need to be famous even if it's as an infamous multiple murderer. Just as I was dropping off to sleep, for some reason – feeling understandably spooked – I got up and hid the transcripts and photographs beneath a carpet tile under the middle of the bed.

From where I'm sitting right now I believe it could have saved my life, because I woke up with the point of a silencer sending me boss-eyed. The gent on the other end was sitting on the bed with a finger over his lips while one of his companions poured me a cup of coffee, asking me, in a languid southern accent – southern as in Alabama or Texas – how many sugars, if any, I required. *Cream?* His other pals were systematically, but neatly, searching the room like forensics officers. I knew they weren't Old Bill, English or American – police don't as a rule use silencers, and the law love to flash a badge by way of introduction. As for asking if they had a search warrant, I wasn't going to waste my breath. They *looked* like law enforcement, or secret service – dark sunglasses, wingtip brogues and summer-weight raincoats – men after my own heart. I didn't feel that scared, didn't welcome their arrival either. If they wanted me dead, I'd be ...

I cottoned on double-quick who they were, realised I'd been expecting a visit. Thinking about it further, I figured that *Miguel's Coca Cola Cowboys* were overdue. *Guerreros mercenarios de Miguel* have understated class compared to Santos' crew; no crashing about for this lot. You'd put your money on them if Santos and this crew started playing kiss-chase. It became apparent that their advanced guard – the ones who'd turned up at the Monarch the other night – had been in London doing their homework. I just couldn't riddle out, at first, why they'd picked me.

They weren't very talkative; every time I asked a question they smiled like rattlesnakes, told me to hush *your noise and drink your coffee.*

After a minute or so one of them pulled up a chair and handed me three pieces of A4 paper. He let me digest the contents – a copy of my hotel registration with credit card details, the itinerary of the flight in from Barbados and a photocopy of my snide passport. They've cyber-crept into the hotel computer and got my assumed name. Then they've run checks and seen when and where I've entered the country. These are guys who can do that as easily as boiling an egg.

Next he hands me a telephoto lens shot of me leaving the Monarch. I was with Morty, so it was last night. Then he hands me a photograph of me coming out of Liverpool Street Station. They've made their point – they can keep up. The chap has the expression of the poker player who's just laid the nuts.

'And?' I shrug – what's your fuckin point?

'Why are you always flitting around on the metro?' he asks.

'The *tube,* you mean? I always *flit* around. Doesn't everyone?'

'You're very evasive. Why's that?'

'I just don't like being followed. Who are you, exactly?'

'Where's your computer?'

'Do you always answer a question with a question?'

'Who told you that?' he says, straight-faced. 'Where's your computer?'

'I don't own a computer.'

'Why are you in London?'

'I'm here because I'm here. A law-abiding citizen. I ain't pointing guns at people.'

'Don't be smart,' he says.

'What is it with you – you and your mate Santos de Lucia? Think you can come over here and start bullying everyone?'

He doesn't like Santos de Lucia, or being lumped in with him. Meanwhile his chums are still searching – everywhere except under the bed, where they might just spot a raised carpet tile. Eventually they run out of road, don't find anything useful – no computers or memory sticks, transcripts or photos.

'I have no computer,' I say, feeling cocky. 'I can barely open an email.'

'See, we think you've been brought in special, to help your friends tackle a software problem.'

'I am here on business but it has nothing to do with any magic wands or memory sticks ... Nobody was interested ... not until you lot started intimidating the staff at the Cosmopolitan and your posse turned up at my associate's club, waving assault rifles.'

'They were pointed at the ceiling, with the safety on.'

'That's all right then. Please forgive me, Mister ... ?' I extend my hand but he doesn't respond. 'Can you see, Tex, how people could get curious?' He's dying to point out he's not from Texas. I continue. 'Specially, Tex, when Mister de Lucia came to my friend's club and offered him a million dollars for some gadget.' Tex whistles low and shakes his head – experts at pretending to be dumb these southern boys, booby-trap you by slowtalking ya. But he betrays nothing. 'But we,' I tell him, 'don't think Mister de Lucia has a pot to piss in ... ' He guffaws in spite of himself, then checks, deadpan again, '... or a window to throw it outta.'

'Would you say you were connected?' asks Tex, grinning. 'Around town? In London?'

'There you go with all the questions again.'

He smiles and winks. 'Someone wants to meet you. I'd be obliged if you'd come along quiet.'

'Are we talking about a party by the name of Miguel Zambrano?'

He ignores my question, and asks, 'You like a deal?'

'Who doesn't?' I reply.

Tex gets up. 'Come on, get dressed, let's go,' he says, and then to himself, loud enough for me to hear, 'Santos ... one million ... What a cheap bastard.'

If ever a remark was calculated to get in my nut it was that one.

We leave the hotel by the back entrance, load up into two nondescript cars and head off. All the time these guys are checking to see they're being followed. We pass along the Embankment in complete silence then up towards Westminster then into Belgravia. The driver pulls into a small mews and stops. We get out and Tex leads us though a garage. Then through tight corridors that eventually open up into a large London townhouse that's full of genuine antiques and bookshelves heaving with leather volumes. I've been kidnapped before – didn't enjoy it – but this time I could almost appreciate their grace. Tex shows me into a reception room, and sitting on a sofa drinking coffee from fine china and talking textbook English into a cell phone is a man I know without introduction is Miguel Zambrano.

Miguel has the vibe of the executive sent over from headquarters to sort out a local difficulty, seems capable of ruthless man-management and extreme prejudice. I know he's twenty-one but he has the assertiveness of a man three times his age. Not flash, but bordering on arrogant. Miguel is handsome, immaculately groomed, and wearing a neat suit, collar and tie first thing in the morning. His call is to an attorney – he's firmly telling them, to *do as we instructed and let us know if anything changes*. He's extremely courteous but the lawyer would be left in no doubt who was in charge. He's no kid. Miguel pours me a coffee without asking if I want one then finishes the conversation – *right now, there's someone I have to talk to. Adios*. He flicks the phone shut and turns to me.

'Do you believe in coincidence?' he asks. But, without waiting for an answer, 'Someone rang my sister from London, or at least it was a Londoner. She got "mixed messages". They had a *contradictory* accent; they'd spent time abroad and they spoke a bit of Spanish. *Habla usted español*?

'Sorry, mate?' I say, acting confused.

'Linguistics and demographics is her specialty. She speaks a dozen languages.'

'You speak very good English yourself.'

'Who could have been ringing my sister? Any ideas?'

'Rare bird, an Englishman who speaks Spanish. Is she at university?'

'Final year. Any other questions?' Miguel asks sarcastically.

'She got a name?' I ask.

'Now you're getting ... too curious,' he says. 'How could anyone in London get her number?'

'From your cousin? Apparently he created quite a commotion.'

'Always does, Cousin Jesus,' he says dry as sand.

'What did they want? Any threats or ransom demands? Just rung to say hello?'

'To check out who she was.'

'But you said they knew already.'

'I didn't – they called her to sound her out.'

'Who?'

'My fuckin sister!' he snaps, losing his temper. 'Who the fuck would we be talking about?'

'See you've mastered the native vernacular.'

'Excuse me,' he says, polite as you like. 'She did say the guy was very articulate, but blue collar. Would you say you were *blue collar*?'

'A lot of my blue collar friends are articulate, much more so than toffs.'

'Toffs?' asks Miguel. 'Toffs are aristocrats, right?'

'Right. Watch yourself with them.'

'That's an English joke?'

'Best bitta advice you'll get all day.'

I ask, in all innocence, 'Who is this elusive Jesus chap?'

'My cousin.' He laughs to himself. 'Jenna's unrequited love ... '

'Jenna?' I ask. This is falling nicely into place. 'Who is Jenna?'

'My sister ... ' he says. 'My twin sister, in fact.'

I put down my coffee on the table and pull my chair towards Miguel.

'Look, Miguel—'

'How do you know my name?'

'Jesus slung it around, like confetti.' Miguel shakes his head. 'It's like this, Miguel, we – my associates – were just doing our business when out of nowhere appears your cousin ... like a hurricane blowing through, but ... he comes, and he goes.' I take a sip of coffee – delicious. 'But next thing, there's *two* teams of Latin Americans in London making threats and disturbing our serenity ... waving firearms and calling people liars ... '

'We'll deal with Santos when we find him again—'

'*If* you find him, same as *if* you find your cousin. My good friend Sonny King is upset.'

'I don't give a fuck about this King Sonny, or whether he's upset.'

'It's Sonny King, not King Sonny ... Your man mentioned a deal.'

'These security people ... ' he nods out towards the door, 'think you were brought in to deal with this, that you're a computer expert. But I don't.'

'That's good.'

'I believe you and your *associates* are drug suppliers. Don't look offended – my family's made their fortune out of supplying narcotics,' he says with a regal wave. 'But I think you're more like a negotiator. You're the dealmaker. Am I right?'

I say nothing – shrug my shoulders – you're-not-wrong. He carries on.

'There is no point having product if you can't bring it to market. A good salesman is worth his weight in gold, more valuable than a million gunmen. I grew up surrounded by gentlemen like you.' His face breaks into a sly smile. '*No te gusta ensuciarte las manos.*'

I shrug again – *no comprende*. But I do – he's not wrong. I wait for Miguel to tell me ...

'You don't like to get your hands dirty.'

'And neither do you, Miguel.'

He laughs. Another time and place, Miguel would be good company, and the ideal connection who could drop consignments of cha-cha on your toes – price on application, cheaper by the ton – sorted with a ten-second call.

'With whom do you do business?' he asks. 'Anyone we know?'

'I would not come to Miami and start asking questions.'

Miguel suddenly makes eye contact, leans forward. 'Is Jesus Zambrano alive or dead?'

'How would I know?'

'Is Jesus in London?'

He's studying my reaction, looking for a chink. I remember Roy's tutorial. I stay still and return his glare.

'What's with the big Q and A?' I say, like I'm offended.

'I'm sorry,' he says graciously. 'It's just ... '

'Fraternal concern?'

Miguel laughs – he recognises and appreciates sarcasm. He carries on, 'Jesus went missing in England. We have established that he didn't catch his train but he had three suitcases when he left the Cosmopolitan Hotel. Do you know anything about those cases?'

'I don't know nothing.'

'That's a double negative – like saying you *do* know something.'

'I wasn't in London when Jesus disappeared. You've got the documentation.'

'If you helped us we would not be ungenerous.'

'Another double negative. How not ungenerous?'

He holds up two fingers. 'A two-part deal. Could you and your associates use a large quantity of grade-one cocaine in return for information on the whereabouts of Jesus Zambrano?'

'You two have got the same surname? Unfortunate.'

'*Extremely* unfortunate, yes.' Said like he means it.

'How much?' I ask.

'That depends on where you take delivery. We have a gent living down the country here who could help out, organise the shipment.'

'Interesting,' I say, nodding my head.

'I'll supply the goods, if you pay the shipping fees to the chap. He'll facilitate everything. He's an Anglophile – English wife – a good man to know. You juice him.'

'Why are you so convinced that Jesus is still alive in England?'

'If not England, where? This is where the trail goes cold.' I wish I could just tell him to pack and go home, that Jesus is dead and buried in deepest Kent. 'Jesus was meant to be on a Eurostar train but he went missing between the hotel and Waterloo Station.'

Something in the way Miguel is slicing an orange with a sharp knife suggests that great harm was waiting for Jesus on that train.

'What kinda figures we talking here, Miguel?'

'Part two of our little deal – I'll supply you with one hundred kilos for the return of that memory stick. Same for Jesus. That's two hundred kilos in total.'

'What's so important with this memory stick?'

'It's a generous offer. But every deal has terms and conditions, my friend. The one condition is that you don't ask questions. Safe delivery of Jesus *or* the memory stick – that's the deal.'

'Any word,' I ask, 'on this Santos dude?'

Miguel pushes a large slice of orange into his mouth. 'Take a bit of advice?' he asks. I nod. 'If I were you, I'd find Santos ... and kill him ... ' Miguel's eyes zero in on mine. 'He's a dangerous dog ... with or without Jesus yanking his chain.'

'Duly noted.'

'Let me run something by you ... ' says Miguel, getting up, starting to pace. 'A scenario ... Someone kills Jesus, they dispose of the body, but then they receive information that a reward is being offered. Would it not be worthwhile for certain persons of influence, in London, to begin to investigate the circumstances of the death with a view to returning the body? We need a go-between ... to our mutual benefit. What you decide to do to with the persons who return the body is up to you ... If they didn't wake up tomorrow, would anyone care? It's worth that merchandise to me, but it's nothing that's of any value to anyone ... It's a family thing, you understand?'

'I don't think I can help.'

'There's no harm in looking, is there?' says Miguel, CEO of the Zambrano Family Corporation. 'Anyway, I'm a pragmatist who likes to use local talent.'

'That's sweet, Miguel.'

'I need Jesus back in his cage.'

'Nobody has a good word to say about the Jesus fella.'

'I'll take Jesus alive or dead. But I will want the whole body ... '

'The corpse? Returned?'

Miguel nods calmly. 'We're Catholics, we need to give Jesus a Christian burial.'

He's had two already, neither of them very Christian. Jesus' *body* could be worth a few million. Can't see Roy digging it up *again*. Miguel's worked out what Mort worked out – the zip drive was secreted up ...

'I'll tell you a little *Jesus* story,' says Miguel. 'You don't know the half of it – that's an English expression, right?'

He laughs while I nod. Bits of this tale I know from the transcripts and the recordings. But Miguel is telling me, in his calculated way, for his own reasons, just enough to get me onside; to get me hating Jesus as much as he does. Miguel wouldn't tell me the correct time if he didn't have an ulterior motive.

It's funny ... you nod your head, make all the right noises, when someone tells you a story, for the first time, that you already know ...

CHAPTER TWENTY-EIGHT

THIS BE DARK

Or fuckin thought I did ... Miguel told me some, then the transcripts and recordings told me the rest. Like Smiler's *file-sharing program – nicking bits of other software and creating a new facilitating host* ... things came into sharp, crisp focus.

Result: the shocking insight into the dark mind of Jesus Zambrano.

Q. Why has Miguel dropped this information on me?

A. To get the London Hounds on his side, to encourage local assistance.

Kids, see ... Miguel knows that one thing that's global is nobody – no matter how criminally immoral – doesn't get angry where kids are concerned. The slightest whiff of kiddie nonsense sends London criminals into a homicidal rage.

Smiler was right. Jesus had an obsessive fixation on his cousin Jenna since she was *seven years old* and he was twenty. Fourteen years ago he told her in all seriousness he was gonna marry her; she found him creepy and never allowed herself to be left alone in the same room. Where Jesus was sexually was anyone's guess, and my guess was that sex was simply an extension of his all-devouring sociopathic behaviour. Jesus woulda fucked the hole in a doughnut. He fucked mostly girls, the younger the better, the dumber the better, but every now and then he'd do the business on a guy, willing or unwilling – a power mechanism rather than sexual gratification. Miguel wanted to pull the trigger on his older cousin five years ago, didn't like this nonsense with his sister. *Really* regrets not doing it now.

The family joke about them one day being an item stopped being funny as Jenna got older. It seems Jesus had seriously thought that he and His Princess would get it together. But she was repelled by the thought – and sight – of Jesus. Papa Vic told Jesus it was a sin in the eyes of God and man. Jesus went to see a sympathetic Catholic clergyman and asked under what circumstances could first cousins be married – *under no circumstances, you sick fuck*, replied the priest.

Jesus decided to ignore the priest, to ignore everyone. He formally asked for her hand at a large family dinner on the candlelit veranda of the Zambrano villa in the hills above Caracas. Jenna was embarrassed. Papa Victor and Miguel said nothing for a good five seconds ...

They looked at one another ... Then they laughed till the tears rolled down their faces, slapped their thighs and held their stomachs. The more they laughed the hotter Jesus burnt. When they wiped away the tears, Miguel asked Jesus to repeat the question. But Jesus was deadly silent. He bubbled with humiliation and rage.

They impolitely declined; they had bigger plans for Jenna. Jenna was an asset, not to be wasted on that prize prick. Her marriage was an opportunity to make an alliance – The Plan discussed in the conversations of Miguel and Papa Vic. Not such an archaic attitude; a lot of people are in arranged marriages, whether they know it or not. Jenna talked to Grandma Zambrano, who explained the family's long history of sacrifice and struggle. Jenna began to accept the inevitable.

In the next few months, Jenna made a mistake – she tried to pacify Jesus and bring him down without a nasty bump. She petted the devil dog. Jesus misinterpreted the signals, because he wanted to. He thought she *really did love him* but was being groomed for higher things *against her will*. Jesus wouldn't take no for an answer, and started driving her mad. Jesus, volatile and disturbed, became her drug-crazed stalker. He travelled to her university in Miami. Threats were made, then local police got involved; they tried to arrest him but he escaped. They asked Jenna who he was, so now she had to lie – family loyalty – *just some guy from downtown, don't know his name*. Students pointed her out like she was a witch – these Venezuelan *Demedos* can't behave. Victor gave Jenna a bodyguard but he disappeared; Jesus' involvement couldn't be proved.

Jenna tried to back Jesus off, sympathy exhausted, her nasty side – the Zambrano side – starting to emerge, but he's around every corner. In between being a nuisance Jesus was doing his monkey business all around Florida – shifting tackle, making money but spinning out of control.

Papa Victor tracked Jesus down, got him back to Caracas, sat him down, had a quiet word with him – uncle to nephew – and very nicely threatened to do him serious and permanent damage if he didn't stop pestering Jenna. Go away, make money, find a girl, settle down, have many children – but not with Jenna, you understand?

Jenna transferred up to Columbia University in New York. Miguel could keep an eye on her there ... Miguel's doing big business in NYC these days ...

But now Jesus has got love and hate working double shifts, day and night. He oscillates between over-romantic, operatic love for his first cousin and ...

I'll show that that bitch Jenna who I love and adore more than anything else in the world, who would complete my world, if she would only love me. I'll show her! I can move and shake and make money – don't need her or her brother or her fuckin father. I'll Be A Somebody.

But the outfits down there in Miami – Cubans, Haitians, Jamaicans – might be criminals but they aren't stupid. Jesus creeps them out, they don't trust him – he fiddles the weight, loads or money are short, he's never where he's meant to be, he lies unnecessarily, out of stupidity. Then he tries to front it out, tells them *they're* the deluded lunatics, got *their* facts wrong. He smashes the granny outta product if he gets half a chance, slaps it *too* much. He gives the impression that he's messy about his business, chatting too much information on the cell, dropping the family name, not paying suppliers, boasting to girls in nightclubs; generally behaving like he could easily get them all pinched or killed or robbed. One day he'll be telling undercover Feds or DEA what a smart cunt he is, who he's connected with, and what he's up to.

There are a lot of people out there who would have slotted Jesus, and buried him as a professional precaution. But he was a Zambrano. Killing Jesus would be an affront. What people didn't know – an ironic contradiction, in retrospect – was that many in the Zambrano clan would have welcomed someone burying Jesus, very dead or still alive. Miguel would shake Twitchy's hand if he could have his cake and his memory stick too.

Sensible, quiet workers gave Jesus a wide, were polite but evasive; kept marching, eyes front, as he waved at them across South Beach nightclubs. Even drug dealers, smugglers, money launderers and crooked lawyers believe Missus Burns' maxim that *you are the company you keep.* Miami is like any place, Bogotá or Lagos, Bangkok or Marbella – everyone is constantly checking out who's with who.

Jesus is always working with entry-level operators or bottom-feeders that he can control. He's never getting fast-tracked – there's no nepotism, and the fraternity have spotted it. It doesn't take a lot of working out that if Jesus could command respect and close a deal, he'd be grooving on behalf of the family firm, the Zambrano Corporation. They keep him where they can keep an eye on him, let him have product at landed prices, extend him credit, let him use the slotting crews if things go bandaloo, but never let him know what's really going on.

Jesus had a fantasy that one day he'd get into something really hot and horny that his uncle and cousin would want a piece of. They'd come grovelling to him, on their knees, looking for a slice, and he'd tell them, politely, to fuck off. If only he could make his fortune independently, he'd win the heart of Jenna. They'd live in a big house on the hill, have bubbas and hold court. And then they, the Zambrano Family, would offer him a seat on the board. Dead simple. Jesus' story takes a turn – turns into a proper Burke and Hare story.

Santos was working for Jesus. His pet soldier, running freelance operations, using the family's facilities – airstrips, diplomatic bags, bent officials, money laundering operations and the Venezuelan army. Santos and his squad of moonlighting Special Forces operators did the schlepping but Jesus always kept control of the money. And Jesus always kept Santos and the *amigos* waiting on payment – they never got paid in full – so Santos never felt in a position to bail. It was *promises* that kept Santos on Jesus' leash. And Jesus could convince Santos of anything. Miguel suggests that because Santos has a rigid, soldier's psyche it makes him easier to manipulate – *less mental flexibility* ... Once you overran Santos' first line of defence you could run riot. Tells you as much about Miguel as it does about Santos.

Jesus had a buyer in Miami for his product, an ambulance-chasing attorney. In the course of an innocent conversation over dinner one night, the lawyer happened to mention in passing that human body parts, vital organs, fetched huge sums of money on the black market. They got to joking ... Jesus asked how much a kidney would cost ...

Did you know that a heart transplant costs one million dollars? Including convalescence, all state taxes, and the beating heart?

The lawyer chappie went on to tell Jesus, who was all ears by now, that certain rare blood groups are found in indigenous Indians – *they have a higher percentage rate than the regular population* ...

The lawyer was doing legal voodoo – defending malpractice lawsuits, liaising with ethical committees and dealing with seriously criminal insurance companies – for the medical centre that was doing a roaring trade in spare-part surgery. There was actually *a shortage of donors* ...

Jesus recruited Santos and his *amigos*, sold them his harebrained scheme. Santos was assured that there was a buyer, a market for the organs. Jesus went to work on him, eroded his resistance – *these Aztec fuckers were sacrificing each other when the Span-yards arrived, cutting out their hearts to pacify the monkey Gods! This ain't nothing new!* On and on ... Till Santos agreed.

Jesus told the lawyer guy that he could get *merchandise* ... Together they would make money. The lawyer switched off the analytical part of his brain.

Off Santos and Jesus and the rest of their crew headed into the remote hinterland where three countries meet – Venezuela, Brazil and Columbia, high in the hills – and began *harvesting*. Men, women and *kids – kids' internal organs are a real specialised market*.

Jesus and Santos used a kidnapped doctor they had terrorised and threatened with castration to remove the organs. Using the same jungle airstrips and routes that smugglers use they transported them overnight, on ice, to Miami, for big money. But Jesus had no proper documentation, or information about where the organs came from – the necessary tests to determine the origin and blood type of the organ were wasting valuable time. It worked for a little while but soon Jesus was making the cargo fit the paperwork rather than the other way round. Jesus saw this *blood groups business* as an inconvenience – *You got your stuff! Why are you persecuting me? Where's my money?* The lawyer decided it had all been a bad idea. Jesus couldn't understand what all the fuss was about, didn't feel the need to justify or explain what he was doing – slaughtering natives for funds to keep him in his dazzling, but ridiculous, finery.

But it's bad karma to be strolling round with an internal organ that Santos' crew murdered, in cold blood, some defenceless, indigenous native to obtain. Then the hospital started asking *serious* questions – medical, ethical and financial questions.

Q. Like?

A. Where the fuck are these organs coming from?

The counterfeit documentation fell apart. There were comebacks that no kickbacks could make go away. Everyone ran for cover. How or when it all went bandaloo nobody really knew. The Zambrano Family, especially Papa Victor and Miguel – not exactly weighed down by heavy consciences – were sickened and knew there would be consequences ... It's the stuff of urban myth, the kinda gruesome tale people love to tell. Soon it will be everywhere ...

The Lawyer arranges a meet – *the usual place.* The Lawyer goes wired for sound; he's maybe looking to cut a deal with the DA. The Lawyer confronts Jesus – *I ain't getting jerked around by some club rat!*

Lawyer's a good old boy, pride of Texas Tech Law School, brought up on preachers who dance with rattlesnakes then sniff coke off alligator-skin bibles. What he doesn't realise is that Jesus has a devil on *both* shoulders. One thing leads to another. The Lawyer thought he was cross-examining Jesus – turned Jesus inside out, got him riled and loose-lipped, like they learnt him at Tech Law. The Lawyer started getting answers – not the answers he wanted. The Lawyer, being a double agent and government informant, threatened to notify the authorities ... Bad move.

So Jesus killed him; not in a fit of rage, more in shame and embarrassment. Jesus found the Lawyer's wire. What me, Mort and Smiler heard last night was the beginning of Jesus' penchant for recording his murders – with equipment courtesy of his first victim.

This attorney guy had connections – *appointments to keep, people to see* – was hotwired-in and middled-up with the FBI, ATF *and* the Aryan Brothers and Dixie Mafia. Not people you need to make enemies with. Rumours spread like wildfire ... The smell wafting back to the ruling junta of the Zambrano Family got worse. *The missing lawyer was last seen in a parking lot, talking, with a party by the name of—*

Don't tell me, I know ...

Jesus was now in grave danger of fuckin up the best-laid plans. This had diplomatic consequences – high-level people started putting distance between themselves and the Zambrano family. Papa Victor rang his disturbed nephew and cheerfully asked him to pop into the Miami branch office next time he was in the locale, just wanted to have a little catch-up ... How about later this afternoon?

Jesus was in Corpus Christi, Texas, doing a trade with some old buddies from Florida State Penitentiary when he got the call. He knew it didn't sniff right. They used Jenna as bait, without her knowledge. *Jenna's gonna be so pleased to see you.* The bait turned into the confirmation of all Jesus' paranoid thoughts – they *were* out to get him. Jesus told them he was coming but went underground.

Jesus' plan to get with Jenna was turning to shit. Doubts creeping in ... maybe he'd got it wrong about the trade in human organs. Jesus decided what he needed was some Positive Mental Attitude. And he needed money to keep him in the style to which he'd become accustomed. He needed a Big Score. Fate played a hand.

Jesus was talent-spotted by a disgruntled accountant who was working for the Zambrano Corporation. Obese and greedy, bitter and twisted, he breathlessly pitched to Jesus in a motel, near

Daytona Beach, over cheeseburgers. Jesus was recording the proceedings – it's all on that little stick, Jesus, everything you need to know. Miguel is planning something really big. BIG! These fuckers are holding you back, Jesus, you're the talent. Just remember me when ... Maybe we could be partners ... What ya saying, Jesus? Me and you?

Jesus was saying nothing. The genie was out the bottle, had its hands around the accountant's throat. Jesus killed him. *Then* he expressed his disgust at this *betrayal* of *his* family ... by this treacherous pig ... this greedy dog upstart ... This ... hold on ... *extremely* fuckin useful source of information ... Jesus – impulsive again – had killed the Accountant before he could fully explain Miguel's BIG coup ...

Jesus stood over the corpse, shrugged his shoulders, then sat down and finished his cheeseburger. Jesus was starting to get a nice warm feeling in his shorts with this killing-for-pleasure lark.

Jesus went underground but he still needed tank money, had to think on his feet, but doors were slamming in his face ... One day he realised he knew a candidate back in Miami – a twilight mover and shaker on the scene, some smug New York banker who'd retired at thirty. And he was an acquaintance of Miguel's. That was a nice bonus. Miguel would be *extremely* upset if anything bad happened to him ... Jesus drove the dead accountant's car down to see Next Victim.

Jesus tortured and killed him, cleared his wall safe out ... his new *modus operandi*. He got that hard currency he needed. *Adios Miami!* Jesus headed east. Next stop, London.

Why London? Nobody can work that out.

Q. Why hasn't Miguel mentioned the three million pounds in the suitcases ... only the cases?

A. Maybe because Miguel doesn't know about any three million?

CHAPTER TWENTY-NINE

PURE TOIL AND TROUBLE

Morty's turned into Roy – talking gobbledygook on the phone to Sonny, using codes – *go west, you get it? He'll know what I mean. Right now. And watch yer back.*

This sideshow is getting dangerous. The Jesus kid is bringing a lot of bad juju and heavy outfits into town; even after death he's a nuisance. Morty wants a meeting with Sonny and Roy *ASAP*, down at Smiler's lay-low.

Morty's head is even more spun than mine. He's angry at the thought of spooks tailing us and he doesn't wanna hear how charming young Miguel is. He thinks the offer – two hundred kilos of coke for the return of the memory stick *and* Jesus, in *any shape or form* – is *chickenfeed*; a better offer than *that cunt Santos*, but derisory. He thinks Miguel has grafted me, which, to a degree, he had.

'It indicates what that gadget's worth – a whole lot more,' says Mort. But just to be on the safe side he decides not to tell the Terrible Twins – *classified information*. Morty wants to keep up a disunited front.

Mort's view – we take the two hundred kilos *only as a last resort* – is not a bad fallback position. And maybe Miguel's right, and the contents of the memory stick are only of value to him – miles and miles of figures, recordings of his cousin doing murders, *boys will be boys*, Miguel's conversations with every Tom, Dick and Horado, and some saucy shots of his sister getting charvered all over a hotel bedroom.

We're not blackmailers, suggests Morty.

We're getting there, I'm thinking.

We made our way over to Smiler's warehouse, making sure we weren't followed. Smiler is excited but Sonny is telling him to shut the fuck up. I tell Sonny and Roy the highlights of the conversation with Miguel – gleaned from the hour with Miguel and careful study of the transcripts – Jesus' infatuation with Jenna, the murders in Miami, the trade in children's organs. Miguel was spot on – Sonny and Roy are *fuckin raging*.

'This finishes now. Straight away!' screams Sonny, stamping up and down. 'A joke's a joke, but carving up kids ain't on! He's going down a fuckin hole! Get everyone out there! Find this Santos! Geezer's an animal! And this Jesus wanted to marry his fuckin cousin since she was *seven*? Seven! Why didn't they pay the nonce years ago?'

Jesus would get more than excrement through his letterbox, broken windows and regular therapeutic beatings if he behaved like that round here. Smiler leans against a wall, arms folded, silent.

'Do you remember where they took you?' Smiler asks me. 'Did they blindfold you? Could you find it again?'

'No, Smiler, they wanted me cooperative. It was cordial.'

Sonny hisses. 'Fuckin *cordial*? Can you believe this cunt ... ?'

'Could you ... ?' asks Smiler. 'If I got you a street plan, work out which house it was?'

'Didn't they give you the address?' asks Sonny, pure sarcastic. 'So you could drop back some time?'

Smiler ain't biting – he appears to be totally zenned-out and bulletproof, the man of the hour. 'If you could listen to the conversations inside that house,' he asks, 'would that help?'

'You thinking of bugging it?' asks Roy, liking what he's hearing. 'They'd be alert to infiltration but I guess you could hit it with directional microphones.'

'Was gonna try something a little old-school, Roy. You're right, the security personnel ain't gonna let ya drop a bug. I was gonna get the rental details, then the landline number, and have a little eavesdrop. Be surprised how many people sweep the gaff but leave the telephone plugged in.'

Roy nods enigmatically.

'You reckon it'll work?' Sonny asks Roy. Smiler rolls his eyes.

'I'm not saying it *will* work ... Might have unplugged the phones. God's truth,' Smiler goes into nostalgia mode, 'we used to listen to the Robbery Squad at Finchley on their own receivers, ones on their desks. Old Bill taught us everything we know. No promises but ... '

Half an hour later Smiler's hunch has paid off and he's dropping the Belgravia house. The security team no doubt swept the premises for listening devices, but a telephone microphone is a listening device, only there's no signal to detect. Smiler found the house, and using the telephones – after running the weak signal through enhancement amplifiers – we can hear Miguel and another Venezuelan talking. Smiler, who appears to have grown into his lab coat, is tweaking the sound, trying to get a better signal.

The talk is mundane – about flights, airports, cars and food. The newly arrived cat obviously likes his grub. Miguel calls the guy *Raul.*

Raul is Miguel's half-brother, the child of Papa Victor's first marriage. Miguel patronises Raul, talks to him like he was backward. Raul is permanently hungry; he wants food bringing in, burgers and milkshakes, in spite of telling Miguel, with some pride, that he ate *three* dinners on the plane, in the business class – *bring me three.* Miguel tells Raul that they'll be going out to dinner but Raul wants a snack to keep him going.

Sonny and Roy are badgering me to decipher what Miguel and Raul are saying but Raul's accent is as heavy as Miguel's is crisp, and Raul's eating non-stop and talking with his mouth full. Whole chunks of Raul remain uninterpreted while Miguel sounds like he's reading the evening news on Venezuelan television.

And this evening's main story is – Brother Raul has brought in some of his top troops. Bad news for someone, possibly us. Breaking news – the generous dowry to be paid to the fiancé's father, the retired general, who is now a senator – *it's a lot of money but it's not our money, it's coming out of the bank* – has been increased. Good news for ex-generals and their bank managers. Spicy gossip – they believe Jenna's fiancé to be a gaylord. Bad news for Jenna, maybe?

Human interest story – the Brothers Zambrano have decided to *smoke Jesus out using Jenna as bait.* Bad news for ghosts.

Hot news – Miguel's father, Victor, doesn't know that sensitive information has been placed on the memory stick. Dynamite, and valuable leverage for later.

Burning ears time ... Raul asks Miguel – do these London guys know where the gadget is? We could go to work on them, Miguel ...

Luckily Miguel don't fancy it and tells Raul that torture and bloodshed could send it where it don't need to go ... like straight into the hands of British law enforcement. Safety first, the prudent Miguel advises his sadistic elder brother. But these *putas Inglesas* – English whores – know more than they're letting on. *I can tell.*

'I had one of them sat right there earlier. You've got to give a little to get a little ... ' We can hear Raul laughing, 'You like that, Raul, I can tell.'

'And?' asks Raul.

'Jesus is in London – dead or alive,' says Miguel, among the white noise. 'The London guy knew all about Jesus *and* Jenna. He pretended he didn't but he knew more than I told him. He knew shit had gone down ... like Jesus had told him ... It was *weird* ... '

'Sure you aren't just paranoid, Miguel?' says Raul.

'Trust me, Raul; I've a feeling ... This outfit know something.'

'How do we know Jesus didn't use the information already?'

'I think we would have heard, Raul, don't you?' says Miguel, loaded and condescending, a gnat's from sarcasm. 'Shit would be flying ... The General would be ... you know?'

Raul grunts in agreement. Miguel starts getting animated. He reminds Raul that if certain information gets revealed *we're dead a hundred times over. These mothers will be looking for people to roast alive, starting with me, then you, Raul! Then Jenna!*

Very good news for us. Then Miguel is calm again. 'But if we keep our nerve ... get that gadget ... no more delay ... maybe this is a sign ... we need to get it done ... '

Suddenly the line goes dead. Smiler shrugs. 'Nothing lasts for ever.'

'Do you think they've tumbled?' asks Morty.

'No rhyme or reason,' says Smiler, getting up to make himself a cup of tea. 'Could be good as gold later.'

Sonny turns to me. 'Did that make sense to you?'

'Bits and pieces.'

He turns to Smiler, 'How are you getting on with that memory stick? We any the wiser?'

'It's interesting, the underlying framework employs Austrian German.'

'*Austrian*?' asks Sonny. '*German?*'

Smiler marches on, 'It's ingenious what he's done, the guy who wrote the program, but I don't think he *finished* the program. I think there's meant to be *two* memory sticks with different data. It ends prematurely, falls off a cliff.'

Sonny turns to me but points at Smiler. 'Do you know what he's on about?'

'Kinda,' I reply. Sonny's not happy with this answer.

'But the good news is,' says Smiler, stirring his tea with his pen, 'we've got the fucker open and it's starting to make sense. We've got *two* sets of figures, thousands of sixteen-digit passwords ... ' Smiler is excited that he's opened up the gadget but is trying desperately hard to be blasé.

'Why didn't you tell me earlier?' asks Sonny.

'We was busy.'

'Can you move money, Smiler?' asks Sonny, like he's exercising extreme self-control.

'Not at the moment,' says Smiler. 'There's a cipher involved, in this case an Austrian fairy story ... a way of matching up the passwords ... ' He walks to number one laptop and hits the *print* button. Immediately paper streams out the printer – electronic ledgers, miles of them. 'It's two sets of accounts, real and fraudulent. One for public consumption, one for those *in the swindle*.'

Sonny starts clicking his fingers; like he's just had an idea. 'You know who's the man for this?' he says. 'Giles. Crooked cunt's a lawyer. He'll know what they're up to.'

'*I* can tell you what they're doing, Sonny,' says Smiler.

'Smiler, switch off,' replies Sonny. 'We've got our man – Mister Giles.'

Smiler can't make up his mind if he's offended or hurt. He's dying to tell *someone*.

'See this, Sonny,' says Smiler, pointing at a column of figures.

'Smiler ... ' says Sonny real slow, 'you don't get it, do you? I want Mister Urquhart, not you, to tell me. To tell me tomorrow.'

'But ... You don't wanna know *now*?'

'No, Smiler,' says Sonny flatly.

Smiler looks distraught, whereas me and Morty are just confused, looking at one another and shrugging.

'We can't exactly get Giles down here, can we now?' says Roy, indicating Smiler's humble abode. 'It's like a fuckin squat.'

'You're not wrong, Roy,' says Sonny, pulling a face. 'It's a bit scruffy.'

'I'm sure,' says Morty, 'Smiler can rustle up some Earl Grey and take down his pin-ups.'

'I think, Mister Mortimer,' says Sonny, voice of reason, 'everyone's getting a bit sarcastic.'

'Sonny,' says Morty, 'it's a fuckin warehouse. Giles won't give a fuck.' Morty flicks his cigarette butt across the floor. 'And Smiler's worked real hard – you might wanna try saying thanks. Been working day and night ... ' Morty points at Smiler but zeroes in on Sonny, 'never knowing if a team of Venezuelans ain't gonna come steaming in and cut his bollocks off.'

Smiler visibly gulps, Sonny crosses his arms in defiance. Roy raises the alert level – to state of emergency.

'You're right, Mister Mortimer!' shouts Roy, pointing at the ceiling, big eyes, 'Tonight, we double the guard!'

'What a mad cunt,' mutters Morty.

CHAPTER THIRTY

RIDDLES AND FIDDLES

Giles didn't get his Earl Grey; didn't want it. Thought Smiler was trying to be funny. I can smell jealousy on the wind, not class war, just simple jealousy. I get it now – Sonny wants top toff Giles, not round-the-flats Smiler, to tell him all about the Zambrano's skullduggery, to get Giles colluding in the scheme. Sonny wants Mister Giles Urquhart *on the firm*.

And Giles, being a Toffia Capo, and not some middle-class shitcunt, knows that sometimes you have to get your hands dirty. He tucks into his bacon sandwiches, washed down with mugs of splosh, with prep-school gusto. Real toffs are taught the art of adaptability in drafty dormitories and cold baths; flexibility is intelligence and all that. Giles' attitude appears to be *when in Rome ... or Acton ...*

Formalities over, Smiler presents Giles with a hefty lump of printouts – page after page of transactions. Sonny's briefing was just that, extremely brief. Giles implicitly doesn't want to know the origin of the information – Giles has a *code of conduct* – but he's in a warehouse, with a group of gentlemen who, if they weren't here right now would either be shifting industrial amounts of cocaine or *conspiring* to shift it. I can't believe that Giles doesn't know that.

And all the jumping about and chopping over cars to get here – Roy's *code double red* – *might* have made Giles suspect that skull runnings was afoot. All that parking up around the back of garages, hiding the motors and then marching at a gentle trot might have got him wondering ... During the journey Sonny asked me to provide Giles with a thumbnail sketch of the players. Again, at certain points, Giles halted the proceedings if he felt that his *professional boundaries* were being overrun, certain *criminal enterprises alluded to*.

But now Giles sits pondering, turning the pages, absorbing

every figure. The numbers, the ledgers, the credits and debits, are telling their story. At one point Giles discards the heavyweight staple holding a bundle of papers together and places sheets side by side on the dusty, grubby floor – so much for Giles being too effete. He sits on Smiler's office chair, bent over double, wheeling himself backwards and forwards, while studying the pages, making connections. I can only hear the hum of multiple hard drives, the traffic on the main road and Giles' brain calculating.

I've seen Giles' breed of lawyer before – he *loves* criminals. Doesn't find them a trifling bore or an occupational hazard. He actually likes, even identifies with, the criminal mindset. He thinks Sonny and Roy should have their own TV show – a double act worthy of the greats. He's amused, flattered and intrigued by them.

Smiler overcomes his envious streak and acts as Giles' private secretary, and when Giles asks for a specific article of paperwork, Smiler has it to hand in seconds flat. They make a good team. Giles asks for 'articles of incorporation'; Smiler whistles them up. Giles asks for a document isolating a certain account number from thousands; Smiler returns with a page of transactions in one neat row. When Giles asks Smiler if he happens to know where a sort code is located, he either knows off the top of his head – *First Bank of Panama* – or glances at a list and furnishes the answer in seconds. Giles, being a well dragged-up sort, doesn't ask about Smiler's lab coat.

But Giles *does* ask Smiler about ciphers and codes, passwords and sinks, shadow accounts and *phantom bottom lines*. Smiler has been living behind the lines and knows the terrain, knows what's what, and no mistake. Eventually Giles quietly asks Smiler if *he* knows what *they're up to*; Smiler nods and shrugs – *'course I do*.

I've also done my homework – been up late reading transcripts and studying ledgers till the digits danced – and I've got a good idea of what they're up to. I feel a presentation from Giles coming on. I think Giles spots what they've been doing straight away but lets Sonny roast.

A gentle smile begins to appear around the corners of Giles' mouth. Giles is deep in thought, hitting a few revelations and liking what he's discovering. Giles is sniffing big readies down

the pike. Giles knows why Sonny and co have sent for Mister
Giles. Giles knows that Sonny knows, instinctively, that he's out
of his league with this financial voodoo. Giles starts to drum out
a tattoo with his fingertips ... but says nothing.

Giles is trying to work out where the payday, the treasure, is in
all Smiler's neatly presented documentation. He'll get there in the
end because that's what high-caste geezers like Giles do. We're
speaking *historically* – purebred Brahma is Giles Urquhart. He
feels the answer is closer than a nose hair. He can smell big money
like a sniffer dog smells skunk. If Giles had a tail he'd be wagging
it because Mister Giles *knows* he's looking at a fortune in those
columns ... and it's of no fixed abode, homeless. Giles is getting
hotted-up ... he loosens his tie, undoes his top button.

Sonny is being remarkably patient, flicking through a pile of
tabloid newspapers, smoking one snout after the other. Morty
looks ready to drop off and Roy is staring into the distance,
spookily quiet after all the trouble he's gone to to retrieve the
gadget. Just when Sonny's patience is about to snap, Giles
suddenly jumps up, rubbing his hands.

'It's *awfully* clever what they've done.'

The Zambrano Family have enterprisingly bought an
off-the-shelf bank in the Cayman Islands, with operating bases in
New York, Miami and Caracas. The transcripts start to make
sense. But nobody from the family is on any of the paperwork.
They are employing a thicket of front companies and nominee
bankers, but the Zambrano Family are the controlling power.
They sink all their dirty cash into the bank, and being generous
people, they let other dark-side operators in on the secret. The
Zambrano Family give a few dozen *acquaintances* the heads-up
... then it goes criminally viral. It's all good but ...

The Zambrano Family are operating what is called a Ponzi
scheme – a criminal chain letter or pyramid-selling operation.
First in – and out – gets the spoils. The bank is simply flipping
new deposits back to *initial* investors as make-believe profit so
more investors are beating a path to the bank. Depositors are
begging to be *accepted* by the Cayman Island Bank. If something
appears too good to be true, it usually is. It's financial alchemy –
turning digits into gold. Criminals are always looking to wash

their black cash. This solves their problem *and* brings a tidy profit. It's just a game to these guys – accumulating money. They don't know how to spend it – *most of them are dumb as farm boys.*

But the Zambrano Family have taken the swindle one stage further by being the clandestine instigators *and* Judas sheep in the swindle. They are secretly *agenting* their bank to international criminals. To encourage them in, the duplicitous nominee bankers, on instructions from their secret owners, are paying extraordinarily large returns. The bankers are talking the usual gibberish about High-Yield Investments and Equity Income Strategies to send their clients giddy, and get them salivating. It's all based on exploiting the greed of the victims. In this case it also exploits the criminal vanity of the mark. *I am an instigator of crime, not a victim.*

Giles is trying to explain a Ponzi scheme to Sonny, who ain't getting it. Investors speculate on large profits; the bank has suggested that they have schemes, not strictly legal, that will make large but very *quick* returns on their investment. The involvement of the Zambrano Family is all the recommendation some folks need. Little do they know ...

Any bank works on the principle that all the money doesn't have to be in the one place at the one time; if it did, they'd be bankrupt. That's why banks can loan out other people's money, charge interest and make a profit. The deposits are represented by digits on a computer screen, as opposed to bullion in vaults. This bank's assets are in two, or twenty-two, places at the one time. All banks spin money but the Zambrano's scheme is pure robbery.

Sonny still doesn't get it. Investors invest, with the promise of a quick, high return. And they get it, too. The *second* lot of investors pays the *first* round of investors' profit. And the second lot get paid out by the next investors who tail them in ... and so on and on.

Q. Like a pension scheme?

A. Exactly! Like a pension scheme! Pure fucking robbery!

Then it goes into the stratosphere. Eventually all the investors feel so confident, get so greedy, they begin to bring even more cash and leave their *imaginary* profits in the bank to turn over again – *be silly not to.* Soon they aren't receiving cash plus twenty percent, they're receiving *statements*. Statements with increasingly large balances. Statements are just figures. You can manipulate figures.

The Ponzi scheme is booming. They are gleefully stealing – *more or less with their consent* – from thieves and drug traffickers, arms dealers, corrupt government officials, canny but cash-rich individuals who simply want to evade punitive taxation. This bank *prefers* the criminally inclined. Word has hit the jungle tom-toms and the nominee bankers are working their way *down* the criminal totem pole, towards *bottom feeders* who still have tens of millions of grubby dollars to wash ...

This is where Giles Urquhart reveals how sly he is, by spotting how crafty Miguel has been. The Zambrano Family have employed a clever tactic. The guys near the top of the criminal food chain are getting massive *genuine profits* – so much so they're bragging – but they're being *incriminated*. They don't know it. They're deliberately being made to look like they're implicated in the swindle. The blame is shifting further away from the Zambrano Clan. It's clever – playing people off one another, creating suspicion for later ...

Come Big Meltdown Day ... Chaos is your friend ...

Q. And who do we think thought this up?

A. It's obviously the kind of thing that happens if you parachute a gentleman like Miguel Zambrano, who's grown up at the knee of serious international criminals, into a respectable business school – he starts to see opportunities. Miguel's attitude is that checks and balances are only in place so the gentleman of superior intelligence can circumnavigate, or exploit, them.

Miguel has created a merry-go-round, deliberately designed to send you dizzy – to throw pursuers off the scent. Giles estimates that only about twenty-five percent of the financial traffic flowing around the bank is real. The rest, he surmises, is to give the illusion of weight going through the coffers – *same way you'd ramp up accounts to get a mortgage*. It's not real; it's the same funds recycled. But a cool two *billion* dollars in cold cash has been dropped into his Cayman Island Bank.

Giles has also worked out that every time the carousel goes round a large drop of change spins off into bank accounts in New

York City. This is one-way traffic – funds go in and never come out. Smiler had spotted it too because these were the files that he found the hardest to crack. They show numerous shadow destination accounts with very healthy credit balances with New York BICs – Bank Identification Codes. *You wouldn't wanna risk your swindled funds in some banana republic*, muses Giles. So the money drops out of sight into secure banks in a stable part of the world. Giles suggests that these New York City accounts combined contain, appropriately enough, *an American billion* – one thousand million dollars. Access to these accounts, Giles surmises, is *tonight's star prize*. But the passwords on the flash drive – sixteen figure combinations of letters and digits, upper and lower case, *like Chinese algebra* – can't be married up to the right accounts. Not without a cipher, a codebook, and the knowledge of how to apply it. Match the right passwords to the right accounts and you end up fantastically rich, but there are *thousands* of passwords for a dozen accounts. You might get lucky but you might alert the banking authorities or worse, Miguel, that someone's knocking on the door.

Yet another smart move by Miguel: steal a billion ... and leave a billion in the jug ... for everyone else to rip each other to pieces over.

'So ... tell me ... ' asks Sonny, with one eye shut and furrowed brow, 'how did the Jee-zuss kid get the three million quid out?'

It's Giles and Smiler's turn to pull the puzzled faces. Neither of them can work out how headbanger Jesus got the three mill – that ended up in Barbados – out of the accounts. Maybe the mystery guy Jesus met at the Cosmo, who ended up deaded, was the computer genius? But why did Jesus want bulky cash? Why was he jumping across borders with suitcases when he was in touching distance of billions? Nobody can work out why Jesus Zambrano was even in the UK. To rinse out the buckshee accounts it would make more sense to head straight for New York.

Q. How will all these double dodgy financial shenanigans end?
A. In tears.

When the scheme runs out of new investors, and old depositors start to realise that their money isn't really in the bank, it's evaporated, it becomes a fast, messy, violent implosion.

Come the meltdown the Zambrano Family will be indignant,

screaming they've been swindled. I'm sure Miguel can be convincing when he's pretending to be betrayed. There'll be a firestorm, but the "straight" game is far more dishonest than the crooked one. The nominee bankers can hide behind accountants, lawyers, police, heavy muscle, legal anonymity and governments. They can utilise the secrecy laws that protected the scheme in the first place, and the corruption that oiled its wheels.

And the criminal factions that co-existed relatively peacefully will quickly, in an atmosphere of mutual mistrust, go into internecine combat, maybe wipe each other out. Maybe Miguel planned it that way. Culls are good for business.

They'll need scapegoats come the endgame – someone to catch the blame when it all goes bandaloo. The Zambrano Family, under Papa Victor, Big Raul, with their own private armies, will be strong enough to withstand any onslaught. They'll need to *keep their nerve* and hope the other investors don't tumble that they're the cause of all the aggravation. They need the information *contained*. Jesus, alive or dead, could get them all killed; funny, but one prick like Jesus can send a billion-dollar swindle haywire.

The Family are running a game on some very heavy guys. If they get tumbled, no acts of contrition will absolve them. They've robbed criminals who can't be *seen* to be being turned over. It could ignite a sequence of events that sees the Zambrano Family consigned to history. This isn't about the Zambrano Family looking bad; it's about survival. It's the crime *and* the getting caught. If Giles was privy to the full contents of the Zambrano Papers, he'd realise that the scheme is part, along with Jenna's arranged marriage, of the family's drive towards respectability, a burnt-bridges, scorched-earth exit strategy. Done right, the Zambrano Family will end up with a laundered fortune to rival the great dynasties. And they'll have access to the political power to con*solid*ate it. Solid – the meaning is in the word – firm it up. They will be respectable. Respectability can be bought. Miguel will push on to make them genuine *multi*-billionaires. And with that they'll be untouchable.

But the best-laid plans ... Jesus gets found by Sonny King and sawn in half by that well-known magician Roy Twitchy Burns ... and Miguel has to have a major rethink. And bide his time.

'So, Giles ... ' says Sonny, holding up the memory stick, 'what do we do with it now we've got it?'

'Good question, Sonny,' replies Giles thoughtfully, 'good fucking question ... I believe you've reached an impasse, a stalemate ... but in this instance, you both need one another.'

'So what do we do?' asks Sonny. 'Blackmail them?'

'Strong word, that,' says Giles with a chuckle. 'What you call blackmail I'd call *compromise* – a nicer word altogether. Maybe you're going to have to learn to love one another. He's an adult, this Miguel Zambrano chap, I'm sure he likes a deal.'

You like a deal, Mister Giles. Two peas out the same pod.

'So what are ya sayin, Giles?' asks Royski. 'We just roll over after all—'

'Don't do anything hasty. At some point you'll need to begin a dialogue with Zambrano.'

'Are you fuckin mad, Giles?' asks Sonny.

'No,' says Giles dryly. 'You ask Zambrano for a share of the money that he has embezzled but cannot access without the equipment that you have in your possession ... and possession is one hundred percent of everything.'

'He'd kill us all,' says Morty.

'And risk losing a billion dollars? No,' says Giles, 'he has to come to the negotiating table. He pays you with *stolen funds* ... They walk away with the majority of the money.' Giles gets up and begins to tidy himself up, redoing his shirt buttons, straightening his cufflinks. He looks at his watch. 'It's time I wasn't here, chaps.'

'Where you going?' snaps Sonny.

'Got to go see another client. No peace for the wicked.'

'On a Saturday?'

'Piece of advice, Mister King – don't be greedy,' says Giles, showing a little steel. 'Think about it over the weekend and come back to me. I'd like to be involved, for a consideration ... '

'How would we do it?' asks Sonny, looking at Giles through narrowing eyes. Giles is preoccupied, brushing imaginary breadcrumbs off the front of his cords.

'You put me, and this man here ... ' Giles nods in my direction but talks to Sonny, 'in a room with Miguel and see what we arrive at. And we have complete authority to do a deal—'

'Why him?' asks Sonny.

'Because Miguel likes him.'

'How do you know?'

'Because he hasn't killed him,' says Giles, drier all the time. 'We offer Miguel the deal in such a way that he believes he's *retaining* ninety percent of the concealed balances—'

'What?' shouts Sonny. 'We only get ten percent!'

'Of a billion, Sonny – that's one hundred million dollars. That's a lot of washed up funds for returning some lost property—'

'No way,' says Sonny, shaking his head and his hands. 'Fuck ten points! I should give *him* the fuckin ten points! *He's* the fuckin kid!'

'Alexander the Great,' says Giles, with a shrug, 'was twenty when he conquered the known world.'

'This *kid's* got backup,' says Morty. 'Serious fuckin backup.'

'No, fuck that, Giles,' screams Sonny. 'I'd want at least half—'

'Half?' Giles is getting irritated now. 'Sonny, you asked my advice. These are Latinos. I know what they're like. Trust me. Let them think they've won. If you drive them into the ground, they'll do the deal—'

'Too fuckin right they will—'

'And kill you after … '

'How are you gonna spend your poshes if you're dead, Sonny?' says Morty. 'Listen to the man.'

Sonny says nothing. I ask Giles a question. I've decided I quite like Giles.

'Who put all this information on a memory stick?'

He thinks about the question, buttoning up his jacket, and then unbuttoning it again.

'There's a degree of vanity in putting that data on that stick ... It's backfired badly.'

'You think it was Miguel who put it there?'

'Who else?' says Giles. 'If you've got a theory, let us have it.'

'One of these banker fellers he was working with.'

'That's a good shout,' says Giles, nodding.

'The photos and recordings of the conversations were put on *after* the account details.'

'I wish you'd told me that sooner.'

'It's about time,' I tell him, 'we gave you a more rounded picture of the situation ... ' Giles nods, winks, then heads for the exit. 'But Giles, I wouldn't wanna violate your code of conduct.'

'What code of conduct, was that, bud?' quips Giles, over his shoulder.

I cut out a little after Giles. Smiler slipped me a brand new transcript. Giles' analysis had got my nut and I wanted to check out some things. I went back to the hotel in the late afternoon, took a bottle of wine from the mini-bar and went up on the roof away from everything and everyone. Twenty-eight floors up, the sun slowly heading towards the horizon in the west and, out to the east, a stunning view out to Kent and Essex. But my thoughts wandered across the Atlantic to Miami, and Jesus and murder. Curiosity has got the better of me. The banker Jesus killed before he left Miami thought Miguel had sent Jesus to kill him? It's a theory – *I won't talk; tell him I won't talk*, he repeats over and over. *Tell him I'll go away, I won't say anything. He can trust me. Take them and go! Just go!*

Maybe the dead guy was one of the nominee bankers who helped Miguel Zambrano put the Ponzi thing together. Jesus lucked out – the Banker was covering his back or was going to double-cross Miguel, skim out some funds. I think the guy handed the memory stick over to Jesus; only then did Jesus begin to realise it had real value. He bottled the gadget and headed out to Miami International Airport, on his way to London.

My phone rings. It's an unknown London number. I answer it. It's a woman's voice.

'Good evening,' she says, with a slight Spanish accent.

'Good evening,' I reply. 'Who is this?' I know the voice from somewhere.

'This is Jenna Zambrano. I'm in London. I wondered if you'd like to meet for a drink?'

CHAPTER THIRTY-ONE

ANOTHER TIME ANOTHER PLACE

This is where the head chess starts, gathers a momentum of its own ... Can't argue with the venue. I can see Jesus' ghost haunting this place ... loving every nook and cranny ... Jesus' home from home, the Cosmopolitan bar, long and narrow with huge mirrors to make it look larger, but dark and plush, with high stools, and a million backlit bottles of exotic spirits, gold and rich and enticing. There's a scattering of early evening drinkers. I sit, perched on a stool, at the far end to see who's coming, to cover the exits.

Jenna wants to do the Jesus Zambrano Heritage Tour – the Cosmo, the Monarch and Bond Street – the Golden Triangle. Miguel gave her my number, said I'd make a good native guide. They're skunking me out into the open – deliberately provocative with a veneer of innocence. I can't *not* meet her. Everything I told Sonny about *appearing* to be innocent is winging back to me. I'm double fucked because I can't tell Sonny and Roy that I made the call to Jenna.

I rang Smiler – my co-defendant – had a surreal conversation.

'She'll know it was me, Smiler, who ... '

'So change your voice—'

'Don't be a cunt, she's a linguist—'

'Isn't that pasta, thin stuff? Or is that linguine?'

'Don't even *try* and be funny, Smiler. You bring out the bully in people.'

'So don't be getting irritated.'

'Smiler, you've grown balls. Anything on your listening device?'

'Nothing. Only Raul eating what he calls chips – what we call crisps. Try not to talk too much ... like your swell pal said, if they was gonna kill ya, they would've done it by now.'

'It could be an ambush ... Could have handed the job to Big Raul ... '

There was silence on the other end for five seconds, then Smiler played his trump card, knowing full well the suggestion was absurd. 'I'll tell ya what ... ' he says, droll, bordering on sarcastic. 'Just don't go. Dead simple. Stay home. Turn the phone off. Watch a blue movie.'

He knew I was going. A switch had been flicked.

'Did you read that transcript I gave you?' he asks nonchalantly.

'Some of it.'

'Read it all before you go anywhere, boss. That's what yer dealing with. It's the Has-Oose fella in London.'

'What's the gist?' I ask.

'Yer gotta read it, mate. Was dictating his memoirs. Thought he was famous, fuckin loon. It's the blow by blow, "for the record". Poor dear's worried about who's gonna play him in the movie, whether they'll do him justice. Any thoughts?'

'On Jesus?'

'On actors.'

'Listen, Smiler, something's been bothering me.'

'Oh, yeah? You surprise me.'

'Has Sonny ever showed any interest in reading those transcripts?'

'Sonny can't read,' says Smiler, dry as a biscuit, 'not proper ... skims the papers, I've watched him, never stops to read anything. Maybe Roy Burns reads him the juicy bits.'

Makes perfect sense in a mad way – Sonny King, multi-millionaire, criminal businessman being illiterate, being more a weights and measures man. I put the phone down on Smiler and made my way over to the Cosmo P.

And the head chess continues ... One thing I know for certain, Jenna's going to be late ...

Riddle me this: is Jenna bait to smoke out Jesus? They still believe he is alive, they think Jesus will break cover for Jenna.

Or maybe *you're* the bait, sunshine, dangling temptingly for Jesus. Maybe *you're* being sold as the new focus of Jenna's affection. But I know something they don't know – Royski killed Jesus once and buried him twice.

Maybe Jenna and Miguel are colluding to retrieve the memory stick; Miguel doesn't want Papa finding out about the possible scrutiny he's exposed the family to, and Jenna doesn't want him finding out about the sexual liaisons that could put her marriage in jeopardy. Should I sound out Jenna about having a meet with Miguel? And what would Brother Mortimer say if he knew I was here?

'*Don't fuck her whatever you do, okay? This is business. This is not a fuckabout, you get it?*'

'*Mort, it wouldn't look good if I didn't show.*'

'*Tell her your missus wouldn't like it.*'

'*I couldn't lie, Mort.*'

'*You're one big walking, talking lie. And why haven't you told anyone – not me, not Sonny, not Twitchy, that you're here? Aye! Nobody except that gobshite Smiler. What's all that about?*'

'*I dunno, Mort. What you driving at?*'

'*You fucking know, you horny little cunt! It's you getting hotted-up by some saucy photos—*'

'*Behave, Mort!*'

'*Don't tell me to behave, pal! It's you gonna get us all killed with that fuckin dick of yours—*'

'*Switch off, Mort. You ain't exactly a fuckin monk.*'

'*I. Fuck. Civilians. She's the daughter of a South American warlord, who will—*'

'*Warlord! You're being dramatic now, Mort.*'

'* ... take a dim view of you having liaisons with his daughter.*'

'*Liaisons? I never realised you were so morally upstanding—*'

'*Who promised her to some senator—*'

'*She's an adult—*'

'*Don't talk to me like I'm a cunt, you hear?*'

'*Oh, look, Mort, would you believe it, that's Jenna Zambrano just walked in, fuck-in-a-maz-ing figure, curves in all the right places, a dream in a spray-on dress, maybe no underwear—*'

'*You're getting ahead of yourself now, pal.*'

'*Certainly no Miguel. Or Raul. She must have one of those nasty subconscious desires to slip the leash, to get fucked senseless all night long. A rampant harlot on the loose! Run for a constable! Oh, look; she's walking this way. Nice and slow, no rush. And you know what, I think she's hoping that I'm the gent she's come to meet.*'

'Tell her it isn't you!'

'See ya later, Mister Mortimer. Don't wait up.'

I pretend not to recognise her ... never seen her before.

Jenna is far better looking in reality, sexier in the flesh, the kind of woman you'd call handsome rather than pretty – stunning rather than simply attractive. Sometimes beautiful woman aren't that overtly sexy. Sometimes women can be incredibly sexy – stop you in your tracks – without being especially beautiful. But Jenna is both, striking and intensely sexual. Her photo doesn't do her justice. Jenna has an aura. Other guys in the bar get on it too.

I imagined Jenna as a girl but here she is fully-grown up and looking to see what's on offer. The diplomatic marriage makes sense now. I imagined her as some passive participant in the transaction but I get – in a flash – that Jenna is doing it because it takes her, Jenna, where *she* needs to go.

I can see how a loose screw like Jesus would have been driven mad by her shows of affection and then blatant rejection. A lot of relatively sane men would lose all sanity around Jenna. Jenna is walking directly towards me. Maybe she's seen Miguel's spooks' photos of me.

Her hazel coloured eyes zero in on mine. She's assertive beyond her years, but there's something unspecified in the eyes – maybe it's mischief, maybe it's lust, maybe it's my imagination playing tricks.

'Hello, Mister English,' she says.

'Sorry?' I reply. 'I believe you must have the wrong person.'

'No,' she says, slipping onto a bar stool, and getting comfortable, 'I don't think so.'

'You're Jenna, right?' I ask. 'Jenna Zambrano?'

'Dead right, Mister English.'

'Who is this Mister English chap?'

'I think we know,' she says with a wink.

The barman appears and she orders a spritzer. I order another vodka and tonic. I realise I'm doing a Sonny King – talking in a posh voice.

'I needed to clear something up, about your cousin.'

'Let's not talk about Jesus. Everyone's chasing around after Jesus, the little ... '

'Little what?'

'It's funny, your voice is different but the syntax is exactly the same – ex-act-ly. *Entiende usted*? You understand?' I shrug. She continues. 'I think we're acquainted already, Mister English. You called me in Miami.'

Jenna looks for a reaction. Roy's 'How Not To Lie' tutorial is getting replayed – resist the temptation to look over her shoulder – eyes straight ahead – look straight into hers, her dark eyes. She has one eyebrow raised, dead cocky, waiting for an answer, like she's used to getting answers.

'So,' she asks, 'if English isn't your name, what is your real name?'

I tell her my name. She slowly, and with great care, licks her top lip – just the tip of her tongue on the edge, taking longer than it should ... considering something. Her lipstick is glossy, dark scarlet. Then she begins to betray the barest hint of a smile.

'You know,' she says, 'I don't wish to offend, but I prefer *Mister English* ... suits you better.'

Jenna goes into her handbag and pulls out some American cigarettes. She puts one in her mouth, the barman rushes to light it for her. She pulls on her cigarette and lets the smoke waft up to her nose before she draws it in – effortlessly seductive. She understands sex is power, this woman. My eyes can't help but drop down to her cleavage, her tanned breasts filling her dress with ease. She's faultless. She's class. I'm breathing through my nostrils.

'Does your brother know you're here?'

'I think he might suspect.'

'That's an ambiguous answer.'

'To a strange question,' she shrugs. 'I'm a big girl now. Mister English, it's not a problem if you called me, you just got me curious ... '

'Curious enough to come to London?'

'Tell me.' She sips her drink. 'You're only telling me something we both already know ... '

What the fuck. 'Okay, I was *told* to check out certain people, *entiendes?*'

'English, please, Mister English.' She laughs at her own joke.

'It's interfering with the smooth running of business over here – Venezuelans making threats. They've got curious.'

'Who's *they?*' she asks with an edge.

'My bosses.'

'This club owner?'

I laugh, shake my head, 'No, not the club owner. I'm talking about *bosses*, high up, *connected* people. They do big business, can't have attention ... The British police can't be bought ... ' Jenna looks sceptical. 'Santos started terrorising the staff here,' I say, meaning the Cosmopolitan. 'Came to the club, and caused murders – that's an English saying.'

'Santos is a rabid dog,' says Jenna, looking almost undignified.

'Miguel told me about their escapades – the organs ... the kids ...' Jenna shakes her head. 'My bosses didn't like it ... not kids ... So now *we're* looking for Santos and Jesus. And *you're* looking—'

'Miguel is not me. Miguel is looking for them—'

'We got Jesus' phone bills from the reception—'

'How enterprising.'

'Not difficult,' I shrug. 'And we checked out who Jesus was calling – you. A great deal. A name and number are very easily married up.'

'Showing plenty of initiative, Mister English.'

'We can't have gents turning up and threatening people on the payroll, can we now Ms Zambrano? Where would that leave us? In a state of anarchy ... '

She laughs. '*A state of anarchy?* If you think this is anarchy, you should come to Venezuela.'

I didn't notice it before – wasn't paying attention – but Jenna has two bodyguards sitting by the door drinking club sodas, trying to look inconspicuous. Bodyguards are not unusual in this neck of the woods.

'Are those two with you?' I ask.

'My family worry about me,' she says, knowing what I'm looking at. 'Especially Miguel, with Jesus on the loose.'

She orders two more drinks without asking if I want one. They've *doubled the guard*. Jesus disappeared one bodyguard to show her how much he loved her. Miguel got it covered up; bet he regrets it now. For the next half hour Jenna's kicking back, relaxing. She's telling me stuff I know from the transcripts. I realise that the bodyguards are gone.

'Jenna, your guys have gone.'

'I know,' she says, 'I sent them away.'

'I didn't notice.'

'I told them if I was still here in twenty minutes to wait outside.'

Jenna gets me talking about myself, telling her more than I should. She tells me about her studies in New York, her love of America. London? *Business or pleasure?*

A bit of both, I hope, she says with a tiny wink but a very straight face. Suddenly she leans forward, her face close to mine, studying a point just below my right eye.

'You have a stray eyelash on your cheek,' she says.

I go to brush it away. She shakes her head. 'It's still there. I think you just rolled it along ... maybe ... perhaps ... '

She comes closer, delicately licks the end of her little finger and tries to remove the eyelash.

'Is it gone?' I ask.

'It doesn't want to go.'

I can smell cigarettes, wine, her body smell, her perfume, her hair, hear her breathing. She licks her lips, slowly, like an old-school film starlet, then puckers them into a perfect ring and blows the eyelash off my cheek.

'There,' she says. 'Gone away.'

I feel self-conscious; it shows. She laughs. Jenna's still in close. Her hand is planted on the top of my thigh.

'I've embarrassed you, Mister English. I'm sorry.'

My dick's getting interested now, attention seeking. She spots it.

'I've been keeping too much male company lately,' I say.

She laughs again. 'Do you know what a French date is, Mister English?'

'No,' I say, 'but I've got a pretty good idea, the French being the French.'

'A man and woman come together, no flowers, no candles, no dinner, no pretence, and pleasure one another, because they like one another, have lust for one another.'

She looks down at my crotch, pats the side of my thigh, stubs out her cigarette, sits back on her stool.

'I'm flattered,' I say.

'I wanted to check you out. I liked your voice, Mister English.'

'And?'

'I could have easily pretended I wasn't Jenna Zambrano, left you hanging ... '

'Could have done.'

'But I quite liked what I saw.'

'So did I, Miss Zambrano.'

'Come on, Mister English,' says Jenna, getting up to leave, 'we might have to leave the Monarch Club for another night. Let's get a room.'

'I've got a room – across town, away from prying eyes, and bodyguards.'

Jenna hums salsa rhythms – clicks her fingers, teases and dances – as she gets undressed, making me watch from the bed. As she strips I feel like howling. The image of her stepping out of her dress, to reveal her black lace underwear, will stay with me forever. She likes to be in control; no harm in that. I like Jenna. She's a giggle, fun. Says she used to be a tomboy, definitely isn't anymore. Jenna's full of tricks she didn't learn in the Girl Guides.

Jenna puts the condom on with her mouth, then gets on top, straddling me, then fucks me fast, then slow, stops as I'm about to come ... She remains still as a statue, blowing on me, gently caressing me, whispering to me, *comportese*, behave, kissing my neck, calming me ... Then after about half a minute she starts rolling her hips again, rhythmical, like there's music playing. She's licking my fingers and getting me to work her clit ever so gently with my thumb, telling me *exactly* what she needs.

And she's talking to me the whole time, in a mixture of English and Spanish, giving instructions, coaxing me, always stopping and starting, driving me mad. But in the end she times it so we both come at the same time – screaming and tearing at each other, ecstasy and relief. The best sex I've had since ... I don't know ... I could be happy here ...

After a minute she rolls off, still breathing hard, her hair stuck to her head, salty sweat dripping off her, staring up at the whirling ceiling fan, mesmerised.

'I needed that,' she says with a laugh. 'It's been a little while.'

I catch a sad look in her eyes – but only a glimpse – then it vanishes.

'*Muy bueno*, Mister English, very good ... but I have a confession.'

'Confession is good for the soul.'

'There was no eyelash on your cheek.' She laughs. 'What do you do, Mister English? For *your bosses*, that they would accommodate you in such a fine room?'

'I'm a broker,' I say, 'I have come to London to broker commodities.'

'Commodities from South America?'

I nod. 'But I've been diverted.'

'By Jesus and Santos?'

'Correct ... and by Miguel and his generous offer,' I reply. 'If we were to find that memory stick, what would we find?'

'Information. And Miguel would pay you well.'

'Is that why you—'

'Hey! Back up,' she says, jumping up, slapping my thigh, 'I'm not a whore.' Her eyes are full of anger. 'Do not offend me now.' But as fast as she gets angry, she calms down again. Jenna kisses me on the lips, by way of apology.

'Tell me about Jesus,' I say. 'Won't be able to find him if we don't know about him.'

Jenna looks apprehensive but begins to talk, slowly at first, then gathering momentum, about her deranged cousin. At times she gets animated, at others sad, angry, even scared. I wanna tell her she's scared of a ghost. But after twenty minutes her eyelids get heavy; Jenna suddenly looks like she's stoned. She puts a finger over my lips – *no more talking*. She puts her head on my chest. After a couple of minutes Jenna's breathing has become deep and steady. She's fast asleep ...

But I'm wide awake – electric. The head chess started again ... This was a ceasefire, not a truce. I give it a few more minutes, and then, as Jenna sleeps, I slip next door to read all about her. If it feels like deception and betrayal, it's because it is. There's a part of me that feels like I'm behaving like Jesus, like Jenna's number one stalker. But I reach into my hidey-hole and pull out the next instalment – Jesus' memoirs.

CHAPTER THIRTY - TWO

A DAZZLING STAR DIES

Makes you wonder why Jesus Zambrano didn't eliminate Cousin Miguel while he was still in Miami. Jesus' memoirs are chock full of venom and extreme vitriol – a coke-fuelled, self-absorbed tirade against Miguel, who he sees as the cause of all his problems. Through the transcript Jesus' bitterness *grows* in intensity – hours of hatred, spat out onto his tape recorder. In an insane way it pulls together the loose threads from the previous transcripts; throwaway lines and off-hand comments suddenly make sense. And Smiler's right, it was recorded in Jesus' room at the Cosmopolitan Hotel. Jesus Zambrano, live and direct from London Town.

Jenna had spent a lot of time in the US; too much time, her grandparents would have said. She'd learnt bad habits – good habits, any boyfriend would have told her. If they knew how Jenna behaved they would have swagged her off to a nunnery. Jenna is sexually proactive rather than waiting to be asked – she likes to have her tummy tickled.

She'd come back to Miami from Columbia University one weekend and bumped into Miguel and his cohorts. She developed the roaring hots for this Austrian guy who was hanging with Miguel, some computer *wunderkind*. Miguel and him were doing some *massive venture* together. But Jenna didn't like her brother knowing too much of her business, and one of Miguel's little maxims was that business and pleasure should never mix.

On the QT Jenna and The Wunderkind got acquainted, got revved up, hung out in South Beach. She introduced him to the strictly-invite-only parties in the poolside bungalows at the Delano or the Shore Club, kept him away from the spring break shitkickers from Kentucky State, or slimy, lecherous lawyers from Texas Tech *who seemed to think they knew* her.

All the surreptitious creeping about suited The Wunderkind. He didn't need anyone telling tales about his sexual liaisons with

Jenna, liaisons that could see him deaded or enrolling in his own version of the Witness Protection Program. He knew these Latinos were funny about their daughters', or sisters', reputations. Jenna sure didn't want her father to know she and IT Kid had been fucking each other senseless. Miguel she could deal with; he was a pragmatist. And she knew enough dirt on Miguel ...

A few people had given The Wunderkind the heads-up that Jenna had this weirdy-freak cousin who was obsessed with her – *be fucking careful* ... They weren't joking ...

Jenna had told Jesus she was marrying the Senator's son to get him off her back. Marrying Jenna into the legit élite was planting the flag, making a statement; herding the waifs and strays of the Zambrano Extended Clan onto a lifeboat and calling in the airstrike. It was about permanent severance. Miguel, meanwhile, did a smart thing – he stuck a trio of his top bodyguards on Jenna's fiancée; it wouldn't do to have him getting killed. The guy's father, The Senator, didn't care who Jenna slept with – either now or in future – but he didn't need it in his face. The Senator needed the deal as much as the Zambrano Family, but for different reasons. He'd worked out that his son and heir was a galloping homosexual. He didn't want it becoming common knowledge in case people suspected something fishy in the gene pool. He'd given up conspiring to kill him – committing filicide – and come around to thinking the marriage was the answer. An eight-figure dowry, paid into a Panama City bank account, and an alliance with an ambitious criminal family wasn't such a bad thing.

Jesus obviously wasn't privy to the internal business of the family. They thought he was just a volatile liability to be kept pacified and watched closely. Someone took their eye off the ball and Jesus went bandaloo – macabre bodysnatching expeditions down the jungle. Papa Victor wanted a word, but Jesus was not answering his pager ...

One weekend, feeling the heat and the humidity of Miami, IT Kid and Jenna drove down the Keys. But they were being followed, by Jesus, who was on a mission; part jealous admirer and apprentice blackmailer. Jesus was *fucking raging* – Jenna was a woman who liked to do her own thing and had rejected his overtures.

She's obviously a woman who likes a bit of rough and tumble in a hotel room but sadly not with poor Jesus. He was embedded nearby, plugged into his snide photographic equipment, getting self-righteous and hypocritical, taking his compromising smudges, sucking his thumb, while Jenna was enthusiastically sucking his rival's dick.

After their fuckfest Jenna shipped back to New York leaving The Wunderkind down in the Keys. He liked to have peace and quiet to do his calculations – the logarithm of twelve-digit numbers, in his head, for fun. Didn't need paper, let alone a calculator. He was listening to the waves gently lapping along the shore. This kid could one day send shockwaves around the world with his innovations – you'd like to buy start-up stock or futures in this guy – but for the time being he lived well, travelling the world, whistling up software programs for whoever was prepared to pay his sizeable per diem. This was a guy who had good looks, a thoroughbred's physique, talent, charm and dignity – everything that Jesus Zambrano lacked. And Jesus knew it.

The Wunderkind had an agent of sorts – a godfather – a friend of his late father's, who kept a parental eye on him and connected him with borderline organisations who could use his talents. Pop's old mate was a traditional money launderer and tax-evasion specialist. He knew the future was electronic and passed the baton to his godson. This old generation of Swiss, German and Austrian bankers didn't think of their clients as *strictly criminal*. These moneymen were gents who knew it was a game – *obviously* you cheated. But you didn't get caught. The law was the law. They were above it. If it wasn't illegal everyone would be at it.

So The Kid was sitting on the private deck of the bungalow at the end of the pier in the five-star resort hotel drinking a Martini, no landmass between him and Mexico. Jenna had deliberately asked for the most secluded bungalow – actually *over* the water, out to sea, a long schlep for busboys or maids, away from eavesdroppers – so she could holler if she felt like it. The Wunderkind was gazing out as the sun was disappearing magnificently into the sea when there was a polite tap at the door.

When he opened the door Jesus was stood there dressed in brand new, brilliant white tennis gear. He was practising forehands and backhands with an equally new tennis racket, returning imaginary balls, deftly dropping shots over the net. The Kid interrupted and asked how he could help.

'I'm the tennis coach,' replied Jesus.

'No shit, Sherlock,' said The Kid, trying to be an American.

'It's time for your lesson, sir.'

'I've got no lesson booked,' said the Austrian. 'I don't play tennis.'

'Someone's *obviously* made a mistake,' said Jesus, playing a drop shot.

'*Obviously*,' echoed The Kid.

'Can I use your house phone?' Jesus asked The Kid.

'Come in, please do,' he said, holding the door open.

As Jesus skipped inside, the Austrian genius had a rethink.

He asked, 'Isn't it getting too dark for tennis?'

'Floodlights, sir.'

'If I was having a tennis lesson,' asks Wunderkind, 'wouldn't I meet you at the court?'

Jesus *didn't like his tone*. The Wunderkind got posted missing. Over the next week sections of the body washed up along the coast. Everything except the head – the head that was going to revolutionise the world. Miguel was getting late-night updates from his various connections giving him the sweet and low ... *funny, he was paid for his head*.

Q. Jesus' motive?

A. Jealousy – personal and professional. The kid was a genius with a computer. It was him who wrote the software that took Smiler days to decipher. The saving grace was that the memory stick was locked in a banker's safe in Miami and not about his person.

Meanwhile back at the Zambrano Palazzo in downtown Miami, The Kid's Official Guardian was cursing the Zambrano Family. He'd flown in from New York City especially to abuse them. Young Genius had gone missing while under their protection; they were responsible. Papa Victor *suspected* that Jesus was somehow involved but had a loyalty to the family. To Miguel – who *just knew* Jesus was involved but couldn't prove it – his cousin was becoming a dangerous liability. This latest business was more than an embarrassment. All the chit-chat about respectability seemed delusional while they had to contend with a livewire like Jesus.

As much as they insisted that they knew nothing about the disappearance and that Florida was a dangerous place, their protestations didn't ring true. The Austrian starts maligning them in just the circles that they want to move into, all because Jesus couldn't get his own way ...

Papa Victor was old school too, thought he could send a team to kill The Austrian, but it would compound the problem. They would be prime suspects. It wouldn't exactly be good PR, would do enough damage to the reputation of the Zambranos that all their respectable political allies, at home and in the US, would bolt. So they had to suffer it, because these establishment fuckers ultimately run the game. Miguel consoled himself with the thought that one day *they* would be the establishment. He realised that if The Austrian Godfather found out The Wunderkind had been fucking Slick Miguel's twin sister, Juicy Jenna, and got killed by his homicidally jealous cousin, Jesus the Madhead, it could all appear slightly slack, a wee bit like soap opera.

Papa Victor, heavily influenced by Miguel, starts thinking of Jesus' branch of the family as *The Deadwoods – They can't behave. Can't help themselves. Greedy fuckers. Either at your feet or at your throat. Been letting them do the business under the corporate banner ... And what thanks do we get?*

Papa starts to think it's time to do a little pruning. Miguel, looking up from his projections and spreadsheets, tells him, *good idea, Father. It's definitely time to downsize.*

Jesus is still apparently eavesdropping on Miguel. And Miguel's having trouble working out exactly what The Wunderkind had done with the records he had encrypted on the memory stick. The Kid was smart enough to build in a few cyber trapdoors. Around this time Miguel began to hear whispers about Jesus and Santos' exploits down in the jungles. Miguel was business-like, a different kind of sociopath ... Jesus would have to go *to heaven or hell* ... he was just going to send him on his way.

Jesus was getting more deranged, fast becoming addicted to murder, humiliation and torture. They were providing euphoric highs that class-A narcotics could only hint at. Ketamine couldn't touch the sides. Jesus told himself crystal meth is for sissies. Your fucking mummy takes cocaine. And Satanism's for girls! Homicide is the new black, baby!

Q. How did Jenna feel about Jesus offing her boyfriend?

A. Sick. Shocked and stunned. A little bit over-responsible. But older heads told her *you can't negotiate with madness*. The killing confirmed everything she'd ever thought about Jesus – he was a dangerous piece of shit who thought the only way to get attention was through causing mayhem. Cousin Jesus now brought out Jenna's heartless side. When she heard whispers that Miguel was making plans for Jesus' funeral – date To Be Confirmed – she bought a Chanel outfit to celebrate – high-heels, a low-cut white blouse, black suit, with the tightest pencil skirt, had the jacket especially tailored to push her glorious breasts up into deep cleavage.

The old family retainers discovered a new trail of murder and chaos in Florida. Jesus had started killing prostitutes to keep his hand in – more bad news for Miguel. He offers a bounty on Jesus and the memory stick; fuck the family edict – he don't need a serial killer with the same surname for a cousin. It's the sorta thing that people remember – *any relation to Zambrano the Florida Strangler?*

And neither does Jenna, because Jenna has political ambitions. There must always be distance between Miguel's operations and Jenna's public image; he needs things *compartmentalised*, she needs thing *deniable*. Seems the Zambrano Twins are planning on taking over Venezuela in years to come, *a whole fuckin country*. Miguel's going to fund her, using the obligatory ill-gotten fortune from the Ponzi scheme. And Jenna's providing star quality. The marriage to The Senator's son is only *Stage One* of The Plan – the one they have been hatching, and refining, since they were teenagers.

Jesus thought there was a deal to be done, was prepared to sell his side of the family down the river for money. He would sell the incriminating photos but only negotiate through Jenna, hence the late-night calls. Jenna was not entertaining him – *fuck you, Jesus, speak to Miguel. I don't know about any memory stick.* She was hitting the red button on the phone every time he rang, before he could deliver his pitch.

Stop. Fucking. Ringing. You. Mad. Murdering. Motherfucker.

Jenna only started to take notice when Jesus revealed the existence of the compromising photos. He sent her JPEGs, via the *complimentary in-house Internet facility* at the Cosmo P.

SUBJECT: FYI JENNA – I LOVE U – JESUS – XXXX

They landed in her inbox with a thump; no good for the family album, but they got her attention. Jenna wasn't privy to the inner workings of the clan – strictly *deniable, need-to-know basis* – but suddenly she starts taking a necessary interest. She didn't want to *think* about allowing Miguel the moral high ground, but she didn't want her father seeing those photographs either. But if they didn't listen to Jesus' demands – sent through intermediaries in various Venezuelan embassies – the Senator, and a few other prominent figures, would get, in the post, the full set of his future daughter-in-law performing. And Jesus knew that spiteful loser ex-boyfriends posted photos of former girlfriends in compromising positions on the Internet. Jenna knew once those pictures hit the net, they were gone forever, blown to the four corners of cyberspace. Any political career would be in shreds; she'd have the wrong type of fan club. The Plan was going bandaloo. They needed to get the toothpaste back in the tube ...

They looked high and low, lit up the sky, looked in all Jesus' hangouts, hunted down all his associates. They couldn't find Jesus. They dropped cash and broke bones but nobody knew where he was. Miguel sent word – if any harm came to Jenna, Miguel wouldn't kill Santos and his team, he would decimate their families – he'd kill them all. Jesus had already alighted in London.

Q. Why London?

A. The shopping and the history?

Jesus knew the memory stick was important. He wanted to feel power. Wanted a reaction. To make them sweat. *This* was what he was looking for from the organ-harvesting fiasco – recognition.

But Jesus had no idea of the real contents. He only got as far as Roy – rows and rows of impenetrable hieroglyphics. Jesus never riddled out what Miguel was chatting to his cohorts about; he knew nothing of Ponzi schemes or nominee bankers siphoning off hundreds of millions of dollars into shadow accounts in New York. He thought the photos and Miguel's malicious conversations were the story.

Jenna's campaign and reputation as the future dazzling star were temporarily on hold; lost, but within touching distance. Miguel was considering a deal, but knew it meant a lifetime of headfuck, knowing he'd been had over by Jesus. The Zambranos' slotting crews were kicking their heels, oiling their guns, but their target couldn't be found. Then came a break in the case ...

One sunny day they got an anonymous phone call from a place called Pad-Ding-Ton Station. The caller, a Venezuelan, declined to give his name but had heard on the grapevine the family was looking for the elusive one. This was the as yet unidentified gent who Flavio had saluted as he got in his taxi outside the Cosmo P. *If things go well*, the caller told them he'd be looking for a favour – *quid pro quo*. He informed them the buffoon Jesus was in London but was shipping out to Paris, on the Eurostar, *departing Waterloo*, ten o'clock, the next morning. The Zambrano Family sent a team overnight to retrieve – or dispatch – the errant cousin before he could do more damage. They could take out Jesus either at Waterloo or on the train ... or even wait till he reached Gare du Nord ...

But they hadn't factored in the phenomenon that is Roy 'Twitchy' Burns and his equally twitchy Skorpion semi-automatic.

CHAPTER THIRTY-THREE

TODAY'S DILEMMA

'Why did Jesus have to kill all these guys?'

Jenna looks at me like I've just asked a silly question. 'You never knew Jesus Zambrano, did you?' I shake my head. 'You two never met, did you?' she asks, eyebrows up, waiting for an answer.

'No. He'd take a dim view of this, us being in the kip, but why would he kill—'

'For fun ... ' she replies, dry as a twig. 'So he could tell his *next* victim about the *last* victim.' She shrugs, 'He was never right ... I always knew it, even as a child ... '

'He was some flower, your cousin,' I say off-hand.

'*Was*?' asks Jenna, quick as a flash. 'You said, "*was*".'

'I was speculating. You need to calm down, Jenna.'

'No, I think *you* need to calm down, Mister English.'

It's the best place in the world: Sunday morning, hotel room, curtains open, bright sunshine, room service, nice breakfast, big hard-on, beautiful woman going down on you ... Our clothes are still scattered on the floor from last night.

Strewn. Underwear. A wonderful pair of words. I think these South American women employ this simple method of keeping their geezers under control – plenty of sex. There'd be no need to stray too far from Jenna – you'd be too exhausted. Ambitious women, like ambitious men, have a very high sex drive.

I'm relaxing a bit ... If Jenna's using me as bait to smoke out Jesus I can live with it ... I know something they don't ... And now I'm reaping the benefits of an American education; they must teach blowjobs in the tenth grade. It's all about getting the breathing right – out on the down, in on the up. She's hit her rhythm now, hitting the right strokes. I'm rocking and rolling, arching my back, like the fella in Jesus' smudges ...

But then I catch some movement out of the corner of my eye

– something strange. Roy's raincoat – which I now have on permanent loan – is being tugged across the floor in increments, disappearing out of view as if giant mice are gently dragging it. The raincoat is sliding across the carpet, edging its way out of sight.

But I can't bring myself to stop Jenna; the head's gone west, odd dilemma. Suddenly a figure breaks cover – a scrawny, chalk-white London junkie with mad blonde hair sticking out from under a cap. He's made a lunge for the raincoat, deciding it's the prize. He looks at me boldly. Something registers with me – recognition, maybe. He's fearless, this geezer, or whacked out. His eyes are pinned; he's smacked-up – oblivious to danger but together enough to know the game's up.

The geezer's hit the door and stepped out, with Roy's raincoat over his arm like he's going for a stroll. I'm shouting, slapping the bed, but Jenna just thinks I'm coming. She carries on regardless. I almost have to wrench her away. She is oblivious of any sneak thief. I'm breathlessly trying to explain that someone sneaked in and stole my raincoat.

'You expecting fucking rain?'

I jump out of bed, open the door and look down the corridor, left and right. Two chambermaids are outside my door; one giggles, looking straight at my hard-on but the other covers her eyes. I realise that if the wallet in the pocket – containing the ATM cards and false driving licence – goes missing, I'll be in serious trouble. Not with Sonny and Roy, but with Ted and Sister Bridget. I won't be able to tell them it was stolen while I was getting a BJ.

But the thief is calmly standing at the lift, trying to act cool. He's put the raincoat on, got my sunglasses out the pocket, and is using the lift door as a mirror. A couple of other guests are looking at him curiously. I run back inside and grab some clothes, pull them on double quick, hopping on one foot, trying to put on a stubborn loafer.

'Someone was in the room?' Jenna is standing on the bed, seriously upset. 'Someone was here! Who?'

'I don't know,' I say, but Jenna is now across the room, blocking my exit.

'Some sneak thief,' I say.

'How did they get in?'

'I don't fuckin know, Jenna. Slipped in with the room service ... hid in the bathroom.'

'It was Jesus!' she screams. 'He's here!'

'No, Jenna, it was some creeper. I've got to get my wallet back. It can't be lost.'

She hangs on. 'You can't leave me here!'

'I'll be gone a minute, Jenna. Please, get out of the way! He's getting away. I'm gonna go.'

I push past her, out the door, but the lift – and the thief – has gone. I watch the indictor counting down fast.

The lifts stop on every other floor; I run downstairs from the twenty-seventh floor to see if my luck's any better one flight down. The lift is stationary on the top floor. I push the button, hear it moving. It arrives. I get in, hit the G button.

On the tenth floor the lift stops. Some other guests get in. They're wanting to wait for their dozy mate who's meandering up the corridor. I tell the geezer to take his hand off the 'doors open' button – *I'm in a hurry, stop fuckin about.* He looks me up and down. If he wants a scuffle I'm up for it. He takes his hand off the button. We continue down to the lobby. Out of the lift. No sign of the thief.

Q. Could this be Jenna setting me up, a distraction?

A. Possibly. Can't think about that right now. But I think she'd send some ice-cold mercenary to dangle me out the window, not some roasting sneak thief.

And she'd be fully clothed when they arrived.

I rush out the main door, cursing. *It's futile* and *I'm fucked.* Then I spot Roy Burns' raincoat and a floppy baker boy hat disappearing around the corner about a hundred yards away. I trot off in his direction. *Fuckin lib – junkie cunt – disturbing my thing.* I'll catch him easy. He can't be that quick or alert. If I can't catch a skaghead whose only exercise is building pipes and running to reload I'm in trouble. I'm fifty yards behind, but holding back.

Big trouble if that gunnif disappears with them cards, serious implications. And I guess Royski will have something to say if his precious coat goes AWOL. But I know that chalk-white face from somewhere back on the old manor ... it's in the back of the canister ... Fuck it!

I *do* know him, the thieving cunt. He's one of the notorious O'Malley Family, one of the gearhead younger brothers. Young Stevie O'Malley. Proper dildo kid, not all there ... A specialist scavenger, getting his tackle creeping City hotels over this side. A fuckin sneak thief, slipping in after cleaners and room service, hiding in wardrobes and shower stalls. Of all the hotel rooms in all the world, he had to sneak into mine ... I've been on red alert since I landed, now I'm a victim of pussy blindness. Maybe I even left the door open after I rapidly ushered the room service porter out.

The whole O'Malley family are loons. I can't apprehend Young Stevie and ask nicely for my stolen property back. I could kill Stevie or do him serious damage on the sly but if I hurt him and they find out there'll be repercussions. And the O'Malleys, being certified lunatics, would pay me no matter what anyone said to try and pacify them.

Stevie is up ahead, no doubt dying to get into the parcel he's just chored. It makes sense to go somewhere secluded to have a peek into the wallet ... I can wait, get Stevie away from the public, avoid a scene. I was spooked; it might have been some manoeuvre from Jenna, or Brother Miguel. Now I'm bizarrely reassured that I know the guy who's robbing me.

I'm getting closer all the time. He's across a set of traffic lights, dodging cars, does a sharp right then swerves round a corner. When I turn the corner I spot Stevie about fifty yards away wrapping Roy's coat around him, over and over again; skipping and bowling along, looking in a shop window, checking his new shades. I've got to be cute, maybe collar Stevie and tell him he can keep the cash but I've got to have them cards, wallet and raincoat back. To him the cards are worthless PVC – be lucky to get a tenner each.

Stevie suddenly turns and starts walking backwards, scanning the street to see if anyone is following. I dodge behind a parked van, get a snide look off the driver, ask him nicely if he's *got a fuckin problem*. I wait until I see Stevie turn to face front again before continuing up the street. I can imagine Stevie getting tingly, knows he's had a touch, telling his mates *the mug was only getting a blowjob while I chored his fuckin coat. Nice bird, though, nice coat too, might keep it for a coupla weeks ...*

Stevie's gathering speed again. Why the fuck he would want a raincoat on a lovely day like today is beyond me. Roy would have a right royal moan-up if that bitta clobber got mislaid cos you know it's got to have talismanic qualities. It's no doubt Roy's lucky raincoat, for warding off evil. I couldn't say I'd lost it, not with Roy in his present state of mind. What a turnout that would be if Stevie turned up down the AKQ Club wearing Royski's old faithful.

I've changed my mind; gonna fight fire with fire. Going to sit on Stevie, follow him till we're safely away from Joe Pub, then I'm gonna jump all over him, get a bit old neighbourhood with him. Get dark before he gets a chance to hurt me. Gonna dislocate his arm at the shoulder then kick it in all directions till he comes under manners. Gonna make him hurt. I've lost patience with the Stevies of this world. Starting to see how Sonny and Roy use violence therapeutically.

If Stevie O'Malley fucked the likes of Sonny or Roy he'd be gone – hole dug deep, *adios* Stevie. Hope it doesn't end up going bandaloo. I need that wallet and fuckin raincoat. Stevie ain't gonna be telling tales to his brothers. If he does Mort'll square it off – a few quid compo, few rounds of drinks down those stinky drinkers the Mad O'Malleys frequent.

But now Stevie's half trotting, heading for Tower Hill tube station and the westbound rattler home. It's getting more crowded, I shoulda jumped on Stevie earlier. He's swerving and darting through waves of tourists, like a locked-on missile on final approach. I'm limbering myself up. Gotta drag Stevie down an alleyway, away from the crowd.

You're Stevie O'Malley. I'm from the neighbourhood too. You've gotta help me out, Stevie. I really need your help. Confuse him. *I ain't angry, Stevie. Hurt, not angry.* Then one knee up hard in the nuts, to double him over. Sharp pain to shock the system, then work the diaphragm. Knee in hard, three or four times. Aim to maim. Get the fight out of him as soon as. No oxygen, no strength, no resistance. This is war. This is survival. You or me, Stevie. Gonna be dark style, might as well enjoy it.

Stevie's no doubt got the classic junkie high pain threshold – *is that your best shot?* But I ain't got time for negotiations, had the piss taken out of me royally. What did Jenna say? You *can't negotiate with madness.* Can't negotiate with headbangers named O'Malley either.

I manoeuvre myself out of his sight line. He turns nonchalantly, all in one movement, checking out the street again, walking backwards ... He's thinking he's clean away, breathing out, relaxing ...

Now Stevie reaches a traffic light but this time he stops, waiting for the little green man. He's talking to a young woman who's waiting as well. She's a tourist – American I'd wager – with a group, doing the Old World tour. Stevie's doing small talk – *where you from, America?* Stevie's bouncing from foot to foot, excited. The day couldn't get better. She smiles, instinctively puts both arms around her handbag, hugs it to her chest. Might be from Bumfuck, Idaho, but she can spot a wrong 'un. Steve's a frog. She's a princess. Don't kiss frogs. The rest of her party is nervous, thinking Stevie's out to rob them all. He'd be outraged if he thought for a second ... *Theft, sir? How dare you?* They're still waiting on the light.

Got to make my move before he hits the tube, far too public. Better make it personal with Stevie O'Malley. It's now or never, bud. Use the Yanks as a distraction; get on Stevie's blind side. Time to move. My heartbeat's pumping. Think of the consequences if ...

Suddenly a gent in a dark suit and large wraparound sunglasses bumps past me. His shoulder collides with mine. I go to say something but he strides on. Big strides. The guy's wearing leather gloves – gloves in August? Hang on ... he marches with purpose, straight towards Stevie. He's ten foot away. His right arm comes up. His left hand comes up to meet it. Now he's got both hands now on – oh fuck, a shooter! The guy stops dead, bends his knees a touch ...

He shoots Stevie twice in the temple, rapid succession – doff, dooff – using a silencer. Blows Stevie's hat off – clean fuckin off.

Stevie crumples, falls. Lifeless. Red mist where his head was. Dead before he hits the floor. Executed.

Nothing moves. The Princess is covered in Stevie's blood, outta Stevie's brain. Then a woman faints. Another tries to scream but no sounds emerges – just a strange, low, painful wail. The gunman has disappeared, vanished completely. Stevie's been slotted by a professional. The law are gonna be all over this place in seconds. If they find that wallet it's trouble ... I need it away from Stevie O'Malley. Away from a crime scene. Exhibit in a murder trial. They'd run those cards through a reader, get all their data in seconds ... This is the Metropolitan Police Force ... no joke ...

I begin walking fast. A large puddle of the darkest crimson blood is flowing from Stevie's head. I'm straight through the gawping crowd. They hold hands to faces, bewildered, trying to comfort themselves. The blood-covered Princess is screaming hysterically now, still clutching her bloodstained handbag. *What happened? What just happened?*

I crouch down, pretending to be a doctor testing for a pulse in Stevie's neck. Trying not to get blood on my shoes. His eyes are still open. His death mask still registers shock. Stevie thought he'd cracked it one minute, dead the next. I shut his eyes, half expecting them to bounce back open – being from a family of awkward bastards.

Maybe you shouldn't touch him suggests a forensically aware punter. I turn and tell him, assertively, that we need to establish that life is extinct. The guy looks slightly ashamed but I don't want him looking into my face too much. I duck my head down.

People take orders from people who they *perceive* to have authority. Get these women away – screaming and weeping – I tell busy punter, the know-all-cunt. The wallet is, amazingly, still in Stevie's hand. I coax it from Stevie's grip. He resists, a little. I knew he would.

I need that wallet in my pocket, not in some evidence bag – the telltale break in the case. Just the thing those Scotland Yard detectives love. I test the pulse in the wrist, for appearances. Then I palm the wallet like a card cheat, shaking my head and shouting for space and air.

Then I tell the busy cunt, shout up at him, to ring the police. He's rung. *Well, ring them again!* All eyes turn to him. In one hit I slip the wallet down the front of my trousers. I stand up, shaking my head, muttering about waste, muttering about *too late for a doctor*. My hand's over my face, rubbing my eyes, pulling downwards in frustration, distorting my features, avoiding recognition – now or in the witness box. Stevie would have heartily approved – *needs must, bruv, couldn't have ya getting swagged. Get on your toes, quick sharp.* I hear the first sirens. *Slip away quick, son. You got the prize, job done.* Stevie would have applauded. Bewilderment, confusion and chaos; Stevie O'Malley died like he lived. Roy's raincoat is a write-off, covered in claret, fit only for the bin or the forensics department. I'm about to disappear when ... fuck!

The bill from the Cosmopolitan Hotel bar is in the inside pocket of that raincoat. Big clue. I crouch back down. I slip a hand into the pocket of the blood-spattered coat. I find the bill straight away and palm it. I move my hand from the raincoat to my own pocket, with less grace than before. An onlooker tumbles that I've dipped the pocket. He starts squeaking. 'Did you just go in his pocket?' he screams. 'Did you see that?' he says to another onlooker.

He says to me. 'You took something from his pocket, I saw you!'

'You didn't, mister,' I say, and regret it. 'You've made a mistake.'

'Show me your pocket!' he demands. 'Show me your pocket then!'

'Fuck off!' I snap before I can stop myself. 'Fuck right off!'

'Are you even a doctor?' He answers his own question. 'You're not a doctor at all, are you?'

'Does he look like he needs a doctor?' I say, pointing at Stevie.

He takes a step towards me. 'I think we should wait for the police,' he says, going to grab my arm. I shrug him off but he's looking into my face, preparing the description he's gonna put in his statement. I wanna step back and nut him but I'm edging backwards. Everyone else is transfixed on Stevie's dead body, or hugging one another for comfort, but he's silently pointing at me, remembering me. Attention to detail. New arrivals are pushing through the crowd – *what happened? Fuck!* Then wishing they hadn't.

Q. Why did you do that? Look at the dead man – his head half gone?

A. Dunno. Was. Both. Fucking. Bizarre. And. Stupid.

I'm moving backwards all the time. The wallet sits awkwardly down the front of my strides. I'm hoping it doesn't fall down my leg. That could be trouble ...

A police car sweeps into the street, almost knocking people over, sirens blaring. It skids to a halt. Two shirt-sleeved cozzers jump out, both with semi-automatic rifles tight across their chests. It makes sense – reports of a shooting, make that random shooting. Could be a lunatic on the loose. They see it for what it is straight away – a murder inquiry. Another cozzer jumps out, on the radio the whole time, whistling up reinforcements. The three of them push people back, set up a tight perimeter. Without panic – well-mannered assertiveness – *nothing more to see.* I'm told to leave, don't need telling twice. Mister Busy is badgering the cozzer with the radio, pointing in my direction. The cozzer is taking no notice, telling him to get back, *out of the way, please, sir, right now, please, sir.*

I imagine Stevie telling me to stroll away *nice and easy. And burn them clothes. New address, bruv, quick-sharp.* I'm doing a Roy; thinking Steve's ghost is cheering my getaway from the other side. I back away slowly, inconspicuously, looking over the cozzer's shoulder the whole time, like I'm arriving not departing. Cozzer's got his arms wide, sweeping all the onlookers, and potential witnesses, up the street and away.

Please move back. Show's over. Nothing to see.

Q. When confusion reigns?

A. Chaos is your friend.

CHAPTER THIRTY-FOUR

CRUEL IRONIES

Walk fast but not too fast, straight into the hotel lobby and the lift.
Don't look right or left. I hit the button. Retrieve the wallet from
down my strides. Open it. The cash is gone – no surprise, in Stevie's
kick, no doubt, but the cards look intact. Gotta get gone, though, get
across town. Alibis are no good; ain't even meant to be here. Sort
the nodder out later. You have to be a bit sociopathic, sometimes,
to get through this life. How the fuck did Santos find me? Was that
his handiwork? Wouldn't be Miguel's. If Santos wanted to ping me
he coulda slipped in the room. If a madhead like Stevie can sneak
in, Santos' crew would find it easy. I think them bullets were meant
for me.

Out the lift, sharp right, down the hall. Chambermaid's trolley
parked up the corridor. I walk past my room – the Do Not Disturb
sign dangling off the door handle – and over to the trolley. The
maid is working three doors down. I take what I need. Heavy-duty
sprays, cloths, rubber gloves, then double back to my own room.
I slip the keycard in, with a moment of hesitation ... then enter.

Jenna is gone; there's no sign of her. I take off my clothes, put
on the gloves and clean the room. Every surface. Paranoid? I don't
want my DNA or prints hanging around. Go heavy with the
bleach. Clean everything that doesn't move. When I'm done I run
the shower over my head and comb my hair. Overload the
cologne; looking presentable but feeling debauched. Where did
Jenna go? Double-check everything. Making good time. Time to
get icy calm. Deep breaths. Can hear sirens down below. But if I
don't check out properly it could be conspicuous ... If I was to just
disappear the hotel might report me missing. The police might
even think I'm the victim of the shooting ... They'd go to work on
the credit card the reservation was made with and that could
attract unwanted attention.

Everything in the holdall. Travel light. Get dressed in different clothes. I head out. Downstairs in lift. Am I walking straight into Old Bill? The lobby is empty. We're five minutes from the scene. I tell the receptionist I need to check out.

'Any problems, sir?' she asks.

'Like what?' I say, startled.

'With the room?'

'Oh, no,' I reply.

'Only you're booked in indefinitely.'

'I fancied a change of scenery.'

She laughs a corporate laugh. I tell her *sadly there's been a change of plan*. Not exactly a lie. She asks for the credit card I used to book the room. Could be a problem. I tell her my human resources department takes care of these things. She scratches her head. *But if you tell me the last four digits ...*

She does and I go into the wallet and check the card numbers, pull out the one I need. It's got more than traces of congealed blood on it – a nasty streak of incriminating evidence – fuck knows how it got there. I almost drop the card. I ask to check the items on the bill. *Some go on expenses ...* I'm sweating. I ask for a tissue. She points at a box on the desk. I wipe the card while concentrating on the itemised bill. The card is gleaming, literally presentable. I hand it to her. She sweeps it through a reader, hands it back, no problem. She hands me an envelope with my receipts and bills, and a customer survey – *did I enjoy my stay? Would I recommend it?* Could win a *spectacular prize* in their draw.

But I'm marching – out the door, looking for geezers in dark suits with guns. I dodge the taxi rank and walk, not really knowing where I'm heading. Ten minutes up the road I dodge into a payphone and ring Morty's work phone. Sunday morning he'll know it's an emergency, condition black. I need a laylow. Till I know the score.

Morty answers the phone, sleepy, irritated. *Someone done one up close, in the nut, who was wearing the fella's coat. Mistaken identity. Was meant to be me.*

'Get a hat. And glasses – any glasses – from a chemist. Don't be a tart. Get a tube two clicks north of where you met the twitchy fella the other day. Don't bring a mess. Turn left out the station, do another one, then turn into the first left you see, there's a square, walk to the far end.'

'What's the square called?'

'Not over the air. I'll see you there.'

'I'll ring if I get lost.'

'Not on this phone. It's gone.'

The phone goes dead. Go to the Angel, Islington, sit in a square, wait on Mort.

Thirty minutes later, sitting in his motor, after I've confessed to the meet with Jenna, given him a blow-by-blow account of the shooting of Stevie O'Malley and my escape from the hotel, Mister Mortimer asks me, 'What are you?'

'A cunt,' I am forced to reply.

Morty shakes his head. He's still dressed top-show but I don't think he was off to church. 'Are you sure it was Stevie O'Malley that got popped?'

'I never forget a face, Mort.'

'Fuck!' screams Morty, most out of character. 'Listen, you say nothing to Sonny, or Roy, or Ted, okay? Not yet, we need to think this through.'

'I'm saying nothing, Mort,' I say. 'I'm meant to be dead.'

'What do you fuckin want? Fuckin counselling?' says Morty, looking at me in disbelief. 'This could get worse – the O'Malleys might think you had something to do with it.'

The O'Malley tribe will soon be on the loose, looking for the people who shot their kid brother – a bizarre bonding experience. They won't be listening to reasonable argument, that Stevie was the architect of his own demise. If they find out we're even remotely involved they'll be looking for blood, or blood money – a drop of compensation for their most heartfelt loss.

I knew Stevie's older brother, Gerry – who'll be either MIA or banged-up somewhere – from early childhood. We were at infants' school together, lived in the same block of flats, so I knew his layabout, alkie father – *too heavy for light work, too light for heavy work*. Also knew his bruised saint of a mother and all his big piss-poor family. The Old Bill was always turning up, blue lights flashing, because of the eruptions going on in their tiny flat. The whole family would turn on the cozzers and chase them away

mob-handed. They'd be slinging anything that came to hand –
furniture, pots, pans, beds, chairs, flaming mattresses – off the
balcony onto the patrol cars below. In the end the law would only
go in with riot gear, to drag away one of the brothers. To the other
residents it was a nuisance, but to us kids it was cheap
entertainment. A huge family of eleven, the older O'Malleys were
all mad alcoholics while the younger ones were lost to the brown
and the white.

Morty is driving and he's livid; not a good combo. You'd think
it was him they'd tried to shoot. He's seriously berating me for
even entertaining Jenna, can't be sidetracked by accounts of her
expertise. For once he *don't wanna know*. He tells me – *do not tell
Sonny and Roy*, till it becomes irritating. It doesn't register with
him that I'm meant to be dead. Morty suggests that *maybe Stevie
had enemies*.

'Mort, geezer was a pro. Was a proper wet job.'

'Then you had a lucky escape.'

Morty drives in circles. Eventually he takes me to a safe
apartment in a mansion block in Swiss Cottage, complete with
underground car park so the inhabitants can slip in and out without
anyone seeing. Gents in my world love an underground car park.

The apartment is sterile but stocked up with frozen food and
gallons of drink. There's videos and a thin layer of dust on
everything, plus a few scattered cobwebs. Nobody's lived here for
months – it's soulless but functional, the safe house every firm has
tucked. You could live here indefinitely but it would drive you
crazy.

'What are you gonna tell those two when they ask you why you
moved?' asks Morty, and as he does his phone begins to ring. He
looks at the ID on the phone.

'Talk of the devil ... it's Sonny.' He answers the phone,
'Yeah?' He listens, a curious expression breaking out. 'Yeah, he's
here. Why do you ask? A few minutes away ... Now? Not the
park? Why? Show me what, exactly? Don't get all fuckin cryptic
with me.'

Morty finishes the call and looks even more puzzled.

'Sonny want us to come over to his gaff, right now, wants to
show us something.'

'Show us what?'

'Dunno, wouldn't say ... '

'What about—'

'Don't worry, I'll buy Roy a new raincoat,' says Mort. 'What Roy wants with a fuckin raincoat down in Marbella is beyond me.'

As me and Morty enter Sonny's des-res the huge plasma TV is booming – rolling news – but the screen shows a flickering image in freeze-frame, like it's been cued, ready to go, four zeros in a neat row in the bottom right-hand corner. I get a nauseous feeling in my guts. Unseen reporters are shrieking – *Bogus doctor ... sneak thief ... police have not identified the victim ... robbing the dead ... callous beyond belief ... part of the execution squad ... speculation ...*

Roy stands to attention, holding a remote control, with a court martial face.

'What's it all about, Sonny?' asks Morty, but he's tumbled that our news embargo is over.

'Sit down, get comfy,' says Sonny, indicating the plush sofas. 'Maestro ... Mister Burns,' he says with a flourish, 'if you would, sir ... '

Roy pushes the play button. The screen is filled with news footage of me removing the wallet and bar bill. It doesn't look good. The anchorman is suggesting that the perpetrator, i.e. me, is *robbing the dead*. The station is running the footage, repeatedly, on a loop, using all their trickery to blow up the footage so it's pixellated. Roy has recorded it.

'The footage was recorded by a tourist,' says Sonny with a certain amount of glee. 'A Japanese one ... one of those camcorders. Personally, I think it's a fuckin liberty.'

'Liberty,' echoes Roy.

'Is nothing fuckin sacred? Point a fuckin camera at anything, some people. You could sue.'

'This is a recording, yeah?' says Roy. 'You getting it?'

'Loud and clear, Roy,' I say.

Sonny is studying the footage, waiting for something ... Sonny clicks his fingers. Dry and crisp. Roy hits the pause button. The screen is filled with a grainy image – my close-up.

'See ... ' says Sonny, pointing, 'I reckon that's you.'

'Could be,' I reply lamely.

'Do you mind if I ask a question?' he asks gently. I nod. Sonny adopts a passive expression, an open posture, speaks slow, 'What the fuck is going on?' I look over at Mort. 'No good lookin at him,' says Sonny. 'Is he your brief? Do we need to play it one more time?' He nods at the telly. 'Need an encore?'

'That's unnecessary,' says Morty.

'See, that's worldwide fame. Global human-interest story. Be on everywhere,' says Sonny, buzzing on my misfortune. Your crisis, my victory. 'And you got a tiddy-wink to blame.'

'Japanese ain't chinks, Sonny,' says Morty.

'Don't fuckin care, Mort. That's our kid here,' nodding at me, 'dipping the pocket of a dead man ... And Roy's got it into his head that that's his raincoat ... all covered in claret.'

'Not a theory. That's my coat,' says Roy, starting to get twitchy, 'the one I borrowed you in Barbados.'

'So?' says Sonny. 'Are ya gonna tell us or what?'

I tell Sonny and Roy, more or less, what happened, leaving out Jenna. That it was Stevie O'Malley, who crept my room, stole the raincoat, who got shot – make that assassinated.

'Stevie O'Malley! That's Special Needs Stevie on the deck, there, dead?' says Sonny, pointing at the screen. 'When was you gonna fuckin tell us, exactly? *Was* you gonna tell us?'

'It was meant to be me.'

'And is that my raincoat?' asks Roy, pointing, childlike, at the screen.

Before I can answer, Sonny's turned to Roy, 'Will you shut up about your fuckin raincoat!'

'But it's my property.'

'Roy,' says Mort, 'someone's trying to kill yer man here, and managed to kill Steve O'Malley instead. It's about perspective.'

Roy doesn't like it but says nothing.

'So who fuckin shot Stevie?' asks Sonny, as his phone starts to ring. He studies it; the caller ID has him perplexed. 'I've a feeling,' he says, 'that this might have something to do with it.'

'Who is it?' asks Morty.

'Santos,' says Sonny, as he answers it, puts it on speakerphone.

'Mister King, good morning,' says Santos, 'or should I say good afternoon. You would have no doubt heard the bad news. I must apologise but we felt it was necessary, for you to take us seriously.'

'Go on, Mister Santos.'

'It's Mister de Lucia, actually. We had *the counsellor* executed to show we mean business.'

'I did hear. He was one of my closest friends.'

'This is the nature of business we are engaged in, Sonny,' says Santos, dead theatrical.

'What exactly are you after, Santos?'

'We would like Jesus Zambrano returned to us, dead or alive.'

'I'm not sure I can oblige you.'

'Or the memory stick he was transporting.'

'Again, I can't help.'

'Jesus had come by a lot of money. We would like that money returned to us ... for the inconvenience.'

Sonny mimics Santos, '*For the inconvenience*? Well my buddy getting shot dead is an *inconvenience* to me.'

'Please take us seriously, Mister King. We are hoping you are a reasonable man.'

'Why does everyone think we had something to do with Jesus' disappearance?'

'The last time I spoke to Jesus, he told me that he suspected that he was being watched.'

'By the police?'

'By your organisation, Mister King. He feared having his funds stolen.'

'Well,' says Sonny, 'he got it wrong.'

'We will shoot another one of your team, Sonny, starting with your sidekick.'

'Didn't know I had a sidekick.'

He describes Roy Burns – *rather nervous, a paranoid, perhaps?* They've obviously been baked-up outside the Monarch. 'Is he your *Head of Security*, Sonny? He rather let your *counsellor* down, didn't he?' says Santos, with a melodramatic laugh. 'Think about what I've said. The channels of communications are open.'

Santos abruptly finishes the call. 'That cunt's dead,' says

Sonny, looking at the phone. 'We get this cunt found and paid. You hear that, Roy. He's coming after you next.'

'Maybe, Sonny,' says Morty, leaning forwards, 'you'll wanna start thinking about a deal with Miguel.'

'Not for anything less than half,' says Sonny, shaking his head. 'Anyway, first things first.'

So I'm right – it's all a tragic-comic case of mistaken identity, Roy's raincoat the misleading clue. I'm conflicted, but not *that* conflicted that I'd swap places. *A man is dead*, was *meant* to be me. I wonder how Santos found me. *I* can't ask him; as far as he's concerned I'm dead.

'Listen,' says Roy, looking hurt after being called *a paranoid*, 'we should get the O'Malleys out looking for Santos.'

'Good thinking, Roy,' says Sonny, slapping his thigh.

'I think we should keep quiet,' says Morty.

'Suddenly you two have got *very* secretive,' says Sonny, nodding at me and Mort in turn, 'all for keeping things to yourself.'

'How well do you get on with the O'Malleys, Sonny?' asks Morty, like it's a loaded question.

'I get on alright with 'em ... ' shrugs Sonny, 'considering they're a load of lagging boats and smackheads.'

'But who do we parley with?' asks Roy.

'He knows 'em,' says Sonny, pointing at me.

'I know Gerry, from time.'

'Morty, could you talk to Patsy?' Roy asks.

'Patsy's a drunk. Get more sense talking to his dog.'

'Chip's the one to talk to,' I say. 'He's half sensible.'

'They could find Santos in no time,' says Sonny, rubbing his hands.

'They couldn't find a hooker in King's Cross,' says Mort.

'I don't think they've got the required aptitude to find death squads,' I say.

'*Required aptitude*?' says Sonny, imitating me. 'I was thinking along the lines of using them as attack dogs, knocking on doors, banging on dustbins, get Santos flushed out.'

'They'd start a fuckin war,' I say.

'Right,' says Mort, shaking his head. 'Get Old Bill livened up. I don't think this is a good idea. Could backfire. Badly.'

'Nah, nah,' says Sonny, wisely waving a finger. 'Blessing in disguise, believe me.'

Sonny – being an instinctive, survivalist little fucker – is looking for alliances. And now he's recruiting the O'Malleys as his penal battalion, the shock troops. There is no question of where to find them – the Paddington Basin Members Club, the home from home for the O'Malley Clan.

'Twelve o'clock on a Sunday?' asks Sonny. 'They'll be there. Death in the family. Good excuse for a piss-up.'

'Don't think they need an excuse,' says Morty. 'I think we should let them know we're coming.'

'Do you think they'll know yet?' asks Roy.

'Good question, Roy,' says Mort. 'The law might be reluctant to tell them, but I guess they watch television same as everyone else ... Wouldn't wanna be the one to tell Patsy.'

'They'll work out that it was Stevie who got shot,' says Sonny. 'Was their fuckin brother, after all.'

'We wanna remember that their kid brother is dead ... And Stevie was a ... ' Morty searches for the right word ...

'A retard,' says Sonny. 'Let's have it right, Mort.'

'Feelings might be running high.' Morty gets up leave, then sits back down. 'You know what, I don't think it's a good idea ... It's a bit desperate.'

'Wrong word, *desperate*,' says Sonny, shaking his head. 'Come on, let's go.'

Twenty minutes later we arrive at the drinking club, a converted coal barge that's permanently moored on the canal in Paddington Basin. After our extensive detours Roy is satisfied but still double-checking the locale as we walk along the towpath; he's checking out the obvious sniping opportunities. Everyone is taking Roy's security procedures seriously all of a sudden. Boats are slowly chugging up and down but most are tied up at anchor around the basin. There's little movement. I don't know if the O'Malley family will even remember me. I don't know if I'm needed here. Morty leads the way up the gangplank. Above the door is a hand-painted 'Members Only' sign and a few bits of tattered bunting flutter in the gentle breeze. The atmosphere is more skull and crossbones than Royal Navy ensign.

Inside it's dusty and damp, a twilight zone after the sunshine outside. The nautical theme continues with ropes and knots, signals and flags, and the barman, a lump who looks like an off-duty wrestler, wears a tee shirt bearing the legend *The beatings will continue until morale improves* ...

Surrounding the bar, at the far end of the club, is a group of about twelve men. I recognise a few of the brothers and several of the darker madheads from the manor. Bad news travels fast. They put down their glasses and march towards us. It turns into a cavalry charge up the long, tight bar. They've spotted *that cunt* and immediately want to attack me, string me up ... Transpires they *have* seen the footage; it's playing on a TV above the bar. Morty and Roy block their way, as politely as present circumstances will allow. Sonny stands aside after a token effort, seems happy to let them rip me apart, but steps in at the last moment, tellingly – after the pushing and shoving, screaming and cunting, when the danger has passed – to calm things down. Never one not to exploit a situation, Sonny.

Six of the O'Malley brothers are there – all except, thankfully, Patsy, the eldest, infamous drunkard and man mountain, the nutter's nutter ... And my old ally Gerry is absent. *You are the company you keep*, Missus Burns would suggest. The O'Malleys pull every hound and growler for miles into their orbit. Some of these disciples are buzzing on the drama of Steve's death. Together they make up a scary posse, looking to get a rope around someone's neck.

The years have not been kind to *the boys* ... There's a strong whiff of stale sweat, A and E departments, custody suites, stinging medication and crack. They're rashy and itchy in well-worn tracksuits and greasy overcoats. All of them are caned – pinned or bloodshot eyes. Half are clucking, the other pissed and gakked. The *halfway sensible* one, Chip – real name John, could be forty, fifty or sixty – shakes hands with Morty but deliberately ignores Sonny.

So Sonny does his usual hearts-and-minds tactic – sets up a large round of brandies. When everyone's got a half-pint tumbler

Sonny herds the brothers into a corner, leaving behind the entourage. The brothers all know who, and what, Sonny King is. And the brothers know that this is not a courtesy call.

Sonny gets straight to the point – he explains that a Venezuelan gentleman named Santos de Lucia killed their brother Stevie. 'He was trying to kill him,' says Sonny, nodding at me, 'but shot Stevie instead ... '

'How do we know yer man, here,' says Chip, 'didn't shoot Stevie?'

'You gotta take our word for it, gents,' says Sonny on my behalf.

'He was stealing from Stevie,' says Chip, pointing at me, talking to Sonny. 'Saw it on telly.'

'Don't believe everything you see on television, Chip,' says Roy, with a glint in his eye.

'I promise ya,' I say, hands raised, 'I didn't shoot your brother. Sonny's telling the truth.'

'See,' says Sonny, 'we need the geezer who's doin all the shootin found.'

Chip asks why Sonny would want that. And in a blatant display of self-important point-scoring, Sonny declares, patting me on the shoulder, 'I need this man alive ... '

'Why was Stephen shot, then?' asks Chip.

'Simple case of mistaken identity,' says Sonny, arms open, palms up. 'They were both leaving a hotel at the same time. Stevie was in the wrong place at the wrong time. This Santos fella sent a geezer to serve this one,' meaning me, 'but he shot Stevie instead.'

Over the bar there's a small, muted television playing the camcorder footage on a loop. I can't take my eyes off it. I didn't shoot anyone, but I'm suffering from survivor's guilt. If I wasn't here in London Stevie would still be alive. Stevie nicked Roy's raincoat and the consequences were grave. I start to think about Jamaica – seems peaceful and safe – start getting homesick for Sundays, everyone dressed up in their best clothes, making their way to church, chubby mamas with flowery hats.

Roy is now explaining to Chip that Stevie was stealing *his* raincoat, and that's why he got shot. It's *simple karmic retribution, reaping what you sow.* Chip is unimpressed. His brothers look increasingly quizzical. It's a bit too esoteric for Chip but he's starting to get his head around the idea that Roy is blatantly suggesting that Stevie was *to blame for his own death.* Morty is looking embarrassed while Sonny, seems to think it's a bitova laugh – give Roy enough rope ... 'It's fate, destiny, Chip. This life, a past life or the next life, there's a price to be paid, see?'

Morty interrupts Roy, shuts him down. Thank God.

'Sonny has a proposal for yer, Chip,' he says. 'Ain't yer, Sonny?'

'Oh, yeah,' says Sonny, 'a proposal. We'll pay you compensation, to find Santos—'

'Compensation?' asks Chip, eyes narrowing, 'You mean blood money?'

'No, no,' says Sonny, shaking his head, 'not blood money.'

'Cos compensation would imply,' Chip gets eye-to-eye contact with Sonny, fearless, 'that you were somehow implicated, guilty of the boy's death. Stevie didn't deserve to get shot like a dog cos he got mixed up in one of your schemes. All this talk of the boy being in the wrong place at the wrong time ... '

Chip is capable of coming over the table and biting Sonny's nose off. And Sonny's looking at him like he picked on the wrong O'Malley to negotiate with, thinking maybe this wasn't such a good idea. But Sonny offers *a reward – make that finder's fee* and *reasonable* funeral expenses if they find Santos. Morty is resisting the urge to bury his head in his hands.

It's become apparent that the O'Malleys don't like Sonny – too big-time – but they will cooperate with Morty to find *this de Lucia.*

'If we find this Santos character,' says Chip, turning deliberately to Morty and offering him his hand to shake, 'we'll call you, Mort, okay?'

'Suppose it's gotta be that way,' says Morty.

'That's the way I'd prefer to do it,' says Chip, 'if that's okay, *Mister King*?'

Chip sends a brief glance in Sonny's direction.

Morty fills Chip and *the boys* in with the details and a few clues of where they might find the elusive Santos and his crew, then

Mort gets up to leave. *The boys* can sniff readies; they're pragmatists. 'Has anyone seen Patsy?' Mort asks. 'Wouldn't want him to get the news ... out of the blue.'

'We can't find Pats at the moment ... ' Chip says, 'but thanks, Mister Mortimer, for your concern.' He gives Mort a small, dignified nod.

Just as I'm thinking that the O'Malley brothers have mellowed over the years, Chip calmly gets a knotted plastic bag out of his jacket – a couple of ounces – and begins to undo it with his teeth.

'Rack 'em up, Chip,' says one of the younger brothers hopefully.

'Fuck off!' snaps Chip. 'Get yer own!'

I look at the crew in front of me – there is no way this firm of headbangers will be able to find a clandestine, military-trained, operator like Santos de Lucia.

We turn to leave, get halfway up the bar, and then Chip hollers after us, 'Oi! Mister King!' Sonny turns back to face him. Chip has a mad grin on his face. He's pouring dangerous rails of cha-cha onto the table. 'Any possibility of an advance, *Mister King*?' asks Chip O'Malley with lashings of sarcasm. All the brothers laugh.

CHAPTER THIRTY-FIVE

SPICK 'N' SPAN

Last night I hit the brandy and blanked calls from Jenna looking to hook up. There's a part of me that thinks Jenna is from a species that kills and eats their partners after sex. Could induce a degree of performance anxiety. Survival instinct, for once, won out over sexual desire. And I'm dog-tired. If all the television stations are rerunning the footage of Steve O'Malley's *assassination*, so am I – the whole show on a loop – so I had disjointed sleep but I'm still up and out. Duty, or my employer, calls. First thing this morning Bridget rang and said Ted wanted to see me straight away. On my own. I told her I wanted to miss the rush hour for obvious reasons.

It's mid-morning and nobody's looking at anybody. Weaving about on the tube is now second nature to me, I do it without thinking. I don't feel like anyone's gonna recognise me but I've bought a linen hat and a pair of lightly tinted shades. I'm hidden away behind *The Times*, reading about Stevie – a strange case of murder, victim still unnamed, police conspicuously quiet. Now I'm selling newspapers, I need to start seeing readies out of this. That might appeal to some criminals' vanity, but not mine.

Yesterday Morty was badgering Sonny but Sonny just got more entrenched – he won't trade that memory stick until Miguel gets down *on his knees and begs him*. Sonny, as he's fond of pointing out, is *in no hurry*, and it's *his* property. Me and Morty were seriously in dispute with him. Sonny is proud of the fact that he doesn't *need the money*. *Let them cunts roast* appears to be his attitude. Sonny hasn't actually met Miguel but that doesn't stop him disliking him. If you told Sonny *not* to sell the memory stick he'd wanna sell it, but it's senseless having it if you're not going to do anything with it. Morty suggested he might wanna *think* about being a bit more diplomatic. Sonny did not disappoint – 'Fuck diplomacy!' he told us. After Giles revealed the stick's contents Miguel's proposition of a couple of hundred kilos of cocaine does seem insulting, so Mort and me decided not to bother Sonny with it.

The fact that Ted and Bridget have not been in contact has suited me up till now. I was told to hit the ground running but so far nobody's come my way. If it wasn't for this bitta mischief, I'd be in the City Hotel, waiting on phone calls and human contact, getting lonely.

After Bridget's call I made a *pragmatic* decision to inform them about the memory stick, the Zambrano family, Santos and Jesus – I'm here on their dollar so it's only courteous. But I have other less noble motives. I need a good tale as to why my mooie's all over the television and papers. And I also think it's time to put Ted and Bridget, who I realise now are a double act, in the swindle. There's plenty there for everyone. I'll tell Bridget and Ted, and then Sonny can do what he wants. I'll say I was offered no alternative but to give Bridget the heads-up. What's Sonny going to do? He ain't gonna kill me; that would cause too much aggravation.

Hopefully Ted might come back to life and put subtle pressure on Sonny and Roy to do a deal with Miguel. Ted will want it sorted – he couldn't exactly stand up to police scrutiny. At the moment it's stalemate. Sonny doesn't wanna approach Miguel. *Explore the possibilities*, Giles had suggested, and having a big cat like Ted Granger onboard carries weight, makes us look like serious people. Ted's whack would pay for itself; at the moment we're carving nothing.

Sonny's need for secrecy is habitual – *tell nobody nothing.* He's buzzing on watching Morty, Giles and me with our tongues hanging out. I also have a theory of my own. It comes from those psychology books, back on the veranda in Negril – psychology is simply mental mechanics.

I think that Sonny is worried about having to step up to Miguel's level, moving out of the comfort zone where he can bully and control, to break bread with a young thoroughbred like Miguel Zambrano. He fears, unconsciously, that Miguel will *mobilise, or liven-up,* all his suppressed inadequacies. Like The Wunderkind did with Jesus.

Meanwhile Giles is getting impatient, speculating that Miguel himself will run out of patience and start a campaign of terror, tell the Cowboys to *utilise their persuasion techniques*.

Something needs to give, Giles told Sonny last night. Sonny takes notice of Giles only when it suits. But *I* took notice of Giles – *we need an icebreaker* could have been directed at me. I like Giles; he's sly in a good way.

I jump off the tube at Holloway Road, walk around the block a couple of times, dodge through a council estate, stroll across a park and finally I arrive at a dry cleaners back on the main road, one of a large chain owned by Bridget Granger – Spick 'n' Span. She also owns a string of launderettes; taking money laundering seriously, and literally, is Bridget.

I open the door, a bell rings. The guy on the counter calmly lifts the hatch, and nods me through into the back room without saying a word.

Ted and Bridget are sitting on plastic garden furniture, drinking tea. Bridget is wearing a yellow nylon coverall over her, no doubt, expensive Johnnie Versace creation, with a pair of matching rubber gloves tucked in the pocket. She has a patience-of-a-saint expression because Ted is half-reading the racing pages and is mid-way through a serious moan.

'Smell them fumes? How do they do it? Work here all day? Don't it send ya fuckin doolally?'

He's not wrong. Space is tight, and the huge, clattering steel cylinders full of heavy-duty chemicals give off nasty fumes. My eyes begin to water. A Hoffman press hisses next door and Radio Sedation struggles in the background – *all those songs you prayed you'd never hear again*. A massive industrial fan redistributes all the fluff and dust, trying, without success, to keep the temperature down to a humane level. Ted sees me but ignores me, and I wouldn't interrupt a chap doing the thing he loves. Ted relights his snout in spite of all the fluorescent orange signs – STRICTLY NO SMOKING.

'Them fumes, they'd give ya lung disease,' says Ted, coughing, missing the irony. 'Aren't there rules? Ain't you worried about being had up?'

Bridget patiently points at a health and safety declaration on the wall. Transpires Bridget owns the chain but she isn't actually the *registered* owner. An old Greek fella in a grubby vest walks silently backwards and forwards with hangers full of shirts slung over his shoulder. Ted gets on it.

'Is he fuckin deaf, that fella?' asks Ted.

'As a fuckin post,' says Bridget.

'Must be – so noisy in here, Bridge ... This tea, too much milk.'

'Do you ever stop moaning, Ted?' Bridget asks her twin in all seriousness.

'Stewed an' all. Tastes like piss. Too much milk *and* stewed. Don't know how you do it.'

'Fuckin make it yourself next time!'

'Oh, yer here, are ya?' says Ted, looking up, studying me. 'Glad you could make it ... '

'Morning, Ted,' I say. 'Morning, Bridget.'

'What with yer busy schedule,' says Ted. He folds back the page in the tabloid that features a pixellated television still. 'A very good likeness, don't you think?' I say nothing. 'This could ruin everything. You're here to do a job, not rob wallets off dead people.'

'I didn't want the card to end up with the law,' I say. 'They would have traced it—'

'If you hadn't of had it thieved offa ya,' says Ted, solid in his argument, 'you wouldn't of had to steal it back.'

'Do you wanna tell us,' says Bridget, 'what the fuck is going on?'

I start to tell them the whole story, but Ted interrupts.

'We know the story, beginning to end. Fuckin intriguing – magic sticks, Sonny being stubborn, *two* lots of Venezuelans,' he adds sarcastically.

'You know all this?' I say.

'We wanted you to come clean,' says Bridget.

'Well, I haven't seen you,' I say, 'since your funeral.'

'Well, we're here now,' says Ted.

'So you know?' I say.

'We know,' says Bridget. 'Know everything.'

'Morty told you?' I ask. I wish he'd told me.

'No, young Giles.'

'Giles the lawyer?' I ask. 'You mean Giles the toff?'

'Giles is *our* toff,' says Ted.

'Yeah, Giles *junior*,' says Bridget. 'Our pet brief.'

I sit down as well. 'You're gonna have to explain this.'

Transpires Giles is *their man* and he's been feeding information back to Ted and Bridget, keeping an eye on Sonny on behalf of Ted. And how did a swell like Giles Urquhart establish a connection with a wolfpack like the Granger Family? Giles' *father* was the Granger family lawyer for *donkeys' years – it's generational, son, a family business both sides.* And when Giles Senior died unexpectedly – heart attack while sniffing amyl nitrate during an energetic session with *two* hookers in Bayswater – Giles Junior *inherited* the Granger Family. Giles Senior had got Ted out of messes in the past, and as Ted got cuter he wasn't getting pinched ... but he still needed a crafty brief in the hedge.

'How do you think,' Ted asks me, 'a fuckin sye like Sonny King got a gentleman like Giles Urquhart as a lawyer?'

'You arranged it?' I ask, knowing the answer.

'*We* arranged it,' says Bridget, nodding at Ted, 'to give the boy a leg up.'

They both have a little smirk at Bridget's well-practised sarcasm.

Two years ago, after a series of manoeuvres, introductions and chance meetings, Giles was *appointed* as Sonny's lawyer. Round-the-flats kids like Sonny are impressed by aristocrats, even if they are duplicitous cunts.

Ted drops his butt into his cup. Bridget doesn't like it but says nothing.

'Don't let this distract you,' says Ted, waving a finger.

'Not a lot seems to be happening. Is there a problem?' I ask Ted.

Bridget answers. 'You gotta sit tight, everything is on hold—'

'We're having *small* problems,' says Ted, 'The supplier has suddenly gone missing.'

'Might be away, you know, over there,' says Bridget with a shrug. 'Not unusual in this game, is it?'

'Was gonna arrange a meet down in Spain but he's ... ' Ted shrugs at Bridget.

'See, the cargo was going to be delivered to Spain,' she says, 'for Ted to slip into the UK.'

'Maybe he's heard?' says Ted to Bridget.

'Heard?' says Bridget. 'About all the bollocks?'

'About Stevie O'Malley?' I ask.

'Yeah,' says Bridget. 'Poor Stevie. Bit backward, wasn't he?'

'Apparently,' I shrug. 'But I don't see how it'd make this supplier go under.'

'You know, killers on the loose,' shrugs Ted, 'shooting people at random.'

'It wasn't at random, Ted, the geezer was trying to kill me.'

'How can you be so sure?' asks Ted.

'Because, Santos *told* Sonny King he had already killed me. This Santos thinks I'm dead. We have something in common – people think we're dead.'

'You're sure it was this Santos geezer?' asks Bridget.

'He *rang* Sonny King—'

'But you're *absolutely* sure?' asks Bridget *again*, getting on my nerves now.

'I'm sure, okay?' I tell her.

'And you're trying to find him?' Ted asks me, 'This Santos?'

'Sonny's got troops out looking ... And he's offered the O'Malleys a reward to find him.'

'Waste of time,' says Ted. 'Was that Sonny's idea?'

'Roy's idea,' I say.

'Jesus wept!' says Bridget rolling her eyes. 'Fuckin Twitchy?'

'It's not such a good idea – they'll cause eruptions.'

'That was Morty's opinion.'

'The O'Malleys'll only find him,' says Bridget, 'if he hides down the Basin Club.'

'You know where I'd hide if I was this Santos geezer?' Ted asks me, dead serious.

'Dunno, Ted. Where?'

'In Patsy's house, under the soap,' he says, then cracks up laughing. 'Come on, Patsy's pickled,' says Ted, 'and the rest of 'em, they're bonkers.'

'Is that why you got me over here, to tell me the O'Malleys are mentally unstable?'

Ted doesn't answer. He gives me a serious look, then goes in his inside pocket and brings out a sealed envelope. He hands it to me, tells me to open it. A United Kingdom passport drops out, nicely aged, with airport security stickers overlapping each other on the back. As a connoisseur I'd say ten out of ten. I shuffle to the back and open it up. The passport photograph, one of the four I sent Morty, is of me. The surname on the passport is Berkeley – same as Sonny's moniker at the Conciliated Bank of Barbados. Ted nods gently, the baby blues fixed on me, pulling an expression that tries hard to be a smile but ends up a scowl.

'You getting it now?' asks Ted.

'Kinda,' I reply.

'Shame, we've been saving that for later,' says Ted, looking at me with one raised eyebrow. 'But you might as well have it now, seeing as you're on telly, wanted ... '

Bridget burrows about under the table and brings out a couple of Gucci carrier bags. She asks me to have a look inside. There's shoes, a shirt and tie, a belt, even socks – all from Gucci. I shrug, fail to see the significance.

'These are for you ... ' says Bridget, 'for Mister Berkeley.'

'Well, well, all these presents,' I say.

Bridget goes over to a rail crammed with suit bags and takes one down. Again, it's from Gucci. She begins to unzip it.

'Isn't unclaimed cleaning, is it, Bridget?' I ask.

She gives me one of her withering looks – intended to shrink your nuts – and hands me the suit bag. 'Aren't ya gonna try it on?' she asks.

'Why are you getting me clobber?' I ask.

'Humour her,' says Ted, rolling his eyes.

'Well, try it on,' insists Bridget.

'Where?'

'Right here, don't matter,' says Bridget, bit too casual. 'Don't worry 'bout me. Got brothers – seen it all before.'

Under Bridget's watchful eye I try on the outfit from Gucci, with her having a reef around – a freebie, truth be told, getting tactile adjusting the tie. The garbs fit but it's *too* crisp, *too* neat. But I think that's the idea – to make me look like a chap named Berkeley turning up to do his banking. Bridget approves. She has me peel it off again and packs it in the bag it came in while Ted gives me the pointy finger and eye-to-eye contact – *be ready to leave, suited and booted, at any time* ...

'You might wanna tell me what you have in mind.'

'All in good time,' says Ted.

'Hold fire,' I say, 'I was brought here to shift product—'

'But now,' says Bridget, 'you're trying to extract money out of a notorious South American criminal—'

'While we pay your hotel bills,' adds Ted.

'Or did, till you had to trap cos you had yer coat nicked, while you was stuck up his sister.'

'Not exactly diplomatic, kid,' says Ted.

'We've advanced you money,' points out Bridget dryly, 'that you've transferred—'

'Okay, okay,' I say, holding my hands up. 'Is there anything you *wanna* tell me?'

'Sonny,' says Ted, 'is gonna help us out – a loan, short term, low interest.'

'You won't need a loan if we sell this merch back to the Zambrano Family.'

Bridget asks Ted, 'Do you know this little firm, Ted?'

'*Big* firm – *everyone* knows the Zambrano mob, Bridge. *Semi*-legit, am I right?'

'Correct,' I say. 'They're trying to get *totally* legit, wouldn't wanna risk fuckin it up now.'

'You ever see Sonny King with a briefcase, a Gucci one?' asks Bridget, out of the blue, leaning forward. 'See, we've checked the Hampstead gaff *and* the Monarch Club ... ' Roy was right when he said someone was plotting up. 'It's only ... ' she says with a shrug, 'we've looked everywhere but we don't seem to be able to find it.'

It's my turn to pretend to be indifferent. Ted studies me hard. 'I think you know where it is ... I'll tell you what ... ' says Ted, 'tell me where you *think* it might be, and I'll *think* about having a word with Sonny ... '

I tell them it's somewhere in Missus Burns' flat. I could have said nothing. But I've riddled something out ... passport, suit, briefcase ... *I'm* gonna be negotiating the loan.

'Ted,' I say, 'it's time you broke cover to Sonny and Roy.'

'The time ain't right,' says Bridget, 'not yet.'

'Look,' says Ted, '*you* don't graft *me*, okay? Sometimes doing nothing is the best strategy.'

'While Sonny risks them turning nasty?'

'I'm fuckin waiting,' says Ted, annoyed. 'I'm going to sit tight and see what occurs.'

'And ... ' says Bridget leaning forward, slapping my knee, 'we didn't have this conversation, okay?' The done thing is to ask *what conversation?* 'As far as Sonny's concerned,' she continues, 'I don't know nothing about this gadget. And Ted's still dead.'

'My lips are sealed,' I say, nodding, giving Ted a wink, getting up to leave. 'We done?'

Ted shrugs. Bridget flicks the kettle on. ''Nother cup of tea, Ted?' she asks.

'Not at the moment, Bridge,' says Ted, ringing a horse, 'I'll have one in a minute.'

I slip back out into the shop with my bags, and out into the street. My instinct tells me I've just witnessed a fine display of studied indifference. Those two are a bit more worried than they care to admit. They're giving me a lot of information – to jam my circuits – but what's *really* bothering them, they ain't saying. Ted's not faked his own death for the good of his health. But something's got them spooked good 'n' proper, and plotting to turn Sonny King over is a bold move – desperate, even. But I'm starting to get irritated; people are getting on my fuckin nerves. I didn't come halfway round the world to be fucked about.

CHAPTER THIRTY - SIX

SAFE JOURNEY HOME

Marching down Holloway Road to the tube, nicely revved up. All I've got to do is convince Ted and Bridget that they have no need to be turning over Sonny. The man in the middle is often the man with the real power. And the man I need a proper sit-down with is Giles Urquhart Junior – the man with the power and, I believe, the plan.

Fuck all that dodging about, ain't got time. I jump straight into the tube station. Soon as I arrive on the platform there's a train coming. I don't bother to sit but I'm spying out the carriage – mostly tourists and a scattering of backpackers, this being August, and a couple of well-dressed Italians, maybe father and son, who got on at the same station but were on the platform before me. I work out my route – Holloway Road to Holborn on the Piccadilly Line, then the Central to Bond Street, change to the Jubilee Line over to Swiss Cottage and home.

I've got a theory – those psychology books again. Bridget's hygiene fixation is resentment and anger, mixed with suppressed sexual desire. A little knowledge can be a dangerous thing. And Ted and Bridget's desire to *borrow* Sonny's money appears very short-sighted and motivated by hatred rather than greed. It could endanger us getting funds from the Ponzi scheme. My hunch is that Bridget rather than Ted is the instigator and she is, beneath it all, the dominant twin. All theory, but it kills the time to Holborn.

As I walk towards the Central Line interchange I realise that the Italian dudes have broke cover and are now front and back of me – one a few metres ahead and the older one lagging behind. They are overly calm, deliberately ignoring me. I sense mischief. The platform has emptied out. I stop dead, to let the tail overtake, to see what he does. He stops too. The lead guy turns to face me. A look passes between them, over my shoulder.

The lead guy, the younger one, starts to pull a gun from under his jacket, but it gets stuck on his belt for a split-second. Wasn't in the plan. He's tugging, struggling to untangle the gun. I run straight at him, instinctively know he's off-balance. I headbutt him. My forehead – his cheekbone. He topples, tries to remain upright but slips, falls off the platform, onto the track, with a scream of pain. He lets go a shot into the ceiling. He's panicking about the electric current, and still firing shots. He bangs his head on the running rail, tumbles down into the suicide pit – the trench between the rails, designed to catch falling bodies – dropping his shooter. It rattles around, dinking off concrete, lands with a metallic chink. He looks terrified, shouts something to his pal – maybe a dialect, maybe Galician, between French and Spanish.

His pal has also pulled a gun – same make and model, with a silencer. He begins to walk towards me. I back off down the platform, away from the exits. He's worked it that way. He's cornering me, in no hurry. I have nowhere to go, only to retreat further down the platform.

The younger guy is screaming, wants to be pulled up out of the track. He's scrambled up the side of the suicide pit, has his arm outstretched waiting for a hand up. The older fella is wondering whether to shoot me dead first then tug his protégé out of the track or ... He compromises. He lets go three shots in my direction – droff-droff-droff, chipping tiles, ricocheting off the walls – to keep me on the back foot, away from the exits.

The young guy's shouting – I think it's Portuguese. But you can guess what's being said. The older dude is coolly telling him to retrieve the gun from the pit. I'm retreating, running backwards, along the platform, towards the tunnel, where he wants me.

The young guy disappears then reappears, waving the gun. The older guy quick as a flash reaches down, arm extended, one foot on the running rail, and hauls him clear.

I've sprinted up the platform – away from the exit. The board says two minutes till the next train. I spot the older gunman taking proper aim. I dodge backwards and forwards – zigzagging, no static target. I hear bullets hitting fire buckets, whizzing above my head, round my ears. I hear their curses. It's all going wrong, it was going to be easy. He's going to find his range. And soon there'll be two guns firing. There's no alternative – I jump down onto the track, carrying Bridget's bags, and dart into the tunnel.

I'm running down a gradient, further into the darkness, back the way I came. Picking up momentum, slipping in my loose loafers, leather soles ain't right. I can't stop. I'm laughing nervously. It's not the ballast that's the problem, it's the loose pebbles on the concrete floor between the sleepers – subtle mantraps, out to twist my ankle, to send me flying. It's tight – no room – that's why it's called the tube. If I go over here I'm fucked. I carry on sprinting, bobbing and weaving, skipping over cables and rails. Every noise, every metallic crash, is amplified. There's a rumble of a train in the far distance, maybe miles away. There's weak tunnel lights – hundred watt bulbs every few yards – fighting a losing battle against the dark.

I look back and see the silhouettes of the assassins trotting after me. I keep running, jumping from one side to the other, so the old fella can't take aim. He's the specialist. One of them is limping, but limping real fast, stopping to take aim. Bullets thud into cables, little deadly missiles. Sparks fly. Something's whistling past my head – very close. *Too* close. Keep moving. I can still hear their curses – hear every-fuckin-thing echoing and crashing.

Away from the station now, up by a junction lit by dim lights. Don't be a silhouette. The air is full of soot. I'm covered in sweat. Still got the bags. A train rattles by on the next track, losing speed, coming into the station, blue sparks flying as its conductors pick up the current. It's deafening.

I run, adrenalin pumping into every capillary, heartbeat punching behind my eyeballs, legs getting tired. To stop is to die – no room for negotiations. You see what happened to Stevie – no mercy. Two in the can. Steve's coming back to me, giving me a tailwind. Bullets skim through the tunnel – like kids throwing stones, ricocheting off walls.

Should I try to hide in the darkness? Double back? Not a good idea.

I run into a cavern, like a junction, damp creeping down the walls. Fat drops of dirty water – dripping, creepy but regular. Dead fat rat, on the track, tail as long as yer arm. Keep on fuckin moving! More bullets whistling by ...

A sudden points change. Hissing as the rails shift. Mechanical efficiency – red turns to green. The train's on its way. That's me fucked – crushed to death or shot dead.

I jump on the rails and dance over. Wouldn't wanna fall now, get flattened by a hundred-ton train, mangled in the points or fried to charcoal by the juice pumping through the skinny rails – no doubt lethal, judging by the chunky cables.

My shoe slips off. Forget it, don't even *think* about ... I hear a train arrive at Holborn Station. Got hearing like a bat – hear train doors open and then shut, hear the train leaving the station. Fucked.

I spot a bolthole – a coffin-sized gap – room for one but snug for two. The cables flow up and over. The edges are painted with a luminous paint to make them stand out in the gloom. Some comic's painted a skull and crossbones above. I dodge in, breathing hard. This could be good, a break – if those two don't find a bolthole. I'm peeking around the edge. The train is approaching. Huge fucker, scarier from the front. Lights like monster's eyes.

The train is on top of me, the noise deafening. Wind gale-force, throwing around litter – cans and paper cups. Carriage lights illuminate the tunnel, every nut and bolt, blinding light that leaves me squinting.

I glimpse passengers in a blur, snapshots – strap-hanging, reading papers, bored, tired, faraway eyes, not focused, some in snooze mode. The train passes, the roar fades. I wait for a count of five, poking my head out ... hoping they got hit.

I hear the two shooters screaming and cursing – something about the younger one getting his clothes dirty. Fuck it! Musta found a bolthole ...

I see two shadows begin to creep up the tunnel, hoping to find me smashed to pieces. I dash out, begin running all over again.

I'm making ground, getting further away, spinning around to catch a glimpse of them. The younger guy's limping, dragging his leg. Being economic with ammunition, less scattergun. Waiting their time?

I keep on running for another couple of hundred yards. The track is full of bends and gradients. Now I can hear another train coming, the noise growing louder. I need to time this right – can't hide too early, give them time to catch up. I carry on running till I find a bolthole. I jump in. Clearance is minimal. I peek around the corner ...

The train is getting even louder. They're still fifty yards back. The shooters have started panicking – running backwards, forwards, tripping and slipping, bumping into each other – evil slapstick. They find what they're looking for – both run for the same bolthole. There's a scuffle, seems there's something stored in there. Only room for one, at a squeeze. It's a deadly, primitive battle – wrestling each other, pushing and punching with their free hands. The old boy is coming off worse. As the train rounds the corner, comes into sight, he tumbles over the rails. The train's still twenty yards away, bearing down on him – its brakes full on, skidding. There's a screeching whistle. And grinding, steel against steel.

The old guy is lying over the rails. He raises his weapon and shoots back into the bolthole. I can see the shots but can't hear them. Huge flashes of orange and red flame. He's screaming curses – *Filho da puta!* Son of a bitch! *Desgragado!* You disgrace! More flashes. He empties his gun then throws it at his ungrateful protégé. The train is skidding towards him – slowing ... but not enough.

The old fella struggles to get up, but falls over again. He bounces up but there's nowhere to go, no room – *it's why it's called the tube*. He tries to press himself against the tunnel wall, make himself small. It's no good. I hear a sickening thud – a skull hitting a train. He tumbles and bounces – spinning between the tunnel wall and the train – then he disappears, under the first carriage.

The train halts, stopping twenty feet from where I'm hiding. It's silent, except for horrific screams. He's alive but dying horribly. The driver climbs down through a door in the front of his cab. He peers down the tiny gap between the train and the wall. I can hear radio traffic.

I creep out of my hole, trying to be quiet, surreally tiptoeing along. I can hear the protégé now as well, dying in his bolthole. Crying, screaming – *Mae! Mae!* Mama! Mama! Same in any language. A dozen shots at point-blank range – won't be surviving. Won't be able to find him, to get him out. Entombed by the train.

The driver suddenly shouts – must have spotted me. I run though a cross-passage onto the parallel track, away from the carnage. I'm sweating like a miner, covered in soot. Running hard uphill now – could that be right? My throat's dry, too painful to swallow. I'm overheating, dehydrated. My shins are killing me. I'm fuckin crippled – need oxygen – feel like throwing up. But then I can see the light at the end of the tunnel.

I emerge on the platform, up a ramp – at Russell Square Station. The waiting passengers are shocked, frightened by my appearance. They jump out of my way. Got my head down cos of the CCTV; no busy station staff, I ain't in the mood. Passengers looking curiously down the tunnel, wondering where the train is. They don't know if I'm a victim or a perpetrator. Not hanging around to explain. There's a mess back there – firearms, mangled torsos, buckets of blood, foreign nationals bleeding to death. But I'm still moving up the platform, looking for the exit sign.

Off the platform. Another lift. Too claustrophobic in a lift, taking no chances. Up the stairs – more fuckin stairs – hundred and seventy-five, two at a time, then three, breathing hard but slowing down at the top, trying to appear like I ain't got a care in the world ... I jump through the automatic barriers like shit through a goose, then out into the midday sun. I pull on my buckled sunglasses, making me look more manic. Think I hear sirens – but I hear sirens in my sleep nowadays.

I hit the backstreet and head north, keep going till I fall in a heap round the back of a university building, still, miraculously, with both Gucci bags and suit. Snot coming out my nose, my lungs fit to burst. Gonna get a nosebleed, or a heart attack, real soon.

I wait a coupla minutes, catch my breath, then walk for a while, walk fast till I find what I'm looking for – a pub khazi with an entrance on the street. I dodge inside and clean myself up – just my face and hands, smooth my hair out. Then I jump into a cubicle and put on the Gucci outfit. I pack my soot-covered clothes and one shoe into the Gucci bags, then cut out.

I bob and weave through the tight backstreets and lanes,

looking respectable now, a pinstriped city banker. I cut across the Marylebone Road round the back of Great Portland Street and head into Regent's Park where there's hopefully no CCTV. I head for Swiss Cottage, across the park, dumping the grubby clothes, one by one, in waste bins as I go, then the Gucci bag. I get to the apartment, check the gaff out thoroughly, then slip in through the underground car park.

I double-lock the door, drink a gallon of water, cough up soot, then fall asleep on the sofa, in my two thousand-pound suit, exhausted and paranoid, sweating buckets. Wondering ... how the fuck did Santos find me again? I was careful ... But as I drop off ...

Unless someone's trying to send a message to Bridget ... or Ted ... cos ... fuck's sake, who'd wanna keep trying to shoot a nice guy like me?

CHAPTER THIRTY - SEVEN

PRELUDE TO MADNESS

I wake up on the leatherette sofa, suit damp with sweat. The mobile's ringing. It rings twice then stops, then starts again straight away. It's spooky, glowing in the twilight. I was having strange dreams – the Bengal werewolf is back.

I press the green button. It's Morty, calling from a payphone. He's *on his way up*, *has seen the fuckin news*. There's something accusing in his tone, like I bring this shit on myself. The phone goes dead.

I find the remote for the television and try to find a news channel ... then I wish I hadn't ...

The ten o'clock news is showing grainy CCTV pictures of me leaving the tube, walking fast, head down, across the lobby of Russell Square station, *and* the aftermath of the shooting of Stevie – they're linking the two events. So will the law.

Apparently, I'm now an unnamed, but highly wanted, fugitive. I ache all over and I'm still thirsty as fuck but glasses of water don't touch the sides – I need salt tablets, vitamins and minerals. I've got blisters on the foot that the shoe stayed on and small cuts and abrasions on the one that I was running on barefoot. I'm still coughing and spitting soot. I'm starving but I ain't hungry, got a dull ache in my guts.

Ten minutes later Morty arrives, all coded knocks and sunglasses. He's got some Indian food that smells delicious and repulsive at the same time. I just shake my head, *ain't interested.*

He lays out his wares; he's been to the chemist, a few different ones by the looks of things, and bought hair dye, electric clippers and nerdy, chunky glasses. And bought some new clothes, nondescript – white and khaki, no labels or logos, no identifying markings.

'They're talking dissident IRA factions. You haven't joined the IRA, have you?' asks Mort with a straight face.

'Twice in two days,' I say. 'Can't work out how Santos found me.'

'You can ask him yourself,' says Morty, 'if you want ... in a while.'

The O'Malleys have sent word – they have *pinned the tail on the donkey.*

'You know they're insane, don't you?' I say. Morty shrugs – tell me something I don't know.

Turns out they found Santos' death squad in a holiday rental flat in, ironically, Paddington, the happy hunting ground of the O'Malley tribe, and from where the Zambrano Family got the tip-off call about the whereabouts of Jesus. They *strangled* all the crew ... except Santos.

'Strangled?' I say, incredulously. 'Strangled?'

'I fuckin know, mate,' says Mort, surreally, 'who strangles people anymore? In this day and age?' He answers his own question, 'The O'Malleys, that's who.'

'They didn't do Santos?'

Real-time sit-rep – the O'Malleys have taken Santos *and*, bizarrely, the bodies, to a disused factory in Wembley, out by the North Circular Road. Santos insists he has *valuable information to trade*, has explained to the O'Malleys that he has had *communications with Mister Sonny King*. Didn't go down well. The O'Malleys don't like Sonny. Roy they don't mind – Roy's a turn. Santos has kept his nerve and told them he has also had dealings with *el hombre negro grande, Sonny's counsellor.*

So now he wants to speak to – the big black gent. They have *had a previous acquaintance*. The O'Malleys have told Santos that Jesus is dead, he's on his own. *No problemo* – Santos is prepared to take his chances.

So after demanding the Geneva Convention to protect his human rights, Santos is ready to happily trade-off his unit, no concern for anyone but himself. True sociopathic behaviour is, by its very nature, extremely hard to diagnose in oneself. This example of restraint is out of character for the O'Malleys; Chip must have the stripes. I would have thought they'd have ripped him apart by now.

'So, we're going to Wembley?' I ask.

'Before we go anywhere,' says Morty, 'we need to sort you out. Go and have a shower. Give me a shout when you're done.'

Morty goes in his magic bags and pulls out a bin liner.

'All the clobber, in there. Every bit.'

'Bridget Granger bought me this suit ... ' I say. 'She told me to—'

'Let's not worry about Bridget,' shrugs Mort. 'One crisis at a time, okay?'

As I turn to leave Morty tells me to have a shave – *get rid of that poncey stubble and take your sideburns up to the top of your ears.*

When I'm done Morty finds me a towelling robe and brings a chair into the bathroom. He sits me down and competently clippers my longish hair down to a neat number four crop – apparently he was the barber among the chaps while serving his birdlime. Then he leans me over the bath and dyes the remaining blonde, sun-bleached hair a very convincing chestnut brown. Then he produces the chunky glasses, puts them carefully on my face. He then nods gently, like he's completed his masterpiece, declares himself satisfied. He tells me to check myself in the mirror. The guy looking back is totally unrecognisable – short, brown hair, side parting, clean-shaven and – the *pièce de résistance* – nerdy, slightly tinted spectacles.

I dress in the gear Morty brought – white tee shirt and linen strides, white Converse. Essentially nondescript, definitely no raincoat. I look like a million other bods.

It's eleven o'clock. I feel better, not great. Just as we're about to leave, my mobile starts to ring.

'It's Sonny,' I whisper unnecessarily.

Morty shakes his head. I let it ring.

'Oh, by the way,' says Morty, unlocking the door, checking the corridor, 'Ted says you're to stop getting in trouble.'

Morty's car is a few streets away. It's a hot summer's night. Now I'm out in the open I feel understandably exposed. We zigzag our way to Wembley – *let the fucker roast*. The Stadium and its twin towers – instantly recognisable and foreboding on the skyline – is waiting to be demolished. We park up and march for five minutes, then Morty makes a call. One of the O'Malley boys,

Thomas, comes to meet us outside the factory. He leads us through the labyrinth of corridors, up stairs, through rickety swing doors, into a large factory floor where the rest of the O'Malley boys are eating buckets of fried chicken, washing it down with brandy. There's puddles of stagnant water and broken windows, a smell of shit, stale piss and blocked-up toilets. The electricity supply remains connected; the room is dimly lit by the few remaining strip neon lights, some of them flickering on and off like ice-blue dry lightning, and a couple make an intrusive, dangerous crackling noise.

In the middle of the room Santos is strapped into a metal chair with about sixty heavy-duty cable ties. His clothes are dishevelled, bloodstained. I'm guessing it's Santos because he has a plastic bag placed over his head – more as a makeshift hood than a suffocation device. Santos would miss the irony – Flavio would pull it tight, till his sphincter went.

Chip gets up to greet us, the others remain sat on battered office furniture. *The boys*, six of them – still no Pats – look strangely contented, feasting after their hard work.

'Where's the rest of this mob?' Morty asks Chip in a half whisper.

'Downstairs in the wagon,' replies Chip taking a bite out of a chicken drumstick.

'They gonna be okay?'

'They're going no place, Mister Mortimer.'

Maybe to hell. Chip strolls over to Santos and pulls off the bag. Santos is bruised and bloody. His lip is split, his eye purple and half-shut. Around his neck he has a dog collar and lead, the end wrapped around an iron column. He's dragged bolt upright and looks like he's in some mad gimp scene that got out of hand. Chip holds the chicken leg to Santos' mouth.

'Wanna bitta chicken, soldier?' he says.

Santos doesn't answer. He spots Mister Mortimer, graciously nods in greeting, trying to retain what's left of his dignity. The brothers get up and start to form a semi-circle around him, but Santos is studying me, trying to disguise his curiosity and his I-know-you expression. Santos doesn't quite recognise me ... he's confused.

'*Buenas noches, Señor de Lucia,*' I say. 'You don't remember me?'

Santos riddles it out, suddenly gets it. He's shocked to see me alive.

'What's the matter?' asks Morty. 'You look like you've seen a ghost. You wondering who you shot?' Santos looks worried. 'Haven't you told him, Chip?'

'You know ... ' says Chip, swigging from the brandy, 'we hadn't got round to it ... '

'You're joking?' says Mort dryly, then seeing Chip's shrug, 'You're not kidding, are ya?'

'No,' says Chip. 'Was waiting for you.'

'Do you know who you shot?' says Morty, in close. Santos says nothing, but looks like he doesn't wanna know.

'Was their little brother,' says Morty, nodding towards the O'Malleys. 'Case of mistaken identity.'

Santos looks worried. 'I am of no value to you dead,' he declares.

'You are of no value to me alive,' replies Morty. 'You idiot, you shot the wrong person.'

'Shot my little baby brother,' says Chip, zeroing in on Santos.

'An error,' says Santos without a hint of remorse. 'My apologies, sir.'

'*Apologies*?' asks Chip. 'Did you say apologies?'

'Please, let me explain,' says Santos. 'One of the men you killed earlier ... *he* killed your brother. He was a hothead. *I* didn't tell him to do it ... but once he did, to my shame, I tried to use it to my advantage.'

'You're lying now,' says Mort, nodding at me. 'Twice you've tried to kill this geezer.'

'Once,' says Santos. 'One time. An error.'

'What did you say?' asks Mort.

'One time we tried,' says Santos. 'If we thought we had succeeded, why would we try again?'

'Once?' asks Morty.

'I told Mister King. The counsellor is dead. Why would I lie? They persuaded me – I ordered the assassination of the gentleman in the raincoat – him,' says Santos, nodding at me. 'We found his hotel—'

'So who tried to shoot me today?' I ask Santos. Funny but I believe him.

'I do not know,' says Santos, all indignant. 'Why ask me?'

'What time did they try to shoot you?' asks Chip, sucking his chicken bone.

'Around midday,' I tell him.

'Well, in that case,' says Chip, 'I can provide him ... ' he tosses the bone at Santos' head, 'with an alibi. They were out looking for *you* ... ' Chip nods at Mort. 'To kill you, no doubt.'

Morty waves a finger under Santos' nose. 'There's *two* rewards out for you,' he tells him, 'One from Mister King and one from Mister Zambrano. Must be nice to be popular.'

'You will need me,' says Santos, smug, like he's got a hidden ace, 'I promise you.'

Morty turns to me, 'Tell him he's a dog. Tell him in Spanish – nothing but a lowlife dog and a child killer.'

'It doesn't translate—'

'Just tell him!' snaps Morty.

'My colleague says to tell you that ... ' I'm fishing for the words, '*Alguien que mata a niños no es más que* fuckin *perro.*'

'But without *the fuckin dog,*' says Santos, 'you won't get the information you need.'

'Oh, won't we?' says Morty, suddenly angry. He pulls a gun that's been hidden in his belt and pushes it hard into Santos' forehead, as much to my surprise as Santos'. 'I don't care what you've got for me, you hear?'

'He knew,' Santos screams. 'Jesus knew!'

'Knew what?' asks Morty.

'That they were following him. Mister King and his acolytes, your gang.'

'*Acolytes*?' says Morty. 'Anyone ever tell you your English is *too* good?'

'There's money!' screams Santos.

'Give me one good reason not to blow your head off.'

'I'll tell you where he got the money in the suitcases.'

'Ain't interested, don't care. I came here to do a job.'

Morty moves the gun, quick as flash, from Santos' forehead to his mouth. Santos resists. Morty pushes hard. A horrible sound of gunmetal on teeth. Morty cocks the gun and looks Santos in the eye. Santos is begging, mumbling – bloody spittle and white froth running down onto his chin.

'What are you saying, man?' asks Mort. 'You're not making any sense at all.'

More incoherent gibberish. Morty pulls the gun out of Santos' mouth and pushes it under his chin.

'There's more!' Santos is screaming. 'Trust me, hear me out! There's money! As good as money!'

'What are you saying?' says Morty, with malice.

'I beseech you! It's why Jesus came to London!'

'Go on.'

'The bonds,' screams Santos, 'they didn't know about the bonds!'

'What fuckin bonds?'

'The bearer bonds!' screams Santos. 'The ones Jesus boosted in Miami!'

'Speak fuckin English, man!'

'Stole! Stole!' screams Santos.

'So tell me ... *Mister de Lucia* ... you fuckin dog,' says Morty, taking the gun from his chin, wiping blood and spittle on Santos' jacket, 'why did Jesus come to London?'

'I tell you – you let me go?' begs Santos. '*Please,* I just wanna go home.'

Morty spins round, winks at Chip. 'We'll consider it ... ' he says, places a chair in front of Santos, 'but we want the truth ... ' Santos is nodding. 'Remember, *hombre*, you're a long way from Caracas.'

CHAPTER THIRTY-EIGHT

WHO'S SAMMY LANIADO?

Nine months ago, around Christmas 2000 – Jesus had found out about Miguel's plan to marry off Jenna to the Brigadier General's son. He also found out that Miguel had set up, one year before that, strictly on a need-to-know basis, a bank, one of those offshore outfits where you could effectively do as you pleased. And he riddled out, correctly, that it was très fish.

A few months later, after the shambles with the organs – and other assorted hijinks – an elusive Jesus was trying to lay low, but Santos tracked him down in Miami, looking for money to *pay the boys*. Jesus thought Santos was there to kill him and was relieved when he only demanded money. Jesus told him to fuck off, said the racket was a busted flush, gonna get them all pinched, get them life plus thirty up in Florida State or extradited back to Brazil, or Columbia to be roasted. Told him about the dead lawyer and his deadly new hobby. Santos didn't react kindly to the news but they got drunk together. Jesus told Santos he could always use a military man, *for the next project*. He told him about his scheme to blackmail the Zambrano Family, revealed more than he should. Jesus figured Santos was useless without him – Jesus – pulling his strings, *don't know shit from chocolate chip*.

So Jesus enlisted Santos, the man with the intelligence expertise to bug Miguel, but Jesus would take the incriminating photographs of Jenna personally.

Santos requisitioned the kit from the Venezuelan Army, and they set to work eavesdropping Miguel and planting bugs to record his telephone conversations. Santos thought there was a payday in it somewhere. Jesus headed off down to the Keys to smudge up Jenna and kill The Wunderkind, while Santos kept Miguel, who he had, like Jesus, grown to hate with a passion, under observation. Jesus got his photos and accomplished his mission. Together they built their case against Miguel, the antichrist. Jesus was geeing up the troops, but knew he was going to abscond before pay-off time.

We'll hit the road. Bring the boys, can always use bodyguards – we'll go underground. Jesus filled Santos' head with magic – *London, Paris, Zurich! We'll show those motherfuckers!*

Jesus would come to the next day in the early afternoon, have a brief recollection of the previous night, punch the mirror, call himself a bigmouth.

Jesus was in Miguel and Papa Victor's bad books after they found out about the trade in organs and the dead lawyer. Now there was heavy circumstantial evidence surrounding the disappearance of Das Wunderkind. They sent for Jesus. He thought they'd found out about *Project Miguel* and the photographs of Jenna. He got paranoid, panicked, broke cover. He kept a rendezvous in Daytona – some slippery bookkeeper who had ideas about how to get money, but it wasn't instant enough. Jesus needed tank money, to travel first-class, like he's accustomed to. He's holed-up with various desperados and misfits – the kind who might kill and eat him – overstaying his welcome every time.

Fate played its joker. Jesus had his brainwave. He trotted down to see Miguel's NYC banker at his South Beach condo. The Banker was by chance holding the memory stick. He thought when Jesus arrived unannounced that he had been sent to retrieve it, or was there – acting on Miguel's orders – to kill him. But Jesus tells him about the incriminating information and photos he has squirrelled away, asks him if he wants to become his partner in blackmail. The banker is baffled, thinks it's a trap and tells Jesus – *ain't interested.* Jesus changes tack and asks, in his madness, for a loan. The banker is confused – *is this a bad fucking joke? Not if you can't collateralise. Do you have any tangible assets, Jesus?*

Jesus felt slighted. He began to feel the vicious compulsion rise, then snap like a plastic spoon. This was the end of Jesus' very short-lived attempt at diplomacy.

The banker was also holding some US government bearer bonds – nine million dollars – *for personal use.* Jesus found them in his wall safe while he was torturing him – standard operating procedure. He tied him up and battered him, half-strangled him, to soften him up. *Tried being nice ... and it just don't work with some people.*

Jesus interrogated the Banker to find out what the bonds were exactly. The banker delivered a tutorial about how the bonds were as good as money – negotiable, convertible. *That's the beauty, man* – they were *already* laundered, the hard work done. But alas, the tutorial went over Jesus' head. Like most sociopaths and other borderline narcissists, Jesus *just don't listen* – after ten seconds it became pure static. Doesn't pay attention, even when it might be incredibly financially advantageous.

'Can I get cash on these?' asks Jesus.

'They fuckin *are* cash, you asshole!' screams the Banker in frustration.

'Don't be smart,' Jesus tells him. 'You are not in any position to be smart.'

Bearer bonds are king; more elaborate than any banknote and worth a whole lot more. You don't *sell* bearer bonds, you hang on to them. Bonds are money. Bearer means owner. Bond means obligation. Bearer Bond means obligation to owner. Whoever owns them *owns* the obligation. You slide them across the desk of the privacy suite and the amount is credited on your account – flushed money, ready to spend. The irony is that if Jesus had a compliant chap like Mister Curtis at the CBB, he could have tipped up and done the business over a cup of Earl Grey and Sonny and Roy would never have got involved. But Jesus completely misses the point, thinks he has to creep around and sell these on the QT. The banker is begging Jesus to take the *memory stick and go* – this memory stick seemed to be incredibly important ... *so what the fuck ...*

Then Jesus killed him, and left with the bearer bonds, the memory stick and twenty gee in thousand-dollar bills. Jesus thought the cash was the prize. But he *didn't* head straight for Miami International – he was on a roll.

Instead he took the memory stick to Santos' resident IT genius Little Pedro – Smiler's soul brother – to see what the fuss was about. Without telling Santos. But Pedro couldn't get it *de*crypted. Jesus thought he was stalling. Jesus also wanted all the negatives of the Jenna photos plus the tapes of Miguel's conversations, to decamp with, but Pedro explained *it's all digital*. He could download the data onto the memory stick – *there's plenty of room. Travel light, hombre, just find a compatible computer the other end*.

Jesus wasn't convinced – the gadget was smaller than his pinkie – until Pedro gave him the demonstration, showed him the photos and replayed, pitch-perfect, the exchanges between Miguel and his bankers, relatives and connections. *All off that?* So now it was all in the one place – the memory stick.

Jesus *was* going kill Little Pedro because he thought he was a bit too tricky. Jesus hated duplicity in others. He thought the ironically named Little Pedro – twenty-four stone – would tell Santos all his business. But suddenly Pedro, sensing what was coming – Jesus was innocently winding a printer cable around both hands – sprinted for the window, jumped on a stool, crashed straight through the glass, fell two floors, rolled down a veranda roof and landed with a bellyflop on the roof of a stationary taxi cab, breaking his neck but saving his life, doing the driver serious physical and mental damage. Jesus watched them struggle to carry Pedro into an ambulance then got a cab out to Miami International.

Instead of jumping on the shuttle flight down to the Caymans or Panama City, Jesus, thinking too fast, headed out to London, and the one person he knew could get him cash-money on these bits of paper, who had the expertise and was in the market for any financial hocus-pocus – Samuel Laniado, the low profile, ex-Venezuelan resident living in deep cover in the genteel Home Counties. Sammy was one of those geezers whose history was vague, to say the least. His appearance was deliberately unremarkable, best described as darkly dignified – anonymous tailored suits, bespoke shirts and tasteful ties. His age could be anything from fifty to sixty. He spoke a dozen languages like a native.

The other advantage of dealing with Samuel was he was no friend of the Zambrano family, having had beefs with them over – no surprises – money. Sammy had relocated to help various European outfits clean up their *schwarzgeld*. Jesus could shift the bonds and later sound out Samuel about helping him decipher the gibberish on the memory stick. But first things first ...

Jesus arrives, resolved to keep a low profile. He hides the bearer bonds in the false ceiling of his room at the Cosmopolitan, the memory stick up his light and bitter and makes *initial contact* with Samuel. He wants to sell some merchandise that has come into his possession – can Sammy help? Samuel knows Jesus by reputation. He thinks it could be some trap, thinks Zambrano's people are sending this buffoon to skunk him out.

Sammy puts in a couple of discreet calls to Miami and Caracas, learns that Jesus is wanted dead or alive, by his own family, hears a whisper that Jesus is peddling stolen property. Sammy clarifies that Jesus is not an *official fugitive*; the law aren't looking for him, only the Zambrano's recovery crews.

Samuel has a two-second crisis of professional conflict – *Those Zambrano whores never did me any good. But The Loco Kid's here in London, ready to do business. After our trade ... if there's a reward ...* It don't smell right but he's gotta take a chance.

Jesus spent the rest of the day obsessively buying clobber on Bond Street and airline tickets on Piccadilly, before heading out to make his debut at the Monarch Club. Next afternoon Sammy and Jesus met at the Cosmopolitan. Jesus shows him the bonds. Samuel asks him what he wants. Cash. *Three million pounds – this is fuckin England, Pops.*

Sammy can't believe his eyes and ears. The paper is as good as gold, proper bona fide bearer bonds – that's nine million dollars in your inside pocket, or in your wall safe for a rainy day – rare tackle these days. Sammy could sell them for a lot more than nine million.

Jesus is trying to be cool, aloof, but he shoots his bolt like an anxious chimp. Sammy stays silent, lets his silence do his talking. Sammy stirs his Darjeeling – black *with Sicilian lemon* – eats his complimentary biscuit and thinks, *maybe ... this shlump might be for real.*

Then Sammy changes tack, jollies Jesus along, tells him about the need for strict confidentiality, even from your family – *we've had our troubles in the past.* He tells Jesus it's *all very doable,* while all the time thinking *knowledge of your whereabouts will do as token of my goodwill.*

Jesus wants and needs cash – *rapido, you understand?*

Samuel barters for the sake of appearances, pours more tea, plays for time, surveys his elegant surroundings – the parrot flowers and the Art Deco vases, the minimalist temple that is the Cosmo P. – decides it's some fruit hangout. *You don't have to be homosexual to be a fag these days.*

Sam's thinking, these bonds are a gift from heaven, but Jesus is looking for, and settling for, less than *half* their value – *in cash, big notes, understand, old man?*

Samuel nods slowly, eyes betraying defeat, like he's saying *you drive a hard bargain* but he's thinking *you runt, they should have drowned you at birth.*

'Cash!' says Jesus. 'Fast!'

'I'll do what I can. That kinda money takes—'

'Do what you can,' says Jesus, 'but do it quickly.'

Neither of them can believe their luck. Jesus is a bad criminal – doesn't *really* understand the game he's in. He's just swindled *himself* out of a few million dollars. Sammy has clients who need to spin out of readies, got more cash than they know what to do with. Cash is a nuisance, cluttering up the place. These geezers fantasise – shut their eyes tight and dream – about Negotiable American Government Bearer Bonds.

And Jesus *wants* cash – bundles. He doesn't understand – *that's a lot of paper* – three bags full, sir. He doesn't want an attaché case of five hundred Euro notes, he wants sterling. If you gave him a letter of credit, drawn on a Zurich bank *and* a complimentary first-class Swissair ticket, he'd wanna cut your face open.

The kid's a throwback, thought Sammy Boy, all the way back home to Berkshire, *like all those Zambrano bastards ... with their air of superiority.* As Sammy pulled up at his front gate – *if this isn't a trap, it's a wet dream ...*

Sammy could just sell the bonds but he has a good night's sleep and decides *no, this is all mine.* Samuel goes to work rounding up readies – three million in high denominations. Cash is king again. He *buys* from his clients with cash-intensive industries – industries like drug dealing, trafficking and smuggling. Sammy spends his mornings parcelling up chunks of a hundred grand, packing them in shrink-wrapped plastic. Sammy's busy in Berkshire but Jesus is happy in the Golden Triangle – the Monarch Club, Cosmopolitan Hotel and Bond Street.

With one bit of business in motion Jesus contacted the Zambrano Clan – re: Blackmail Attempt. Jesus sent *tasters* – attachments speeding across the Atlantic, snatches of conversations and indiscreet smudges – *no demands as yet.* Getting them off-balance with snippets and snapshots. Placing untraceable follow-up calls, pretending to be in Hawaii. Jenna got her email, called Miguel straight away on the hotline, had a screaming match. Jenna wants Jesus *sorted once and for all ...*

Miguel passed the file to Raul. He responded by rounding up Jesus' immediate family and starting a campaign of 'proxy torture' – torturing relatives to ascertain Jesus' whereabouts. Raul let Jesus know; Jesus *couldn't give a fuck.* People are pliable if their kin are suffering but it didn't work with Jesus. Plus torturing Jesus' folks meant torturing Auntie and Uncle, who Raul was *incredibly fond* of. Someone suggested torturing someone Jesus has an emotional attachment to. They couldn't think of anyone, except Jenna.

But Jesus is tubbed-up at the Cosmo, drinking and sniffing, getting more deluded and lovesick for *his fiancé.* Jesus is caning the trombone while the hooker or the new squeeze – or both – sleep restlessly on. But Jesus is getting no response, no grovelling or pleading from Jenna or Miguel. Jesus needs a reaction, so he's on the phone to Santos, bragging, but won't tell him where he is – *I could be anywhere, fuckhead. Fuck body parts, we shoulda boosted bearer bonds. Dead. Fucking. Easy. I've got three million in sterling on the way.*

Santos *does the math.* Santos ridicules Jesus – *you are one fuckin asshole, Jesus! Bonds! He should be paying you, ya prick! He's dumping all his green on you, sucker!*

Santos signed Sammy's death warrant for him. Jesus puts down the phone ... and flips, raging against *that bastard Sammy fuckin Laniado.* He almost had to *beg* him to buy the bonds. Suddenly Jesus *is* listening, and *he's* being swindled. Massacres and murders are forgotten. *He's* being made a fool of. And *he is not a victim, no, sir.*

Jesus begins to make amendments to the arrangement, recalls the humorous story of the gent who sold his dog over the other side of town. When he got back home the dog was there to greet him, wagging its tail and licking his master's face. The guy sold the dog many times.

Samuel knew that story too ... Samuel had sold many dogs, many times. He hires a pair of bodyguards – great big 'roidheads, all muscle, dense as poured concrete. Old wisdom – you pay peanuts, you get monkeys. Sammy didn't wanna frighten Jesus off, didn't want him thinking the thicknecks were going to turn him over. And he didn't want these fuckers getting ideas when they heard seven-figure sums. So he has them keep their distance, tells them to keep the show under surveillance. They shadow Sammy on the meets, and take his money – *piss-easy, this body-guarding lark.*

Samuel tells Jesus that *for a consideration* he'll get him a home for his readies, a personal introduction at the premier VIP account at a compliant bank in Brussels. *That's in Belgium—*

'I know where fuckin Brussels is, you—'

'You drop what money you don't need that day in the bank, all neat and tidy.'

Samuel don't wanna *properly* explain money laundering, not that Jesus would listen – *attention span of a fruit fly* – too busy thinking about flash clobber, wet pussy and getting his ticket punched down the Monarch.

But now Jesus was ringing Santos back in Miami – drunk, coked to the gills – oscillating between smug dude and dumb bastard. Jesus was *uncontained*, he couldn't keep himself to himself. Jesus tells Santos – *it's been a mistake, Santos, fly in and meet me. I'm in London. I'll go down Piccadilly in the morning and buy you flight tickets.* Jesus tells Santos he has a feeling that he's being followed in London, that the room safe has been opened but nothing taken. His paranoia tells him that the *slick concierge i*s feeding information to a nightclub owner.

Then Jesus passes out, wakes up at midday, puts the phantom pursuers down to paranoia, and regrets the things, if he can remember, he did eight hours ago. *What was I thinking of? Getting that meathead Santos over here. He'll go ruining my spot, man.*

But there's no stopping Santos now. London, England, was Santos' spiritual and sartorial home – pack the fuckin tweeds, men! Santos was getting ready to ship out while Jesus was down Piccadilly buying even more tickets to leave. So that's how the Santos fella arrived in London. No time to check out Buckingham Palace or the Changing of the Guard – too busy chasing ghosts.

Ironically the problem started on the day of the trade. Sammy was delivering the money – three suitcases, one hired car – to Jesus at the Cosmopolitan Hotel, as per arrangement. The money was in the hired car in the underground car park. Sammy opened the case Jesus selected, pulled out a package at random, counted it and, satisfied, they told hotel security to watch the motor and headed upstairs to the breakfast room for tea. The bonds were in a copy of the *Herald Tribune*. Both of them arrived with a copy under their arm; both of them left with the one they didn't arrive with.

Meanwhile Sammy's bodyguards spotted Roy and his men, whispering into radios, creeping up stairwells, making surreptitious signals to the concierge. Then they spotted Sonny King, *obviously* the Gov'nor, sitting in an anonymous motor, eating a corned-beef sandwich, drinking from a polystyrene cup, *like cozzers on the telly*. They assumed they were heavyweight detectives baking-up on Jesus and Sammy, ready-eyeing them, getting ready for the flop. The bodyguards fled – weren't getting nicked for monkey nuts.

Roy didn't want to take out Jesus at the Cosmo, didn't wanna bring attention on Flavio, didn't want cozzers quizzing him. Needed distance between the hotel and the ambush. Roy pointed out that Flavio was *not trained in counter-interrogation*. And it could go bandaloo with people ending up dead on the premises.

So Sammy does the trade but can't find the bodyguards. He gets didgy thinking that Jesus has got some back-shooters himself but why should he worry, he's got the bonds. Sammy insists he keeps the hired car to schlep the cases to where they need to go. Sammy, keen to get gone, jumps in a taxi to Paddington.

Sammy's got a train to catch but he stops at a public phone on the concourse, heaps bundles of change into the slot, and punches in an international number. He lets one of Miguel's Yanks know that Jesus is leaving tomorrow morning on the Eurostar out of Waterloo, bound for Paris. Tells the guy he'll be in touch – to accept his reward ... *hope it goes well*.

Sammy's hedging his bets. That's what smart operators do.

CHAPTER THIRTY - NINE

JESUS' INFERNO

Samuel Laniado heads west on the fast service to Reading. His head's spun. All he knows is he's got the genuine bonds; he was half expecting a switch, a conjurer's sleight of hand. It's what he woulda done. He changes trains at Reading, gets the local shunter along to Goring and Streatley, where he gets the local cab driver to drive him home to his secluded house up on the Downs.

Jesus meanwhile, sits in the Cosmo Bar, getting seen. He waits until things have settled down for the night. *No Monarch Club tonight, Mister Zambrano?*

'No, no, I leave in the morning.'

'You'll be missed, sir, if I may say so.'

Jesus doesn't trust any of the hotel staff. He orders up room service, eats in his suite, leaves the tray outside the room and hangs the 'Do Not Disturb' sign on the doorknob. Roy's crew were still in situ, but they had stopped paying attention, been taken in by Jesus' simple deceit; if they had known the prize was three million they might have been more alert.

Jesus wanted to smoke out Sonny and Roy, weigh up the enemy's strength, and assess intelligence, before proceeding. He, one by one, rolled the suitcases into a cleaning cupboard he'd *acquired* a key for, then crept back to his room. Risky? The cases were empty, a decoy; Jesus had removed all the bundles of cash and carefully hidden them in the false ceiling of his room – like paper bricks, the weight evenly distributed. Jesus patiently waited another *two hours*! But nothing happened, no robbery; he was half hoping he was right. Then he slipped out of his room, down the back stairs to the car park and into the rental motor. He drove up the ramp, into Park Lane – surprised that nobody was following – and headed into the west himself, just as a light drizzle started.

Soon he's out in the country, driving fast down a dark road, on the *wrong* side, in the torrential rain, the windscreen wipers going full blast, trying to light another cigarette *and* tune in the radio to a news station. And the gas station map is upside down.

Up on the Downs? What kinda English bullshit is this?

Q. How did Jesus know where Sammy lived?

A. The Zambrano Clan always knew his whereabouts and had *pragmatically* put him on ice, never knowing if they'd need him to do trades. They didn't like one another, but that never got in the way of business. In happier times, Jesus was going to go to England and kill Sammy, to court favour, but Papa Victor graciously declined his *kind offer.*

Eventually Jesus finds the house up on the Downs, the Laniado Residencia. It's proper, genuine Georgian – all belled up, alarmed, of course, and CCTVed-up. But as luck would have it – lucky for Jesus, but definitely not for Sammy – the alarm was not actually *on.* Sammy's wife was out for the evening with her girlfriends down the local tease-spot. She had never really got the hang of setting it and was forever sending false alarms. The police thought it was a joke, were always ringing up to ask if they should send a patrol car. Jesus parked the rental down the lane, nicely outta sight.

Cut to – Sammy upstairs, lying in bed, silk robe on, feeling horny, like he always did after he'd had a touch, flicking through the television stations, trying to find something to catch his imagination. Sammy's telling himself that everything's locked up or nailed down, that nobody could find him here; even his dozy missus can't find her way home half the time.

Ironically, just as Jesus crept through the undergrowth with his improvised bag of tricks and surprises, Sammy was considering putting the alarm on and calling the missus to tell her that she'd better ring him when she got home. Sammy wasn't the type of guy who was weirded right out by every inconsistency, but there was a nagging feeling ... Fuck those bodyguards – *paira apes ain't getting shit.* Sammy carried on flicking through the TV stations.

Meanwhile the rain has stopped. Jesus is creeping through the wet garden in his Bond Street finery, dodging the discreetly placed cameras. There's dry lightning over the hills in the distance. It's that horrible British summer damp, followed by sticky humidity. Reminds Jesus of being up in the jungle, deep in the hinterland, border country, while he was overseeing his last ambitious, but doomed, project.

Jesus slips in through the corrugated plastic skylight on the roof of the garage – *the coach house*, Samuel would insist. Jesus flicks open the lock on the connecting door into the house using a room service fork from the Cosmo.

Maybe I should have a look round, maybe get my Beretta from the you-know-what, thinks Sammy, just as Jesus is creeping up the stairs towards the sound of the television.

Sammy goes for a piss in the en-suite bathroom. Jesus enters the bedroom; no Sammy. Jesus hears sounds from the bathroom. Jesus creeps up, throws a nylon garrote around Sammy's neck and drags him back into the room and onto the bed. Sammy's tongue is sticking out and turning blue. Jesus has to check himself to stop from killing Sammy. He might be a compulsive murderer, but he knows a dead Sammy Laniado is no good to anyone. The bonds could be in a million and one places but they're probably in the wall safe, and Jesus is no safecracker. Jesus has Sammy standing on tiptoes, fighting for air. Jesus is taking time out to enjoy the moment, breathing long and hard.

Sammy, meanwhile, has soiled himself, which Jesus finds *absolutely fuckin disgusting*. Jesus can't acknowledge that he's actually the cause of Sammy's severe distress. All he knows is that *he's* offended. He curses Sammy for a whore. Sammy knows he's in trouble. He *wants* to tell Jesus where the bonds are – he's choking and fighting for breath – and is seriously regretting not pulling the same stunt on Jesus.

Jesus lets Sammy drop, then drags him out of the bedroom and down the stairs. Whether Sammy knew he was dying or not is debatable but the odds weren't looking good. Jesus appeared to be mucho happy in his work. Torturing information out of victims was Jesus' new hobby – *I'm getting good at this,* he's thinking.

Jesus has a plan for Sammy ... Jesus needs to shift an uncomfortable nagging feeling that just won't go away ... That horrid feeling of being ridiculed and laughed at, by *all those people,* over *all those years* ... Sammy is symbolic.

Q. Why didn't Jesus just turn over Samuel Laniado somewhere between Park Lane and Paddington ... or on the train to Reading?

A. Because it wasn't in Jesus' *plan* for Sammy.

Jesus' plan amounted to what psychiatrists call 'annihilation' – mastery through destruction, control through obliteration. Sammy, and Jesus' other victims, were taking the blame for the other's misdemeanours and general fuckery, and he was gonna wipe them off the face of the earth, remove all evidence of his *perceived* humiliation.

Retrieving the bonds was relatively simple; Sammy knew when to offer resistance and when to comply. Sammy had a decoy safe full of bogus paperwork, ready for getting turned over by bogeymen or law enforcement, an occupational hazard. But Sammy, knowing he was dealing with an inept criminal, and possibly someone who killed for pleasure, quickly bypassed the decoy safe, all the time trying to pacify Jesus, telling him he could *sort him out proper money, sackfulls, in the morning*, trying to cut a deal ...

'In case you haven't noticed ... ' Jesus told Sammy with a twisted smile. 'You are in no position to negotiate.'

Maybe Samuel, in his wildest dreams, thought that Jesus would just cut and run once he got the bonds. Sammy opened his real safe – outside in the barred gazebo, behind a double-locked gate, away from the elements, hidden under an artfully disguised flagstone, *in-fuckin-genious*, surprisingly big, for plugging up all that bulky cash, but now it was very empty. A small strongbox sat in the corner. Sammy, under Jesus' watchful eye, unlocked it, opened it and returned the bearer bonds to Jesus. There was no cash – Jesus had already cleared him out – hence all the space in the safe. There were a few other bits and pieces – false passports and open business-class plane tickets, coded address books and a Beretta pistol – but nothing of value to a hothead like Jesus. Jesus wanted to take the pistol, but thought better of it. He was crossing international borders tomorrow. He was home free and nothing was standing in his way. What the fuck did he need a weapon for? Little did Jesus know what Royski had in store.

Jesus dragged Samuel back inside the house. Sammy was dragging his heels so Jesus pulled the nylon noose even tighter. Samuel kept begging and screaming, getting on his nerves, so Jesus pushed a crushed velvet scarf in his mouth and knotted it hard at the back. Sammy carried on groaning and begging, but muffled now. Sammy looked ridiculous – regal purple scarf in his mouth, noose round his neck, blood dripping from his nose, split lip, elegant silk robe hanging open, shit down his leg, dick shrunk to nothing.

'We're going on a little trip ... ' Jesus Zambrano tells Samuel Laniado, dragging him down the hall. 'Just me and you.'

Just as Jesus was about to open the big heavy front door he heard a key in the lock ...

Jesus motioned to Sammy to remain quiet, like it's a surprise party, but kicked Sammy hard across the jaw anyway ... Jesus tiptoed, like a pantomime cat, behind the door. Missus Laniado didn't stand a chance. Another glass of Chardonnay, *one for the road, darling*, would have saved her life.

Jesus dragged her body down the cellar stairs while Sammy screamed and wriggled in torment upstairs because he knew he was going to die.

Then Jesus had a brainwave. He hauled the wife's heavy body – it's not called deadweight for nothing – back upstairs, out to the gazebo and put her in the empty safe. She's still gotta be there, poor dear. Jesus shut the door and spun the dials, dropped down the flagstone, double-locked the gate and congratulated himself on his ability to improvise.

Jesus drags Sammy out into the garden, down the lane to the car. He throws Sammy in the boot and jiggles a plastic petrol can under his nose. Sammy starts crying – *no más, no más* – weeping like a child. Jesus starts laughing, sniggering like a maniac. He shuts the boot on Sammy.

Jesus drives back towards the motorway, finds the junction he needs but turns right instead of left, heading, unknowingly, in the wrong direction, towards Rural Fuckin Wiltshire instead of London. Through the whole drive, Sammy is banging, begging, crying, gasping for air, wriggling and screaming, and all this muffled agony floats Jesus' boat ... for a little while ... Then his tolerance increases and Sam's humiliation isn't enough anymore.

Then Jesus starts seeing old faces in the lights of the motorway, the condescending faces of the people who did him down. *I'll show them*, he tells himself, *I'll come for you ... In the dead of night. And you'll all fuckin beg like Sammy fuckin Laniado ...*

And Jenna? She can fuck right off, the two-faced cunt ... And cousin Miguel? I'll cut his fuckin head off and keep it in the icebox ... Jesus is getting nicely ratcheted up.

Then Jesus looks at the road sign and realises he's been travelling, for the last hour, *in the wrong direction*. After his illusion of power and control, he hits Reality like a fly on the windscreen.

Jesus – building to frenzy now – pulls off the motorway at the next junction and begins driving very fast down dark lanes again. He makes no alteration between his speed on the motorway and the tight narrow roads. The rear wheels skid and slide. Sammy slips and slides in the boot as Jesus pushes the car round tight corners. He drives faster, more suicidal than homicidal, pedal to the floor, grit and dirt hitting the undercarriage, headlights on full beam, faster and faster, down the local Lover's Lane. Suddenly he stops with a skid, sending up a cloud of dust. Jesus jumps out of the motor, rushes to the back, opens the boot and drags out the terrified Samuel Laniado. Jesus throws a fresh garrote around his neck.

Jesus pulls and pulls, the veins in his biceps bulging. Sammy has no fight left in him; he goes into spasm, he's dying. Jesus thinks he's fighting back. Suddenly Sammy's body goes limp but Jesus doesn't notice. He draws blood, splits the main artery, it sprays out, in pulses, like Sammy was still alive. Jesus releases the garrote and Sammy slides down the motor into the dust, almost under the rear wheel. Jesus retrieves his plastic container of petrol from the boot, still sparky, electric, out of control, spitting and dancing, threatening a dead person with death. Jesus douses Sammy in petrol. It's become a rite of destruction, a chasing away of bad spirits and curses going back years. Samuel Laniado has become the personification of all that has been, and will ever be, wrong in Jesus Zambrano's life.

Then Jesus lights a match from a box of Monarch Club matches, sets the whole box ablaze and ceremoniously drops it onto the now lifeless body of Samuel.

Samuel instantly catches fire ...

But so does the rental motor ...

Ain't funny. Jesus watches, powerless, as a trail of flames runs straight to the motor. It instantly ignites – a sudden whoosh – then a blaze, a huge fireball. Jesus runs to the passenger door, flicks it open at arm's length, and retrieves the bearer bonds from the front seat. In seconds the whole car is ablaze, sending up thick black smoke. The plastic interior drips and spits fiery blobs. Flames curl out of the windows, over the roof. The blaze is rampant. Fuckin spectacular! A joyrider's Valhalla! The paint blisters, peels in the heat. The windscreen pops. The tyres melt, revealing steel ribbons. The steering wheel buckles. Jesus howls like an animal. He's been denied and swindled, made to look a fool. Sammy shrivels, devoured by flame – an unrecognisable black mess. Beyond belief and identification. The flames quickly reach their peak, lighting up the surrounding fields, scorching the leaves and the branches of the close-by trees. Jesus sees hellfire everywhere. Jesus thinks the world's gone fuckin mad, not him. Me? Mad? Never!

Ancient wisdom – only a madman never questions his own sanity.

The petrol tank explodes. Jesus is blown off his feet. In seconds the blazing car matches the inferno that is the inside of Jesus' head. It's become the perfect flaming symmetry, an exact reflection of all Jesus' uncontained rage and bile. Jesus picks himself up, bounces back to his feet and screams and spits at the blazing car. But now Jesus thinks he *really* is jinxed, a curse, a fuck-up. He *knew* it; he was right all along. Sometimes it's not so good to be right.

On a practical level he's fucked, stranded in Rural Fuckin Wiltshire.

Jesus leaves the burning car and the remains of Samuel Laniado behind. He trudges aimlessly for a while – dishevelled, covered in soot and mud and blood, like a fashion victim scarecrow, still clutching the boosted bearer bonds. At first light, he finds a car to steal, hotwires it, drives off with the alarm wailing, manages to kill the noise, heads east, towards the M4 and London. An hour later, near Heathrow Airport, he sees a minicab office, orange light flashing outside. He dumps the car and walks into the cab office, asks for a taxi.

No Cash, No Car says the sign. Jesus' banknotes are damp from sweat and rain and bloodstained from ... So are his clothes. The taxi driver, a Somalian, isn't going to be helping anyone with their inquiries, but Jesus tells him he's been to a *wild fuckin party, man!*

The driver nods and grins, doesn't speak much English. Jesus thinks this is wrong – *driving an English car on English roads for English men and English women and you can't speak fuckin English? Can't talk to the passengers?*

There's nothing worse that a self-righteous psychopath. But Jesus has got a call to make, then a train to catch ... Jesus gets the cabbie to drop him off around the back of the Cosmopolitan.

Jesus crept back to his room just as Roy's ambush team were receiving their final briefing. Jesus had a swift wash and brush-up, the bone-warming shower, while all the time repeating his new mantra – No Sleep Till Paris.

Jesus was exhausted but he knew he couldn't sleep, had to keep on moving. Jesus liked his sleep, was usually going to bed around dawn. Missing his kip made him irritable, argumentative, explains why Jesus was so abrupt with Royski later that day ... Maybe he thought, when he saw Roy's Skorpion, *here we fuckin go, another round of persecutors. I knew it ... Nothing goes my way.*

Jesus retrieved and reloaded his suitcases, just as the cleaning staff were coming on duty, but he needed recognition, like vampires need blood, so Jesus took time out to ring Santos who was in Heathrow arrivals lounge. Santos and the three *amigos* had just got off the red-eye – Miami—Heathrow, coach class. The promised upgrade hadn't materialised. Jesus *had* to tell Santos all about Sammy – to *share*, as the Americans say. Jesus couldn't *contain* himself, couldn't wait. Santos sat on his suitcase listening to the details, *couldn't get a word in.* Santos is thinking he's gonna have a nice couple of days in London, before splitting to Paris ... Jesus eventually tells Santos to get a cab into town. He's waiting, *looking forward to seeing his old friend ...*

Jesus calmly checks out of the Cosmo, *adios London*, skips into his cab for Waterloo, loaded up with The Three Samsonites. Not a vocal harmony group.

With friends like Jesus, who fuckin needs ...

CHAPTER FORTY

PATSY, YA GOTTA LOVE HIM

'So Jesus ... have I got this right?' Morty asks Santos, 'Was crossing borders with three million?'

Santos shakes his head. 'Jesus was a lunatic but he was far from stupid ... '

Jesus was taking the suitcases to a freight shipping firm near Waterloo Station. He'd negotiated, over the phone, late at night, a drop of diplomatic immunity; the three suitcases were going into one larger container, to travel to the Venezuelan Embassy in Brussels as a diplomatic bag. Jesus was going to kill a day in Paris and then get reunited with the bags in Belgium – *nice* – then deposit the money with the guy the late Sammy Laniado had recommended.

Santos doesn't know about Roy's squad ambushing Jesus but he knows where Jesus had hidden the bonds for safekeeping.

Sonny, or Roy, have never mentioned any bonds. Is it possible that they never knew of their existence, the same way that Santos or Jesus didn't know the true value of the information held on the memory stick? But knowing Sonny, he wouldn't have been able to contain himself if he'd stumbled onto nine million dollars in bearer bonds, *plus* the three mill sterling. Too much of a coup – he would have had a gloat-fest with Morty and me in Barbados, wouldn't have been able to keep his mouth shut.

Jesus thought the memory stick was a bumper jumbo blackmail package – the nonsensical hieroglyphics, incriminating recordings of Miguel and his sexually explicit photos of Jenna. Got to be worth another five million dollars. Jesus was selling himself seriously short.

Chip clicks his fingers and gestures to one of his younger brothers to give Santos a swing on the brandy – *fuck me, he needs it.*

'Jesus is dead?' asks Santos, brandy running down his chin.

Morty nods.

'And his money, Laniado's money?'

'Gone,' says Morty, 'but not my way.'

'But the people who stole Jesus' money didn't know about the bonds, no?'

Morty shrugs, shakes his head.

'There's a deal to be done,' says Santos, spitting out blood like a boxer. 'My safe passage for the information – where I believe the bonds to be located ... '

Santos is getting self-satisfied again, the devil returning to his eyes. *You will need me and I will need you.*

'Where's these bonds now?' asks Chip. 'Did this Jee-zuss fella have them when he left this hotel?'

'With respect, *señor*,' says Santos, 'I think we need to talk terms before I part with that sort of information.'

'I could easily beat it out of you,' says Chip.

'That's unnecessary, my friend,' says Santos. 'What difference does it make to you if I'm alive or dead?'

'You killed my brother—'

'I'm trying to make it right, with nine million—'

'Dollars?' Chip asks Morty. 'What's that in real money?'

'About six mill, Chip,' says Morty. 'A nice pension.'

Santos is looking from face to face. Chip is weighing up his options on behalf of the brothers, who are eerily quiet for once. Do they kill their brother's killer in revenge, or take his blood money as compo? Morty is studying Santos with narrow eyes.

'How do I know you're not lying?' asks Mort.

'No more clues,' says Santos, 'it's not a game. And ... ' he adds, getting eye contact with Mort, 'I will only do a deal with you. You may be a Negro but I feel you are an honourable man.'

Morty tries not to laugh, 'That's very nice of you to say so.'

'So it's up to you ... ' says Santos, dramatically, looking for a drum roll, 'the location of the bearer bonds for my life. You get me on a plane or to my embassy – I have contacts there. I will say I have been the victim of a traffic accident. I have a wife and small children at home in Venezuela ... I just want to see them again ...' Santos holds his composure well. 'One more dead South American to dispose of *or* the chance to get your hands on nine million dollars ... I know which one I would choose ... '

He leaves it hanging in the air like cigarette smoke. Suddenly the swing doors fly open. A huge silhouette fills the doorway – pure John Wayne. Could be the law – guns suddenly appear and point at the figure, then they drop. The eldest, biggest brother – man mountain Patrick, six foot twelve – has arrived, making an entrance like something outta an opera.

Patsy marches across the floor, a huge pistol held straight out, obviously in a blind rage. He aims, goes to shoot Santos – *just like he killed Baby Stevie*. Patrick O'Malley, the legend, was never bright, he didn't have to be, but now he's paralytic, been heavy on the bereavement lash. The rest of the brothers jump in his way. Patsy raises the gun, lets one go, straight into the ceiling. *Fuckin stand aside*, he roars. Everyone ducks. The bullet ricochets around, bouncing off the concrete walls. Patsy's making animal noises and roaring incoherently. Suddenly there's guns waving everywhere. Patsy marches on, swaying slightly, taking one-eyed aim at Santos' head. The brothers jump on him; there's a melee.

Morty tries to intercede but Patsy roars *this is your fault, you*! Brothers are holding onto Patrick's back. He's delivering old-fashioned haymakers with his free hand. The junkie pups are like dogs on a bear. Santos is too bewildered to be scared.

'Listen, Patsy, there's millions!' shouts Chip above the noise.

'Fuck off!' screams Patsy. 'Get the fuck out of my way.'

'Bearer bonds, Pats!' shouts Chip.

'Fuck bearer bonds, whoever the fuck he is!'

I move backwards. The other O'Malleys scream at Pats that there's a colossal earner in this, all shouting over one another. But Patsy raises his gun again and points it towards Santos. Pats is about to pull the trigger but one of the juniors hits him across the head with a metal chair *to calm him down*. It draws blood – nasty gash. Patsy sees his own claret running into his eyes – never a pleasant sight.

Patsy goes ballistic. The brothers leap on him to restrain him but Patsy wrestles free and holds the shooter in both of his huge hands, shuts his eyes, and squeezes – yyyyyyyyyyaaaaaaaaaaaarrrrrrrr he screams, like he's having a orgasm.

Patsy shoots Santos in the temple at point-blank range. Santos' head explodes, sending blood and grey fat flying – up the cast iron column, along the floor. Santos slumps in his chair, dripping onto the dusty floor.

Always had perfect comic timing, the O'Malley clan. It's sad, a geezer dying like that, but Santos was undeniably an evil cunt. I wonder if he ever imagined he'd end up getting shot in the wigwam by a notorious Kilburn drunk? I guess there's a dose of karma in there somewhere and *one more dead South American to dispose of.*

Goodbye bearer bond payday. The brothers are arguing and fighting amongst themselves, bodies and chairs flying. Chip fires shots into the ceiling; they ricochet around. Brothers are roaring at Patsy but he's wailing, making no sense, oblivious to anything. Suddenly Pats stops dead ... then he rocks ... his eyes roll up in his head, he crumples, then collapses in a heap. His head hits the concrete with a clunk. It's dead silent ... for a count of four ... then Patsy starts to mumble. His brothers then carry on fighting and shouting recriminations, not that interested in Pats.

Morty stands with his arms folded. Patsy goes off to sleep with a snore, still holding his gun. Chip goes over and takes the gun out of his hand. The brothers begin to accept the situation. Things begin to go quiet again.

Chip turns to Morty. His expression says *well, what now?*

Morty shrugs, an exaggerated look of recognition on his face, as if to say *well what*? *You and yours just shot the golden goose, sunshine, not me.* 'We all need to get gone, Chip,' he says.

'What about these bonds?' asks Chip.

'Gone, mate,' Morty nods at the dead Santos. 'Forget it – needle in a haystack.' Morty pulls Chip closer. 'Now, this is important. You've got to impress upon your boys that they're to tell nobody, not a fuckin soul, okay? This is murder, remember that, no matter what he did or didn't do. It's murder times four.'

'What about Sonny King's reward?'

'Sonny wanted him alive, to talk to him ... Not much chance of that now. You could ask Sonny for readies but ... '

Mort shrugs. Chip looks sick. Chip is halfways sensible. Chip saw the possibilities but ... Too late now. Damage limitation time ...

'This didn't happen, Chip,' says Mort. 'I can make a call ... to

get rid of the bodies. If the law get on this, they'll charge everyone
– that's twelve heads in the dock.'

Morty goes into his pocket, puts out a chunk of cash. 'Take
this, leave the other bodies, but we better get it done. And not a
word, okay?'

Chip shrugs but says nothing.

'Not even to Sonny or Roy,' says Mort, leaning in even closer,
'if you should meet them on your travels, you understand?'

Chip nods and takes the money. 'Fuck Sonny King,' he says to
himself.

'And, Chip, tell Patsy, when he wakes up, to keep quiet, okay?'

'To be honest, Mort,' says Chip, turning to leave, 'I doubt very
much if Patsy'll remember a thing.'

We cut out, retracing our steps. It's getting light. We drive for
five minutes then Morty pulls over at a parade of shops with a
phone box in front. He pulls out his phone and finds a number and
makes a point of repeating it to remember it. He tells me he's
going to be one minute and trots over to the payphone, leaving his
mobile on the seat. I pick it up, curious to see the number – it's
listed in his speed dial as *Miss B wrk*. Could this be Bridget
Granger's work phone? Could she have a little sideline in
disposals? Guess it's better than having parties where they sell
saucy underwear.

Part of me that thinks those bonds and the O'Malleys would
have brought big trouble. It's a lethal combination, raw shitkickers
with high expectations. I knew I wasn't going to be in the final
bust-up and it would get ugly and chaotic before the end. *The
boys'* greed would be up and running, fuelled by alcohol,
handguns and drugs. The O'Malleys never learnt to share. Half a
minute later Morty trots back to the motor.

'You understand why we're doing this?' he asks, then answers
his own question. 'Them lot would fuck it up, leave 'em to rot,
get us all chored. Best get 'em shifted.'

'Would you have let him – Santos – go home, Mort?'

Morty starts the engine and pulls away. 'You shouldn't ask me
questions like that.'

'Do you think he was bluffing? Did he know where those
bonds were?'

'Who knows if there *were* any bonds,' says Mort. 'That was a man fighting for his life.'

'He might have got away with it too, if it wasn't for Pats ... '

'He was never going to see Caracas again,' says Morty pulling onto the dual carriageway. '*You are a noble negro – you I do a deal with ...* ' He starts to laugh. 'For the time being ... ' says Morty – I know what he's going to say before he says it – 'let's agree not to tell Sonny or Roy about Santos, yeah?' He gives me a little wink. 'Strictly need-to-know.'

'They won't hear it from me,' I say.

Morty drops me off a few streets away from the luxury flophouse, tells me to get rid of all the clothes I'm wearing and to have a good scrub down. It's dawn now. I could kip for a week. But then I can't sleep – it's that speculation business, burrowing further into the psyche. And more gruesome images to keep me wide awake.

Riddle me this. Santos denied sending shooters to kill me in the Underground. He admitted killing Stevie; why deny the second attempt? So who tried to shoot me in the Underground? It would be pointless Miguel's firm trying it; they need me alive, out looking, hoping to cop a reward. While I was in Wembley Miguel's crew kept leaving proxy phone messages, *on behalf of* Miguel, about the conversation we had – *did I have any further thoughts*? Miguel's behaving like a proper CEO – delegating, distancing himself from the frontline. He believes he's recruited me to the firm.

If Miguel wanted me dead he'd send one of his Americans. They'd know how to do a wet one ... I'd be dead and buried. So who? I think there's something woven into the fabric of that memory stick that lets them know that it's lit up, that it's in use in London ...

Fact – someone followed me from *Bridget's* dry cleaners. Someone's trying to get at Ted? He thinks nobody knows he's alive; maybe a little conceit on his part. Someone knows he's alive ... They don't want him dead but they want to send him a message?

Tossing and turning, legs still aching, blisters playing up ... Speculation – the late Samuel Laniado was the evasive connection that Ted Granger was going into business with. The timing of Sammy's disappearance would correspond; lots of heavy circumstantial evidence. Where's the merchandise Ted said was on its way?

And in the further speculation department – I think Sammy Laniado, although he didn't know it, was Miguel Zambrano's UK connection, *the Anglophile, living down the country*, who would organise the reward consignment of coke if we returned the gadget ... That would mean that Ted Granger could be buying – indirectly – from the Zambrano Family.

Small fuckin world we live in.

CHAPTER FORTY-ONE

WRONG PLACE, WRONG TIME

I know this meet with Ted and Bridget's going to go bad. Morty
didn't wanna come, didn't like any of my speculative theories.
If I could do it on the phone I would, but bad news needs to be
delivered personally so I wait by the open-air theatre in Regent's
Park until Bridget speeds up in her Range Rover to collect me. I
jump in. She seems unconcerned about being followed. Bridget
is *almost* compassionate about me *almost* getting murdered
twice, tells me she'll have to find me a new suit. *Morty told me
the old one couldn't be dry cleaned.* She says it like someone's
died, sympathetically pats me on the thigh; bit over-friendly, to
be honest.

We take off. Bridget drives like a nutcase – it would be hard to
keep up with her. She's yawning at the traffic lights, like she's had
a late night. I make no mention of her sideline. She's happy in her
work – it's not like she needs the money – come rain or shine
people always need clean clothes.

We weave through the back-doubles to Bridget's apartment
alongside Regent's Canal, beyond Little Venice – the top two
floors of an old converted factory with a private lift. Bridget leads
me upstairs to the main living area. The whole top floor is
massive, tastefully but minimally furnished. Down one side are
sliding doors from floor to ceiling with a tint in the glass. The
kitchen area is cleaner than an operating theatre, with a gentle
waft of bleach in the air. It's colour-supplement chic but
beautifully done. I'm surprised for a minute, but then it makes
sense; Bridget is extremely wealthy. The only pieces of the
dream-lifestyle jigsaw that don't quite fit are the lingering smell
of fried bacon and the pint of milk sitting on the stainless steel
worktop with the tinfoil top neither on nor off. Bridget would
never allow such shoddiness but it tells me that Mister Ted
Granger is now in residence. Bridget studies the milk through

narrow eyes. She grinds coffee, slings a tea bag into a mug for Ted and accepts my compliments about her taste with calculated nonchalance.

The canal is narrow at this point and Bridget's apartment is overlooked on the other side by old industrial buildings. Down below, canal boats chug by, but heavy glass doors that lead out onto a deck insulate against noise, creating a tranquil cocoon.

Ted appears, dressed in pressed slacks and polo shirt, trying to be relaxed, but his furrowed forehead betrays worry and foreboding – *he wouldn't be here if it wasn't bad news*.

'What the fuck have ya done to yourself?' he says by way of greeting. 'Dyed yer hair? Jesus wept!'

Bridget hands Ted a mug of tea while the smell of brewing coffee begins to fill the apartment. Ted sits down on the sofa opposite me, sips his tea. 'What's it all about?' he asks. 'Yer man,' I guess he means Morty, 'wouldn't say nish, just said you might have something to tell me.'

Bridget hovers, her eyes locked on me.

'Did you ever hear of a chap by the name of Samuel Laniado?'

Ted leans forward. 'Go on ... ' he says.

'Laniado's dead.'

Ted goes crazy, instantly. He turns red with rage, puts the mug down slowly. He's breathing hard through his nostrils. Ted runs his hand down his face, wiping away frustration, then massages his temples.

'You didn't know he was dead?'

Ted's face answers my question ... He didn't.

'No?'

'Fuck off!'

'Don't shoot the messenger, Ted.'

Bridget – pure poker face, inscrutable – turns and goes to see how the coffee's doing.

'What happened?' Ted asks. 'Tell me.'

I tell them how Jesus killed Laniado. Ted explodes at the end. 'This is all Sonny King's fault! That Fuckin Sonny King!'

'He didn't kill Laniado,' I say, but Ted ignores me.

'I want that fuckin gadget everyone's getting sticky knickers about – as compo.'

'You didn't wanna know.'

'That was when I thought I had a bona fide supplier, ready to go to work.'

'I don't think Sonny will want to put you in it ... not without some persuasion.'

'Fuck Sonny King!' says Ted, 'He'll get some fuckin persuasion, all right!'

Ted isn't thinking right. If he wants to *take* it ... could be a big problem. Could get fuckin ugly, fuckin quick. Small-scale civil war. This requires diplomacy.

'If I might make a suggestion, Ted,' I say. 'Giles Urquhart is the key. Get him over here, explain the problem. Get him to work Sonny.'

'This is what we're gonna do,' says Ted with a degree of finality.

And this is Ted's initiative – arrange a meeting with Roy, get him to convince Sonny to do a deal with Miguel, create a united front in negotiations. Ted believes he can manipulate Roy because Roy believes in *the code-of-the-road and all that old bollocks.*

I suggest, as tactfully as I can, that, 'This might not be such a good idea. I don't wanna talk ill of Roy's mental state but ... Sonny told Morty that Roy's screaming in the night, having nightmares, more paranoid than usual.'

'No, no, Roy's cool,' says Ted, believing what he wants to believe. 'He's a soldier, is Roy.'

'See, you're meant to be dead, Ted.'

'And?' he says, with a shrug. 'What's that got to do with anything?'

'It's easy to put ideas into Roy's head, but it's a lot harder to get them out again.'

'What the fuck you on about?' Ted asks.

'It'll spook him. He's just got his head round the fact you're dead,' I say. 'Giles is your man, Ted. Sonny respects him.'

'We're gonna do a pincer movement on Sonny King,' says Ted, with a trace of a smile, 'come at him from both directions.'

Ted laughs, coughs. Drinks his tea.

'Can I tell you something?' I say. He nods. 'You don't need to turn over Sonny for the money he's got plugged in that bank.'

'Turn over?' says Ted, all offended. 'Since when do you have the gall to tell me what to do?'

'Listen, Ted,' I say, starting to lose patience, '*I* need this fuckin deal. I need away. I'm *wanted*, remember. There's a settlement to be negotiated with Miguel Zambrano.'

Something moves out of the corner of my eye. I look around; someone's creeping along the corridor, heading towards the stairs. I do a double-take and see an apparition, a face from the past – older, more malnourished than when I last saw her. Evey, the volatile ex-girlfriend of Sonny King is stood in the hall, looking dazed and confused, pale as a ghost.

'Is that Evey, Ted?' I ask, surprised, pointing back into the hall.

'Yeah, right fuckin string vest 'n' all she is,' he says. 'Come in a taxi, potless. No fuckin money. Bridge has to go down to pay the fare. Liberty. Parks her up ... detoxifying, ain't she?'

'Oh, yeah?' I say. 'Detoxing, you say?'

'Offa drugs,' he says.

'To be honest, Ted, I wouldn't want Evey to see me here, you know what I mean?'

'You're not wrong. Got a big mouth that one. I've tried telling Bridge ... but she says Eve's so whacked ... ' He points at his temple, makes a circle, as if to say she's too shot-away.

'All the same,' I nod towards the decking. 'Shall we?'

Ted gets up, wanders over, fiddles with the catch on the window and slides it open.

'Come on,' he says. 'And bring that phone – you're gonna ring Roy Burns.'

Ted leads us out onto the deck. It's like something from an upmarket resort, with chairs and sun umbrellas, loungers and tasteful wooden furniture. The view is across the rooftops of west London but it's a sheer drop six floors down to the canal below. There's a large brick barbecue against one wall, and running along the edge of the decking there's waist-high boxy privet hedges, watered and lush, in heavy aluminium planters. They look like they've been clipped only this morning with nail scissors and a set square, not a little leaf out of place.

Ted sits us down under a large sunshade. Ted lights up – *Bridge don't allow smoking in the house.* Once he's settled and sparked up, Ted half-orders me to call Roy – *prime him for a surprise, then hand the phone to me, okay?*

I ring Roy's number. He answers, sounding dead suspicious.

'Are you with our royal friend? No? Okay. Calm down, mate, it was only a question. You're alone? Now someone needs to talk to you, on the QT. But here's the thing, Roy, this might be a bit of a shock.'

Ted is bristling with impatience, gesturing for me to hand him the phone.

'Hiya, mate,' says Ted with far too much bonhomie, 'this is your old mucker from over there, you know who I mean? Good ... Now I know what you heard, mate. You shouldn't believe everything you hear.' There's a brief pause. 'No, no, I'm in the best of health ... Now, listen, mate, I need to have a meet with you, yeah? But nobody's to know – not your pal, not anyone. Good, no problem. Need-to-know, mate,' Ted gives me a little wink. 'I'm gonna get my man here to sort it. We'll speak later but it's very important that you don't tell the other fella. He'll be told in time, but not now ... You getting it? Sweet. See ya later, fella.'

Ted hands me back the phone. I push the red button to finish the call. 'I still think you getting Giles to graft Sonny would be a better idea.'

'Shut up, will ya, please,' says Ted, suddenly looking tired. 'Give it a rest ... Divide and rule ... '

'Meaning?'

Before I can get my, no doubt ambiguous, answer, Bridget walks out onto the decking with coffee cups and a cafetière on a tray. She trips, falls forward, curses – *cunt!* She recovers her footing but simultaneously the enormous windowpane behind her disintegrates with an almighty crash, as if by magic, leaving shards of razor-sharp glass swinging from the plastic sun-protection film. Bridget drops the tray. I'm gone like a whippet, instinctively back inside, over the glass, straight through the space where the window was. I know it was a bullet that did the damage.

Ted and Bridget both hit the floor immediately and roll over to the planters on the edge of the decking. They huddle up behind it like two children playing hide-and-seek. I peek back around the corner.

More shots are coming in, but *silent*, skipping across the deck. A gunman is firing with a silencer; a professional with a high-powered rifle. Bullets begin to clunk into the steel kick plate, pass through them with ease and ricochet, hitting the wall behind, huge chips of brick flying. The sniper's laying down a steady hail – got his rhythm now – a second between shots. The bullets are coming in almost level, a position slightly higher than the decking. Bridget crawls one way, Ted the other. Shots begin to rip up the planters where they've just been. The soil absorbs the impact, but holes the size of sausages are getting punched in them.

I can't hear the shots; only see the bullets hitting targets. The sniper's keeping a rhythm going, skunking them out – trying to coax Ted and Bridget out into the open – but they're edging along the planters. The shots are calculated and accurate. The rounds are big; I know from the ricochet. The sniper hasn't worked out where they're hiding. But he's still accurately placing rounds into all the places they *could* be.

The firing appears to be coming from a disused factory over to the right. To their credit, neither of them is scared. In fact I think they're enjoying it. I swear I heard Ted giggling but he has more sense than to get up and make a run for it.

The shooting suddenly stops. I creep along inside, flick the locks on the door at the far end, and in one fast movement push the door open so Ted can jump in quick. I can see both Ted and Bridget breathing heavy. Ted's inching slowly over towards the open sliding door, using his toes to propel himself along, slithering like a python – looking like a snake, but thinking like a sniper. What would he do?

Go quiet, that's what. Wait. Let the targets think you've fled. When they get up to brush themselves down – whack! One to the canister!

It's *too* fuckin quiet now. I can hear my heart pumping. My mouth's dry again.

'Maybe they've gone, Ted,' shouts Bridget from the far end of the decking.

Right on cue Bridget gets her answer. Bullets – a *silent* hail – immediately impact against the walls, clunking into the steel railing, bouncing off the barbecue, thudding through the metal base plate, ripping up the planters, sending privet leaves everywhere. The shooter has put his weapon on automatic mode and a full clip in, and is letting go, looking to create carnage. Now it's a free-fire zone. The shooter has moved position; the bullets are coming in from a different angle. Ted and Bridget are dead still, every part of them pressed into the wood. Bullets smash into the decking, turning the furniture to matchwood. Lamps above the barbecue explode. A bullet flies through another window, leaving a perfectly round hole in the shattered pane. The bullet ricochets across the room inside, zinging around the corners. Then thumb-sized holes get poked in a sweeping row across the plasterboard wall at the far end of the room. The plasma telly takes a direct hit. I hunch down lower. Suddenly a shattered windowpane drops away into a neat pile, leaving only its tattered film of plastic and glass. Windows have taken shots; only the plastic coating is holding them together. The barrage stops as suddenly as it began.

'He's changing the magazine!' shouts Bridget. 'Quick, Ted, get inside!'

Ted shouts back, 'Stay fuckin down, Bridget!'

But Bridget makes a run, almost doubled-over, towards the door, the length of the decking. As soon as she breaks cover the firing starts again. RIP Bridget. But like the war hero charging the machine gun, bullets are hammering around her head, behind her, in front, and where she's been the split-second before. It's a miracle. A window gets blasted, the glass drops away and Bridget – like she'd anticipated it – jumps through the space where the glass was. She rolls, then lies flat on the floor, desperately trying to catch her breath. The firing stops again. She crawls over to me.

'Thought he was changing the clip,' she says calmly. 'Where're they firing from?'

'It's the red-brick building, deffo, up to the right,' I say, pointing. 'Don't know what window. They changed places.'

'Need to know if the law are comin,' she says, crawling over to the decking, towards Ted, still cowering beneath the planters.

'Where's the scanner?' Bridget shouts over to Ted.

'In the tool box under the sink,' Ted shouts in reply.

Bridget ducks low, makes her way over to the kitchen. She finds what she's looking for – a gadget like a cell phone with a sturdy antenna. The police frequencies have been pre-programmed in. Bridget listens for a second to mundane radio traffic – *suspected prowler, message timed at ...* – then pushes a search button. The scanner dances around till it finds another frequency. Bridget's concentrating hard, listening for any mention of a firearms incident, anything code red. All appears quiet on the airwaves and outside.

Ted begins crawling towards us to safety, staying low the whole time. Suddenly Ted leaps up and runs for the open window. He does a little zigzag but then heads straight for us. There's no firing. But he stumbles and falls. He's gotta be dead. But he bounces up, sprints through the doors, without any shots being fired.

'Do you think they're gonna storm the gaff?' he asks Bridget breathlessly.

'How the fuck would I know, Ted?' replies Bridget, real droll, like he'd asked if it's gonna rain.

Bridget keeps pressing buttons, sending the scanner onto different police frequencies.

'No police,' says Bridget. 'Nothing on the normal bands ... Don't mean to say ... ' her voice peters out. She holds up her hand, motions to us to be quiet. Bridget has tuned into voices talking on two-way radios somewhere nearby, talking in an odd *dialect* of Spanish.

'It's Spanish! These cunts are fuckin Spanish!' screams Ted.

'It's fucking Italian!' counters Bridget.

'No, it's South American Spanish!' says Ted, 'Listen!'

'Italian!' spits Bridget.

'Do you understand that?' says Ted, turning to me, but shouts, 'You Spanish cunts!' at the scanner before getting an answer.

It's neither. I've riddled it out. It's Portuguese, with a brutal

South American inflection – same as the geezers on the tube.
There's two shooters, and they're Brazilian.

Ted desperately wants me to translate but they're talking too
fast, the accents too heavy. One is the shooter, the other the
spotter. They're wired up, got earpieces and stick mics, like airline
pilots ... or professional snipers.

They're quarrelling about not getting paid – *no kill, no money*.
One's mocking the other for ridiculing the pair who got killed in
the metro tunnel – now *you've made a mess yourself*.

They have a scanner too, tuned to the police; we can hear it
in the background. One's talking about abandoning the mission
at the *first sign of policias. We could storm in and finish it*. The
other disagrees, *it's London not Sao Paulo*. They're cursing and
arguing, in a calm but chilling way. They want *someone* alive?
Vivo! Who the fuck do they want alive? They thought the sister
would be there *sozinha* – alone. They were told *just kill the
sister – the woman. Don't kill the guy, that's what they said.
Don't kill the Duppy man or they'll never get paid. Should pay
his bills ... pay what he owes ... pay the bosses ... not charity ...
good work for us ... extra ... want it done quick. He's not meant
to be here – shall I shoot him? No! More money for us – we
come back again, stupid ... to kill him. Want her dead, and him
scared.*

'What are they saying?' Ted shouts at me, 'Tell me!'

'I'm only getting the gist, Ted.'

'What's the fuckin *gist*?' he says, regaining his belligerent
attitude.

'Stay down!' screams Bridget. 'For fuck's sake, stay down,
Ted!'

'Don't talk to me like a cunt, Bridget!' shouts Ted, right in
Bridget's face.

'Okay, Ted,' says Bridget, strangely cool. 'Get yourself fuckin
shot if you like.'

The spotter tells the shooter to retain his *disciplina de rádio*!
Retain radio discipline! People could be listening! There's rank
involved, and one of them has just pulled it – they sound vaguely
military. *Let them think we've gone – then we kill her, not him,*

okay! Keep the doors and stairs covered. Should have killed her in the street.

The gist is that the two guys have been sent to kill Bridget to frighten Ted because he owes money, but their boss won't get paid if Ted is dead. It explains why they didn't shoot Ted when they could.

'Fuck this,' says Bridget, dodging into a blind spot in the kitchen, 'I'm not waiting around to get ... '

Bridget grabs a claw hammer from the toolbox and starts to smash a hole in an innocuous plasterboard panel. She reaches in and pulls out an ugly, short machine gun wrapped in greasy canvas. She hunts around the hole, pulls out an oily bag and brings out three clips of ammunition, then a naughty-looking silencer. She assembles and loads the weapon in double-quick time, shouting to me and Ted to keep our eyes on the building *across the way*, for signs of movement. The scanner is spookily quiet. Bridget creeps back over to us. 'Might have another team out the front,' she says. 'It's what I'd do.'

'They ain't talking to anyone else, Bridget,' I say.

'We could break out,' says Ted.

'They have the stairwell covered,' I tell Bridget. 'They're regretting not shooting you on the street.'

'Me?'

'It's *you* they're trying to kill ... to scare Ted ... I'll explain later ... we all need to explain a few things.'

Bridget appears very comfortable with her machine gun nestled in her shoulder. For once she's not worried about the mess. For the time being it's stalemate – just gotta hold yer nerve and keep your eyes wide open. So we wait ... I almost feel like putting the kettle on.

But then I catch the tiniest glint of light in the darkness of one of the windows in the building opposite – a flash, a watch face or sunglasses. I count the windows in from the side of the building then point it out to Bridget – *four windows in, top floor*. We're ducked down low, peeking around corners. Trying to not present a target. Bridget studies the window hard but does nothing.

'We just sit here and wait?' asks Ted.

'What do you fuckin suggest?' replies Bridget.

'We need a decoy,' says Ted. 'For them to show themselves—'

Bridget quickly interrupts. 'What, you want me to fuckin go out there again?'

'That's not what I said.'

'Sounded like it, Ted,' says Bridget. 'First chance I get I'm going to rip those fuckers apart. Italian cunts.'

'Bridget,' I say, 'they're Brazilian.'

'Shut the fuck up!' replies Bridget. 'They won't know what's hit 'em. Gonna get a dose of my naughty-naughties.'

Hollow-tipped bullets, filed flat – against the rules of war – expand on impact. Bridget would like a rocket launcher. I feel strangely protected by her; she won't go down without a fight, our Bridge.

I look down the room, through the wreckage. At the far end, Evey is wandering ghost-like towards the decking, over the glass and debris, floating on a cloud of heavy lockdown medication. Evey looks with childlike curiosity at the devastation as she meanders out onto the deck.

Bullets start thudding into brickwork behind her head. She looks open-mouthed at the dents in the wall. Bridget jumps out onto the decking and begins firing, fearlessly, aiming at the building opposite. A chain of tracer rounds zero in on her target – the sniper's window. Rounds bounce and crash around their hidey hole. Then Bridget's naughty specials ricochet around inside. She empties the whole clip in seconds.

Too late. Evey gets hit in the head – killed instantly. Head flies one way, feet the other. Lands in a heap. Lifeless.

Bridget jumps back inside. She lets the empty clip drop to the floor and grabs another one. She's raging, screaming angry, struggling to get the clip in the slot. I grab her arm – hold on tight – and shake my head. I nod at the scanner. Bridget's hit one of the snipers. There's screams coming from the scanner – no radio discipline.

The spotter has a shattered shoulder – *losing blood* – crying for morphine, for his mother. The wounded man is already in deep shock. *Aborto, aborto*! He's screeching, in agony. The shooter is distressed by his comrade's wounds. Sounds like the shoulder is completely gone – no artery, no tourniquet, no chance – caught the full impact. We can hear gurgling sounds, and the wounded man fighting for breath, both of them crying.

The scanner goes silent, abruptly – their radios turned off. Bridget pushes the search button again. It scans the airwaves – mundane police radio traffic, no sirens or flashing blue lights. She turns down the volume switch, rolls backwards, lies on the floor, her eyes closed, the fresh clip still in her hand. Her old pal Evey is rapidly making a dark puddle on the decking. Bridget opens her eyes, stares at the ceiling, at something far away, or long ago. I see a side of her I'm sure she wouldn't like me to see – her bottom lip quivering, eyes watering, close to tears.

CHAPTER FORTY-TWO

JUGGLING BIG TIME

We went to the park. It was full of nannies and kids on summer holidays. Sandpits and face paint – a long way from gunfire and corpses. We sat in the cafeteria. I was a regular here, on nodding acquaintance with the staff, winking terms with the waitresses. We felt the need to clear out for a while, to let the smoke settle, clean up later. Evey was left on the decking, with a tarpaulin thrown over her. Can't stay there forever, of course ... but you never know who might be in the vicinity.

The snipers had troubles of their own. Bridget wanted to chase them down, get revenge for Eve, but I couldn't see the point – accelerating a slow death at much risk to ourselves was futile and dangerous. Following blood trails to find them could be like cornering a couple of extremely desperate rats. Maybe his buddy administered the *coup de grâce* before heading back to Brazil. Taking a dying man to hospital and risking getting police involved was, to the survivor, pointless. The wounded man was on the way out – trauma was gonna kill him before blood poisoning. He might be dead in that building across the canal. Bridget insists that she'll check it out after dark – corpses littering the neighbourhood, in high summer, isn't good.

Bridget is understandably gutted about Evey, someone she'd taken under her wing when Bridget was in big school and Eve still in the juniors. And now she's invited her in, to look after her, and a gun battle's broken out. These things happen in Evey and Bridget's world. She ain't handling it too well ... giving Ted a hard time, maybe thinks Ted wasn't pulling his weight back there. It's also time to fess-up – get a confessional as to why two geezers are trying to kill Sister Bridget – to fill in the blanks. I know bits but not details. The geezers were sent to frighten Ted into paying for some cargo that he's already had. They couldn't kill Ted or they would never get paid; it's that South American proxy intimidation again.

And me? I'm extremely alert, frightened *after* the event. Only after a genuinely life-threatening experience do you feel just how good it is to be alive, same as only after your liberty is threatened do you find your sense of freedom. The other irony is how getting shot at, repeatedly, with a high-calibre assault rifle, and escaping alive, is a bonding experience for the three of us, but especially me and Bridge. I'm trying to work out who'd wanna shoot Bridget Granger. Who exactly *isn't* trying to kill Already Dead Ted? Can't be the dead Santos. And Miguel doesn't know Ted Granger exists ... unless Miguel blames Ted for the death of Laniado. Could it be Sonny's manoeuvre? Could Sonny rustle up Brazilian shooters? Has he got a sniff about their little scheme?

And I've got the raging zig with Ted – I've put part of the jigsaw together. The monkeys on the tube were shooting at me because they figured I was part of Duppy's organisation; understandable after I walked into his sister's dry cleaners with only a folded newspaper and reappeared, half an hour later, carrying the Gucci bags. Maybe they thought I was carrying either cha-cha or mucho readies and they'd be in for a hefty payday, a bonus. The attempt was a memo to Ted, but he kept it under his hat. My hunch is that the firm he owes big money to have lines of communication open with Ted; they're calculated enough to know a dead Ted is a worthless Ted.

'This is getting too heavy for me,' I say, 'assassination attempts, machine guns, Eve dead back there.'

'What ya saying?' snaps Ted.

'Might just head off back to Jamaica—'

'Bollocks,' he says. 'Yer bluffing.'

'Might be. Try me.'

'What, walk away from that gadget?'

'No good to me dead.'

'I might be able to help you there,' says Ted. 'Could work on Sonny.'

'I think it's *you* rather than me who needs the help.'

'You cheeky cunt!' roars Ted, but Bridget, seething, hisses at him – to tell me *the whole fuckin story, now!*

What emerges is a sad story – not a tearjerker but a sobering, cautionary tale – and it makes Ted Granger appear even more like a throwback to another time. Like those eighteenth-century wastrels and spendthrift ruffians, united in a mad punt, doing their bollocks at the racetrack, or the smoky card saloon.

Ted The Duppy Granger is a skint member – not a fuckin penny to his name, except for a couple of properties in Spain that will need taxes paid on them before Bridget can inherit, sell them, and move the money over to Ted.

Being boracic is hard to stomach after watching millions go through his muckies over the years. Where's Ted's accumulated funds? His lifetime's work?

He never really got ahead; betting all his money on unreliable gee-gees – *that's where the millions went*. When Ted wanted a punt the bookies would be laying-off all along the Costa del Sol. If he lost tens of thousands he'd be chasing it with *hundreds* of thousands. This was a man who did mega bets – hundred kay on a four-horse accumulator – but now he's down to borrowed tenners and looking for shrapnel down the back of the sofa.

Will that be on the nose or each way, Mister Granger, sir?

What do you think I am, pal, a fuckin deadbeat?

Ted was like the junkie who hated the dealer while begging to be served; Ted detested and resented the bookies who took his millions.

Ted had also given away millions to friends and family, operating like a one-man charitable organisation – from hospital bills to four-bedroom houses in Willesden Green, to taking planeloads to Florida Disneyland. Ted's heart was in the right place and people appreciated his generosity but now he was starting to think about all the beneficiaries who perhaps hadn't fully valued his gifts, and who had the audacity to stop saying *thank you, Uncle Ted* after a few years. The criminal trust fund was empty.

But Ted was a proud man, so he let the antipathy fester ... He needed to get to work ... That Sonny King was shifting untold product and the warehouses were beginning to look threadbare, in need of replenishment. Not having liquid assets was not a problem for a man with a reputation like Duppy.

Everything is bail or mace – credit – in the wholesale game; everything is done on good faith. Ted's credit rating was good.

He'd shifted a lot of gear over the years so he didn't need capital. He ordered the gear, *down there*, at approximately fifteen hundred dollars a kilo, arranged delivery to a small port in eastern Brazil, and got it on its way across the Atlantic on a trawler that had its own onboard canning plant so it could be at sea for months without attracting attention. It was going to be Ted's last mission; the consignment would keep them going for years. Most of it was going into deep freeze, to be brought out when required. Bridget, in charge of the family piggy bank now, was going to invest his share in a dozen buy-to-let apartments in Docklands to provide a pension for Ted's senior years. His whack would be enough to retire on.

The Atlantic crossing was a breeze, but as they prepared the cargo to be landed in Kerry, Southern Ireland, fate, and inclement weather, were waiting to play a hand.

The picturesque but remote southwestern coast would be, in normal conditions, an ideal place for a peaceful motoring holiday or to smuggle ashore a large consignment of cocaine under the harvest moon. They have a long history of smuggling in that part of the world, be it Libyan arms or French brandy. But beware; the undercurrents along that seemingly calm stretch of coastline can be extremely treacherous, even at the best of times, and the weather susceptible to rapid change.

While unloading the consignment from the mothership onto an ocean-going yacht – to ferry the gear ashore – the wind started getting up, getting blustery, but the cargo was safely stowed onboard the yacht behind specially constructed bulkheads. As they waved the trawler goodbye and it headed back to Brazil, Ted turned down the wireless on the bridge, decided to ignore the *incredibly pessimistic* weather forecast.

They were heading straight into the heaviest storms in County Kerry in forty years! Hundred mile-an-hour winds! Flooding everywhere! Rivers breaking banks! Gardai out in force but seriously distracted ... *in normal circumstances a Godsend.* Bridges washed away – *fuckin biblical!*

On the storm-lashed high seas, as they tumbled and rolled, Captain Granger cried, *Break out a double ration of valium and rum!* Then the overloaded craft began to sink. They couldn't exactly call the lifeboat, send up a flare or a mayday signal – not without getting banged-up in Portlaoise, Ireland's premier double-A-cat jail, for double figures. Meanwhile the Coastguard had called upon the Customs and the Irish Navy to help; the emergency services were fully mobilised – *getting fuckin busy.* Everyone put to sea to help boats in distress.

In a room in a cliff-top hotel, as the merciless gales lashed the coastline, Bridget was watching the chaos on television, thinking about *those cunts in peril on the seas*, waiting for the one-word call sign on the two-way radio to head to the rendezvous, to load the cargo into freezer lorries. A bad feeling was growing in her guts, just as the massive consignment of coca was hitting the seabed with a glug-glug-glug ... Bridget's instinct was right. The cargo was ruined – washed up on the rocks, smashed to pieces in the waves.

The crew didn't give a fuck about product any more. They were lucky to get ashore in rubber dinghies – almost drowned – wouldn't be attempting a lunatic stunt like that again in a hurry. One guy got both legs shattered after getting repeatedly smashed against the rocks before his pals managed to drag him onto the sand. If the crew had been observed landing, if a passer-by had quite innocently called the police, intending to help, they could have been in severe trouble; Kerry's remoteness makes it a hard place to get out of if you're a fugitive.

After the yacht sank it left Ted owing money to the cartel who had supplied the goods, *in good faith*. Ted and Bridget had fucked up big time, lost a consignment – enough to keep Sonny King going for years to come, no excuses. That's why they're playing catch-up.

'How much we talking, Ted?'

'Thirty million.'

'Oh, dear. Dollars or pounds?'

'Dollars.'

'How much was there, on the yacht?'

'Twenty tonnes.'

'Tonnes? Twenty tonnes!'

'Sounds more than it is. That's metric tonnes – twenty thousand kilos.'

Worth a lot more than thirty million dollars landed on UK soil; stick a couple of zeros on the end of that. Ambitious or not, it's still got to be paid for. The supplier's agent expressed their disappointment. *Señor Ted, Mister Amigo, it's unfortunate, a force majeure, an act of God, but now it's the silver or the bullet – which you gonna take? You've a big family and these devils don't care – it's how it works with these people. Ruthless isn't the word. They will find a way ... I'll let them know ... See what we can do ...*

They weren't sympathetic but they would take instalments. Ted had missed a payment. He was juggling, robbing Peter *and* Paul.

Bridget was in charge now. They pulled together what they could – a couple of million assorted pounds, dollars and euros. If they ever got out of this, Bridget told him, she was going to look after his money, pay him an allowance and keep him away from the bookmakers, card schools and hard-luck stories.

Yeah, I know, Ted – all this fuckin palaver over a poxy thirty million.

You're right, Bridget, so fuckin right.

I was being fuckin sarcastic, Ted.

Ted needed to get back in the game with new suppliers – cue Sammy Laniado – to repay the money. Ted had a comeback strategy – orders, contacts and a dynamic sales force, had Sonny King all revved up. All he needed was product, before word crept back to his creditors. Things needed to happen quickly. Desperation was the wind in Ted's sails.

The late Sammy would supply the tackle, and I would lead the fire sale. Ted was *looking for readies up front* in exchange for keen prices – unheard of. That's why he wanted a man of mystery – me – to do his bidding.

The plan was to turn over the shipment of cocaine into ready cash as quick as poss, and give the Brazilian suppliers some love. If that means driving an over-fished market down, dropping the price and nicking business, so be it. It's a case of needs must. The debt must be paid and although they had been understanding – relatively speaking, for international drug suppliers – they can't appear to be mugs.

Ted, the elusive pimpernel, doesn't wanna end his days rotting down some Spanish gorge.

So Ted started collecting false IDs. And buying IDs started giving Ted ideas ... But Bridge was there before him. They knew, through Giles, how much money Sonny had in the CBB. Sonny's money was paid by credit transfer – *to keep the paperwork down*. Sonny was anal retentive around his money; the very thought of gambling on anything he couldn't dominate or control was in-con-fuckin-ceivable. But, strange as it may seem, Sonny barely checked the statements; kept it all in his coconut, under his hat – a by-product of Sonny's illiteracy and belligerent nature.

Ted and Bridget started planning on *diverting* some of Sonny's funds – *a bridging loan*. They need to drop a chunk into a Brazilian bank account as a *good faith* payment, and the amount of good faith would be dictated by the amount they stumped up.

Curtis would be able to smother it if Giles told him to; Giles didn't wanna see his pet gangster, Ted, murdered beyond repair. Maybe the funds *can be in the two places at the one time*, suggested Ted – *fuck me, they're only numbers*. As long as there isn't an audit they'd be okay. But Curtis didn't like it, wanted an out if the scream went up. Wanted to be able to say the mischief was getting done over in Europe, didn't want Giles' Pikeville 'clients' shitting on his well-scrubbed doorstep. Oh, and Curtis wanted *a drink* outta it.

Bridget was cultivating her resentment of Sonny because of his treatment of Eve. A plan was taking shape, but Sonny's trip over to Barbados was a godsend for Ted and Bridget. Once Morty mentioned that I was out in the Caribbean, having a spot of cash-flow bother myself ... and Sonny and Roy were on their way out to deposit a large amount of cash, Ted and Bridget put two and two together and got ... *Mortimer's old chum, what's-his-name, over in Jamaica? He's a sensible chap ... What if, we could work it ... two birds, one big stone.*

Then Morty mentioned that I might possibly have a spare passport photo knocking about ...

They were going to fly me into Amsterdam and pitch me their idea about me being their number one salesman. Apparently I'd been elected to become *Mister Berkeley*. But when they heard that

Sonny was making calls to Giles – to get the sweet with Curtis about some *freelance cash Sonny wants to lose* – they decided to send me on a detour, to get a visual on Curtis, chief jug wallah at the Conciliated Bank of Barbados. And for Curtis to meet and greet me. *Always best to know who you're dealing with, even if you don't know you're dealing with them.* When the cute girl back at Curtis' Bridgetown bank thought I was Mister Berkeley she was ahead of the game.

Ted wanted to appear flush, to get me onside; made a point of advancing me a *non-returnable* hundred and fifty grand. I'd made a point of transferring the sweetener from their Belgian account back to an account I held in the Jamaican branch of a Canadian bank. Just as well it was gone before Ted asked for it back to put on some nag who was gonna end up in a tin of dog food. It was Bridget's shoebox money – *the smash* she keeps for emergencies.

All the preparation was done, they just needed my cooperation, but they were convinced I'd have no problem with the scheme, seeing as Sonny King *was such a complete cunt*. But when a boisterous Sonny turned up in Bridgetown to deposit Jesus' readies he attracted the wrong kind of attention, upset some church-going disciples, pissed off an anonymous worker ant, and they alerted someone upstairs who got a bit busy, descended on Curtis' fiefdom and wanted to know what was going on. Curtis covered it but told Giles to *hang fire* with the secret personal loans until his superiors went back to the Royal Westmoreland Golf Club. It was about picking the right moment. Meanwhile – prompted by Kevin the Cab's terminal prognosis – Ted revived an exit plan that had sat on the backburner for a little while.

Q. Would Sonny have been repaid?

A. Tricky question ... but if anything untoward happened to Sonny ... I don't believe Ted would be informing Sonny's next of kin ...

With the best will in the world Bridget and Ted might be convinced they would repay Sonny ... but wake up one day and decide that it's too much aggravation ...

It's all a bit too fuckin messy, Ted ... putting stuff back ... it's not what we do.

You're so right, Bridge ... Pass the marmalade.

Bridget and Ted are insistent, swearing on bibles, that they would have repaid the funds to Sonny after they got up and running with Sammy Laniado's zip; they also needed Sonny King, he made them lots of money, and that rankled. But self-righteous indignation, coupled with greed, can have us doing some strange shit. I couldn't condone murder, not to thieve a man's money ...

Their bizarre justification for taking liberties with Sonny's identity is they wanted revenge for Evey, on account of the Infamous Airport Abandonment. They seem to think it was a seminal experience in Eve's insane life. But Eve was never right in the first place and she wasn't going to be seeing any of Sonny's money ... And now Evey was dead.

And what does my old pal Mister Morty know about all this? Maybe he believed that the readies would flow back to Sonny. He bought into Ted and Bridget's sneaky condemnation of Sonny's despicable behaviour.

Ted's Lazarus Project was slightly desperate; not well thought through, now they're displaying a high degree of criminal vanity. There's a lot of conceit in Ted's deceit. Sonny would not skip lightly into the night. The Brazilians obviously didn't buy Ted's death – they sent a *couple* of teams over to investigate and apply pressure. The exits were shutting. Sammy Laniado, the key piece in the plan, has been cremated like most people think Ted has. Two weeks ago the suppliers also sent another red letter – *do not ignore this notice*. Where's our fuckin shekels?

Ted had missed a payment instalment. The Brazilian suppliers had eventually found Ted and issued an ultimatum. They wanted to be taken seriously. The tube shooting was a warning, but that went very wrong for them. Today's attempt on Bridget is them upping the ante. It's all *fuckin messy*.

Ted now wants Giles and me to do the deal with Miguel *as soon as*. We still have to get the memory stick; Ted believes this will *not be a problem*. I agree, but on condition they *don't* kill Sonny.

'I thought you didn't like Sonny?'

'I don't particularly, but it's not right to *borrow* his funds ... or serve the geezer.'

Ted shrugs. He wants to roll on, put a meet together with Roy for this evening.

I feel like telling Ted to fuck off. I'm a bit fragged with all this criminal hierarchy bollocks. A couple of days ago I wanted Ted to influence Sonny but now I don't want Ted, with his history of finesse, anywhere near me or the memory stick. These Brazilians might send a fuckin army or call in an air strike.

'We don't know, do we, Ted, who these Brazilians will shoot next. Could be Sonny, or Mort, or me, or Bridget. Could be anyone, except you, cos they want their money.' Ted says nothing. 'This is the deal, Ted, we can get you out of your difficulties with the Brazilians. Hopefully all those guys who died are just hired help. You reckon you can influence Roy – we'll try it your way. We'll make it a condition of our deal with Miguel's people that your debt gets paid or discharged. I think Miguel may have some influence ... but if anything happens to Sonny King, the deal is off.'

'What yer saying?' asks Ted.

'I will square it with Sonny and I will personally safeguard his interests.'

'*Safeguard his interests*,' mimics Ted, 'Oh, you fuckin will, will ya?'

'Yeah,' I say, meeting his eyes.

'Who give you the shout?' asks Ted, dead stroppy, leaning forward. 'Since when did you—'

'Ted ... ' says Bridget, interrupting, looking at Ted, nodding towards me, 'people are trying to kill him ... and me ... yeah?' Ted nods, lips zipped. 'So just shut the fuck up for once and realise you've got a deal, okay?' Bridget goes to get up. 'I better get back ... get it sorted ... ' Get Evey vanished, pulped in a concrete mixer, poured into oil drums. Where Santos ended up ... Business is good for Bridget's sideline. 'Don't like the idea of her being out there ... all on her own ... '

Bridget walks towards the cafeteria exit, with Ted tailing her out. She stops, turns back to whisper in my ear, 'Best we don't tell Mortimer 'bout Evey – know what I mean?'

I nod, then Bridget whispers one more thing ... and leaves.

CHAPTER FORTY-THREE

BROKEN SOULS

Morty picked me up outside Tottenham Hale Underground station. Ted has decided to go seriously cloak-and-dagger and made a meet on the edge of town – *Royski likes all that skullduggery* – away from prying eyes and accidental encounters.

Morty doesn't think it's a good idea for Ted, recently deceased, to graft Roy, apparently going bonkers, to graft Sonny, one greedy fucker, to do a deal with Miguel – still an unknown quantity – *don't think it's a good idea to have Roy sit down with a dead person*. I ask if he's got a better idea ...

'I can't see why you and Giles don't go and explain the benefits of the deal to Sonny again – properly gang up on him this time.'

'We'll call that Plan B. Got to give Ted one bite of the cherry, even if it's to prove he's wrong ... '

'Strange way of doing things ... ' says Morty to himself.

We drive on in silence for a while, then we turn off the dual carriageway into a light industrial area. A huge area has been laid waste for redevelopment but then been forgotten about. It's a blind spot, hemmed in by the railway tracks around two sides so there's no through traffic. The railway is on two levels, one on the ground, the other over an old viaduct. The arches have businesses in them. A freight train rattles across the viaduct, shaking the street. Motor oil and brake fluid is spilt over the road, and old, unwanted engine parts are strewn about randomly. There's a scattering of recently broken car window glass that glistens nastily in the late sunlight. Morty stops the car, gets out the motor, looks both ways up and down the street.

'Fuckin hate comin up this end ... '

'Do you think the motor'll be okay?' I say as we walk away.

'Probably not ... ' he shrugs, then laughs. 'Maybe we'll have to walk home. Come on, we're late.'

We walk slowly up the street. It's now dusk, the sun's going down, throwing long shadows. There's nobody about, only a lone tipper lorry and a couple of trucks creeping in and out of yards further up the street. Scrap yards, car-breakers and heavy plant hire firms run off in all directions, enclosed in corrugated steel fences with barbed razorwire running along the top. Some of the gates have heavy-duty chains and padlocks, crude signs warning people away, while others have the doors hanging wide open to welcome in business. Even the lampposts have been vandalised. Peeping over the top of the wire there's cannibalised motors and builders' skips that have been piled precariously high. In one of the yards I can hear a vicious dog howling and barking, and another replying. From their ferocious barks you just know they've tasted blood and liked it.

Tumbling out of a couple of torn rubbish sacks are piles of everyday bits and pieces, somebody's personal belongings. It's like some poor soul's been evicted from life – like their house contents have been bagged-up, cleared out and discarded, for whatever reason – in this out-of-the-way backstreet. In this case it's a curious mix of well-worn platform shoes in bright primary colours – purpose-made for kinder whores, perhaps – and some frayed, supposedly sexy underwear that's anything but. And a poignant and colourful collection of flattened plastic toys, dumped and crushed by the kerb.

The hound-from-hell's barking is getting louder and closer. The evening sun still sends up a haze. Morty leads the way, all the time a couple of steps ahead of me. He picks up a stick and drags it along the corrugated iron fence, making an irritating clicking sound. We come to a yard with figures chalked up on a tatty blackboard – today's prices for lead, copper, aluminium, and wire – stripped or burnt. And prowling at the end of a chain is the dog we heard down the street – a big, woolly Alsatian, more wolf than dog. When he sees us he comes alive, leaps at us, straining at the end of the long choker chain, desperate to get at us, snapping and snarling. The dog's protecting a bleached-out bone that looks like it came from an elephant. Morty walks just out of his range and the dog begins to strangle itself but still won't give up trying take a bite out of us. Morty ignores him, marches into the yard that's piled high with scrap metal – radiators, neon light shades, drums of heavy-duty copper cable and mountains of jagged, metal offcuts. A soapy geezer is operating a crane with a humming electromagnet, loading metal onto a conveyer belt. The metal leaps to the magnet. It raises it up, and as he releases a pedal, the magnet is no longer a magnet – the humming stops – the load crashes noisily onto the belt. It gets carried up to a menacingly loud crushing machine. The mesmerised operator doesn't acknowledge us or look in our direction.

Morty leads the way through the yard over to a prefab office. There's a battered Volkswagen Polo parked outside that could be scrap, but I've got a hunch it's one of Roy's anonymous work cars. Mort knocks, and without waiting to be asked, enters. I follow him in. It takes me a second to adjust after the sunshine but when I do, I realise that Ted and Roy are sat on either side of a metal desk that's covered in piles of untidy paperwork, newspapers, dirty chipped mugs, sandwiches in their plastic wrappers and biscuit crumbs. Everything has a thin layer of grimy dust.

Ted's looking incredibly relaxed – for Ted – feet up on the desk, leaning back, puffing on a matchstick-thin rollie, and chewing gum. The muscles in his jaw and temple pop and bounce, making his head look skull-like. Roy's twitch, on the other hand, is going full blast – Condition Red. He's trying to interrupt Ted.

'Simple, Roy,' says Ted, 'I'm *entitled* to a bitta that gadget everyone's getting excited about.'

Roy goes to talk. Ted silences him – a finger up to his lips. Behind Ted's head there's a handwritten sign, yellow and curly, stuck with rusty pins.

'You Don't Have to Be a Cunt to Work Here, but It Helps.'

'What's the problem, Roy, stop worryin. You'll be able to go back down to Spain, switch off.' Ted turns to Mort, acknowledging him for the very first time. 'Tell him, Mort – tell him it makes sense.' But he doesn't wait for Mort. 'We need a united front. We go for a *percentage of the account balances* on the memory stick.' Giles has, no doubt, explained the practicalities, and Ted is repeating, parrot fashion. 'The funds are easily transferred. This is my business now. You two, you and your mate Sonny, made it my business.'

I'm not sure how Ted works that out, but Roy's job is to convince Sonny that this is the best deal for everyone. Roy is on the ropes – Ted follows up.

'This business with the gadget has wrecked my business. There's plenty there for everyone. This Jee-zuss kiddie has killed my connection. I want my debts removed ... This Zambrano geezer is *capable of exerting pressure*.' Ted – calm as a duck pond – is suggesting a pragmatic approach, far too simple to explain. 'I want you, Roy, to convince Sonny that your share of this stick is with Morty and yer man. Can I trust you with that job?'

Roy needs to think about it; the more he thinks the harder it becomes. There's another masterpiece of wisdom among the curry house calendars and faded pin-ups, entitled 'Stress Management Device' – a felt-tip circle has been drawn with 'Bang Head Here' written in the middle. Roy looks like he could use it.

'Okay,' says Royski, pulling a grimace, 'I'll talk to Sonny, but what about the Santos fella? He's still on the rampage, looking to do a number on him.' Roy nods in my direction.

'The Santos geezer is history, Roy ... It clears the way for a deal. We use it – *a sign of good faith*, a gesture to show willing.'

'Did you kill him, Ted?'

Morty interrupts, 'It's not important, Roy.'

But Ted replies to the question, 'I never laid eyes on the geezer, alive *or* dead. And Mort's right, it ain't—'

'But you've killed people, right?' asks Roy, almost innocently.

Morty cuts him short, 'Nitto, Roy ... '

Roy doesn't appear to hear Mort. He carries on, eyes locked into Ted's, half-intimidating, half-pleading. 'You've served people. I know you have. And did you feel the need to confess, to unburden yourself?'

'Listen, Roy,' says Ted, 'this is too fuckin weird.'

'That's not an answer, Ted.' But then Roy asks him, matter-of-factly, 'How do I know *you're* alive, Ted?'

'Do what, son?' asks Ted, concerned about another plan going bandaloo.

'You could be a ghost, Ted,' says Roy with a small laugh.

'That's not funny,' says Morty.

'It's not a joke, Mort,' says Roy. 'How do I know Ted here's not come back to life?' Roy waves around the cabin with a manic smile and knowing eyes. 'How do I know this is happening?'

'Enough now, Roy!' snaps Mort. 'Shut up!'

'See,' says Roy, suddenly angry, standing, but close to tears, 'everybody's trying to shut me up. I'm not havin it!'

'Listen, Roy,' shouts Mort, pointing, 'Ted was never dead. It was a get-up – he was being threatened. He's not a ghost.' Morty slaps Ted on the arm, 'Look, flesh and blood, Roy, he's all here – living, breathing.'

But Roy's a long way from home. Something's snapped, something that's been bending for a while. Roy flips. Roy thinks Ted is a dead phantom *bringing a message from Jesus Christ, who died on the cross for all our sins* ... He starts chatting madness, karma, fate, synchronicity, serendipity, ghosts, prayer, and spooks – and it's all pure psychosis. He's accelerating, head gone, like he's possessed. It's ugly. *There are forces we don't understand, can never understand. If a spirit dies in violent circumstances* ...

Morty tries to grab him, talk sense to him, but Roy wrestles free and grabs Ted's arm, gets on Mort's blindside. Roy tells Ted he feels *compelled* to confess to the local Catholic priest – *O'Fallon, the Paddy, the one who taught me to box, years ago – I coulda turned professional except for ... what happened ... with the other priest* ...

Roy stops dead still, deep in his own past. A single tear rolls down his cheek. Then Roy spits, returns to his mad rant, talking faster but getting tongue-tied, frustrated. He feels the need for absolution for his sins, for my sins, for *all our sins*! Roy's brain is bouncing. Scattergun. 'Remember where that stick came from? Down that hole! His eyes, they wouldn't stay shut, staring at me, even in the pitch black. It was on me – on me, you hear! And I was searching. The smell was choking me ... not shit, rotten meat ... the worst fuckin smell ... Can't get away from it! No matter how much I wash ... it's like I've swallowed it, can't get rid. Was like sludge in that hole – like hell! Can't eat, not for days.'

Don't bear thinking about ... Roy spits again, repelled, nausea growing. 'It's killing me. I dream of the cunt! Tried pills, vodka, to knock meself out. But I still dream of him. Grinning at me, like a loon! Calling Mum names, saying what he's gonna do to her –

dirty cunt! Can't kill him twice? Wish I could! He's dead already!'

Roy, his face a snarl, reaches out – hand spread like a claw – like Jesus' face was in front of him. Roy wants to erase Jesus' memory, wants to crush his skull, grind it to dust. Only Roy knows what madness he's seeing.

Now it's Ted who's spooked. Roy changes tack, feels betrayed, breaks down again. He begins to weep pathetically. He grabs Ted, *and Sonny's taking the piss. You're a soldier, he said – it's a mission.*

'Sort this out, Mort!' cries Ted, pushing Roy away, 'Sort this mad cunt out!'

Roy is across the table – one big leap. He grabs Ted's throat with both hands – *I ain't mad, ain't fuckin mad. Tell me I ain't mad! Tell me!*

Ted's overwhelmed, amazed at Roy's agility. Roy's shaking Ted, seeking reassurance. They're grappling in the tight space. If Ted was cuter, he'd pacify Roy – *Sane? 'Course you are, son.*

Morty grabs Roy's shoulders, tries to wrench him back. Roy instinctively wriggles free, like he's been greased. Morty tries to get Roy in a headlock. Roy won't have it. He's still got Ted around the throat. I'm half-across the table now too, trying to prise Roy's hands off Ted. Roy is oblivious, fearless, gone. Roy's not trying to kill him; he's trying to squeeze something out of him – *no, Roy, you're not mad.* If Roy was trying to hurt Ted he'd wrench his windpipe out or snap his neck. It's symbolic. Ted doesn't see it – he's choking, spluttering, punching and trying to kick out. Ted's pinned against the wall but edging himself towards a cabinet that's half under the desk, his hand extended towards it just as Roy's had been – grasping. The other hand is trying to push Roy's face backwards. Ted is getting redder, fighting for breath. Morty is reaching but can't get at them properly. He's punching Roy in the head, the kidneys, trying to incapacitate him. Morty's blows bounce off, do no damage. I'm hanging on Roy – see his hands, up close, white and bony, trembling. Roy's clamped on Ted's throat, scared to let go, childlike; wants to be told he's sane, but acting like a madman. Suddenly Ted pushes a thumb hard in Roy's eye, drawing blood. Roy groans, twists and turns – still hangs on. But I let go of Roy. It allows Ted to drag Roy far enough across the table to knee him in the diaphragm. Roy coughs and chokes. Ted seizes his chance, moves towards the top drawer of the cabinet – something's gonna save him. Roy's hands are *still* around Ted's neck.

Morty spots Ted straining and throws himself across the table, but Roy's blocking his path. Morty goes to grab the drawer handle but Ted gets there first. He opens the drawer, comes out quickly with a handgun in his free hand, his other hand holding off Roy. Roy sees the gun. He turns his head side-on to Ted, his eyes squinting, fear on his face. I jump back.

Ted fires – at the closest range. Ted blows the back of Roy's head clean off, sends blood, brain and bone splashing over the wall. It's a blur, a micro-second. Roy's hands drop from Ted's throat. He slides off the desk ... then stands dead straight, standing to attention, supreme effort, like he's gonna salute. He remains upright, eyes wide open – head half gone – then his arms go out in front of him, like a toddler trying to walk. Then he slumps backwards, bounces off the wall, crumples in a pile on the floor.

I can't breath. There's no oxygen. The air is full of cordite. The cabin has gone deathly silent. The clanking and crushing goes on outside. A freight train rumbles over the viaduct. I'm frozen to the spot – spooked – ears ringing. The smell of blood makes me wanna vomit; I'm trying hard not to retch. Don't wanna look at Roy but can't turn away. A puddle of dark, thick blood is creeping across the floor – same as Stevie, as Evey, Santos. Morty flops down on a chair, lights a cigarette, takes a long drag.

'Ted,' he asks quietly, politely, 'what the fuck did you do that for?'

'He was trying to kill me!' says Ted, trying to catch his breath.

'He was ill!' Morty hisses. 'Not right in the head!'

'He was trying to strangle me!'

'It could have been dealt with, Ted! You didn't have to fuckin shoot him! He was harmless!'

'Harmless! It wasn't you he was trying to fuckin strangle! It's all right for you to say!'

'You was told ... ' says Morty, looking at the floor, shaking his head. 'Told he wasn't well.'

'He was talking about confessing, to a priest. What do ya think a priest is going to do with him?'

'You didn't need to—'

'Send him to Old Bill, that's what. Confessing to murder. They'll rinse him out, take advantage. He's mad!'

'Not any fuckin more he ain't!' screams Morty, losing his temper. 'He's fuckin dead!'

'They'd know everything Roy knows. And he's an encyclopedia. Roy knows everyone's business—'

'*Knew*, Ted, fuckin *knew*. We coulda got him down to Spain, found a doctor, straightened him out.'

'I'm not being funny, Mort, but you've allowed this to get messy. I ain't blaming anyone but ... '

Morty looks like he can't believe what he's just said. Morty leaps up, screams at Ted. 'You what? You stupid fuckin cunt! I shoulda walked! Fuck you! If you hadn't lost that load we wouldn't be in this mess!'

Mort's being sharp considering Ted's got a gun and we're witnesses to murder.

'Oh, fuck off,' says Ted, with a dismissive wave of the hand. Too dismissive.

'What did you say?' asks Morty, his eyes locked on Ted's. 'What did you just say to me?'

Suddenly Roy's heels start drumming on the floor – a rapid, relentless snare. Roy's gone into some posthumous spasm, like he's throwing an epileptic fit. Morty looks sick, sits back down, but now Ted's twitching, like Roy used to. Ted is desperately trying to cover his embarrassment – strange word in the circumstances. He slings the gun on the desktop and begins searching for a live match in his box of dead ones, won't ask Mort for a light. Ted finds a match, lights his snout, oblivious to Roy's spasm.

Suddenly as he started, Roy stops, stops dead. Like someone pulled the plug. His eyes are staring straight ahead in shock, mouth hanging open. Morty brings out a hanky, tiptoes over, and carefully crouches down. 'Why couldn't you, Roy, just for once, shut up?' Morty reaches over and, tenderly, shuts his eyes. 'You couldn't just go away. Had to be around for the finale.' Morty stands up. 'You better get this cleaned up, Ted,' he says, 'before it starts ... to be a problem ... ' Like Roy was the remains of a takeaway.

Ted nods at me. 'Is he gonna be alright? Only his suntan's gone.'

'Probably not,' shrugs Mort. 'But to be honest, *I* ain't all that clever ... Come as a shock.'

Ted shrugs, nods down at Roy.

'It's a shame ... I used to like Roy. Shame it wasn't Sonny ... '

'You're right ... ' echoes Morty with dry sarcasm. 'Yeah, given the choice.'

'Now, if you're feeling queasy ... ' says Ted. 'If it's gonna be a performance, I'll straighten this out.'

'If that's alright with you, Ted?' says Mort.

'Yer man has gone white,' he says, pointing at me. 'Looks like he's gonna be sick ... '

Ted had got his mojo back. Didn't take long. He opens the door just enough to let us out.

'Don't forget Roy's motor,' says Mort, nodding at the Polo.

'I'm on it,' says Ted dryly.

'You couldn't be in a better place to get rid—'

Ted interrupts, 'If you're going, go.'

We step outside, glad to be back in the air again. Morty turns back, an afterthought.

'Ted,' says Mort, 'we don't say anything to Sonny ... ' Ted nods. 'And don't tell Bridget – she was fond of Roy.'

Ted nods again and shuts the door. We walk back across the yard. The guy playing with his magnet wouldn't notice a bomb exploding; appears heavily sedated. The dog snaps at the end of his chain. Plump bluebottles buzz around his bone. We get back to the car. The sun is going down on a warm late summer's day. Royski picked the wrong venue to have his psychotic episode ... So much for his theory about having his own personal guardian angel.

The car is untouched. We haven't been away ten minutes. Morty stops before he gets in.

'You wanted to be back in the swindle,' says Morty, twitchy, 'well, now you are. Happy?'

No, not really. I wanna burn these clothes, get back in the shower, and ponder some tricky questions.

Q. Can Ted Granger be charged with murder?

Q. Can a dead man be charged with murder?

Q. Why do people keep getting shot in the head around here?

A. That's not the right question. You're not getting it, are ya?

Q. Why do people keep getting shot in the head around *you?*

CHAPTER FORTY-FOUR

WHAT IS MADNESS?

Madness is never having to say sorry.

Madness is thinking Twitchy was the mad one.

Madness is the darkness in your head, the restless one percent that wants to push strangers under trains.

Madness is thinking there's easy money.

Madness is making reality the enemy.

Madness is retreat from the world.

Madness is shooting people in the canister, thinking it's justified.

Madness is shooting people in the head and saying he asked for it.

Madness is Duppy Granger.

Madness is Mort thinking Roy's corpse is *a mess* ... Telling me Roy *was never going to make old bones.*

Madness is Bridget Granger sawing up frozen bodies of old playmates.

Madness is Bridget rubbing her hands at the thought of dead Venezuelans.

Madness is a trio of dead Brazilians a long way from home.

Madness is Patsy O'Malley shooting Santos de Lucia in the GHQ and forgetting to remember.

Madness? Nice place to visit but you wouldn't wanna live there.

Madness is sucking yer thumb like an imbecile. It's not funny anymore.

Madness is a feeling you've been swindled outta yer whack. It's not going away ...

Madness is thinking people are laughing at you.

Madness is thinking everybody's mad.

Madness is paranoia made normal.

Madness is when the mundane is insane, the insane mundane.

Madness is burning down the house ... seeing the funny side of burning down the house.

Madness is the expression on Duppy's face as he pulled the trigger – one for the family album. Seared on the memory.

Madness is getting blasé about madness.

Madness is wanting someone to drill a hole in yer skull, to let the demons out.

Madness is assisted suicide – Kevin the Cab thinking Ted's doing him a favour.

Madness is Ted very kindly agreeing to kill Kevin – *only cos I like ya, Kev.*

Madness is what happens to ordinary people in mad situations.

Madness is having the power of life and death over someone ... a chap called Sonny King.

Madness is Bridget, whispering in my ear ... in a park, around kids – *if you change yer mind 'bout Sonny, let me know.*

Madness is having a fifty-gallon oil drum with Sonny's name on it ... ready to rock.

Madness is Bridget making concrete jam outta Evey.

Madness is Miguel, charming industrial psychopath.

Madness is Jenna, her men in specimen jars.

Madness is Jesus Zambrano – but at least you know where you're at with Jesus.

Madness is wishing you were dead, or more alive.

Madness lives in the head, rent-free.

Madness is effortless self-persecution ... never seeing, or sensing, or feeling any contradiction, or expressing any contrition.

Madness is telling yourself that you should have seen it coming.

Madness is thinking you can predict the future, while sitting in a jailhouse, doing birdlime.

Madness is believing you rule the world, thinking you control the universe.

Madness is ruling your known world, every day, for years ... getting madder every day.

Madness is fun for a little while, then gets dark ... then darker still.

Madness shuts the door behind you, tells you everything's gonna be all right.

Madness talks in riddles, shouts and rages.

Madness gets its way in the end.

Madness takes no prisoners, isn't your friend.

Madness wants your soul.

SOULS WANTED. Best prices paid! Instant cash waiting! What are you waiting for?

Madness is a master of disguise, it goes underground.

Madness is God. Or thinking you are God.

Madness is hearing voices ... angels in the ether, but listening to the wrong voices.

Madness is thinking you're God *and* the Devil ... at the same time.

Madness is out there, where we live – everywhere; horrific snapshots, that won't go away.

Madness isn't forgetting the dry cleaning or the coriander ... It's more serious than that.

Madness enters as a friend.

Madness is contagious, cunning and *I'm sure he wouldn't mind me saying but* ... Madness is a cunt.

Madness is the snidest geezer you ever knew ... mercilessly derides your dreams, ridicules your desires ... but you *like him anyway ... because ... he's never boring ...*

Madness tells you you're the mad one, tells you you're going mad.

Madness is not to be believed ... but is *so fuckin* convincing.

Madness has you asking for forgiveness, begging for understanding.

Madness can be charming ... if it suits its purposes.

Madness turns in the witness box – turns informer – blames all its transgressions on you.

Madness laughs all the way home ... at your misfortune.

Madness is spiteful, and malicious ... when it isn't being charming and amiable ... and contagious and dark.

Madness has you punching the air because you pulled fifteen years; you expected twenty.

Madness waits behind the cell door.

Madness is thinking there's an element of control to be had.

Madness is thinking you're in control of an incontrollable entity.

Madness is poking yourself in the eye with a fork ... might be fun ... least you won't be bored ...

Madness is getting lost in a strange country ... not knowing how you got there.

Madness is off the map ... The one you bought at the petrol station ... *off that funny-looking man.*

Madness isn't for kids. This is grown-up stuff. Isn't one sandwich short of a picnic. Oh, no, madness is a *very* serious business.

Madness is not for the fainthearted or weak-willed. Madness takes commitment, untold strength of personality.

Q. Trying to negotiate with madness?

A. It's a mug's game, guv ... send ya mad ...

Madness wins every time. Madness is thinking there's gold at the end of the rainbow or millions in offshore accounts, waiting to be plucked. Madness is thinking there'll be no consequences, when *everything* is consequences.

Madness is lying awake, speculating on the nature of madness ... when there's an airport down the road ... many flights to many destinations.

This is Madness. Welcome home. Been away, on yer holidays? Nice suntan, mate.

CHAPTER FORTY-FIVE

PLAN B

What is required is a one-man delegation – thinks Giles. I voted for Morty. Everyone else voted for me – on account of me volunteering to *safeguard Sonny's interests*. Problem is ... I feel I'm cracking up. Didn't sleep much last night – too busy thinking about madness – was seriously worried, for a while, about my own sanity.

I have what a shrink might term a backlog of emotions that need *processing*. I think the renewed offensive on Sonny would come better from me *and* Giles, but Morty and Bridget seem to think that Giles would be a touch delicate for the AQK Club, where Sonny is in residence. Plus, it's been pointed out, Miguel Zambrano wants to do business with me, not *King Sonny*. Bridget believes all this palaver is unnecessary – a *coup d'état* could be organised, not a bloodless one, and the *fucker* retrieved. She's *not wrong*, except for the fact that Sonny has taken the prize into custody, from Smiler in Acton, *for safekeeping*. Morty has another hunch – Sonny's hidden the prize in the same place that Jesus had ...

We can all get out alive, with a tidy payday, nobody else has to get killed. So I've been delegated to *sound out Sonny, see where his head's at*. Try and make Sonny see sense before Miguel decides that diplomacy is futile and lets Raul go to work. I've been given twelve hours to convince Sonny to cooperate or they will instigate *an intervention*. I don't want Sonny on my conscience. Bridget is all for killing Sonny and sparing Roy. It had to be pointed out that would leave us without the kit. She doesn't know about what happened ...

A cat like Ted will have his own resources to dispose of a body. Roy'll end up dropped in a pine-dipping bath or down a deep hole, out in the countryside ... *it don't bear thinking about* ... Ted'll maybe feed him to the yard dog. But nobody will be finding Roy ever again. The person most concerned about Roy's whereabouts

– for selfish reasons – will be Sonny ... And he doesn't wanna meet in the park – insisted I come over here, *no debate, no chit-chat.*

I get a cab over to the AQK Club. I've been briefed by Mort to *forget about what went down with Roy. Plead ignorance – you can do that, can't you?* If Sonny asks, Mister Mortimer is out and about, with Patsy, Chip and the rest of The Flintstones, looking for Santos. The AQK has a slight siege mentality – can you have a *slight* siege mentality? The habitually suspicious clientele have been given something to get paranoid about. The guy behind the jump has been told that I'm coming, so without a word he leads me through the downstairs café, out the back, to a staircase, and points upwards.

I follow the stairs up three floors, then a guy appears in a dank corridor, silently beckons me towards him, pushes open a door and nods inside. It could be night or day. Sonny has taken to the lockdown lifestyle with ease. He's been doing coke, swigging vodka, and getting paranoid; wearing his bulletproof vest over a towelling bathrobe. One of his soldiers is checking for bugs. He gives me a sweep then Sonny dismisses him with his eyes. After the guy leaves I ask, with all the sincerity I can muster, 'What's the story, Sonny?' pointing at the firearms scattered around. 'And where's Roy? What's going on?'

'Roy ... ' says Sonny, looking cagey, 'has gone missing ... '

'What d'ya mean?'

'I mean *missing.*'

'Ain't like Roy.'

'Fuckin *know* it ain't like Roy. He's left all his tackle, his passports, everything. He was checkin in, every hour, on the hour. Was driving me mad, to be honest, but it ain't like Roy to go through the slips, not without letting anyone know.'

'His phone might be dead.'

'No, *he* might be dead.'

'Since when?' I ask. 'Since when's he been missing?'

'About half seven last night. His phone went off, switched off or died, but Roy would get a message through. You know what he's like ... codes and contingency plans.'

'Might have been kidnapped.'

'No contact. You don't kidnap someone then keep it a secret. Not how it works, mate.'

'So, what's your theory, Sonny?' I ask. 'What do you reckon happened?'

'I reckon Santos must have found him, weighed him in.'

'If Santos had killed him, he'd be in touch – like when he killed Stevie, but thought he'd killed me ... '

'Good point,' says Sonny, nodding his head. 'So this Miguel geezer must have killed Roy, for serving his cousin.'

'It's not his style. Miguel fancies himself as more of diplomat – far too sensible.'

'You defending him?'

'Just saying, it's not his MO. If it's anyone's it's Santos'.'

Sonny is deep in concentration, rubbing the stubble on his chin, weighing up scenarios.

'You don't know he's dead yet ... ' I say.

Sonny seems upset about his buddy, after years of taking the piss. *You're a soldier, he said – it's a mission.* He suddenly clicks his fingers, gets up – a decision made – walks across the room, empties out a bag of sportswear, pulling off tags, getting dressed double-quick.

It's a tricky manoeuvre – jogging pants, tee shirt, Kevlar bulletproof vest, tracksuit on top, fresh trainers. He's cursing Santos, cursing Miguel, cursing Ted – *gonna get more firepower out there, find this fuckin Santos once and for all.*

I hope the O'Malleys can keep their mouths shut ... but it's only a question of time ...

'Anyway ... ' Sonny stops dead, 'what the fuck are you doing here?'

'I've got a proposal – a few things you need to be aware of.'

'If ya wanna talk, we'll have to do it on the way.'

'Where are we going?'

'To Roy's mum's. Talks to his mum every day, Roy.'

I'd forgotten about Mum. My head is spun enough already. Missus Burns is the last person on earth I wanna see right now ...

Sonny takes two guys as bodyguards for the drive around to Roy's mum's. Sonny wants to know what the score is, but I won't talk in the motor – *don't wish to be rude.* One of Sonny's guys gives me a look like he'd like to wrap me up and put me in the boot, work on me later. I'd like to get it sorted before we arrive at Roy's mum's so I don't have to go up there but I can't bail out and leave Sonny to go up there on his Jack – would be bad form.

When we arrive at Missus Burns' block, Sonny's straight out the motor, looking left and right. We leave the guys outside. We slip in through the security door, while it's open – the postman was leaving – and together we trot up the stairs as I try to get Sonny to listen to The Miguel Deal – *say they wanted to do business* – but Sonny refuses to listen. *Let's get this sorted first.*

'Sonny, we ain't got time to fuck about.'

'What did I just say to you?' says Sonny, as we hit the corridor.

'At the moment you've got the gadget but—'

'Dead right I've got the gadget.'

'But you've got one hundred percent of zero.'

'I've got readies.'

'Sonny, what deal would suit you?'

'Fifty-fifty – yeah?'

'Not going to happen – they'd start popping us before they'd give us half their money. Miguel's the easy option.'

'*Miguel*?' Sonny stops abruptly. '*Miguel*? Have you been talking to this *Miguel* already?'

'Not yet, but I wouldn't wanna lose the opportunity.'

'Only, you seem very pally with *Miguel*.'

'He knows we have what he wants, Sonny.'

'Good, we'll let the cunt roast – he mighta topped my pal.'

'I don't think he did.'

'You seem to know what he knows, and what he doesn't.'

'That gadget has got some Judas device, some tracking system.'

'Don't care,' says Sonny, walking towards the door. 'Fifty, fifty. Tell your South American mate, *Miguel*, I'm gonna let him keep half ... ' Sonny rings the doorbell. 'If he behaves himself.'

I can hear Missus Burns fumbling with the bolts and catches. I have the power of life and death over Sonny – a tricky dilemma. I want out; the authorities are hunting me and Sonny is holding everything up, but everyone's losing patience with *me*, not him. They know it's pointless getting angry with Sonny. They think

I'm delaying a lucrative deal, think the time for *chit-chat and diplomacy* has passed, that I'm *being a stubborn cunt*. I could have Sonny killed with one call. If only Sonny knew how I look out for him.

Missus Burns opens the door. 'Is Roy with you?' she asks, looking hopefully down the hallway. One look at her tells you she's worried.

'No,' says Sonny, trying to appear calm. 'I haven't seen him. I popped round on the off-chance, to collect my briefcase.'

'What briefcase is that, Sonny?'

'I left it here the other day, when I was here with Roy. I didn't want to bring it to the club with me.' Missus Burns looks unconvinced. 'It's on top of the wardrobe. Roy put it there.'

'Best you come in then,' says Missus Burns bringing us through to the living room – and its shrine to Roy. 'I'll make some tea – are you hungry?'

'Not at the moment,' says Sonny. 'Not sure we've got time for tea. You haven't seen Roy then?' he asks, trying to sound calm.

'No, I'm sorry,' says Missus Burns, apologising. 'I'm a little worried.'

'Oh, yeah?'

'Roy was meant to pop round last night. He said he had an appointment to keep.'

'What appointment was that?' says Sonny, getting curious.

Missus Burns turns to me, her wrinkly hand on my sleeve, 'He calls twice a day, wherever he is in the world, Spain or the West Indies—'

'One second,' Sonny interrupts her, an edge in his voice. 'He didn't say who he was going to meet, did he?'

'No, Sonny, just that he had someone to meet and he would come after. Are you sure you haven't seen him?'

'Not since yesterday morning,' says Sonny.

'I just worry that he might have had an accident, got in some trouble.' Sonny has a frown across his forehead, trying to riddle out who Roy was meeting. 'Should I ring the hospital, do you think?' she asks Sonny.

'He's only gone missing one day, Missus Burns. They might not entertain yer.'

'But he's usually so regular, with his calls, I mean ... And I tried ringing his phone this morning, but it said that the service was unavailable. What does that mean, Sonny?'

'Means his phone's turned off, or run out of battery. Maybe he met a girl,' says Sonny with an unconvincing tone.

'He'd still ring me, Sonny,' replies Missus Burns with a hint of anger. 'Now where did you say this case was?'

'Top of the wardrobe, Missus B,' says Sonny moving towards the door. 'I can get it, no worries.'

'Maybe I should ring the police,' says Missus Burns.

Sonny stops dead. 'I don't think Roy would like that.'

'No?'

'No, Missus Burns,' says Sonny with an edge. 'See, Roy had problems with the police, didn't he?' She nods. 'People pick on Roy, for some reason ... police did as well. Remember, he had that trouble ... They made allegations they couldn't prove ... It's why he had to go away ... ' Missus Burns is nodding furiously. 'See, I don't think Roy would want you ringing the police.'

'No, you're right, Sonny.'

'I only wish I had a mother like you, looking out for me,' says Sonny, and then to me, 'Don't you wish you had a mother like Roy's?'

'Yeah, I do,' I reply, but I feel like I'm gonna vomit all over her carpet any second. This is day one of Missus Burns' life as a mother of a *desaparecido* – a disappeared – never being able to grieve or go to a funeral, because Roy is gone to an unmarked grave or disintegrated back to dust, a victim of a double life his little old mum knew nothing about. And Missus Burns would defend Roy's reputation to her dying breath. I see Roy's face now like Roy saw Jesus' yesterday, can hear Roy now – *do you feel the need to confess, Ted, to unburden yourself?* – his redemption mantra, can smell his blood and the cordite. Trouble is, the only way for Roy's mother to get answers is for me, Mort and Ted to be either in the witness box or the dock ... Life is a contact sport – someone is going to end up carried from the field.

'Are you okay there, son?' Missus Burns asks me. 'You don't look well.'

'I'm okay,' I reply. 'Could I get a glass of water?'

'You won't have some tea?'

'No, water will be fine.'

Missus Burns goes into the kitchen. Sonny is looking at me with an intensity that could burn through steel, looking *into* me – almost a smug expression – nodding to himself, like he's got a clue ... Missus Burns comes back with a glass of water and hands it to me.

'If I may, Missus Burns,' says Sonny, 'could I get that briefcase? I know where Roy put it.'

'You help yourself, Sonny,' says Missus Burns.

Sonny dodges out the living room, into the bedroom leaving me alone with Missus Burns.

'You look like you need a good feed ... ' she half-whispers to me, 'and different company.' She takes my hand in her dry, bony one, 'remember, you are the company you keep.' Her eyes dart, for a split-second, towards the bedroom, contempt in her eyes. 'Always remember that, son.' She pats my hand. 'Is my Roy okay, son?' she asks.

'As far as I know, Missus Burns,' I lie. I feel like crying.

I want to wrench my hand away and run but she lets it slip away as Sonny returns with his briefcase.

'Best we be going,' he says, moving towards the front door, knowing it can be an elongated process leaving. But today Missus Burns appears tired, and half shoos us out.

Sonny walks fast to the stairs, breathing heavy, swinging his case. Suddenly he turns to face me. I push past him, almost tumbling down the stairs, but he keeps getting ahead, intercepting me.

'What was all that about?'

'What?'

'You know. I saw your fuckin face.'

'What the fuck's that supposed to mean?'

'I think you know something about where Roy was last night, and why he isn't around this morning.'

'I don't know nothing about Roy – you're getting carried away.'

'Oh, yeah? So, tell me, where were *you* last night?'

'Leave it out, Sonny. This is hysteria—'

'*Hysteria*? You cunt! My pal's dead—'

'We don't know that. His mum's worried about him, and you're starting a witch-hunt—'

'So? If it's all a loada bollocks, where were yer?'

'I ain't gonna get into this—'

'Maybe you were out with yer pal Miguel, planning to row me out ... '

'Leave it out, Sonny—'

'Maybe you were trying to bend Roy's head, and he weren't having it ... ' He leans in close. 'See, I know stuff about you, your old boss, how you put one in his can. You ain't all sweetness and light ... ' What the fuck is he on about? I trot past him down the stairs. 'See, I know you've put people away.'

I stop at the bottom of the stairs, turn and face Sonny.

'Hang on, are you saying *I* killed Roy? Are you mad?'

'I ain't mad, pal,' he says, trotting down the stairs, 'but there's shit going on that I don't know about ... that worries me.' I push open the security door. We pass through. It shuts automatically, with a clunk, but he's in front of me again. 'Hang on,' he says, looking left and right, 'where's them two boys? Where's the motor?'

The Range Rover is gone. The street is deserted. Quick as a snake, Sonny grabs me, his free hand on my throat, and pushes me against the brickwork. 'What you know about this? What do you know about Roy, you cunt?'

I'm wriggling, choking, trying to get his hand off my neck. He's crushing my adam's apple, but suddenly a huge motorbike roars into the courtyard and skids to a halt, fifteen feet away from us. Two people are on the bike, both with crash helmets with dark visors, wearing cheap wedding suits like the ones Santos' crew had on ... and gloves.

The passenger aims a semi-automatic pistol with a silencer directly at Sonny, both hands on the gun. Sonny swings me round; I'm a human shield. The shooter lets go two quick shots – doff, dooff. They shatter the wired glass in the door behind us. Sonny uses all his strength to manoeuvre me between him and them. The shooter takes careful aim again. Two more shots. We duck. This time they clunk into the brickwork, just missing Sonny's head.

Sonny is moving like a boxer, bobbing and weaving. The gunman is calmly pointing at Sonny with his gun, gesturing for me to move aside. It's Sonny they've come to execute – they're stalking him. The shooter lets go two more shots. They miss by a whisker. Our luck's running out. Sonny starts to drag me backwards. The two guys on the motorbike appear remarkably calm.

They're professional, have done this before. Neither enjoying it nor scared, nonchalant. Imagine them cursing – fuck it! It's annoying, getting messy. Meant to be two shots in the head.

The driver calmly guns the engine and rolls the bike to a better angle, like he's got all the time in the world. Sonny drags me backwards. We take cover behind a metal dustbin, dodging backwards and forwards.

'Ask them what they want! Tell them they can have the fuckin thing!' Sonny screams in my ear. 'You talk their language!'

'What fuckin language?'

'Just fuckin tell 'em!'

'It's too fuckin late for that, Sonny!'

The shooter starts putting rounds into the huge dustbin – they ricochet, echoing – someone's hitting a gong with a hammer. They reposition the bike again, both slowly shaking their heads. They're impatient. They could so easily just shoot me to get me out of the way. I'm dispensable. Sonny retains his grip on the Gucci briefcase. With the other hand he's holding on for dear life. The shooter goes to get off the bike, to come over and finish us off, but the driver taps him on the helmet and shakes his head. The driver rolls the bike closer.

Sonny, not missing a trick, suddenly sprints – *behind* the bike, zigzagging as he goes. Moving fast, faster than he should for a guy his build, across the courtyard, *away* from the street and the gun. It confuses them; the shooter gets off a shot but it misses. The driver lumbers the bike around – there's cursing under helmets – been *too* casual. But Sonny's hit fifth gear. He's heading for a row of old sheds at the far end of the courtyard. Sonny, on the move, throws his briefcase *over* the sheds. He hits one of the doors at full speed with his leg almost straight out. It gives him enough momentum to grab hold of the ledge on the top and scramble up onto the roof. In double-quick time Sonny's *rolling* across, and dropping down out of sight. This confuses the assassins. They speed the bike over to the sheds and the passenger quickly clambers up onto the roof. He looks around then jumps down, indicates to his pal, in basic sign language – a shrug and a circular movement of the gun – that they must go round the back to find Sonny. But they don't know how to get to the other side.

They zoom out the yard, ignoring me. I'm taking no chances. I cut out, in the other direction, skidding around corners, feeling the ache from my jog in the tube all over again.

I retrace the route I took with Sonny and Roy – through the alley, over the railway bridge, tumbling down the other side, up the terraced street with its bijou cottages. I keep on running through backstreets, across Paddington Recreation Ground. The game's up – Sonny's dead, the gadget lost.

I don't stop till I hit Maida Vale, staggering like a drunkard. Then I collapse in a shop doorway, an untidy heap of limbs, huffing and puffing ...

Sonny has assumed that this is Santos' handiwork ... So did I, for a minute, losing all reason, you do around firearms. But squatting in my comfortable doorway, getting my breath, and my composure, back, I realise I've seen that weapon before ... And I know where. When you're terrified, adrenalin pumping, you've got the snout of a dog.

Versace perfume ... on a Venezuelan gunman? Don't think so ...

Just you wait till I see that bitch Bridget fuckin Granger ...

Gonna thank her very much for not shooting me – *thanking you most kindly, Miss Bridget.*

CHAPTER FORTY-SIX

THE BRIGADIER'S COUP

'If Bridget wanted you, or Sonny, dead, you'd be dead, but she didn't – it was a negotiating technique. Anyway, she says he had his fuckin hands around your throat, was gonna squeeze the life outta ya—'

'Don't be so fuckin dramatic, Mort!'

My favourite waitress turns round. Morty smiles at her, raises his coffee cup in salute. 'Keep yer voice down,' he tells me, still smiling, leaning in closer. 'Did he or did he not have his hands on ya? Yes, he did. She was keeping an eye on yer. You do get she was shooting to miss?'

'Shoulda given me a bitta warning—'

'Couldn't risk it. He might have riddled it out, mate.'

'Don't call me *mate*.'

'We didn't know he was gonna head for Roy's mum's. Fortunate, I call it, having Bridget tailing you. Saved your life. She thought Roy might have come out blasting ... still don't know he's ... '

'I might have had a fuckin heart attack, bullets whistling round me head. I just wanna get that kit and have the sit-down with Miguel.'

'We all do, mate,' says Mort, overdoing the amicability.

'Miguel's lackeys keep ringing, enquiring about my whereabouts.'

'That's nice.'

'Jenna too.'

'Very nice ... But if I were you I'd put business before pleasure. Sonny will be a bit more willing to do the deal now.'

'Or he'll go completely under, never come out again.'

'Now who's being dramatic?'

'Has he been in contact?'

'Not yet, but he will. Sonny's not a quitter.'

'What happened to Sonny's two geezers in the Range Rover?'

'One tap on the window and they were gone – no loyalty, some people. Told you they were mediocre.'

'So what do we do now?'

'Wait,' says Morty, lighting a snout and pouring more coffee. 'Things are in hand.'

'Is there anything more you wanna tell me?'

'Wanna or gonna?'

After we've hung out in the park for half an hour, watching the world go by, Dougie Nightingale, of all people, rings. Transpires Sonny is seeking refuge with Dougie – he *doesn't trust criminals anymore*. Sonny is convinced that Santos' team is still trying to kill him ...

Dougie rang Sonny a little while after the shooting, over something trivial, as Sonny was making his escape; perfect or bad timing, depending on your point of view. Dougie, realising Sonny was in trouble, and being a charitable soul, offered his partner and friend a sanctuary, so Sonny headed over to see him, to lay low. Morty convinces Dougie to put Sonny on the phone.

'We need to have a serious chat,' says Morty. 'You're gonna need a second. Bring yer lawyer, if ya like. In fact, I insist, mate.'

'*I insist*,' I can hear Sonny say. 'You've been having it with that cunt too long.'

Smart move, getting Giles to come along.

'See you in a while.' Morty ends the call. 'Come on, let's go.'

'Where?'

'We're gonna go and see Dougie Nightingale. You might have met him – you wouldn't forget Dougie.'

'Did Sonny ask about me, if I'm alive?'

'What do you think?' says Mister Mortimer.

We drive the long way to Dougie's apartment; apparently Mort's been there before. Dougie lives in a mansion block just north of the Marylebone Road, the kinda massive block that people seeking anonymity favour – a labyrinth of corridors. He occupies a penthouse overlooking Regent's Park.

Dougie lets us in. He's already charged up on cha-cha, holding a goblet of wine in one hand and a snout in the other. Dougie, apparently, wanted to *facilitate* us on the seemingly fashionable, but fatal, roof terrace but Sonny preferred to be inside, out of the firing line. Dougie is excited by the thought of having all these gents around to discuss *business*.

Dougie reports that Miguel and Jenna are in the Monarch most nights – *always asking about you guys*, always with heavy bodyguards. *Good spenders, though.*

'What have you lot been up to?' says Dougie, fishing. 'No, don't tell me I don't wanna know ... '

'Has Giles arrived yet?' asks Morty, cutting him off.

'Not yet, he's been *sent for*,' says Dougie, pushing the door open to a large dining room. 'Sonny's in there ... ' And then, in a whisper to Mister Mortimer, 'Sort it out, *please*.'

Sonny is sat, defiantly, at the long dining table, Gucci briefcase by his side and a large tumbler in his hand.

'Oh, yer fuckin alive, are ya?' Sonny says to me, setting the tone.

'So it would seem.'

'Knew you'd get away. You're a natural longtail.'

'Why the fuck should I even talk to you? Last time you ended up trying to strangle me.'

'Oh, fuck off,' he says.

'Then you fuckin used me to stop you getting shot.'

'Stop being a fuckin girl! Fuckin holding grudges! We need to get this sorted, mate!'

'Don't fuckin call me mate.'

'You're me mate, ain't ya?'

'Mate? To be honest, Sonny, I always got the impression you didn't like me.'

'What's *like* got to do with it, ya fuckin mug?' He isn't joking. 'You're a good geezer to have on the firm.'

'I shouldn't even come near you. Someone's trying to shoot you.'

'At least I know it's not *you* trying to kill me!'

'You need to fuck off, Sonny.'

'Oh, that's nice, ain't it?' says Sonny, pretend offended.

'I meant get outta London.'

'If I'm going I'm taking that fuckin gadget – it's gonna keep me alive—'

'Or get ya fuckin killed, Sonny. It's worthless to anyone but the Zambranos, you get that?'

'Now listen, Sonny,' says Mort, 'that device is going nowhere. I didn't wanna be the one to tell you this but Roy has been confirmed dead.'

'How do you know?'

'We know ... the English Spaniard's been in touch. The conversation was short, and a surprise. It was a straight hit, if that's any consolation. He disappeared the body.'

'He could be bluffing.'

'So where's Roy?' says Morty with a shrug.

'Roy told his mum he had an appointment,' says Sonny. 'Was that Santos?'

'Dunno, Sonny. We'll get the griff when we find him.' Sonny looks absolutely gutted; his eyes are moist. Mort continues, 'I think Santos was hoping to tell me both you and Roy were dead. Reckons he's gonna kill the two geezers who fucked up your *assassination*.'

'Why weren't they trying to kill him?' says Sonny, pointing at me, like I wasn't there.

'Was meant to be a witness ... bringing back the message – Latino thing, apparently. I don't think they realised it was him ... Santos thinks he's dead, thought he'd killed *the counsellor* already. Santos told us that Roy was dead ... ' Morty shrugs, 'and he's gonna keep after you. Says you've insulted him, and his intelligence. What did you say?'

Sonny shrugs, looks mystified; could be a thousand and one things.

'How did he get your number?' asks Sonny.

'They're military intelligence,' Morty shrugs. 'Guess there's a method to these things.'

'Poor fuckin Roy.'

'You owe me an apology, Sonny,' I say. 'You said I killed Roy.'

'Fuck right off – there, that's yer apology,' says Sonny.

'Cut it out,' says Mort to me. 'Ain't got time for this bollocks.'

We sit in silence. Sonny ponders his options. Then Morty asks, 'You wanna stay alive, Sonny?'

'Did Hitler like a uniform?' replies Sonny. 'Silly question, Mort.'

'Well *I* wanna stay alive ... it's only a question of time before this Santos comes after me.'

'Why would he come after you?' asks Sonny.

'Why *not*, is a better question. If we'd done the deal when Giles suggested it, Roy might be still alive.' That was seriously below the belt from Mister Mortimer.

'Or maybe not, Sonny,' I say.

'I liked Roy ... ' says Sonny, turning to me, 'he was my fuckin mate. I ain't the fuckin psycho you seem to think I am.'

'We appreciate that, Sonny,' continues Mort, 'but this Miguel guy is the *only* option. If Santos starts serving us one by one to get that gadget, he's gonna try and blackmail Miguel. We do a deal with Miguel, Santos is fucked.'

'We should get out there and find this cunt once and for all.'

'You need to be out the way, Spain maybe ... get him chasing shadows ... Then I'll get Bridget to find Santos and do the business.'

'I could keep a low over here.'

'Out the way,' says Morty with a degree of finality. 'Someone needs to sort out Roy's business down in Spain – the bar and that.'

'Gonna be tricky,' says Sonny, 'without a death certificate.'

'I think Bridget knows people down there,' says Morty. Then, calm as you like, 'And maybe Ted too.'

'But Ted's dead ... ' says Sonny, but Morty is shaking his head.

'Ted's alive, Sonny. It was a get-up, to lose Old Bill.'

'Ted's alive! Sly fucker.'

'Was gonna put a bitta distance between himself and a few outstanding warrants but now things have changed ... he's in this arrangement ... and Bridget.'

'Hang on,' says Sonny, 'why the fuck is Ted, and Bridget, Granger suddenly in this?'

'Woulda thought that was self-evident.'

'Well, apparently not, Mort,' says Sonny, sarcastically, 'you're gonna have to explain.'

'Cos they've got a shitload of product but no distribution, no salesman, because you are both – you and our friend from Jamaica here – under some death sentence. So he's got the right zig because he sees it as self-inflicted, the result of you, and Roy, may God have mercy on his soul, turning over this Jesus fella for the parcel that you thought was gonna be a few dozen Rolexes. *Freelance* is when it doesn't interfere with Ted's gig.' Morty is getting angrier, sharper, 'And now it transpires that we're on the verge of being wiped out by some South American lunatic who dresses like Prince fuckin Charles but has no problem ripping the organs out of human beings, kids being a specialty. I had to explain all this to Ted – why you were fuckin about in Barbados. Ted is rightly pissed off. A lot of time and effort went into faking his death. He don't need fuckin dramas or any attention, nothin spectacular like hordes of Venezuelan gunmen, in London, trying to kill everyone, twoed-up on motorbikes, chasing associates down railway tracks or shooting them dead in the street ... People he's sent for,' Morty nods at me, 'ending up all over the evening news. Ted wants a deal with Zambrano. This Miguel is sweetness and light ... but could seriously fuck up Ted Granger's escape plan, if he woke up in a spiteful mood ... '

Sonny is taking it in. Morty continues.

'And to add a fuckin dash of Tabasco, turns out now that Ted Granger and Patsy O'Malley are old comrades ... from some prison riot or some such nonsense. Patsy is thinking his brother's death was something to do with you, Sonny. Not that you shot him, but the killer is in London, on the rampage, because of some mischief *you* instigated.'

Morty leans forward, both hands on the table. 'Now, Sonny, you was *told* not to approach the O'Malleys, but you wouldn't listen – you knew best. And don't even think about blaming Roy ... You was talking rewards, dead or alive, slinging readies around. You got intoxicated, big-time. We shoulda done what we're doing now – called it on with Bridget and let her find Santos. He'd be in his oil drum now – job done. Bridget would have found him, and his outfit, and served 'em.' Morty stops to light a cigarette before continuing, 'This is the consequences, Sonny – you getting it? That's why Ted's in the bust-up, okay? It's compensation. Ted's consignment is coming – just like Christmas – his supplier will still have to be paid. We can't have *three* lots of South

Americans creating mayhem ... ' Morty laughs, 'Would be insane. That money must come from somewhere ... otherwise Ted, *and* Bridget, will not be best pleased.'

Sonny's eyes are widening. He's in grave shit; Bridget Granger, I've riddled out, is a one-stop shop for assassinations, real or counterfeit. Hygienic disposals are her forte. Sonny King's more terrified of Miss Spick 'n' Span than of Santos. The *threat* of Bridget is Morty's doomsday weapon. And Sonny knows Bridge doesn't like him ...

There is a knock, the door swings open, and Giles appears, all fine and dandy – looks like he's spent the morning at a spa. Sonny winks at Giles; the numbers have just been evened up.

'Hello, Giles,' says Morty. 'We've met before, in Acton. We was just explaining to Sonny ... ' Morty gives Giles the Toff what the late Roy Burns would call the sit-rep – his expression instantly changes.

'Roy is dead?' says Giles, suddenly worried. He turns to Sonny. 'This is serious.' Giles sits down, takes one of Sonny's snouts and lights it. He doesn't normally smoke. 'So, what's the deal?' he asks. 'Where's the resolution?'

Morty runs his solution past Giles. Mister King will take twenty five percent of any realised funds. Mister Mortimer and Giles Urquhart will look after his interests but he must surrender the memory stick and leave London, if only temporarily. The funds will be routed to the CBB. This is still dependent on Miguel being willing to do a deal; it might get ugly once he knows we can access the memory stick. Giles sits patiently, listening hard. Then he turns to Sonny.

'Sonny,' says Giles, 'what is your fucking problem? This is about realpolitik. That amount of money will see you out for the rest of your life. Why would you put your life or liberty in jeopardy? With that amount of money tucked away, ready to spend, you could live like a lord for the rest of your days. With what you've accrued already, you're talking about turning it into, over the next few years, *fifty* or *sixty* million.'

'See,' says Sonny, 'I get the idea that you're all spivving me.'

'Sonny,' says Giles, '*you* asked me to come here.'

'Like it's a team effort,' says Sonny, sulky.

'Sonny,' says Morty, fixing Sonny with his eyes, 'this is really a take-it-or-leave-it deal. We get Bridget out there. Miguel will be looking for Santos as well. We put our heads together. It's *symbiotic*—'

'Don't start ... ' says Sonny, glancing at me, 'with the big fuckin words ... '

'But does it make sense?' asks Mort. 'An alliance?'

'I can see the sense in it,' says Sonny.

'This will be a temporary exile, Sonny,' says Giles. 'If you remain in London there's always a possibility that this Santos chap will be watching Miguel, hoping you turn up, planning to intercept you. You're his target. Hopefully we can do a deal *tout de suite*.' Napoleon would have approved – the classic pincer movement. 'Please,' says Giles, 'trust us.'

Without warning, Dougie tumbles, huffing and puffing, into the room. He's alarmed because out of the blue he's received an extremely disturbing call – a package, addressed to Mister Sonny King, has been delivered, by hand, to the Monarch Club. It was opened because it looked fishy. It was found to contain a dead fish with a bullet in its mouth, and a message – on quality notepaper, in perfect English, very formal – enquiring about his health but going on to say *Mister King, you have to be lucky every day – we only need be lucky once.*

Now Dougie is panicking, thinks he's going to get shot in the head before too long – a not-so-innocent bystander. The afternoon coke has cranked everything up a notch.

'I don't know what's going on,' he screams dramatically. 'All I know is someone is trying to kill you, Sonny. *Please*, do whatever these chaps want you to do,' he urges Sonny. 'If there's a shooting at the club the police will get involved. It will be the end of everything I've ever worked for.'

'You've never worked a fuckin day in your life, you fuckin fruit,' snarls Sonny. Dougie is seriously offended. Morty holds up his hand to silence Dougie before he says something he'll regret.

'Hang on, Sonny. Dougie's not wrong,' says Morty. 'If you get shot dead, inside or outside the club, the law will start investigating and the law will end up with that memory stick. You'll be dead and we'll get nothing.'

'Any percentage of something,' interjects Giles, 'is better than a large amount of nothing.'

'This Santos dude has made it personal,' says Morty. 'He's prepared to kill you to force your hand. It's time, Sonny, to give it up. Let your man Giles look after your interests. That's why he's your lawyer. You need to go away for a while, down to Spain, till we sort out you-know-what.'

Dougie, meanwhile, is pacing – no doubt worried about how to safeguard his own health and reputation. Suddenly he clicks his fingers.

'Giles, you could fly Sonny over to France in your aircraft, the one at Elstree.'

Giles shoots Dougie a cutting look but says nothing. But Dougie continues, turns to Morty, 'Giles keeps a light aircraft, at the aerodrome, just outside London – says it's a great way to empty a pair of knickers—'

'It would be easier for Sonny to get on a train at Waterloo,' snaps Giles, obviously not liking Dougie's idea. 'I can't fly in the dark.'

'But it's not dark, Giles,' points out Dougie – literally pointing out the window.

'Not yet, Douglas,' he hisses, the spa glow totally gone. 'Anyway, I haven't filed a flight plan. Are you suggesting I fly Sonny down to Spain?'

'No, just to Paris, Sonny could pick up the overnight express, be in Spain—'.

'Because I wouldn't have enough fuel to get to Spain,' snaps Giles, defensively. 'It's bloody foolish to suggest—'

'We got all the way to Marrakech that time,' suggests Dougie.

Giles clearly doesn't want to be reminded about Marrakech that time. His eyes narrow to slits. So do Sonny's; he's watching Giles like a Doberman.

'We stopped to refuel, Dougie, if you remember, in Le Touquet.' Giles straightens up, becomes the courtroom lawyer. 'Oh, no, you wouldn't remember, Douglas. You were in your usual drunken haze. Anyway, it will be dark on the way back.'

'Dark? Those crates fly themselves, with the GPS, autopilot – you said so yourself. You have them eating out of your hand up

at that airfield, so a flight plan's not a problem.' Dougie turns to
Morty and laughs. 'Airfield? It's a glorified car park, for planes,
with a control tower.'

'Fuck's sake, Dougie!' barks Giles, suddenly irritated. 'You
shouldn't even be in here!'

'What?' screams Douglas, 'In my own fucking house?'

'No! In this fucking room! Discussing these matters!'

'How dare you!'

'It's nothing to do with you, you fucking degenerate!'

'It's *everything* to do with me, Giles,' screams Dougie,
pointing at Sonny, 'if my fucking business partner happens to get
murdered!'

'Oh, stop being such a fucking old drama queen!'

'My life has been threatened on two occasions and you don't
think I have the right to be concerned? Well, fuck you, Giles
Urquhart!'

'And fuck you, Reginald Draper!' Giles retorts with dry
malice.

This really hurts – using Dougie Nightingale's real name.
Dougie regains his composure, takes a standing count. 'Urquhart
... you are a complete cunt ... ' he hisses. 'A cunt with a capital
Kay.'

Giles feigns indifference.

'Oi, Giles ... ' says Sonny, interrupting their squabble.

'Yes, Sonny?' asks Giles.

'Listen to me ... I want you to fly me over to Paris tonight,
okay?' Sonny says it in such a way that it would be foolish to
refuse. Giles has inbred deference, knows when someone is
issuing a command. Sonny isn't finished. 'Then I want you to
come back and sort this business out. You get the memory stick
when I get to France. I'm trustin you, Giles, okay?'

Giles nods his head. 'Okay, Sonny, but ... I think it would be
better if we flew to the south west of Paris, to the field at Le Mans
Arnage. It's suitably provincial ... The security, gendarmerie,
customs, et cetera, are practically nonexistent.' Giles is nodding to
himself. 'You can easily catch a taxi into town and pick up the
overnight sleeper. You might have to lose that briefcase, and look
like a tourist ... You have your passport?'

Sonny taps the Gucci briefcase, holds up three fingers.

'One should be sufficient, Mister King.'

After farewells and token threats from Sonny, he and Giles cut out and head to the small airfield at Elstree. Giles insists that we *don't* accompany them up to genteel, rural Hertfordshire. This was a stealth mission and *one nefarious character onboard is enough.*

'No offence taken, Giles,' says Morty. 'We don't all need to go.' Then he tells Sonny, 'You're in safe hands with Giles. We'll keep you posted ... '

So Sonny leaves, still telling us he wants to avenge Roy, still clutching his briefcase across his chest. Dougie shows them out – *we shouldn't leave together,* Morty insists, *just in case.* And when Dougie returns to the dining room ...

'Well done, Douglas,' says Morty, shaking his hand, 'perfect – a faultlessly executed *coup de grâce.*'

'Thank you, kind sir,' says Dougie with a small bow.

'You ever trod the boards?' asks Mort. 'Only I think you're wasted in nightclubs.'

'Well, I do have a strong element of the thespian,' says Dougie. 'It's a stage, you know?'

'Quite right,' says Mort, dryly, nodding. 'All the world's a stage.'

'And all the men and women merely players,' replies Dougie. 'They have their exits and their entrances—'

'Good thinking, Dougie, let's go and get a drink somewhere quiet,' says Mort, getting up.

'Let us make haste, my noble Lord Mortimer,' says Dougie with a theatrical flourish.

Morty has a very thin smile ... Thinking he might have started something.

And so we wait on Giles in the secluded corner of a pub garden in leafy Hampstead, letting Douglas tell us stories of what goes on in public school dormitories after lights out. Seems to think us lower orders have some perverse fascination with their sexual penchants, pecking orders and domination techniques. Morty doesn't agree with Dougie's argument that *you're not necessarily homosexual* if you sling your tool up another man's back-alley.

Dougie keeps popping off to the khazi for fat rails every twenty minutes. And all the time we're creeping closer to our multi-million dollar payday.

Dougie's reward for his outstanding performance? Control of the Monarch Club, no more interference from Sonny. He's free to rinse it out, fuck it up big style and generally run it into the ground. While Doug's having a nose-up Morty drops an FYI on me. The route that Sonny is using to leave the UK is the same one, in reverse, that Duppy Granger used to attend his own funeral – same overnight train, but going north – certainly the same pilot on the final leg of the journey. Ted arrived in London the exact same time I did.

As the pub begins to shut, at the end of a glorious English summer's day, and four hours after we left him, Giles rings on Dougie's phone to say that Sonny is in France, heading due south to Spain – talking about flying some of his crew into Malaga, for protection against the ghost that is Santos de Lucia. Giles is about to take off on the return leg.

'They want to know if you have *the thing*, Giles,' says Dougie.

'*Mise en place*,' says Giles, laughing against the noise of static and a noisy propeller, '*mise en place*.'

'What the fuck?' asks Morty.

'French, Mort,' I tell him. 'Means everything's in place, means we're sweet.'

CHAPTER FORTY-SEVEN

NEVER TRUST A TOFF

Giles wants to have a pre-meet meeting, just me and him – *to discuss tactics* – away from the rendezvous, at an oyster bar around the back of Piccadilly, before we move on to his private club. So here I am, nice and early, tubbed-up in a booth in the corner.

This is a bit more civilised – we've been jumping about like itchy hillbillies at a barn dance, not like crims at all. Morty is babysitting the memory stick, and neither Giles nor myself have any knowledge of its whereabouts. Mister Miguel, meanwhile, was very inquisitive when I spoke to him on the phone this morning. He was being cute – fishing, trying to keep the expectation out of his voice. Miguel agreed to a meeting and when I told him the where and when, and the fact that he would be meeting a lawyer who *looks after our interests*, he got more curious still. *A lawyer ... ? That's good ...* We made the meet for one o'clock.

Tip for ya: always strike matches away from the body, never keep a monkey as a pet and always arrive early for a meet. Always sit facing the door, rub a smidgen of talcum powder on your hands before you leave your slaughter or hotel room. Blow your nose, dress appropriately, remain anonymous. Don't eat the nuts or olives, that's a schnorrer move, don't want oily hands. Remember who you're meant to be. Sit still in your seat, absorb your surroundings and don't fidget. You're here on business, not to fuck about.

This morning before I left my little hidey-hole in Swiss Cottage, I looked in the mirror and told myself that all I have to do is hold it together – not go insane – for a little while longer, deal with this mad shit later. I dream of Stevie, Santos, Evey and Roy – 'course I do. What else would I do? Madness is what happens to sane people around insane events.

After a couple of minutes Giles arrives. He spots me across the

'But you and Ted helped him buy the fuckin thing, Giles. You, no doubt, hooked him up with your chum Dougie ... or do I mean Reg?'

'Didn't say it was rational, did I?' he says, downing another oyster. 'Bridget ... deadlier than the male ... and the males are pretty deadly ... no offence.'

'None taken.'

'It was Bridget who suggested getting Sonny working for them, doing the you-know-what ... making serious money for them before they swindled him.'

'Before Bridget offed him, you mean, Giles?' I say. 'Let's be adults.'

He nods. 'And all this insanity started over some bizarre story about a mother and child marooned at some airport—'

'Oh, yeah?'

'Couple of years ago ... ' Giles starts on his toast. 'I never got to the bottom of it – suddenly Ted's screaming blue murder, wanting to seriously hurt Sonny King ... '

Mad Eve and Hyper Rory, clucking for smack and e-numbers at the airport while Sonny topped up his tan – the kinda tale that brings out the self-righteous in every crim.

'So instead they go into business with Sonny?' I ask. 'To set him up?'

Giles just shrugs. 'Told you it was mad, didn't I? Sonny made money for them, with your friend Mortimer as a go-between.'

'Sonny wasn't going to retire down to Spain, whether that yacht sank or not, was he?'

Giles ignores the question, catches the waiter's eye and gestures for the bill. 'I think your friend Mortimer kept Sonny alive, for the last two years – kept telling Ted it would be insane to do harm to Sonny ... while Bridget was poisoning Ted, telling him nobody's indispensable. People are strange ... '

There's no answer to that. Bridget wanted to work Sonny hard in revenge for Evey, before she made him disappear. Maybe me arriving was the beginning of Bridget's endgame.

The bill arrives. 'You know what I'm curious about?' asks Giles, getting out his wallet and dropping two twenties on the platter, a small frown on his forehead. 'I don't wish to be personal, or rude – please don't take offence – but you don't come across as a typical criminal.'

'You're right, Giles. I've always believed it's a short cut ... to wealth ... within reason ... I ain't greedy. How rich can one man be?'

'You think criminality is about money?' Giles wipes his hands on a linen napkin then slings it on the table. 'Interesting concept ... ' He looks at his watch. 'Time to go.'

Out of the dozen oysters, Giles managed seven, while I got to make do with five – but who's counting? Toffs. Buggers can't help themselves.

We stroll through the backstreets to Giles' club. I begin to think of Jesus Zambrano running amok in these Mayfair streets a couple of weeks ago. I can see Giles' thinking in wanting to have the meeting here – it's not the sort of place that encourages shoot-outs or kidnapping, with its Grecian columns, Union Jack flags, sweeping flight of steps up to the huge double doors and attentive, liveried doormen. I would prefer somewhere away from witnesses and curious individuals. But this place is semi-public, so Miguel, or more particularly Raul, won't be *cutting up rough*. Giles wants to *repeatedly emphasise that it's a business transaction – plain and simple*. And he thinks Miguel, if perhaps not Raul, will appreciate the sense of history that oozes from the very fibre of the building. I have my doubts.

'Follow my lead,' says Giles, as we enter. 'It's best not to over-rehearse. Let our case unfold slowly so Mister Zambrano can digest it. Remember this is commerce, the bedrock of civilisation.'

'Don't underestimate this guy, Giles.'

'I don't underestimate anybody,' says Giles with genuine steel.

We enter the echoing, baroque entrance hall – cool marble, the air and atmosphere still and calm. There's a lingering smell, centuries old, of cigars and brass polish. Above the reception desk there's a Roll of Honour of past chairmen and a small brass plaque, commemorating three staff members killed in the Great War.

There's no need for Giles to announce himself; he gets shown through to the dining room – *not restaurant* – to a table in an alcove in the far corner. The room is oak-panelled, hung with portraits of dignitaries with insincere smiles, cruel eyes that follow you around the room. They were doing white-collar crime, insider trading, here before it was invented. Other guys in the dining room nod to Giles like he's well-respected in his circle, got a dash of charisma. There's a surprising amount of young geezers in here. You'd think that these clubs would be full of ancient coffin-dodgers and trust-funded layabouts, half-pissed and dribbling, getting ready to snooze the afternoon away in plump armchairs, but the gaff is full of junior swells, the next wave.

I order a Sanbitter, with *only a little crushed ice*, then I sit back to observe.

These aristocratic fuckers didn't stay where they are by being all-round good eggs. They got to, and stayed, at the top by being conniving jackals.

Family mottos: 'Play Both Sides', 'Survive At All Costs', 'Eat Your Young', 'Strike Back First', 'Never Forget, Never Forgive'.

The Toffia could teach a fighting dog a thing or two about survival. They're ruthless, but at the same time they can be charming – the world's their extra oyster and they know it. I've watched Bilkos who run naughty little firms let themselves down badly around genuine swells, but most especially around the gals – they go boss-eyed and bandy-legged, their compass spins out of control. Villains who've clawed their way up from scuzzy council estates can be the worst snobs once they get a few quid.

It works the other way around as well. Toffs love a scallywag – till they actually meet a *real* gangster. Then the *mocking villain that is reality doth intrude*. Some swells, throughout history, have gone slumming and ended up with more than they bargained for. But these aristocrats, despite their squabbles, will always look after their own. You can hate them for it if you want, but it gets you nowhere.

I hear the hall clock chiming. It's exactly one o'clock. As I look up Miguel and Raul are being escorted across the dining room – Miguel is his usual sleek Prada self while Raul, his half-brother, is huge, fuckin obese, breathing heavy, and already sweating profusely. Giles is up on his feet and apologising for them having to leave the hired help outside – *no bodyguards on the premises. I'm glad you understand.*

But Raul doesn't appear to be listening. Quick as a flash, without anyone seeing, after the head waiter has doubled back to base, he pats down both me and Giles – runs his hands quickly over my chest, into the small of my back, and then, double rapido, and completely unselfconsciously, into my crotch. Satisfied, he does the same to Giles. Giles is taken aback. I half-expected it; it's standard procedure for American crims, both north and south. Raul tosses our phones onto the tabletop, and, quick as a conjurer, peels off the backs and removes the batteries. He then places his own phone on the crisp linen, clicks his fingers for Miguel's. Raul removes the batteries so they can't be used to record the conversation. Then Raul pulls out a small electronic device, turns it on and leaves it sitting in the middle of the table. Miguel watches everything like a cobra.

'Microphones. Bugs,' says Raul, breathlessly, in a heavy South American accent, nodding at the device. Raul, it transpires, doesn't speak that much English. Miguel is translating for him but also seriously checking out Giles Urquhart – his attire, his manners. Miguel is a guy who observes and adsorbs. Every now and again someone fits *exactly* your preconception of upper-class English Aristocrat, and this is one of those times. Tall, tanned, well-cut hair, dark navy linen suit, Oxford collar, salmon-pink shirt, purple and maroon tie, handmade pigskin chocolate brown tasseled loafers. Manicured nails. Cufflinks in well-worn silver – definite heirlooms. Battered 24k gold Rolex – vintage, of course. Giles is a geezer who could certainly pull women, and that would score points with Miguel.

But Raul, meanwhile, has trouble fitting into the chair. I think Miguel might be embarrassed by his half-brother's size, but he's inscrutable.

Q. Could this Raul fellow nonchalantly watch somebody being slowly tortured to death while eating a hero sandwich?

A. Without doubt. Raul could slice and fillet, crush and burn, break bones, pull teeth, and then sleep the sleep of angels.

Giles goes into a well-rehearsed thumbnail history of the club – the prime ministers who fought duels, the ne'er-do-well dukes who lost the entire family estate in one night at the gaming tables, the singsongs around the piano during the Blitz.

'Spare me the history lesson,' Miguel snaps. 'You are a lawyer, is that correct?'

Giles nods, but he looks a tad put out.

'You practise?' Miguel asks.

'I represent select clients, whose anonymity is essential. I control investments and facilitate tax strategies.'

'You wash money?'

'No, Mister Zambrano,' says Giles, exceedingly polite, 'I get it to where it can be assimilated back into the monetary system. Let me reassure you, Mister Zambrano, we have a lot to lose, so we must insist that anything that is said around this table, stays here.' Miguel says nothing but Giles continues. 'We are here to solve a problem ... *your* problem.' Giles has suddenly gone into lawyer mode; a harder edge enters his voice. Miguel made a mistake upsetting Giles too early.

'What's this all about?' asks Miguel.

'Shall we order?' suggests Giles calmly. Miguel's eyes narrow while Raul's eyes tell me he's thirty minutes off turning cannibal.

'You want to give me a clue?' says Miguel, knowing Giles' little game.

'Of course ... ' says Giles, picking up a menu. 'The Dover sole – the best I've ever tasted. Judge a kitchen by its Dover sole. The beef and lamb are wonderful, but can be heavy, 'specially in summer.'

Miguel realises he's gonna have to be patient. The waiter comes over and Giles orders the Dover sole three times, but Raul wants proper fish and chips, twice – *Demedos*. And *mucho fries*. Turns out Raul does have a smattering of English – when it comes to food.

Miguel doesn't want to appear impatient but the suspense, and Giles' nonchalance, is killing him. He turns to me. 'So, why did you ask us here today? Apart from the Dover sole.'

I look to Giles, who gives a tiny nod in my direction.

'It's good news and bad news, I'm afraid. We have made investigations and have concluded that both Jesus and Santos are now deceased. After the details of their trade in children's organs got out ... they didn't stand a chance.'

'The irony is,' interrupts Giles, 'that the attention that your chaps, and Mister de Lucia, brought down on Jesus Zambrano, and the importance of ascertaining the whereabouts of a piece of missing kit, instigated something of a treasure hunt.'

Miguel nods. He doesn't bother translating for Raul.

'Furthermore,' I say, 'the parties responsible for the deaths of Jesus and Santos are now dead themselves. Is this a problem?'

Miguel shakes his head. Raul is hungry, eating tartare sauce with a spoon. Giles tells the waiter to bring some bread, *and some butter.*

'So, you brought me here to tell me those two were dead?' says Miguel. 'That's bad news? The *missing kit* ... any sign?'

Giles doesn't miss a beat. 'That's the good news, Mister Zambrano,' he says. 'A third party now has control of the memory stick. Through our connections we have managed to locate it.'

'We don't actually *have* the piece of equipment,' I say, 'in our possession.'

'Or know *exactly* where it is.'

'But we can *get* it.'

'We are operating as *agents* for the party holding the merchandise.'

'And what do they want,' Miguel asks me, 'this third party?'

'The party who hold the merchandise must be pacified. To try and take the memory stick by force would result in a lot of bloodshed in London—'

'Something ... ' Giles cuts in, 'the authorities are not prepared to allow. Internecine hostilities are out of the question. You understand? We need you to help us to help you. Is that possible?' Miguel nods, statesmanlike. 'We need you to actively stop searching for the equipment ... to stand down the guard.'

'Okay, maybe,' says Miguel, suspecting he's being grafted. 'But what do they want for its return?'

'They will be recompensed, if you are agreeable, by you discharging a debt they owe ... ' says Giles. Miguel looks quizzical but interested. Giles marches on, 'They owe thirty million dollars to an organisation in Brazil.'

'Are you seriously suggesting I give some bunch of Brazilians thirty million dollars?'

'No,' says Giles calmly. 'That's the figure they *owe*. I'm

suggesting you, or your family, *influence* them to *overlook* the debt ... Or negotiate compensation ... Make up their loss ... At wholesale prices ... Return goods, to them, product, to the value of the debt.'

'*Influence them*?' repeats Miguel, digesting the information, seeing how it could work, thinking he could be getting a deal with a capital Dee ...

'It's an arrangement that could suit you. Once the debt is discharged they will deliver the merchandise to us.'

'To you?' asks Miguel double-quick. 'Not to us?'

Giles shakes his head. 'They will deliver the merchandise to us.'

'Can they be trusted?' asks Miguel.

'I assure you, Mister Zambrano,' Giles replies, 'this will not be a problem.'

'So how did they come into possession of the equipment?' Miguel asks me.

'For me to ask them,' I reply, 'would be a breach of protocol. It's one of the terms and conditions ... '

'As we say over here,' says Giles, '*no questions asked.*'

'Meaning?' asks Miguel.

'Meaning,' says Giles, like it's fucking obvious, 'exactly that – we don't ask questions.'

'How they came to steal it from the thieves,' I tell Miguel, 'is their business not ours. If you want an explanation, Miguel, you might not get your equipment returned. You might not get both.' Miguel's face says nothing. 'The theory, Miguel,' I tell him, 'is that they stole it from the people who killed your cousin.'

'*Fair exchange is no robbery* ... ' says Giles.

'Robbery is never fair, Mister Urquhart,' says Miguel, pure deadpan.

This kid's been playing poker with grown-ups since he was old enough to count. Miguel doesn't believe me. He's trying to work out how thieves would stumble across a memory stick inserted in someone's anus ...

'Miguel,' I shrug, 'you asked me to locate this thing and that's what I've done ... '

Miguel asks Raul if it would be possible to find and *influence* this Brazilian crew. Raul laughs – grunts – *we find them easy* ... *all we need is a name* ...

'That shouldn't be a problem,' says Miguel. 'So when we *discharge* this debt you return our property?'

'The discharging of the debt prepares the ground,' says Giles. 'It's the first part of the operation. After you discharge the debt, the property becomes *our* property.'

'Meaning what, exactly?' asks Miguel, betraying the first sign of anxiety.

'How can I put this?' Giles asks himself. 'To be precise, it becomes the property of the people I represent ... ' Giles nods at me, 'and the people my colleague works for.'

'Your bosses?' asks Miguel.

Giles nods. 'And they, I'm afraid, don't come cheap.' Miguel looks concerned but Giles continues. 'To put a deal like this together requires a certain amount of trust ... We have partners, junior partners, who must be included in any trade ... '

'This nightclub owner?' asks Miguel. 'Am I right?'

'Correct,' says Giles. 'He and his associate Mister Burns were *conduits,* working backwards and forwards, and were partly responsible for locating the equipment. Santos offered Mister King one million dollars for the return of the equipment.'

'It pricked their ears up,' I say. 'Got them and their connections mobilised, asking questions.'

Back to Giles. 'They retain *an interest* – they're muscle. But we are not here on *their* authority.'

'I would ask you, Miguel,' I say, 'and you too, Raul, not to do anything to anger or antagonise them. We need to keep them out of the way. Please don't give them a reason to get excited.'

'They're hovering,' says Giles, 'but they don't understand diplomacy.'

'Or pragmatism,' I say with a shrug.

'There is a risk, of course,' says Giles, taking a sip of water, 'that this *operation* could bring unwanted attention from the law. You understand me, Mister Zambrano? All this is factored in when calculating, and justifying, our fee.'

'But all the money in the world,' I say with a touch of

resignation, 'is no good if you're not alive, or at liberty to spend it.'

'Alas, money makes sensible people envious,' says Giles, philosophically.

'And a little greedy,' interjects Miguel. 'Do you not agree?'

'Listen, Miguel, you're talking to the government here ... ' I indicate Giles and myself. 'You don't wanna be talking to the army, I can promise you.'

'Ditto,' says Miguel, nodding at Raul. 'Can we talk numbers?' he asks.

'You don't know what we're selling yet.' Giles pulls out of his inside pocket documents, printouts, fresh off the stick, from Smiler's laboratory. 'The people I represent, *my bosses* as you put it, insisted I show you these ... If you'll care to study them you'll realise that the party who hold the originals have only allowed us every fourth page. These are "read only" documents ... samples, as it were.'

Miguel is taken aback, surprised that anyone except the deceased *Wunderkind* could even open the files. Giles lays the printouts on the tabletop, flattens them and points at the page numbers – *every other even number*. Miles and miles, page after page, of figures, enough to send you dizzy.

'You've had personal access to the equipment?' asks Miguel, expressionless, but realising he's been lulled into complacency, ambushed in daylight.

'Just to clarify, Miguel, the files contained on this memory stick are records of numerous accounts held in the Cayman Islands and New York, together with thousands of sixteen-digit passwords.' Miguel's eyes bore into Giles' as he loads it on. 'And an Austrian fairy tale to be used, no doubt, as cipher to place the correct password with the correct bank details. I think I've got that right. Added later are recorded conversations, mostly of you – in fact, exclusively of you – talking with various associates.' Miguel begins to take more notice. But Giles isn't finished. 'Miguel, the device also contains photographs of a woman I believe is your sister in compromising sexual situations. I take it you were aware of the existence of these pictures?'

'I'm going to take the fifth,' says Miguel, starting to look a little sick. Miguel knew they existed but it's impossible to work out if he knew they were on the memory stick. Now he's translating to Raul, relating this sudden turn of events. Raul shoots me a look like he wants to eat the messenger.

Giles continues the case for the prosecution. 'The photographs I have no interest in. The party holding the device let me study the electronic ledgers. After I studied them I left the party holding the memory stick no wiser as to the true content, or should I say, the true *value* of the information contained on them. They seemed to believe the valuable cargo was the compromising photographs – the reason you wanted the device returned immediately. My boss has told me to organise, to negotiate, the discharging of their debt as a *sign of good faith*.'

'Maybe I should be talking to your boss, Mister Urquhart,' says Miguel, leaking a little anger.

'He is a firm believer in delegation,' replies Giles, with pure, solid charm. 'I am only following his instructions ... '

'Where I come from, delegation can be seen as an insult.'

'This is London,' says Giles. 'Things are done differently here.'

'You simply have a more sophisticated form of corruption,' says Miguel with an edge, turning to sit sideways on.

'Touché,' says Giles.

An army of waiters descends and serves up lunch. Miguel asks for a dry white wine. The headwaiter tells him he'll send the wine waiter. 'Please,' says Miguel assertively, 'just bring it.'

Giles is impressed. In a strange way, I think Giles and Miguel are growing to like one another. They respect one another's antagonism. Anyone else but Miguel would have their elbows on the table, head in hands, but Miguel's *been to business school*. Business school is gladiator school. In America commerce is a blood sport – physical contact is mandatory – some brave warrior will be carried from the field with the figurative bloody nose. The waiters disappear leaving Raul with his two lunches, one under a cover to keep warm. Miguel ignores his food as Giles takes up where he left off.

'The ledgers contained on that memory stick are evidence of a Ponzi scheme – I'm sure I don't have to explain the mechanics ...

There are two sets of accounts as well, showing proof of a *massive* illicit transfer of funds. It's not for me to judge, but that might have been foolhardy, or vain even, to place the two sets of accounts in the same place.'

Miguel's eyes look like he would gladly kill that fucking banker in Miami stone fucking dead if Jesus hadn't already done so, but he retains his enigmatic air. It's good news – the memory stick is coming home – but it's going to cost him dear.

'The photographs would only be an embarrassment,' continues Giles, 'if it were not for what you've grandly entitled The Plan – a long-term campaign to promote your sister Jenna as a future political candidate, some kind of Venezuelan Eva Perón. I believe your own cousin was attempting to blackmail you, and your sister, with these compromising photographs.'

Miguel's pragmatism is getting tested to destruction but he realises that unleashing Raul would sever all connection to the memory stick. They realise they have to give a little to get a lot. It's a trade; we both have something the other wants ... Giles is priming Miguel towards what he called *tender blackmail*.

'Please don't think us rude or insensitive,' Giles goes on, 'but as a precaution, we have brought some insurance. And like all insurance we hope we never have to use it. Sealed copies of these documents,' Giles taps the papers on the tabletop, 'and copies of the photographs have been placed in the vault of a firm of solicitors with instructions that they are to open them if any harm comes to my colleague or myself.'

Miguel has his eyebrows raised, watching Giles' performance with almost detached interest.

'Everything is about containment,' says Giles, 'keeping things under wraps. If we're lucky, that piece of equipment will end up with us, and not some incorrigible scoundrels. If those photographs were to fall into the wrong hands ... it could lead to all sorts of despicable behaviour ... Or if they were to realise their true value ... We're speaking *hypothetically* here, Miguel. You do understand, don't you?'

Miguel shrugs and nods. He wants to ask the price but isn't going to and Giles isn't going to tell him till he asks. Our Giles pushes on.

'And it transpires our bosses have "associates" who do business with this Cayman bank. These people – nasty, nasty people by all accounts – have deposited their funds there, in expectation of great returns. It's a small world, isn't it, Miguel?'

'Getting smaller all the time,' says Miguel, roasting beneath the Prada collar.

'Maybe incestuous would be a better word,' says Giles, musing, contemplating this concept. 'But business is still business. Apparently one of our associates buys "commodities" from one of these investors – if you catch my drift – has done for years. In fact, they advised him to deposit his cash in this Cayman bank but ultimately he preferred to keep it under his Swiss mattress. I think our associate would be delighted to hear his instincts were correct. You know what they say about bad news?'

'Travels fast.'

'Correct,' says Giles taking a sip of wine. 'Yes, containment is the name of the game ... '

'See, Mister Urquhart ... ' says Miguel very politely, 'let me know if I'm wrong, but I think you're blackmailing us. I think all this ... is just bullshit to sugar the pill.'

'And the pill is what, exactly?' asks Giles.

'The fact that you're shaking us down, hustling us like a pair of beach grifters,' says Miguel. '*The pill is what, exactly*?' He imitates Giles in a passable English accent.

'The pill, since you ask,' says Giles, getting eye contact, 'is ten percent of the balances of the New York accounts.'

'Ten percent?' asks Miguel, taken aback. Eyebrows raised, quizzical expression.

'Yes, Mister Zambrano ... it comes to approximately one hundred million dollars ... by our calculations one hundred million dollars for the return of this memory stick.'

Miguel leans in close to Giles – a quick glance back into the room. 'Why the fuck should we give you ten percent ... ?' he asks real slow. 'Or ten fucking cents? That piece of equipment is totally worthless to you.'

'You're not wrong, Miguel,' says Giles, 'and it's reflected in the price. But your extremely ambitious future schemes – that's schemes *plural*, long-term and short-term – are in complete and utter jeopardy without it. They're going to melt down, like ice in the sun.' Miguel goes to speak but Giles silences him with his hand. 'We take a "consultancy fee" of ten percent for our help in getting them back on track ... and you get to keep a whopping ninety percent ... enough for Jenna's dowry ... and in later years, her campaign war chest, a few well-publicised charitable works, a hospital dedicated in her name, no doubt. And, I should point out, without being discourteous, Mister Zambrano, that it's not *actually* your money we're using to facilitate the equipment's return.'

Miguel looks at Giles in total fucking amazement, like he can't fucking believe what a sly, slippery cunt this a-rist-o-crat-ic motherfucker is ... I coulda told you what they're like.

'Ten percent?' Miguel asks again, incredulous. 'One hundred million dollars?'

Giles nods. Miguel translates for Raul but Raul has worked it out already; he understands *one hundred million dollars*.

'This is a generous deal, on our part,' says Giles. 'We want ten percent of what's deposited in those accounts in New York. We've studied the figures ... it's a fair solution.'

Miguel turns to me. 'I made an offer to you – it was in product. That's what we discussed.'

'We didn't discuss anything, Miguel. And the commodity in this case is money.'

'Miguel,' says Giles, '*your* cousin started this mess and we are tidying it up, doing *your* firefighting.' Giles taps the printouts. 'When is this *project* going to run to term?'

'Sorry?' asks Miguel, like he can't believe Giles' impertinence.

'When are you hoping to cash out, Miguel?' asks Giles.

'Easy now!' snaps Miguel. 'Back Fucking Up! That's none of your business.' He obviously doesn't like being out-manoeuvred. 'How do I know this will be the end of it?' asks Miguel.

'A deal's a deal, Miguel,' says Giles calmly. 'The people I represent wouldn't want it to become common knowledge that they received funds from a failed bank ... the assets of distraught criminals who deposited their monies there in good faith. They wouldn't want this to come back to haunt them – they hold positions of power in the legitimate world. They would require complete severance. This would be a collaboration ... Think of the fee as a legitimate expense.'

'Your *consultancy fee*?' asks Miguel sarcastically.

Giles nods. 'For that fee, we make sure the information doesn't go anywhere near law enforcement. We would be *colluding* with you, Miguel. Containment is in *both* our interests. Our bosses are also men of their word. They would require complete confidentiality from *you*.'

Giles is going well, careful not to tip the balance between pragmatism and pride. Giles is looking to provide Miguel with enough of a loophole for him, and his ego, to jump through – to grease the sides so decorum is maintained.

'Miguel,' he says, 'let me explain something ... It's not in my interests, or the interests of my associate here,' Giles nods at me, 'or the people we represent, for those photographs to see the light of day, now or at any time in the future. It would bring attention. This is a business transaction. Any commitments we make will be adhered to. You are dealing with reasonable men ... ' Giles takes a sip of water. 'In that respect, Mister Zambrano, you got very lucky ... '

'Lucky?' says Miguel, with a curious look.

'Through sound judgement, or pure instinct,' says Giles with a shrug, 'you approached the correct people in London.'

'I think you're trying to flatter me now, Mister Urquhart.'

'You know something,' replies Giles, 'you're right ... And I would also have thought, Miguel, that one hundred million dollars would be a cheap price to pay when one day in the future you intend to take over a whole country ... after building your twin sister up as a popular idol. Her reputation, and maybe her virginity, will need to be intact.'

Giles' comment stings Miguel but he says nothing. He stares at the far wall of the room – a hint of megalomania in his faraway eyes, his vision of ruling Venezuela by proxy fulfilled.

'One hundred million dollars ... ?' he says, pondering, weighing it up.

'Please let's not haggle, Miguel,' says Giles. 'Let's both retain our dignity ... We know how to keep a secret ... you understand?'

Miguel has the face of a man who's trying to digest something bitter. Then, just as I think Miguel's gonna tell us to go fuck ourselves, his expression changes to one of acceptance.

'I'll pay you.'

'A wise decision,' nods Giles.

'You know why I'm going to pay you?' asks Miguel, looking to Giles and me in turn. 'The money? Fuck the money! My sister's reputation! It's worth every cent! But if those photographs appear in years to come ... I promise you ... ' Miguel gets all Latino. 'I will come back and haunt the pair of you. I will slice your balls off.'

Miguel pushes his untouched Dover sole away. He leans forward, a small glance to the left and right. 'Let me ask you, Mister Urquhart,' says Mister Zambrano, 'what is the market like here for product?'

'Given the right infrastructure and distribution you could recoup your hundred million in no time at all.'

Miguel nods, leans back in his seat. 'One last thing ... ' he says. 'A condition.'

He points at me. 'He stops fuckin my sister.'

'Done!' says Giles. Then he turns to me; this development is breaking news to Giles. 'Have you been fucking his sister? My God, you are a secretive chap.'

Suddenly Raul pipes up – hasn't said a dickie-bird all day. Now he's gone all rapido Español to Miguel. Fuck it! He's only insisting on getting Jesus' body returned – they're devoted Catholics. Raul can go and dig it up himself. Jesus has already caused enough trouble for ten lifetimes.

Miguel politely asks the question on Raul's behalf. Giles deflects it, with the utmost grace and cunning, over to me.

'I'm not sure that's possible ... You see ... the party who had the altercation with Jesus has actually departed this life themselves ... Sadly leaving no clue as to the whereabouts of the remains of Jesus ... '

But then Raul begins chuckling, slowly at first, then gathering in momentum. He's choking, but trying to keep a straight face. Soon Raul is hysterically giggling, rocking backwards and forwards, spitting fish and soggy potatoes over the table.

'Forgive my brother ... ' says Miguel, nodding at Raul, 'he has an evil sense of humour.'

'Fuck him, fuck Jesus,' says Raul, through a half-chewed mouthful, fat tears rolling down his chubby cheeks. 'Let the motherfucker rot in hell.'

North west Kent actually, Raul.

CHAPTER FORTY-EIGHT

COUPLE OF COMPLICATIONS

Giles clarifies the terms – the Brazilian creditors must be paid off, and ten percent of the account balances shown in the shadow accounts must be transferred to the bank where the now grandly named 'London Syndicate' hold accounts. *Time is the essence of this agreement*, Giles tells Miguel. Miguel simply nods.

Miguel then points out that for this to work both him and the memory stick must be in the same room. It will only work if Miguel uses the money in the Ponzi accounts to pay off the Londoners. Okay so far ...

'You said it yourself, Mister Giles, I'm not paying with my own money. Your *consultancy fee* needs to come out of those accounts. You're being naïve if you think I'm paying you out of my own funds. It isn't going to happen.'

'You buy the kit, Miguel,' says Giles, 'we return it to you, then do your business—'

'Hold fire,' says Miguel, 'all you've shown me is some printouts and told us some bullshit about fairies killing my cousin. And you want me to transfer a hundred million dollars to exactly where? With what evidence that you actually *have* possession of the merchandise? You're asking me to trust you and you're not showing a great deal of trust yourself.'

'This is not an impasse,' says Giles.

'Too fucking right, it's not,' snaps Miguel. 'Let's not complicate this. I get in a room with the equipment. I have a foolproof method of matching passwords up with accounts once I've got them all in front of me.'

'This Austrian fairy story?' asks Giles.

Miguel nods, 'I send you your money to wherever it needs to go. You then leave and let me do what I need to do. Let's not make difficulties for ourselves ... ' Then Miguel drops a bombshell. 'But the transaction must be done in New York.'

'New York?' says Giles, eyebrows raised. 'Surely the monies can be moved from anywhere?'

'Not these funds. The procedure was always designed to trigger in New York. The accounts are with American banks. We have our people infiltrated into those banks. We're talking about large amounts of money and years of planning. Show faith, Mister Urquhart.'

'Are the Americans in on it?' asks Giles.

'Enough already with the questions,' replies Miguel, smiling a genuine smile. 'We must retain a little mystique. I wouldn't worry – financially, New York is an open city. You could buy your own bank and transfer the money there, do what the fuck you like.'

'We have acquiescent banks in place already.'

'That's good. In New York?' asks Miguel. Giles says nothing. 'We work in New York all the time,' Miguel continues, 'much prefer it to Miami. There's something solid ... dependable. See ... forgive me ... this is not criticism, you understand, but you English guys don't travel well ... you've got your comfort zone ... '

Miguel gives a regal wave, indicates our grandiose surroundings, then hits us up with an artillery barrage of dazzling possibilities *for you gentlemen to think about* – the quick-fire round.

Incorporate a bank in New York State ... bypass federal taxes and regulations ... the bank is not actually in New York, you understand ... flexible currency regulations ... open an account in the destination bank ... then simply instigate an inter-bank transfer ... we've done this sort of thing many times ... we'll actually be in the same building, a couple of floors apart ... The holding bank and the destination bank will be in the same building ... We'll be relying on you not to make it traceable back to us ... use some hocus-pocus, black magic ... 'Severance' – I like that ... We do big deals ... We transfer funds all the time ... We have global partnerships ...

Miguel is showing off his business school education. He wants to do the deal – no fuckin question. It's suspicious how much he wants to do the deal. Miguel knows it's good business, needs the kit back in his kitbag.

'But ... ' Miguel shrugs, 'nothing can move until we get that memory stick in a computer terminal with our men on the inside. Once your money is moved, to our mutual satisfaction of course, and you get confirmation of the transaction from your destination bank, you walk away, leaving us with the memory stick. You retain your paperwork, your "insurance policy" with your attorneys. You want to do business. This is how *we* do business ...'

Miguel stands up and extends a hand. 'I realise you will need to talk to the people you represent, Mister Urquhart.' He shakes Giles' hand vigorously, and then mine. 'But I feel we have made progress here today. Let's speak first thing tomorrow morning. In the meantime I will begin arranging travel to New York. Till then, gentlemen.' Miguel marches back towards the lobby, with big Raul tailing him out. 'Shall we say nine ... ?' he says over his shoulder. Then they are gone. Miguel didn't eat; his Dover sole went back to the kitchen to feed the cat. Giles is looking pensive.

'Does that make sense to you, Mister Urquhart?' I ask.

'In a mad kind of way, it makes the most perfect sense, but I need to think this through ... '

Morty has been sat in a motor outside since quarter to one with some gents who look seriously capable. With a nod from Morty they vanish into thin air.

'How did it go?' he asks.

'Interesting, Mort. They *wanna* give us a hundred mill but there's one or two complications to be ironed out.'

Morty wants to leave the car and walk before he gets the full sit-rep, stretch his legs. Apparently he watched them come out; Miguel was rubbing his hands.

We walk across St James's Park, past the bandstand, over the bridge on the lake, trying to work out if we're being followed.

'It's good news ... mostly, Mort.'

I explain the situation to Morty.

'Fuckin New York?' says Morty. 'What's Giles saying? Where *is* Giles, by the way?'

'Giles has gone home to put his head in a bucket of cold water.'

'So what are *you* saying?'

'The geezer's prepared to give us one hundred million dollars. I think we might have to prepare ourselves for some give and take.'

'Does that mean we're going to New York?'

My phone rings. It's Smiler.

'I've got a funny feeling that this might be significant,' I tell Mort. 'How ya doing?' I ask Smiler.

'You fancy a curry ... just me and you?' He says in such a conspiratorial way that you know that he has something to tell me.

'Yeah, could be good,' I reply.

'Been eavesdropping, you know?'

'See you at the usual place ... about thirty minutes.'

'Come alone,' says Smiler, melodramatically. 'Don't bring the twins, you know?' He means Sonny and Roy. 'Good news ... if you've got a thick hide ... And don't come with the big fella.' He means Mort. 'This is for your ears only. I want it to be your call. You seem, like, balanced, pragmatic.'

'Thanks.'

'How hot do you like yer curry?' he asks.

'Hot as you can handle.'

'Watch yer Union Jack,' Smiler says as he disconnects.

I hail a cab. I tell Morty I'll catch up with him in a couple of hours, I've got to go and see Smiler, *alone* – he's got what Roy Burns would have called *real-time intel.* Morty just nods.

Half an hour later I arrive at Smiler's lab. Sonny's guys have cleared out but Smiler is still in residence. Before Sonny went to France and Roy went to wherever he ended up, they told him to stay put, so here he is. But he's not been idle. He's been earwigging – listening to Miguel and Raul on their arrival back at the Belgravia hacienda, using the landline telephone as a bug.

Smiler sits me down and we listen to the recording while eating an eye-watering king prawn vindaloo. Transpires Smiler is double competitive where curries are concerned. And Smiler has provided neat English transcripts to complement the tidied-up and amplified recordings in Spanish – *the edited highlights.* I have a nasty feeling in my guts; thought I was home and dry but now I feel a stitch-up coming. *Good news, if ya got a thick hide* is rattling around the canister.

Over in Belgravia, a celebratory mood is the order of the day. Miguel sounds like he's got champagne bubbles tickling his nose. Raul asks him if they'll go through with the arrangement – he could easily get them all wiped out. Miguel tells Raul it would be foolhardy. He's telling Raul to send a team down to talk to these Brazilian monkeys, offer them ten cents on the dollar ... If they refuse, you know what to do ... Have your fun, live ammo practice. It's beautiful. We've just got to make sure nothing happens to these Brits.

'And after ... ?' says Raul, with a trace of hope in his voice.

'And after ... we open up a London office, Raul. Think about it – Caracas, New York ... and London. These guys are looking for good raw product coming in the diplomatic bag. It's wide open here ... we use these guys to develop the market. We landed on the top of the pyramid. If they step up to the plate, great ... If not, we find someone else. I like this place, it's civilised ... Eating Dover sole, sitting around drunk all afternoon. Papa would love it here ... These Brits have got something going on ... it's called class, Raul, and you can't fuckin buy it.'

Change the fuckin record, pal.

'You hear all that bullshit about "*the third party who holds the device as we speak,*" – it's bullshit, English diplomacy. They're past masters. I didn't believe it for a second. I think they were negotiating with the Sonny guy ... The one who stole it from Jesus. They were playing for time, you see? Getting round the security system that that Austrian prick put on without waiting to be asked.'

'So, let me get this straight ... ' says Raul, 'I'm not getting it, Miguel ... We pay them and *then* we kill them?'

'No, Raul!' replies Miguel. 'We go into business with them! Don't you see? These are people who can make things happen. *They* have the connections, Raul – we don't. Raul, you're not going to do anything to sabotage this thing. Promise me, Raul.'

'I promise, Miguel,' replies Raul, no doubt with hand on heart.

'They're wired in at the top and the bottom, Raul. Jesus has done us a major solid. If that prick weren't dead I'd kiss the fucker.'

'So what happened to Jesus?' asks Raul.

'Who gives a fuck? I'll ask them afterwards, you understand – wouldn't be decorum, *old boy*, to ask beforehand ... I'll ask them if they know why he was in London ... And what happened to

Santos ... But, Raul ... ' He adopts a mad English accent, '*that would be totally infra-dig, old boy.*'

I can hear Miguel crack up laughing. Raul don't think it's as funny as Miguel who's obviously hit his own sweetspot and can barely stay the right side of hysterical.

Smiler moves the recording on. ' ... and when Giles said *one hundred million* I thought I'd misheard him,' says Miguel. 'I wanted to run to the bank to give it to him, the sanctimonious prick. Thought he was dealing with idiots. No, Raul, whatever happens these guys stay alive. *Voy a prender una vela en la iglesia pa' que no les pase nada a nuestros nuevos amigos.* I'm going to light a candle in the church for our new friends. Going to pay the priests to say mass for the motherfuckers ... Gonna hire them the best guardian angels money can buy.'

'But,' says Raul, 'they've swindled us.'

'Raul, it's not our money. I can't wait, everything's back on track. I thought I was going to have to pay it out of my own pocket for a minute. One hundred million ... it's beautiful.'

Miguel is laughing, then he stops suddenly. '*Only* one hundred million ... ' he asks himself. 'It makes sense ... but then it doesn't ... '

'Could it be a trap, an ambush?' asks Raul.

'How could it be a trap, Raul? Nothing moves without the device. They understand that, their money's on the memory stick ... '

'Could still be a trick, Miguel,' growls Raul.

'But how, Raul?' says Miguel. 'You tell me ... I couldn't believe it that these London jokers settled for one hundred million.'

I see it now, in hindsight. Miguel didn't miss a beat when Giles said *one* hundred million. It was surprise, not indignation, he was expressing, or suppressing. He indulged in token resistance, for the sake of *form*, this being England. Sonny was right; we should have pushed for more. I feel slightly belittled but it's *my* perspective that has been manipulated. Millions of dollars, washed up, in an offshore bank, with Miguel Zambrano's thanks and blessing – with no comebacks – looks real handsome at the moment. Sonny's greed could be fatal at this stage of the game.

My whack will be in the region of twenty-five million, tax-free, to invest in real estate. I can lose myself again, live off rental income, be set up for life. I know I'm gonna get paid ... get out alive ... I feel something I haven't felt in a long time – relief.

'Smiler,' I tell him, 'I'm gonna make sure you get a bung out of this. How's a couple of million dollars sound?'

'I don't really need a million dollars,' says Smiler, casually. 'I've got more money than I know how to spend. Peace of mind is more important than money.'

'Oh, bless. You've had a revelation, Smiler. How sweet.'

'You just keep me sweet with Sonny and Roy – put a word in when you see 'em. Tell 'em how helpful I was ... Roy 'specially ... He's the real ... you know?'

'I know, Smiler, I'll have a word with Roy, let him know you riddled it out.'

Except ... No Roy. Ted shot Roy.

'Smiler,' I tell him, 'you can pack and go. Thanks for your help.'

'What about all this hardware?' he says, nodding at the computer gear.

'Sling it in a skip ... if you can be bothered.'

I get back on the street and ring Morty.

'What's the verdict?' he asks.

'*Carpe diem*, Mort.'

'Seize the day? Am I right?'

'Affirmative. We get on a plane and ring that arrogant little fucker Miguel from New York City.'

CHAPTER FORTY-NINE

VIVA LA MADNESS

Grantley Adams International Airport, Barbados
Thursday, 20th September 2001

I landed back here on last Friday evening, three days after the
planes hit the towers. I could feel, in the midst of the chaos and
speculation, somehow safe, as if a conjurer's sleight of hand was
diverting global attention far away from me. There was an atmosphere of psychosis in the air but I felt thankful, for once, to be a
nonentity. Truth be told, nobody was looking for white guys,
wearing Ralph Lauren linen suits, travelling on British passports,
that nice Mister Berkeley, perfect gentleman, whose nonexistent
fiancée's old-money parents held land interests in Barbados, Can-
ada and South America. The Bajan border control personnel were
alight, asking the right questions, double-checking passports, but I
knew it was simply a formality. I'd already ditched the passport I'd
travelled in and out of New York on and was travelling on the
passport so kindly donated by Ted Granger, complete with its
indefinite US visa.

Two weeks ago, on the overnight flight from London to New
York, my head started doing a number on me, plotting a
last-minute price hike, the belated *coup d'état*. But then I decided
that I was being greedy and should start to think in terms of
receiving twenty-five million rather than thinking I was getting
swindled out of more. I was in this as the result of Sonny's greed
and inability to let an opportunity to make some easy money go.
I couldn't exactly say I'd *earned* the readies – not with a straight
face. I was in the right place at the right time and greased the
sides. I'd been extremely fortunate. Old wisdom – *don't smack a
gift horse in the mouth.*

Morty was on the same flight but we didn't acknowledge each
other. One look at Mort told me that any dissent at this stage

would be met with disapproval. He wanted *mucho dollar* to set up his kids with parcels of land in far-flung corners of the globe.

For once we were going to do the deal as arranged. We'd get our money to disappear, wipe our mouths and march on. But then events started to get jumbled up; all those old clichés about fact being stranger than fiction started to become self-evident and too fuckin obvious. Just when I thought I was back to reality, getting a handle on life again – without people getting murdered all around me – something comes along to totally jam the circuits. In Sonny's words *some cunts took a massive liberty.* Or, to paraphrase Missus Burns, *no matter how mad you think you are, there's always someone madder ...* And you can't negotiate with madness.

We arrived on the Thursday before, just before midnight of the sixth, and rang a surprised Miguel back in London from JFK. Next morning New York was alive, roasting hot, with painted-on blue skies, just as it should be, but in my paranoia I started thinking *does everybody know something I don't know?* We went underground, up on the Upper West Side, but the deal kept getting delayed. I was getting understandably itchy. Morty – backed-up by a little firm from London, proper grown-ups, not kids – was bodyguarding the memory stick and me, shadowing me to see if I was being followed, but I wasn't.

Miguel had moved fast, arrived in New York on the Friday, at midday, but was immediately playing for time, telling us not to be impatient, turning on the charm and the studied indifference. He made great fanfare of telling us that Duppy's debt to the Brazilians had been *absolved.* Giles let Ted know. Ted's *well pleased*, Giles reported back, and *putting one together* – ordering up another massive consignment ... Same-old-same-old round Ted and Bridget's house then.

Giles and Miguel were getting increasingly cosy. Giles calmly tells Mort and me that Miguel has decided to *cash out* and this *might cause delays.* Everything was happening on Miguel's schedule now, and he was talking his time *to get his ducks in a row.*

It annoyed me and Mort but by then Giles the Toff seemed to be in a different camp, had morphed into Giles the Limey – *he's giving you twenty-five million dollars for God's sake, these things don't happen overnight.*

Then Giles dropped a little surprise on us. He wanted to land
all the funds with Curtis in the CBB, before transferring them to
each individual offshore account. And Curtis was looking for a fat
commission. I disagreed, severely. It almost came to blows one
night in a steak restaurant up on the Upper East Side.

I told Giles I wanted mine paid directly into my own account.
Giles turned – hissing, frowning, showing cold steel – *don't fuck
this up, okay? Don't you fucking dare make me look like some
parochial hillbilly.*

Giles is telling us to *fucking relax*; he can smell the *money
blowing up Broadway* from the financial district. I'll say this for
him, Urquhart couldn't be intimidated, could get shouty with the
best of them – *it's the deal I've done with Miguel. You're making
us look like we don't trust them, like we're buffoons!* He pitched
it like we would be fools to not go ahead, telling us Miguel is *a
fucking genius, hitch your wagon to this chap.* Mort was looking
for a bucket to throw up in but instead he seriously threatened
Giles, *marked his card*, while waving a steak knife under his nose.
Only Giles gets more animated, tells us he's *not an imbecile* – he
*doesn't want to end up dead or to be running for the rest of his
life.* Mister Mortimer made sure that Giles got more than a
glimpse of his slotting crew, anonymously eating rare sirloin at
the next table.

Giles takes a deep breath, tells us that he'll put the CBB
accounts in the name of Berkeley, but separate from Sonny's –
*What more do you want, for Christ's sake? You'll control the
accounts, not me ...* He turns to me, huffing and puffing – *you'll
be the front man, the point of contact. You have the correct ID.*

Then he calmed right down; got chatty, blasé, like nothing's
happened, ordered another vodka martini. *Take a tip, Mister
Mortimer? Twenty-five million dollars is a lot of money. Buy land,
as an investment. It's only going to go one way – up. South
America, especially The Argentine. Have a little holiday down
there. Montevideo and Buenos Aires are fucking extraordinary ...*
Then Giles went to hook up with Miguel. I went back to my hotel
overlooking Central Park.

On the Monday, Giles asked me to meet him in a coffee shop
off Liberty Street, down in the Financial District.

'*We've* bought a closed corporation, off the shelf ... ' he told me. 'You should come and see *your* company ... Pursuit Investments.'

'And where do I find this *Pursuit Investments*, Giles?'

'Slow down, I'm coming to that. We're on floor ninety-six ... ' Giles pointed upwards with his nose, 'World Trade Centre.'

Miguel met us outside, took me and Giles into the World Trade Centre, Tower One. The lobby was the size of a gigantic shopping mall. We got in the fast elevator. Someone pushed the button for the thirty-eighth floor, not the ninety-sixth. We got out, walked through a reception area without a word being said, and onto a mezzanine overlooking a frantic trading floor.

'Down there ... ' said Miguel, waving like a young emperor, 'trillions are moving as we speak. Do you think anyone's looking for our few hundred million? Giles says you've got a problem. Is that right?' I shrugged. 'You ever read much history?' he asked. I nodded. 'You know what this is all about? What we intend to achieve?' I nodded again. 'We'll give you Jenna as a hostage. You sit and wait at a location unknown to us. And when you get the word from Mister Urquhart here, we send Raul to collect her ... '

'How do I know Raul won't ... '

'Kill you? This is commerce. I don't know what Mister Urquhart has told you but we will be going into business together. I've re-evaluated, decided this is an investment, for the future.' He tapped his temple. 'It's about perspective ... The hundred million will be an advance. And it will be recouped.' He let go a rare but genuine laugh.

I was being told I was *definitely* getting twenty-five million dollars but felt belittled, like some snotty shitkicker getting in the way of the adult's aspirations.

'Mister Urquhart may have a position for you,' Miguel said, 'in the infrastructure.'

Giles nodded, dead sneaky. I knew he wasn't going to turn me over, but he had unquestionably switched sides. He opened his briefcase and handed me a CBB new customer pack that had been couriered over. 'As we agreed ... ' said Giles, with a smirk.

'You deliver the equipment to Giles,' said Miguel, 'and we'll conclude our business. I'm not about to put my own sister's life in danger. I want nothing to go wrong ... nothing unexpected. We've hired a suite of offices upstairs ... '

'So I'm told.'

'Good, so everything's good to go. All we need is ... '

The memory stick that Morty, and his squad, was holding across town.

'We go tomorrow,' said Giles.

'Nice and early,' said Miguel.

They had a little chuckle.

I thought the Jenna hostage manoeuvre was designed to get me away from the trade ... and maybe it was. If Giles didn't want me in the building I was going to neglect to inform him where I was tubbed-up with Jenna.

Later I got a phone call from her – *where do you want me?*

Jenna was the most compliant kidnap victim in history. She was apparently looking at her wristwatch when two of Mort's crew arrived at the Paramount Hotel coffee shop to collect her from her bodyguards.

They dodged about, losing any tails, real or imagined. Swept her for trackers, confiscated her phone, and used a device to see whether she was bugged. Their shadows worked out that nobody was following them, or Jenna. They brought her to the Hudson Hotel, over by Central Park.

Jenna asked me, by way of greeting – *Are you this suspicious about everything? You don't get how much we want to do this deal, do you?* But she complimented me on her abduction – *slick, Mister English, muy slick ...*

She rang Miguel to let him know she was safe ... And then slowly took off all her clothes ... so I could *search her properly ...* We both knew what was coming next ... *we've got lots of time to kill.*

It wasn't your usual hostage situation – in bed, hot night, making love, strangely tender, then licking the salt off each other. After the festivities, all the events of the last few days caught up with me. I fell asleep, suddenly exhausted ... like I'd been drugged ... hypnotised by the ceiling fan, but like I was actually relaxed ...

But next morning Jenna woke up weirded-out; she'd dreamt about Jesus. He was laughing, full of his insane, hateful mischief, telling her Miguel will *get his comeuppance.* I was spooked. Jenna was rattling on – reminded me a bit of Roy in the scrap yard –

telling me that Jesus will be *a restless soul*. Jenna swore she saw Jesus' ghost. She *felt his presence* from beyond the grave.

I wasn't that sympathetic, was double alert to a deception. *It was a fuckin dream, Jenna!* I'm telling her, all the time thinking ... *This could turn into a fuckin nightmare.*

Next thing Giles is on the phone, delivering the *real-time sit-rep*. He can hear Jenna in the background. *Is she all right? Don't fuck her, okay! Don't mess this up!*

She's pacing, long strides, talking to herself in rapid Spanish, her fear of Jesus runs deep. Giles is hissing again, telling me to *keep her fucking quiet.* He puts the phone down on me.

Then Morty called, whispering. He'd delivered the memory stick to Giles on the ninety-sixth floor. Miguel was alone except for *a couple of bankers, some computer kids but no muscle ... This could be sweet.*

I put Jenna in the shower. She seemed to calm down. Then I got back on the phone with Giles, checking in – stage-by-stage, step-by-step. I could hear irritation in his voice – *Give us a break. We're starting work now.* I realised I trusted Miguel more than I trusted Giles but soon he lightened up, even had a little chuckle – *fuck me, it's a breeze. They've been in rehearsal. I've got to check something with Miguel ... I'll ring you back.*

The next time he rang, Giles said, *relax, buddy, in two minutes you'll be a very rich man. I'll ring you back ...* Then he was gone again.

Jenna came out of the shower – calm again – kissed me on the lips and half apologised.

Next thing, she's gone again; she seemed to disappear into herself – physically present but mentally absent. Too bizarre. She sat on the edge on the bed staring into space. I wrapped her in a robe, but got more suspicious still, if that was possible. Then Jenna suddenly leaps up. She wants to go to where Miguel is – *right now!* All her usual composure and what was left of her poise gone.

I had it explained later, by Mister Mortimer, no less. It was a curious but not totally unique phenomenon. It was psychic trauma. Her twin was in a place of grave danger, maybe dying at that very moment. And she felt it too, felt it to the marrow of her bones.

I told Jenna to call Miguel, punched in the numbers in the

phone for her, ready to hand it to her when Miguel answered. But there was no answer, just a low, flat tone – no ring. I tried the number again – same result.

I called Giles; his phone was dead. I tried it again and again, hitting the green button repeatedly. No fuckin answer. Now I'm worried. I tried Morty's number; no answer – a recorded message, *number unobtainable*. I got a sickening feeling in my guts.

Jenna was freaked. It got contagious. She tried to get out the door, in spite of only being dressed in a bathrobe. I stopped her. Locked us in – *you're a fuckin hostage, remember? Was your brother's idea!*

I stood in front of the door but I don't know if someone was going to come flying through it to shoot me dead. Jenna screamed at me – *Something's going on. I don't know what, but it is!*

She tried to get out again. I barred her way.

What do you know, Jenna? Fuckin tell me! Is someone coming to kill me?

Jenna stopped struggling, her voice small, tears in her eyes, *something's happening to Miguel. I just know it. What have your men done? Have they killed him?*

I'm asking Jenna if I'm about to be assassinated but she's telling me that I've killed her brother, *after making love* to her, telling me I'm *an animal*. A hostile stalemate broke out. *I ain't a fuckin murderer*. I told her to get dressed, straight away, *right fuckin now*. Jenna quickly pulled on her clothes. I got dressed as well, trying Giles' number the whole time – nothing.

'Where are we going?' she asked.

'To that fuckin office.'

We got in a cab outside. The driver was from Kuwait and had the news station on loud *and* crazy Arabic music, wailing pipes and racing drums. It sounded frivolous and optimistic. I told him he'd get a fat tip if he hurried. He smiled, put his foot down. Me and Jenna were speeding downtown on Broadway, sat at either ends of the back seat. Then the news comes on the radio; reports that Tower One has been hit by a plane – *a fuckin plane?*

The cab driver pulled over to the curb and snapped the music off. We sat in silence, just listening to the news reporter getting increasingly frantic. For a couple of minutes Jenna and me were close – sat together, hugging like kids.

When the second plane hit the driver started crying and praying, quietly rocking backwards and forwards in his seat. Fire trucks, police cars and wagons were all screaming south. I sat in the back of the cab and slowly, selfishly, began to decide that the gods were conspiring against me.

Jenna suddenly started feeling her pain by proxy again. It was eerie – *something bad is happening to Miguel.* She began screaming at the driver, *ordering* him to drive but he just retreated further and further into himself. Then she was out of the cab and gone. I jumped out but I couldn't see her; she vanished, disappeared – headed south.

I didn't wanna leave the driver on his own weeping but I did. I felt awkward stood on the pavement. I dropped a bundle of notes through the cab window then put my head round the door of a crowded coffee shop. Everyone was in shock, stunned, gazing open-mouthed at the tiny television above the counter. I realised I was doing the same, watching two burning skyscrapers. There was gridlock, sirens and a dark vibe on the sunny streets.

The plane had hit around the floor were our Giles had so proudly rented his office. It looked bad. And Morty was missing. The phones are inactive so the only way for anyone to contact me would be at the hotel. Morty would riddle that out – if he was alive – but Giles didn't know where we were at.

Everyone was glued to televisions, or sat on the curb staring, or weeping. I started marching back to the hotel. I felt lonely and a long way from home. I knew one thing – it wasn't another elaborate diversion. I was caught up in the most inconceivable incident in history.

I knew straight away that things were gonna get tricky; the whole of the USA was going into massive lock-down. In an atmosphere of justifiable anger, panic, paranoia and fear the dragnet was coming down. Maybe I should be gone, but back in my room the television was so addictive I watched, transfixed – trying, like everybody else, to process circumstances beyond my comprehension.

Then the first tower came down. I couldn't believe it, thought I was hallucinating. I'd felt, earlier that day, humiliated that I wasn't in that building ... It seems that, for once, there was no swindle. My hunch was Giles and Miguel had sent the money minutes – or *seconds* – before the plane hit. I *was* going to be extremely rich, except ... I felt guilty for feeling that way.

I knew I had to sit and wait. I had no choice. A part of me kept thinking that Jenna was going to return to the hotel but the rational bit of my brain knew it wasn't going to happen. I only ventured out briefly, in case I missed her, or Morty. In Central Park there were preachers saying prayers for the dead, singing hymns, making appeals for forgiveness. Others were screaming for immediate revenge – *punish the evildoer*, quoting Revelations, predicting the end of the world – *The Apocalypse starts here.*

Factions in government were, in Roy's words, *making lemonade*, declaring war, apportioning blame, trying to exploit the lunacy.

Next day I called Curtis. He didn't wanna talk on the phone, just kept asking when *we* would be arriving; refused to transfer any funds without the permission of Mister Giles Urquhart. Mister Cee didn't wanna believe that Giles *wasn't around anymore*. I told him where my share was going but he *wasn't going to do anything*. He told me *not* to ring him at the bank, *under any circumstances*, gave me his personal cell phone number, told me to ring *as soon as I knew my ETA*.

Thursday morning I checked the drafts folder on the email address me and Morty shared. He was alive. He'd altered the draft, left me a riddle; not to spin my head, it was spun enough, but so any FBI eavesdroppers didn't catch a scent.

Happened as planned. Meet me where he didn't get champagne. Check in at the same time.

The Rendezvous Bar on Bridgetown Harbour – keep checking in at six p.m.

Morty wanted to go see Curtis, to make the necessary moves to access the money. I felt kinda weirded-out about the money. Small problem – nothing was flying in or out of the USA. The money was there but we were here. I altered the draft – *ASAP*.

The hotel concierge got me on a train travelling south. A day later I tripped up in Miami where the vibe was seriously muted – wild shirts but sombre frowns. I rang Curtis, left a message, then managed to get a flight over to Barbados. After a stopover in

Puerto Rico, I landed at Grantley Adams Airport three weeks after I left. I got a taxi to the Rendezvous Bar but didn't arrive until half past six on the Friday.

Morty was sitting at the same table we'd sat at with Roy and Sonny, sipping a beer, reading an English newspaper. As I sat down he placed the paper between us. The whole front page was a photograph of the aftermath.

'Fuckin insane,' said Morty, by way of greeting.

'Nice to see you, Mister Mortimer,' I said.

'Likewise,' he replied.

'How come you weren't up there – you know, with Giles and Himself?'

'My ears popped on the way up – it threw me. Once I knew we weren't getting shafted ... there's a smell you get when you are ... The money was sent, you know that, don't you?'

Mister Mortimer had delivered the memory stick to Giles and Miguel in the World Trade Centre then cut out, leaving his hired help to oversee the proceedings. He never did like being too deep or too high ... was *worried about getting a nosebleed*.

'I thought you were in there ... ' says Morty, tapping the paper.

'Why?' I ask.

'That woman, Jenna, the one you was meant to be holding hostage ... ' I nod. 'I swear I saw her, among thousands of people, running *towards* the building ... Everyone else was running away but she was ... '

'Trying to find her twin.'

Morty nods. 'The money ... We've got a problem.'

'Tell me.'

'No Curtis.'

Mort had a hunch – *I think Mister fuckin Curtis has gone through ...*

Morty had *moved heaven and earth*, and paid out a lot of money to jump the queue, found the Bajan community in New York and bought a ticket from a chap who was stranded. He'd got, miraculously, a flight on Friday, arrived in time for lunch, but went to *show me face* at the CBB instead. Transpires *Mister Curtis is on sick leave*, had not been in since the previous morning, not called in either. And now that fuckin bank was fuckin shut till Monday.

We can't walk into a bank and demand the proceeds of a crime. They won't entertain us. They'll call the law or think we're a pair of lunatics.

'You're taking this very well, Mort.'

'What fuckin choice do I have?'

Maybe if Morty or me had got there a day or two earlier Curtis would have simply pocketed his commission and moved our money on ... Maybe if we'd sent someone to sit on him before the trade ... But Curtis got restless; his head did a number on him.

He'd *done a Ted* and disappeared; had a Brazilian girlfriend apparently ... could be anywhere. It makes you wonder – how much would you walk away from your life for? Never see your family again, sever all contact, never go home again ... Some people would walk away for a crisp tenner, others for one hundred million. But Curtis' crimes were of the non-reported variety – the law wouldn't be looking for him – no bells, no sirens, no flashing lights.

'Could be lying low, Mort.'

'Could be touching down in Australia.'

The gardener up at Curtis' house up near Speightstown told us that Mister Curtis had been gone since Thursday – given him a couple of month's wages in cash, then got into a taxi ... no doubt to the airport ... no doubt to catch a flight into thin air ... via the Bridgetown branch of the Conciliated Bank of Barbados.

'See,' Morty told the gardener, 'we're police officers, from England. We need to look inside.'

'Don't insult me,' said the gardener. 'You're not policemen.'

'Okay, we're not ... ' said Mort, 'but suppose we give you a shitload of money?'

Inside the house there was no evidence of someone clearing out in a hurry; the only clue was a pile of empty photo frames. Everything else was as it should be. There was a wall safe behind a large mirror in the master bedroom – closed but unlocked, and very empty. And a cell phone with a few missed calls.

Morty modified his theory – after Giles was killed, with the money parked up in some twilight account, neither in nor out of the system, the temptation was too much for Curtis. We picked the wrong day to attempt large-scale financial skullduggery.

We looked high and low, all weekend, but Curtis couldn't be

found anywhere. And just when we were thinking it's ninety-nine percent certain Curtis has cleared the accounts out, and we were wondering how to break the bad news to a sceptical Sonny ... Sonny got in touch. He tracked Morty down ... They had a short conversation. Mort was in a call box on the West Coast – outside where we'd had our fish supper that night – and Sonny was in Marbella, Southern Spain.

Sonny was *not best pleased* ... The previous day, Friday, he'd walked into a bank in Gibraltar with some slimy lawyer to move some money, to buy into a nightclub – *never idle, that boy* – but there was no money, *not a fuckin bone.*

Transpires Curtis – once Giles, his old school chum, had given him the idea, morally corrupted him, persuaded him how easy it could all be – decided it was time for a change of location. Once you put an idea in someone's head, it's hard to get it out again ... In for a penny and all that ... *Complete severance*, Miguel would have suggested.

'That cunt, that fuckin mouse!' I could hear Sonny screaming. 'That fuckin straightgoer cunt! No more trades with these toffs! They can't be trusted! I'll find that Curtis cunt, I promise you I will. I'll bury him!'

Morty informed Sonny that Giles died in New York.

'I know! It's all over the papers. RIP? I'll kill that cunt 'n' all.'

We could hear Sonny smashing up his Spanish phone box. We left him to it.

'Sonny'll bounce back,' said Morty, looking out to sea. 'Won't take long, either. He's at his best when his back's against the wall. He wanted to know why we were in Barbados.'

'And you told him what?'

'We're on holiday, mate – we're off-duty.'

'You're very philosophical about all this. You haven't got religion, have you?'

'Just glad to be alive, brother.'

First thing Monday morning Morty and me went to the bank, with me clutching Mister Berkeley's ID, armed with the paperwork the late Giles Urquhart had handed over exactly a week ago in the World Trade Centre. We checked out the account; a desperate formality – *maybe he left us a few quid.* Lots of action but zero balance, not really unexpected. And you can't call mum if someone's been naughty. Twenty-five million dollars is a lot of money to lose, even if you've never actually had in your hands.

But just as we were walking out of the bank, we bumped into, quite literally, Pearl, the cute Customer Relations Manager, who'd looked after Sonny when he'd come over with Jesus' loot. Fortunately for us she was late for work that day, first time ever. She asked me if we had come for our suitcases – the Samsonites were still cluttering up the corridor.

'Of course,' said Morty, without missing a beat. 'Why else would we be here?'

Morty took the cases from Pearl, and wheeled them out the door to our hire car. I still hadn't tumbled. We drove right up through Barbados, only stopping at a hardware store to buy some tools, screwdrivers and hammers. We kept going right up to where the Atlantic meets the Caribbean. We stopped in a clearing, off the main road, away from inquisitive eyes, and then Morty began systematically – with a mixture of brute force and stealth, using the screwdriver – taking the cases to pieces, neatly dismantling them. I was catching on rapido ...

In the very last case he found what he was looking for, snug between two plastic skins. Morty had worked out – in a split second, after Pearl's innocent inquiry – that the Samsonite suitcases concealed the bearer bonds that Jesus stole in Miami, sold to Sammy Laniado, then retrieved in Berkshire. Jesus was using the bearer bonds as a bartering device but Roy Burns went to his grave never knowing of their existence. That was the information that Santos was attempting to trade ... before Patsy O'Malley ...

A nice consolation – nine million dollars in negotiable US bearer bonds, for me and Mort to carve. No partners, no expenses; very easy money, but it still feels like the booby prize.

We got our few days knocking about in the Caribbean but it was too quiet, nobody about, and I soon wanted to be on my toes again. A mixture of curiosity and sadness got me ringing Smiler in Brighton and asking for his help. He got busy. Five minutes later he sent me a link to a website containing information on Jenna and Miguel Zambrano – suggesting two ambitious and highly talented Venezuelan nationals were killed in the attack on

New York. I felt sick for them both, but obviously more so for Jenna ... Her beauty and her determination got Jenna into that building – through cordons and police lines – just before it collapsed.

Mort and myself agreed that I should travel down to Uruguay alone, sit tight for a little while, then *get a decent deal on the bonds in Montevideo,* and, working on Giles' tip, *look into the property situation down there.*

I'd nicked a trick from Jesus and hid the bonds in the shell of an attaché case, but even if the authorities had something to say they'd have to prove that they were stolen. Morty drove me over to the airport and bid me farewell – *be careful ... stay lucky ... see you soon* – exactly thirty days after I'd waited for him, Sonny King and the late Roy Burns.

As the plane taxis across the tarmac towards the runway, preparing for take off, it occurs to me that maybe someone should grant Jesus Zambrano's greatest wish and ghostwrite his autobiography; someone who knows all the ins and outs ... has heard the recordings, talked to all the key players ... been there ... Because I'd riddled something out; people know bits and pieces, but nobody knows the whole story. That degenerate prick Jesus would have loved the ending to his tale, would have buzzed, from his dark hole in Kent, England, on the trouble he caused; would have been thrilled by the fatal serendipity of getting Miguel and Jenna into that building; would have cherished the unknown body count, the mindless destruction and the grief of innocents – all in the name of an obsessive but unobtainable cause. Some folks love a drop of madness, whether they realise it or not. Personally I don't. I like to think I've grown out of it.

But then I think *fuck him ... and his memory ... mad cunt ...*

The plane's engines throttle back ... we gather speed on the runway ... then we're airborne ...

Q. A title for Jesus' fantasy memoir?

A. Could only be *Viva la Madness.*

AN INTERVIEW WITH J. J. CONNOLLY

In conversation with Barry Forshaw, author of *The Rough Guide to Crime Fiction* and *British Crime Film*.

Q. What were you trying to achieve with your novel *Layer Cake*?

A. I was trying to write something I would have liked to read myself. I saw a lot of fiction portraying London criminals as thugs and not very bright. I had seen, and met, many guys who were involved in criminality who were far from stupid and to whom violence was very much a last resort. Their reasons for being in the crime business were not to enhance any make-believe reputation but to make a great deal of money: they were genuinely able to rise far and rapidly so. Prohibition – making drugs illegal – had paved the way.

So I think the motivation for writing *Layer Cake* was seeing crime being written about quite badly because a lot of observers were quite naïve about professional criminals. Things needed updating: jump-starting as one reviewer put it. I think on some level I saw a gap in the market and a whole world that needed to be explored.

When the narrator suggests that 'everyone likes to walk through a door marked private' that's the key – no pun intended – to the whole book. The narrator took you into his confidence, because you, you're smart.

I also picked up on the phenomenon that a lot of kids want to be drug dealers; there was kudos to be had. It's a shortcut to riches and maybe self-esteem, but as the narrator says in *Viva La Madness*, 'crime pays, but there's a price to be paid.' It's a fantasy to a lot of people. The reality of selling drugs is that it's a brutal, hard way to make money, even if you don't get caught. You have, as demonstrated in *Layer Cake*, more to fear from other criminals than you do from the police.

I wanted to write something that stretched the characters, especially the main guy, the anonymous dealer. We – or I – start off explaining this really cool set-up, explain his exit strategy, and then watch it disintegrate. Essentially that's the baseline for all good fiction, whether it's crime or historical drama: everything's sweet and dandy ... but not for long.

Q. Did you see yourself as part of a British crime novel tradition, or have you tried to do something different?

A. If I wasn't doing something different I'd just go and open a bar. And probably make more money. I write for the same reasons as those chaps who swim up the Amazon against the current, to turn myself inside out: to challenge and push myself.

What was different about *Layer Cake*? I think *Layer Cake* was a criminal procedural rather than a police procedural; it invited you in. It was written from the criminal's POV. The police are very thin on the ground in both *Layer Cake* and *Viva La Madness*. I always want my writing to be both timeless and date-stamped: contradictory I know, but what I mean is that I want it to really tell the reader something about the times they live in – or we, when we're gone, lived in – and also to be based upon the same human traits and frailties that have always plagued us. I never want to be ghettoised as a crime writer, in bookstores I'd like to be in both the crime section *and* out on free-flow in the general population.

Q. Who are the writers who inspired you?

A. My favourite books are Norman Mailer's *The Executioner's Song*, and *Slaughterhouse Five* by Kurt Vonnegut. I have revisited these books since I was a kid, especially *Slaughterhouse*. I can get through it on a plane journey. To me it's like listening to an old Bowie album. Some writers might teach us to think out of the box but Vonnegut would suggest that there is no box: *what box?* It's about learning to remove any constraints and so allowing our style and imagination to take us where we need to go, to push the boundaries.

Q. Do you try to avoid moral judgements on your characters?

A. Most definitely. It's not my job, it's the job of the reader. I lay out the facts and let people decide the questions of morality for themselves. You have to remember that without the market for drugs, narcotics, dopes of all varieties, there would be no drug dealers and because it's illegal and over-subscribed there's going to be casualties. Likewise without a market there would be no tabloids or supermarket gossip papers.

As a writer what you've got at your disposal is human nature and a hopefully sharp pencil. It's your job to go into the murky, dark places, whether it's in the psyche or the city. I actually think the narrator of *Layer Cake* and *Viva La Madness* is quite a moral guy in a strange way: he dislikes bullies and violence. I think he very often has to push down a compassionate streak. Sometimes more successfully than others.

Q. Did you feel that the film of *Layer Cake* – which was remarkably successful – did justice to the novel?

A. As soon as you sell – remember that word – your property to film producers it's *their* property not yours. I hear writers bitching about film-makers ruining their work but they ran to the bank to cash the cheque. My experience was a good one. I was curious as to how they would adapt it. And they asked me to write the screenplay, whereas a lot of writers of the original material get told to jog. It's one of the few films that did do justice to the novel but it's a totally different entity. Coming from a culture that suggests that nothing is 'as good as the book' you've got your work cut out. Matthew Vaughn, the producer and director, knew that if you try and diligently replicate the novel you're on a loser. You have to create a whole, new, autonomous piece of work. In an hour and forty minutes ... The book is a deeper, more concentrated world. *Layer Cake* the novel would be about thirty hours of screen-time so you can't afford to be too precious. Scenes you love have to go.

The casting was brilliant. The actors really did the screenplay justice. The dilemmas that the central, Daniel Craig character was confronted with really came across on the screen. I was extremely happy with it. It took *Layer Cake* from being a cult novel to being a title that everybody knows. It didn't do me any harm either. It opened doors marked 'private'.

Q. What can you tell me about your new book, *Viva La Madness*?

A. *Viva La Madness* is a sequel to *Layer Cake*. The narrator has been lying low in the Caribbean, then he gets a call from his old buddy, Mister Mortimer. He's older and maybe wiser, been made disillusioned, but I think he'd call disillusionment a gift, a good thing not a bad thing. It's *Goodfellas* meets *Macbeth*. It's gangster gothic. As if international crime organisations had existed at the time of Edgar Allan Poe. It's much darker than *Layer Cake*, and *Layer Cake* was pretty dark. It's also more expansive – *Layer Cake* goes global – full of mad South Americans, twitchy North West Londoners, international drugs smugglers and ladies who do a nice sideline in body disposal. You'd not want to meet them personally but feel happy eavesdropping on their world. It's different but the same, if that makes any sense. It's all the fun of the fair.

Q. In what way does it differ from its predecessor? Did you feel some pressure following up the success of *Layer Cake*?

A. As I say, it gets a whole lot darker. Then darker still. Did I feel pressure? Nobody creates pressure, only ourselves. It's a relative term. I lead a charmed life. Nobody's going to come looking for me if I miss a deadline. But pressure is not such a bad thing. A little pressure gets our creative juices flowing, gets us setting the bar higher. When all's said and done, I'd rather be following up a successful novel than an unsuccessful one.

Q. What's next, or are you still focused on *Viva La Madness*?

A. I've had my head down writing *Viva La Madness* for what seems like the longest time, so now I'm back on the screenwriting circuit. I've got meetings and proposals from a few directors and producers, loads of interesting projects in the offing. Life is good … And at some point I'll be talking to Matthew Vaughn about *Viva La Madness* the movie. Maybe Matt can put in a call to Daniel Craig and we can get going all over again.